CRAVING MY ROOMMATE

ASHLEY ZAKRZEWSKI - AMANDA SHELLY
DENISE WELLS - ILYSE HARTT - KRISTIN LEE
REGINA FRAME - KEIGHLEY BRADFORD
SUTTON BISHOP - SHARON WRAY - EMERY LEEANN
MEG NAPIER - J. KEELY THRALL - JULIE HALPERSON
SKYE NIGHT - SUSANNA EASTMAN - DANIA VOSS LORI
ANN BAILEY - LAUREL WANROW
SKYE BLACKBURN - ALEXIS R. CRAIG
J.T. BOCK - MARIAH KINGSLEY

Copyright © 2024 by all participating authors

All rights reserved.

No part of this book may be reproduced in any form or by any electronic or mechanical means, including information storage and retrieval systems, without written permission from the author, except for the use of brief quotations in a book review.

Contents

Chaotic Love
Emery LeeAnn

Chapter 1	5
Chapter 2	8
Chapter 3	11
Chapter 4	14
Chapter 5	16
Chapter 6	18
Chapter 7	21
Chapter 8	23
Chapter 9	26
Chapter 10	29
Epilogue	31
About the Author	33

Exes & Ohs
Keighley Bradford

Chapter 1	37
Chapter 2	45
Chapter 3	53
About the Author	59

Making the Move
Amanda Shelley

Chapter 1	63
Chapter 2	71
Chapter 3	75
Chapter 4	83
Chapter 5	86
A Note from Amanda Shelly	95

Holly's Hero
Dania Voss

Chapter 1	99
Chapter 2	102
Chapter 3	106
Chapter 4	110
Chapter 5	114
Chapter 6	118
Chapter 7	122
Chapter 8	126
About the Author	131
Read More from Dania Voss	133

All Spun Up
Laurel Wanrow

Chapter 1	137
Chapter 2	143
Chapter 3	148
Chapter 4	156
About the Author	163

Sharing a Bed with Someone Like Him
Susanna Eastman

Chapter 1	167
Chapter 2	173
Chapter 3	176
Chapter 4	180
Chapter 5	187
About the Author	193

The Unicorn
Denise Wells

Chapter 1	197
Chapter 2	200
Chapter 3	203
Chapter 4	206
Chapter 5	208
Chapter 6	212
Chapter 7	216
Chapter 8	224
About the Author	225

Frenching My Flatmate
Skye Knight

Chapter 1	229
Chapter 2	233
Chapter 3	237
Chapter 4	241
Chapter 5	247
Chapter 6	249
Chapter 7	255
About the Author	259

Level Up
Julie Halperson

Chapter 1	265
Chapter 2	268
Chapter 3	271
Chapter 4	273
Chapter 5	276
Chapter 6	278
Chapter 7	283
Chapter 8	286
About the Author	293

My Roommate Confession
Ilyse Hartt

Chapter 1	297
Chapter 2	301
Chapter 3	305
Chapter 4	309
Chapter 5	313
Chapter 6	317
Chapter 7	320
Chapter 8	323
About the Author	329

No More Waiting
ALEXIS R. CRAIG

Chapter 1	333
Chapter 2	336
Chapter 3	339
Chapter 4	341
Chapter 5	344
Chapter 6	349
About the Author	351

ON FIRE
Sutton Bishop

Chapter 1	355
Chapter 2	365
About the Author	379

PUCKING MY ROOMMATE
Kristin Lee

Chapter 1	383
Chapter 2	386
Chapter 3	389
Chapter 4	392

Chapter 5	395
Chapter 6	399
Chapter 7	403
Chapter 8	408
Chapter 9	412
About the Author	419

Roommate Wanted
Skye Blackburn

Chapter 1	423
Chapter 2	430
Chapter 3	436
Chapter 4	443
About the Author	449
Other books by Skye Blackburn	451

Second Chance At Forever
Meg Napier

Chapter 1	455
Chapter 2	458
Chapter 3	463
Chapter 4	471
Afterword	477
About the Author	479

The One That I See
J. Keely Thrall

Chapter 1	483
Chapter 2	489
Chapter 3	492
Chapter 4	497
Chapter 5	506
Chapter 6	509
About the Author	511

The Roommate
Mariah Kingsley

Chapter 1	515
Chapter 2	519
Chapter 3	523
Chapter 4	527
Chapter 5	532
Chapter 6	536

Too Close For Comfort
Regina Frame

Chapter 1	543
Chapter 2	546
Chapter 3	551
Titles By Regina Frame	557

Trapped with Temptation
Lori Ann Bailey

Chapter 1	561
Chapter 2	565
Chapter 3	569
Chapter 4	573
Chapter 5	582
Lori Ann Bailey	589
Also by Lori Ann Bailey	591

True Love Delayed
J.T. Bock

Chapter 1	595

A Room with A Groom
Sharon Wray

Chapter 1	627
Chapter 2	630
Chapter 3	634
Chapter 4	638
Chapter 5	645
Chapter 6	652
About the Author	657

Roommate Deal
Ashley Zakrzewski

Chapter 1	661
Chapter 2	665
Chapter 3	668
Chapter 4	671

Chaotic Love
Emery LeeAnn

*I dedicate this to Brandy Locklear. You are such a beautiful soul and I feel so blessed to be your surrogate mom.
Love you to pieces!*

1

Brandy

I finally finished packing the last box in the U-Haul truck I rented, anxious to get on the road. I was promoted to Branch Manager of the bank I worked for, but I had to relocate. My mother was ecstatic. It meant I would be closer to her.

The only snag I'd run into was the house I wanted to purchase wasn't ready yet. The builder said six more months, and my job wanted me immediately to clean up the mess the old manager had left. I could stay with my mom, but it would be a forty-five-minute commute one way, and that just didn't appeal to me.

Mom had a friend of hers who she'd met at the animal hospital she worked at. She'd known her for years before, tragically, she died of breast cancer. She and my mother became best friends and Mom took it really hard. The woman had left behind two kids. A set of twins - Joseph and Jaelyn. They had inherited the huge Victorian house that they had grown up in.

I met them at college. At that point, they had just turned nineteen;

Jaelyn and I were roommates in our dorm. We became fast friends. She was studying engineering, and I was studying business management. Joseph, her twin brother, was studying to be a physical therapist. We had lost touch with each other since college. Life had gotten in the way.

That was eight years ago. Apparently, Mom had explained my situation to them, and they offered to rent me a room. I was reluctant at first. I really didn't know them anymore, and it seemed odd to me that they were 27 and still lived together. But then I thought about it. It *was* their family home. As I didn't have siblings, who was I to judge?

I just wanted to get there and try to get settled in. It was awkward enough that I really had never tried to reach out to them - but on top of that, I had to deal with walking into a shitshow at work. Apparently, the manager before me had fudged all of his reports and was skimming money from the bank. It was one very astute teller who caught on and called corporate. They offered her my position, but she was an elderly lady and didn't plan to work for much longer. So, they settled on giving her a substantial pay raise, which she took graciously.

I was hoping she would be my guide through all of this. My GPS was saying *turn left at the next street.*

Why can't they have a GPS with a sexy Scottish accent? *Turn left, lass. Then I will lift my kilt.* I giggled as my boring voiced navigator said *you have arrived at your destination.*

Wow. No wonder they wanted to rent a room out. This house was ginormous. It was large and imposing, two or three stories, the exterior consisting of steep, gabled roofs, towers, turrets, and highly decorative woodwork. It almost looked like a people-sized version of a doll house. While I sat there gawking, a knock on my window shook me out of my reverie.

It was a guy in a leather jacket. Sweet Jesus, he was hot. *Down girl, you're not here for that.* I opened my door and got out. "Yes?" I said to the hot meat who had interrupted my thoughts.

"Brandy, right?" His smile was sly and mischievous like he was planning something.

Then it occurred to me. I was so consumed with his looks that I didn't actually *look* to see it was Joseph. "Joseph! Oh my gosh. I hardly recognize you." I could feel the blush creeping up my face. What the hell I was blushing for - I wasn't sure, but damn, he grew up fine!

"It's Joey now," he put his hand in his pocket and produced a key for me. "This is for you. I will help you with your stuff."

"Oh! You don't have to do that. I can manage," I said. "You really have changed!"

"Yeah. I'm not that geeky kid you knew in college. I was a late bloomer, I guess." He shrugged.

"Yes, he does have to help you." A lyrical voice behind us piped in. She was shaking her fist at her twin brother. Jaelyn was absolutely adorable. She had chestnut colored hair, green eyes, and a small petite build. Joey was bigger, I mean muscular, taller, with dark broody eyes, and a smile that could melt my panties off. I was not expecting this at all.

Between the three of us, we only had to make two trips to get everything in. The inside was magnificent. There were large staircases, big mantles, big fireplaces, and half a dozen bedrooms.

"This place is amazing!" It was a shock and awe moment for me. I'd never been in a house this large before.

Jaelyn laughed. "We get that from everyone who sees it for the first time. It's been in our family for generations, which is why we decided not to sell it."

I nodded. I could hear the sincere love she had in her voice as she took me through the house and gave me a tour.

I was apprehensive at first staying with them, it was almost like staying with strangers, but now it may not be so bad.

2

Joey

When I pulled up on my bike and saw the car parked in front of our house, I guessed it must be Brandy. We didn't need the money, we were just helping a friend out. Brandy was the daughter of Roslyn, who was one of my mother's best friends. When Mom died, she came over daily to check on us. As strong as you think you are, you don't know shit until you lose a parent. I'm not sure how we would've fared without all of her emotional help. So, when she asked if her daughter could stay with us for a bit, it was a no-brainer. We would do anything for Roslyn. Hopefully, we could mesh just as well with Brandy as we did in college. Well, hopefully, Jaelyn will. I was at the clubhouse more often than not these days. It did make me feel better to know she wouldn't be alone so much.

What I didn't expect was how fucking gorgeous she was. Not in like a movie star way, but she had curves in all the right places. I loved a curvy girl. Every time I saw a stick thin girl eating a salad, I always want to buy them a donut. You need meat on you. If I wanted to fuck a bag of bones, I would dig up a skeleton. Just my opinion, everyone has one.

Didn't matter. Brandy was off-limits. She was a roommate only. After we took her stuff in, Jaelynn took her on the grand tour, and I whipped us up some lunch.

Jaelyn

It was going to be so much fun having another female in the house. Joey was okay, but a girl he was not! Plus, he usually spent most of his time at the clubhouse. I was a software engineer and worked from home doing my coding. There were some weeks I never left the house. In fairness, this house was big enough that if I walked around it enough times, I'd probably get my steps in for the day.

Brandy still seemed like her old self- very personable. She was in awe over the house. It wasn't a big deal to us because we grew up here. I just loved the look of wonder in her eyes.

I helped her unpack, then we ran downstairs to feed our faces.

Brandy

I felt like I was being transported back to college. We had so much fun catching up, I wished I had taken the bank up on taking the first week off, but I knew I wasn't actually moving in so I told them I could start right away.

Jaelyn told me about her high tech job. It was very impressive, plus she had the extra added bonus of working from home.

When I looked at her brother and asked what he did, he shrugged and smiled that cocky smile and said, "I ride." He flipped his hand towards the outside. "That's my hog out there in the driveway."

I was confused. Why would you ride a hog? Wouldn't a horse be more comfortable? "You have animals here?"

Jaelyn spit her drink out laughing. Joey looked at me waiting for the punchline. I was more confused than ever.

"Uh, no. My Harley Hog *Motorcycle*."

By this time, Jaelyn is holding her sides and snorting, pointing at her brother. "All I can picture now is you sitting on one of those huge hogs gramps used to have at his farm." She was cracking herself up.

He just shook his head and muttered under his breath about never understanding women.

Unfortunately, my eye candy left. Joseph - excuse me - Joey had to go back to the clubhouse. He was an Enforcer. I asked Jaelyn what that meant.

"Enforcers - well - enforce, which mostly means that they make sure everyone keeps themselves to 'the rules', whatever those rules may be."

"So, he gets to knock people around?" I asked.

"Pretty much. But most people don't mess with them, so he is usually safe," Jaelyn replied, her face still red from laughing so hard.

3

Joey

I had to chuckle at those girls. It was nice to see Jae happy again. She tended to cut herself off from the outside world. Now I wouldn't have to worry so much. I'd still come home every night, but at least I knew she could get a hold of Brandy if I'm unreachable.

I was an Enforcer for The Dragons of Death MC, so I was usually busy seven days a week, which was hard on her. Brandy can fill that void.

I'd damn sure like to fill Brandy's void. Fuck, I couldn't seem to get that girl out of my head. Besides the fact she is staying with us, I knew better anyway. Long-term pussy is a distraction. If you have your head shoved so far up an old lady's ass - you will slip up on the job. I can always get a piece of ass if I felt the need from the crow eaters (club whores) because they know it's a one-time deal. No messy feelings involved.

When you're getting ready to bash some heads, you can't be coochiecooing with some chick on your phone instead of doing your job. Priorities. Brothers first - pussy next.

Brandy

Jae and I stayed up watching chick flicks, then went off to bed. I had an early morning, and I was whipped. Sometime in the middle of the night, I heard the motorcycle pull up, but then I drifted back to sleep.

The next morning, I jumped in the shower and walked down the steps to find Joey making breakfast and already pouring me a cup of coffee.

"Cream, right?" He looked at me to confirm.

Yes, there was definitely cream, but in my nether region. Trying to stifle a moan, I just nodded and took the cup from him. The moan made its way out, though, after I took the first drink. "Holy shit! This is delicious!"

He smiled that smile that melted me, seriously, I don't know what is going on with me. He wasn't even my type. I didn't like *barbell heads*. Usually, their muscles were big and their IQ was small. But I knew Joey was smart. He was actually brilliant. I'd always imagined he would go on and start up some hedge fund company and earn millions. I never would've believed he would be in an MC.

"It's a special roast. Vietnamese coffee with sweetened condensed milk," he was saying as I stood there like a bump on a log.

"This may be the best coffee I have ever tasted."

He brought down a coffee thermos. Pointed it at me as if to ask if I wanted one for the road.

"Hell fucking yes."

He chuckled, then went to the stove and stopped me out eggs, bacon, and placed toast on my plate. "There is fruit and juice on the table. I will make more coffee while you eat."

"Wait," I said, stopping him, "aren't you going to eat?" He certainly didn't need to wait on me. I did appreciate it, but I was no prima donna.

He never turned around, just said, "Already ate before you came down."

Shit. Did this guy ever sleep? Just then, Jaelyn stumbled sleepily into the room.

"Mornin', y'all." She yawned.

I giggled. Same old Jae. She hated mornings. She did everything she could to schedule her classes in the afternoon.

"You hungry?" Joey had brought the thermos to me.

"Nah, but I will definitely take some of that coffee." Jae's eyes perked up.

"Coming right up." Within a few seconds, he produced a mug of coffee for Jaelyn.

"Okay, if you ladies are done making me your kitchen bitch, I have work to do."

He laughed as I swatted him with a dish towel. "It does have a good ring to it. That may be your new nickname." I laughed despite myself.

4

Brandy

Jaelyn refused help with the dishes, so I decided to head in early - get myself oriented. It was a beautiful building. Originally it was a small church constructed in the 1800's. It now was newly renovated on the inside - with the exception of the original marble floors, but they tried to keep the outside structure as authentic as possible with keeping the original stone that had been used to construct it.

I had my blue twill suit on with a champagne-colored cami underneath. My pumps were a modest blue color.

I felt like a freak show. All eyes were on me as I walked in and went straight to my new office. I wanted to drop my things off and then meet everyone, especially Florence. She was the whistleblower on the previous manager.

After setting a picture of my mom on my desk and placing my pens and nameplate where I wanted, I took a deep breath and went out to meet the staff.

Because the bank was open, I did it two different times. Half of the staff came to the lounge to hear my *I'm so happy to meet you all, I'm sorry it's under these circumstances,* while the other half worked. After the first group introduced themselves, they then swapped with the first group that was working. I went through my spiel again. Everyone seemed welcoming. This second group had Florence in it, so when the meeting was over, I asked her to stay behind.

She was very astute. My mother would've called her a no-nonsense kind of woman. I liked that, but I could see how easy it would be to misunderstand or misinterpret her or even take offense to what she says.

"Florence, I really appreciate you taking time out of your day to take me around and show me the ropes." I smiled at her.

"Just know that I'll be keeping an eye on you," she replied crisply.

"I would expect no less." I nodded. Some people would've resented what she said and her tone, but I appreciated it.

Florence nodded. "Follow me."

She took me on a tour through the bank. It was a nice branch. It was a shame what had happened. Greed was a terrible thing.

When the tour was done, Florence looked at me. "You can call me anytime. I've been with this bank for over twenty years. I was devastated when I found out what Luke did."

I saw the sadness in her face as she tried to blink away her tears. "I'm sorry. You must think I'm an old fool."

I wanted to hug her, but something told me she wasn't the hugging kind, so I settled with patting her arm. "Not at all. I think you're human. You grew close to someone who you trusted and he betrayed your trust," I pointed out at the tellers, "all of your trusts'."

She nodded her head again. "Thank you, dear. Like I said, you can always call if you need me."

5

Joey

Reaching the clubhouse, I had enough time to grab a cup of coffee with a shot of Jameson before church – our official club meeting.

Going down the steps, I could hear the raucous laughter coming from the room. Walking into the room, they started whooping and hollering.

"Glad you could join us," Deakin the club President, grunted.

I looked at my watch. "I'm not late."

"And yet you're the last one here." He glared at me.

"Just saved the best for last." I shrugged. Everyone burst out laughing, breaking the tension.

Deakin just shook his head. That was the best you could get from him.

"Our Southern chapter needs some help. Four of you will be headed over. Killjoy, Martin, Joey, and Blue. You will be there as long as they need you."

My head started to spin. "Can Rock take my place? I can't leave my sister that long. We discussed this before."

"You challenging me—"

"I really want to go," Rock piped in.

Everyone was silent for a moment. "Fine." With that, Deakin slammed the gavel down to signify the meeting was over. He pointed at me. "Office - now."

We walked to his office in silence. I could almost smell the smoke as the heat was dripping off his pores. He was so pissed.

As soon as I shut the door, he began.

"What the fuck is wrong with you? Is this about pussy? For fuck's sake, don't tell me you finally found some, and you are wrapped around her tit."

I let him get it all out. Then calmly, because with Deakin, if you react to him like he was reacting to me, he would shoot you, I said, "It's about keeping my sister safe. You know what she went through. I can't ever let that happen again. Do you know how stupid it looks that one of our own was raped, and we didn't retaliate?" I stared at him in his eyes.

That was like a bitch slap in Deakin's face. He calmed down. "Joey, I swear to you we will exact revenge on them when the time is right."

"Until your *time is right*," I made quotation marks with my fingers. "My sister relives it every day and night."

"Next time, pull me off to the side. Can't have you deliberately saying no to me in front of everyone."

I nodded. Deakin was a fucking prick most of the time, but he also tried to help if he could.

"And here I thought it was about pussy."

"You know me better than that," I replied, walking out the door. I only wish I believed that myself.

6

Brandy

Work was chaos. I worked a lot of long hours to get this bank back where it needed to be. The things that Luke Perty did actually do, he did wrong. I was not sure if he was an idiot or just a complete imbecile.

How he got away with this for so long was beyond me. One of the duties of the job was sending a report once a month to headquarters. Did he not do it, and they didn't notice?

In the evenings, when I got home, Jaelyn was so excited to see me. I started to notice, though, that there was a look of sadness in her eyes. Her happy face contradicted her eyes.

Maybe she was just lonely. I could see that. So, I figured out a solution.

"Our inside lobby closes at 3:30 p.m. Why don't you bring your laptop down and work at the bank while I work to catch up on some of my mess?"

"Really?" She said, with a little excitement in her voice.

"Yes! I would love to have company. But there's only one rule."

"Okay." Jae looked pensive.

"You bring the coffee!" I giggled.

"You got it!"

Just then Joey walked in. We filled him in on our plan. He looked Jae in the eyes. She nodded perceptively.

"Good. That's great," he said absently.

It was kind of weird, but I brushed it off. We ordered pizza. After eating dinner, Jae excused herself and went to bed.

Joey looked at me, "Can we talk?"

"Of course. What's up?"

"This isn't my story to tell, but since you live here, you should know." He took a deep breath. "Jae was raped last year. That is why she works from home."

A myriad of emotions came through me. I was stunned - how horrendous she had to go through this, revolted - how dare someone shatter her like that, and saddened - my heart was broken for my friend who didn't deserve that trauma.

"D-did they find the bastard?"

Joey

"No," I lied, "but we are still chasing down leads."

"What about the cops?"

I could feel my face stiffen. "The cops are fucking useless. They say because I am part of The Dragons of Death MC that it was probably just retaliation. They won't do anything."

"What the fuck?"

"You can't tell her that you know. She may eventually come around to telling you. Just please keep an eye on her." I grabbed both of her hands on instinct and stared into her eyes. I swore I could see her soul as I drowned in those pools of molten lava.

I couldn't help myself. I bent down and kissed her. Her lips were warm and soft. They parted slightly, allowing my tongue to slip inside.

Our bodies pressed together heatedly against the wall, breathing heavily as I deepened our connection even further.

Finally, I let her go. Caressing her cheek with my hand, "I need to stay the night at the clubhouse. Will you two be okay?"

Her face was flushed, and she was out of breath, but she was able to nod.

I needed to get out of there. I was not sure how much longer I could keep my hands to myself. Roommate or not - I'm going to fuck her.

7

Brandy

Three months later

Finally the paperwork was all in order. The bank was running smoothly, and Corporate was happier than a pig in shit. Florence had been a godsend. I was truly blessed she'd decided to stay on.

Being able to literally work banker's hours now, 9 to 5, I would meet Jae at home. I was seeing Joey on the sly – well, fucking may be a better term, but it was amazing. I knew his lifestyle rarely afforded him time for a relationship,

As I was leaving work, a disheveled man with wild eyes walked towards me at a brisk pace.

"You!" He bellowed. "You took my job!"

Backing up, I looked around and saw everyone else had already left. "Sir, I don't know what you mean," Knowing exactly what he meant but trying to diffuse the situation, "I was transferred from Ottawa to help out. That's all."

He glared at me. Before I knew what was happening, he rushed me and took a swing, knocking me on my ass. Making me hit my head.

Thankfully a passerby saw it and stopped which scared him off. The woman called 9-1-1 and stayed with me until the squad came. She called Jae for me, who met me at the hospital.

When Jae saw my black eye and bruised face, she had a severe panic attack.

Oh shit, I thought, *it didn't occur to me this would trigger her.*

I held my arms out. She came to me and wrapped her arms around me. I scooted over in my bed so she could crawl in. Poor thing was shaking like a leaf.

The police came and I gave them the description of the man, telling them I believed it was Luke since he mentioned I stole his job. I gave them my permission to go into the bank and take the security tape. I called Florence and explained everything. She was absolutely distraught. I asked her if she was up to taking charge until I came back but also told her to be vigilant because he hadn't been caught yet.

Florence said she wouldn't let me down. That much I already knew. I had my arm around Jae, who was still in bed with me when Joey came in. He took one look at my face and spewed a string of expletives.

"Yeah, but you should see the other guy." I smiled, then quickly grimaced because it hurt to smile.

Running his fingers through his hair, Joey asked, "Who the fuck did this?"

"I honestly don't know. I think it might be the guy I replaced, but I've never seen him before." I held my hand out. I was not sure if there was supposed to be a time limit, I mean, we'd only been roommates for three months - but seeing the look of concern on his face - I knew I was head over heels in love with Joey.

8

Joey

When I saw the damage that motherfucker did to Brandy, I wanted to rip him apart. But I knew my girl wouldn't want me to hurt him. She would want the police to take care of it.

Shit. Did I just say *my girl?* Fuck me walking. I'm definitely in trouble.

I walked over and took her hand. I sat and watched both girls doze off for a couple of hours. The nurse ran us out. They wanted to keep Brandy overnight for observation because she hit her head. I called Deakin. He said he would send a prospect to guard her room. Jae sobbed silently as I took her home.

I gave her a sleeping pill so she could sleep in peace. Her doctor prescribed them to her, but she hadn't needed them since Brandy moved in.

Once she was good and asleep, I grabbed my Glock then rolled out on my bike to do some hunting.

Brandy wanted her guy caught and brought to the police. Fine. I could do that. Jaelyn, she wanted retribution. That I could also do. I had to wait for Deakin's approval, and he finally gave it.

The whole damn club who sheltered this rapist would pay. When you fuck with a Dragon (or someone that means something to us), you fucking will get burned.

This was a two-day mission. First, we needed to get this Luke fellow. Finding him was easy. Motherfucker was at his house drinking a beer. Not a care in the world. We opened his front door. He apparently didn't think he needed the added security of locking it, and I shoved my gun in his face.

The fear of failure all over his face, Luke just stared at me. I could see him sweating and trembling. It didn't make me feel sorry for him - just disgusted.

I pointed to an office chair with wheels. "Go sit on that"

"N-no. I don't want you to kill me."

"If I wanted to kill you, I wouldn't waste my breath on you. It pisses me off you get to breathe my oxygen. Now get in that fucking chair and sit down or I will put you there and it won't be pleasant."

Luke nodded, realizing he had no choice.

I brought out the duct tape and rolled it around him, effectively restraining him to the chair. Then I slapped a big red bow on him with a card that said, "Here is the man who beat up Brandy Locklear. You're welcome."

Next, I rolled him outside in front of his condo. I then went to several neighbors' houses and knocked on the door so they would come out and see the message.

The next night would be even better.

Brandy

Finally, they were releasing me. It was only one day, but I'd had to have a two-hour conversation on the phone with my mom to convince her not to come. Although, I was guessing we will be seeing her soon.

Jae came to pick me up and let the man outside my door go home. She called him a *prospect*, which I guessed meant he was trying to become a member of the club.

I was exhausted by the time we made it home. Jae worked in my room so if I needed anything, she would be there. I didn't see Joey the rest of the day.

9

Joey

I smelled of soot and death as we stood there and watched the Hillsong MC clubhouse burn to the ground.

Satch, the one who violated my sister, was on his knees, watching his entire club be annihilated. This was on him. His club should've punished him. When they didn't- we had to.

We put a thick chain around the clubhouse after we snagged Satch and set the place ablaze.

Snatch glowered at me. "Just kill me and get it over with."

"Oh, I'm going to. I just want to make an example out of you so people will know from now on not to fuck with us or our own."

I took a 22 inch wooden dowel, shoving one end through his right eardrum and all the way through until it came out the left. I could see the anguish on his face from the stabbing, torturous procedure.

I looked at the prospects. "Now hang him up." They had screwed in two hooks to hang the ends of the dowel on.

"Joey?" Dean asked after hanging Satch up.

I turned around.

"He's still alive."

"Light 'em up." I shrugged and walked away.

After calling a report into Deakin, I was whipped. I just wanted to go home and crash. That was until I walked past Brandy's room, and she was making little moaning noises in her bedroom. I wonder if she was dreaming of me?

I took my clothes off and slid in bed with her. She woke up and smiled when she realized it was me.

"Can I touch you?"

"Anywhere," she whispered.

I licked the rim of her ear. "Anywhere? Really?"

"Really."

Twisting her neck, I pulled her mouth to mine for a brief, deep kiss, Her lips tasted like luscious berries. And I could feel her trembling while her warm breath embraced my touch,

She let out a choked sound, and I paused. "Okay?"

"Yes." Her hips tipped, pressing her tighter against my hand. "Please."

I lifted my head for a moment, raising myself up on my arms enough to make eye contact, and she groaned at the sudden because I took my tongue away,

I lifted her tank top off, sucking on each nipple, while I massaged the other, which was patiently waiting. I slowly removed her pajama shorts and was pleased to find she had no panties on. I thrust two fingers inside of her. She shivered for a moment.

"Everything okay?" My mouth was wet, her pupils were wide and dark. "If I do something you don't like, just tell me. Or if you want me to stop—"

I kissed my way down in between her legs.

"Don't you even fucking dare stop," she warned him.

I chuckled against her pussy, making her clit vibrate. Suddenly, the dam broke, crackling through her body like summer lightning, and she was flung to the stars, hoarsely screaming his name.

She was breathing heavily, coming down with her orgasmic high. Before she could even speak or say one word, I flipped her over and entered her wet pussy from behind. She clamped onto my cock, slowing down to stave off my own release, I snaked my arm around and grabbed her breast, squeezing it, while my other hand slid down and rubbed her swollen clit.

"Mine," I growled, which sent us over the edge, her screaming my name over and over.

"I love you, beautiful."

She looked at me, her eyes shining.

"I love you too."

10

Brandy

There was a knock at the door – well, it sounded more like someone was trying to beat it down - that woke us all up in the morning.

We all stumbled downstairs in our pajamas. There were two police officers at the door. I figured they were there for me. Hopefully they caught Luke.

Opening the door, they said, "Hello. We are with the sheriff's department. I'm Officer Keith and this is Officer Turner. Does a Joseph Birchfield live here?"

I saw another side of Jae I'd never seen before. "Oh, for fuck's sake. You know he lives here. What are you trying to pin on him now?"

Joey pushed through us, grinning at Jae. She was the levelheaded one. For her to be so pissed, there must be history there.

"What do you want?" Joey asked the officers.

"Can we talk inside?"

"Sure."

Joey let them in, and we all followed.

Officer Keith did all the talking. "I'm going to be honest with you. We have two crimes, and you are linked to both of them. If you come clean now - it can only help you."

"What are these alleged crimes?" Joey yawned like he was bored.

"First, Luke Perty was assaulted at his house two nights ago."

I jumped up. "You mean the same Luke Perty who did this to my face? You honestly have the balls to come here and question any of us about dick that happens to him?"

"Ma'am, we have detained him for his part in your assault."

"His part? He did it all! Are you stupid?"

Officer Turner tried to turn things around. "Now, last night, the Hillsong MC was torched to death."

"The whole club?" Joey tried to look mortified.

The officers didn't answer; they just said, "We have a credible witness that places you at both crime scenes."

"Bullshit. You would've already arrested me."

I stood back up again and looked at Jae. "I'm sorry, we were going to tell you." Then she looked at the officers. "It's bullshit anyway because Joey was home both nights in bed with me."

"Ma'am, do you realize you could go to jail for perjury?"

"Sir, I am not a liar. Do you want my panties as evidence?"

"Um, babe, you didn't have panties on last night."

I was not sure who that struck as funnier, me or Joey.

I looked at the officers. "Now, we will be calling a lawyer, so if you have any more bullshit questions - please go through him."

Epilogue

Brandy

We were so worried about Jae not accepting us, and she turned out to be our biggest cheerleader. I was learning the MC life, and I adored it.

Jae met a woman at her support group, and they meshed really well together, so I kept my plan and moved into my house because Gloria had moved in with her.

Joey moved in with me; the two of us got involved in this crazy relationship, but it worked out well for us. To others, we were an unusual pairing, but we knew this complicated love thing wasn't supposed to be easy.

Our chaotic love was all we needed.

About the Author

Emery LeeAnn is an International Best Selling Author who lives in Ohio with her family. Besides being addicted to coffee, she is a true believer that variety adds spice to your life. Writing in every genre gives her the variety she craves. Her characters like to invade her mind every hour of the day usually waking her up in the middle of the night. Loving the dark and gray side of things, she is exploring her passion with the written word. There are many wonders to come from her in her twisted Wonderland..... Stick around you may find you enjoy her special brand of torture.

Want to follow her?

https://linktr.ee/EmeryLeeann

Exes & Ohs
Keighley Bradford

About Exes & Ohs

Indie is a flight attendant who's returned home from working an international flight, only to find her boyfriend between the sheets with another woman — on their anniversary. She finds herself at the doorstep of her friend's apartment seeking someplace safe to stay until things settle between them. Only, her ex isn't getting the message that they're over, and Indie is ready to finally take the plunge and put him in her past for good.

Xavier adores Indie and would do anything for her — including offering her to be his new roommate...and to be her first-ever hook up after her ass of an ex-boyfriend failed to worship her properly. He isn't afraid of showing her what she's been missing out on. And from the way she moans from his touch, he plans to give her more than one orgasm before night's end.

1

Indie

When I'd got home from the airport after a long-haul flight for work, the last thing I'd expected to find was my boyfriend between the sheets of our bed with another woman. Her hands tied to the bedpost, ass up in the air, screaming how much she liked it. The pair were completely oblivious to the fact I was even standing there, listening to my boyfriend tell his mistress how good she took him.

It was like a lightbulb went off in my head. Suddenly, it all made sense. Our relationship had been doomed from the start. I could never satisfy him in the bedroom, and this was why. I had no interest in any of this....*stuff*...and he did. It made me wonder if that was what all guys were really into.

I didn't stay to ask, though. Nope. I ran out the front door with nothing but my purse in hand. I couldn't get out of there quick enough.

I'm such a fool.

He told me time and time again that nothing was happening between them, and I believed him every single time. He'd made me think I was crazy for even suggesting he'd sleep with her. She's assured me just the same. Yet I'd now seen it with my own two eyes. There was no mistaking that the girl in his bed wasn't me.

I knew he'd lost interest; knew I wasn't satisfying his needs. I was selfish in letting this go on for as long as I had, not wanting to admit that our time had come to an end. Could you blame me, though? Jeremy was the first real boyfriend I'd ever had. I didn't want the happy memories to end, and lo and behold, he'd just tainted all of them.

I couldn't believe I thought dressing risqué and doing a strip tease for him would fix our relationship. I'd spent so much time researching this fantasy too, eager to not disappoint him. Travelling from the airport home in nothing but sexy lingerie underneath a long wool coat had been no easy feat in the summer heat. I'd been ready to compromise and give him something he'd been begging me for, determined to please him for our anniversary. In return, he got me a gift I hadn't asked for — the conniving basted getting caught red-handed screwing his best friend.

What made it all worse? We had a call scheduled for that same time to celebrate. It was how I knew he'd be home, after all. I just hadn't expected he'd have company, since he asked to spice things up for the special occasion. Now I wasn't someone who enjoyed phone sex, but of course, I played along, knowing I'd be home to surprise him with *actual* sex instead. A good compromise...or so I thought. Discovering them together made me wonder if he'd intended for her to be there all along. He was probably going to make her touch him while we spoke, pretending it was me who was getting him off when he knew it was really her. A woman who could actually please him.

I shouldn't have been surprised that he'd strung me along. I knew things had been rocky for a little while now, but to cheat on me? It hurt more than parting ways would've. Cheating said that I wasn't enough for him anymore. Cheating said there was nothing left to save. Cheating was the final nail in the coffin that forced me to say goodbye to what we had. As far as I was concerned, he'd crossed a line he could never come back from. I didn't care how much he begged or grovelled. It was over. I was done fighting for a man who so clearly didn't want me. I wouldn't be that woman. Not any more.

I had no idea how much time had passed, or how long I'd been aimlessly wandering the streets of Melbourne. All I knew was that the sun had long since set, and I'd somehow ended up in the city. My feet had grown tired from the walk, the pain only accentuated by the heels I was wearing. My body was a hot mess as well, undoubtedly made worse by my stupidity in wearing this damn wool coat. Not to mention, my eyes were sore and swollen, a sign of a battle lost to the tears I'd shun whilst grieving what once was. I was exhausted from the jet lag too, which only made this whole situation worse. I feared I could drop at any moment, and I wasn't too keen on the idea of being caught out and about in the city half naked. I'd already received enough odd looks for dressing like this to begin with. I'd prefer to move on and forget this night ever happened, truth be told. That was wishful thinking, though.

Thankfully, I soon found myself at the footsteps of a building I'd only ever been to once before. I probably should've called first, but the truth was, I wasn't sure where else to go. I didn't want to waste money on a hotel — I couldn't risk Jeremy tracking my whereabouts since I'd been boycotting his calls — and I'd already tried my best friend's apartment with no luck, either. She was either deep asleep after our flight earlier or had somehow found the energy to have a fun time with one of her many gentlemen callers. Time will tell.

I knocked on his door and waited for him to open it. For a guy I barely knew, Xavier Carmichael had quickly become one of my most trusted allies. I hoped he didn't mind the intrusion.

"Hey stranger," he said by way of greeting, his face falling as he took me in. I hated to think about how I looked right now. My mascara smudged, if not running down my face. Eyes red and puffy. I didn't need a mirror to know I was a mess. I felt like absolute shit right now, and I'd bet it showed.

"I caught my boyfriend in bed with another woman," I said by way of explanation. There was no point beating around the bush about it. He not only left me heartbroken but homeless. I not only needed a place to stay for the night, but I needed a trusted friend to lend an ear as well. I didn't expect him to offer me both, but just one would be enough to help me see the night through.

Xavier closed his eyes and cursed, uttering, "I'm so sorry, Indie." For some reason, his swearing didn't bother me. Perhaps because there was something about Xavier that made me feel safe. It was a rare quality, especially for a man. Whenever Jeremy swore, I'd always find myself getting on edge, wondering what I'd done wrong now.

I met Xavier in a coffee shop of all places, a little nook of a place in the city not too far from here. Some days I'd just needed to get out of the house and away from Jeremy. I'd lie and say I was seeing Liv, when really, I just needed a break from his overbearing, possessive behaviour. He never wanted me to anywhere by myself, and if he wasn't in the mood to come with me, he'd make me feel guilty for leaving him alone. It was a massive red flag I should've seen sooner. Thankfully, Liv was the only friend of mine he trusted me to be around, and I knew she'd always have my back if I ever used her as a scapegoat as well. As such, it gave me the perfect alibi to sneak out and hang with my new friend. It was an opportunity I took as often as I could.

He gestured for me to come inside. I smiled gratefully and moved toward the couch. My body sagged into the soft cushions with ease, my feet feeling instant relief. Honestly, I began to wonder if Xavier would let me sleep on his couch tonight. It felt so good sitting here, I imagined laying down would be just as nice.

My phone buzzed in my purse. I didn't look at the caller ID to know who it was.

Jeremy.

He hadn't stopped calling and texting me since I saw him with Ebony. Well, since he realised I'd seen him with her. He hadn't a clue I'd witnessed a damn thing until I told him I never wanted to see him again. Honestly, I was a fool to stay with him for as long as I had, but I knew I'd be an even bigger fool if I went back to him.

Xavier sat beside me, a glass of gin in his hand outstretched in offering. "Do you want to talk about it? You can say no."

I shrugged, accepting the glass. "There's not much else to tell. I loved him, but he didn't love me. I came home to surprise him for our anniversary, and instead, he shocked me by screwing his best friend in our bed. Silly me, huh? Thinking I'd do something nice for my man to celebrate such an occasion."

"It wasn't stupid, Indie," he assured me, resting an arm on my shoulder. "If anything, I think the gesture was sweet. The jackass didn't deserve you, and now you know that."

"I guess so," I replied dismissively, not believing him in the slightest.

"There's no 'guess' about it, Indie," Xavier insisted. "Any guy who cheats on his girl is a fucking undeserving jackass, plain and simple."

"I should've seen the red flags sooner," I replied. Hell, I saw them and just didn't care. He loved me. What more could I have wanted from my man?

"Indie, his cheating isn't your fault. You know that, right?"

On some level, I knew that, but what Xavier didn't understand was that it was in a way my fault as well. I fought to keep us together when I shouldn't have. I was the one so desperate for a happily ever after that I drove him away.

I forced a smile. "It doesn't matter. He'll justify it however way he wants to see to it I was the bad guy in our love story. But I don't care. He crossed a line and broke the trust I'd given him. I'm done. We're done. It's over now. I can't forgive him for this. I just can't."

"Where are you staying tonight?" he asked softly.

I sighed. "I don't know yet. I just know I can't go home."

Home. I wasn't sure it'd ever feel like home again now that he'd tarnished the memories I'd had in that house. It was a shame. It'd been my childhood house as well. My parents had left it to me when they died. I'd never lived anywhere else but there, and now I wasn't sure if I'd ever find the strength to step through the threshold again.

He nodded. "Then you'll stay here tonight, and for as long as you need."

"I appreciate the offer, Xavier, but I can't intrude like that. I'm sure I'll figure something out. You've already been gracious in lending me your time."

I had no idea why I was being so polite right now. Habit, I guessed. This was what I'd been hoping for — a place to stay. Why did I turn down his offer?

"You can and you will," he insisted. "You can barely walk, Indie. Don't think I didn't notice that your feet are sore and swollen. Plus, it's late — too late for a beautiful woman like yourself to be walking around the city alone. Plus, that prick doesn't know me. He won't come looking for you here. You're safe and can rest easy knowing that."

"Thank you."

"You don't need to thank me, Indie. Only a jackass would toss you on the street after all you've been through. No friend of mine will ever not be welcomed here should they need a safe haven. Remember that."

"Sorry," I said, shaking my head. "I guess I'm just not used to—"

"A man treating a woman right?" he suggested with a raised brow.

I offered a small laugh. I supposed that was one way to put it.

"I'm not used to people being so generous or kind," I replied truthfully. It was usually the other way around — me giving and them taking. It'd been a long time since someone had given and I'd taken, but, well, this situation called for an olive branch and I'd happily accept it right now.

"Come on, you look beat," he said, offering me his hands to help me stand. "Let me show you to your room."

I flinched as I stood, pain shooting through my feet and up my legs with the weight of my body on them once more. But I forced a smile and swallowed the groan threatening to escape my lips. I couldn't let Xavier see how much pain I was in. After all, I was the idiot who walked around the city all evening in high-heeled shoes.

Xavier led me down the hallway to a room with a beautiful view of the city outside. I was surprised, to say the least. Not many apartments would have such stunning views from every room.

"Here you go," he said to me. "Bathroom is across the hall, kitchen back near the living room. And my room is just down the end there if you need me. There's a lock on your door as well, if you need it."

I frowned. "Why would I need it?"

"Honestly, Indie, I hope you don't need it, however, I am also aware that our friendship is still quite new, and I don't know all the details about your relationship with your...ex," he said gently. "I want you to feel safe and comfortable here. If sleeping with the door locked brings you peace of mind, so be it. I'll take no offence."

I was trying so hard to not break down in front of Xavier. His kindness was stirring things up inside of me and I didn't want to scare him off or make him regret giving me a place to stay for the night because I couldn't keep it together for a few measly minutes. I could cry my heart out once I was safely in my room, where he wouldn't feel the need to console me.

I didn't deserve his kindness. After all, I'd done this to myself. I should've ended things sooner. I knew we were over long ago, I'd just dragged out the inevitable and got hurt in the process. So now I had an ex. My *first* ex at that. Hopefully the first of not too many. It was such a strange thought. I'd gone from having a boyfriend one minute to having an ex the next. Was that what I'd been afraid of all along? The label I'd be assigned if we'd broken up? It didn't seem so bad now that it was done. And at least I was only his ex. To me, he'd always be a cheater. That was so much worse of a memory to have.

"Thank you," I said once again. "You're a good man, Xavier."

"No problem," he replied, a faint blush creeping upon his cheeks. Had I embarrassed him with the compliment? "I'll let you get some sleep. Goodnight, Indie."

"*Um*...Xavier?" I called softly as he began to retreat down the hall toward his room.

He paused and turned back toward me. "Yes?"

"Could I...*uh*...borrow a shirt to sleep in, by chance?" I could feel my cheeks begin to heat as I added, "I...*uh*...don't have anything on under this coat, if you know what I mean..."

I'd never been one of those girls who could sleep naked in bed. Even after sex, I'd have to slip something on before I fell asleep. Sure, I could've technically counted the lingerie I had on as clothes, but as far as I was concerned, this set was getting thrown the minute I took it off. I'd bought it for this occasion and didn't want to be haunted by the memories of tonight after what'd happened. Hell, even this coat was getting thrown. I'd be donating it to someplace. That way I wouldn't feel guilty since I knew how much money it'd cost me. Someone in need could benefit from having it, whilst I'd benefit by forgetting what my... ex...did to me tonight.

"Of course," he said, recognition clouding his eyes. He returned shortly later with a couple of tees and boxers for me. "Just guessing you'll need some clothes for tomorrow too, huh?"

I looked away sheepishly, embarrassed with him knowing the truth of the situation. I was all but naked right now, and I found it hard to believe he hadn't speculated as such when I'd arrived and refused to remove the article of clothing.

"I didn't really think this through, did I?"

He took a step forward, gently touching my elbow as if uncertain if this was okay. "Indie, you reacted like any human would've in that situation. Hell, I know a few women who may have even thrown something at their men for doing what he did to you. Honestly, don't stress about this. Clothes are replaceable, unlike trust. I don't want you stressing about living arrangements when I have a perfectly good spare bedroom that's never been used. You'll stay with me for however long you need. I don't want to hear any arguments about it."

"Xavier," I whispered, meeting his eyes once more.

"Yes, Indie."

"Promise me you won't let me go back."

2

Xavier

Promise me you won't let me go back.

Those words had haunted me since the day Indie showed up at my doorstep. She'd sounded so broken and defeated. As if her whole world had fallen apart, and in a way, it had. From what she'd told me, she and her boyfriend had been together for years. That night was supposed to have been their anniversary. She'd come home to surprise him, and found him with another woman instead.

I'd never met the guy, and for his sake, he better pray that I never did. A man who cheated on his woman was the lowest of lows in my books. I didn't care if they were a friend or foe. Redemption wasn't an option when it came to cheating on your partner, and I reminded Indie of that every time the bastard called or texted. It was perhaps a little cliche, but at the end of the day, actions always spoke louder than words. It didn't matter how often he begged for her forgiveness. If he cheated once, he'd cheat again. It was that simple.

Unfortunately for her, the guy just couldn't seem to get the message that they were over. I could see the pain on her face whenever she saw his name flash on the screen. She was ready to end that chapter of her life, and he wouldn't let her go. His persistence was never-ending; he was contacting her at all hours of the day nonstop. I'd seen the messages he'd been sending her as well. His texts may have been seemingly sweet at first, but that all changed the more she ignored him. He began to act like she owed him; like she belonged to him. His words had manipulation written all over them. I understood why she was worried — she was frightened he'd talk her into returning to him. I wouldn't let that happen, though. She deserved a hell of a lot better than that scumbag, and I'd see to it that she knew that.

Thankfully, she'd accepted my offer to stay with me, so it'd be a hell of a lot easier to achieve that goal with her living under the same roof as me. I'd gone with her to collect her things from her house as well. The bastard was seemingly out at the time for some work thing she knew he wouldn't miss, which was probably for the best. I didn't want to get arrested for beating the man if he'd come at her, and somehow, I suspected that's exactly what would've happened if he'd been home. From his messages, I didn't peg him as a man who'd respect her wishes for space and keep his distance once he saw her again. I was glad she was no longer with him. She could do so much better.

Since Indie moved in, we'd developed a nice routine living together. It was easier than I'd expected, after living alone for so long. I was used to doing everything myself…and it seemed she was as well. It made compromising on household tasks somewhat difficult. I hadn't had to do that since my last relationship, truth be told, and after everything she'd been through, I didn't want her worrying about cooking or cleaning when I was happy to do. Hell, I *wanted* to do those things for her, to make her life easier. Apparently, she wasn't used to that kind of treatment and it showed.

Indie had returned to work earlier this week. Her first international flight since living with me. I had to say, it felt weird not coming home and seeing her body curled up on my couch with a book in her hand. Apparently, I'd quickly grown comfortable with her being here, and that fact didn't bother me in the slightest. I wasn't afraid to admit that it was nice to have someone to come home to, even if things between us weren't romantic in nature.

Not that you wouldn't take her against the door if you had the chance, I thought.

It was hard to deny that I was attracted to Indie. Not only was she drop-dead gorgeous, but she was also sweet and kind. A lethal combination when it came to the appendage in my pants. I liked her brain as much as her looks, and her staying here meant I was only liking her personality more and more as I got to know her. But right now, my attraction didn't matter. She needed a friend, not another asshole taking advantage of her. As such, I kept my feelings hidden and only expressed them when I was in the privacy of the shower. Something I might do before she gets home tonight to ease my wandering mind.

I unlocked the door to my apartment and stepped inside, a huge grin spreading across my face as I saw her beautiful blonde locks in an all too familiar space of the lounge room. I hadn't thought I'd get to see her until morning. Unlike her ex, I was delighted by the surprise.

"You're back!" I exclaimed, making my way toward her. "How was Italy?"

As I got closer, I could tell something was off. Normally she was curled up on the couch with a book. Relaxing, if you will. Her beautiful blue eyes would light up when they saw me. Right now, though, she looked far from relaxed. She looked like she was ready to fight somebody, phone gripped tightly in her hand. *What the hell has that fucker done now?*

"Work was fine, until it wasn't," she replied with a little shrug. "Such is life, I guess."

"What happened?" I asked, sitting beside her. She was playing it off, but I could tell it bothered her.

"Jeremy," she answered somewhat reluctantly. "Apparently he has now resorted to showing up at the airport and waiting for me. I have no idea if he knew my flight schedule, or if he was just guessing and hanging around until I showed up. He'd cornered me outside as well, away from airport security."

Fucking bastard. This was getting ridiculous. Did this guy seriously not understand boundaries or repercussions? Cheat on your girl and lose her. End of story. It shouldn't be that hard of a concept to grasp, so why the hell wasn't he leaving her alone?

"I'm lucky Liv caught up with me," Indie continued, mentioning her best friend and coworker. "I'd been waiting outside for her to share a taxi. Poor thing was crook as a dog all day, yet she scared him off with ease. Threatened to have him blacklisted from ever flying again for harassing airport staff. Thankfully, he backed away. I don't think he followed us, but he could be assuming I'm at Liv's… She's promised to call me if he shows up there, though. I don't want him harassing her, either, especially while she's unwell."

Good. I liked Liv. She was a badass babe. I'd only met her once, but I liked her vibe and made sure to let her know she was welcome to pop by anytime since Indie had been struggling at the time to come to terms with this being her new place of residence. If things escalated with his guy and she needed a safe haven as well, she could stay here, no questions asked. I didn't have another spare room, but she was welcome to mine while I slept on the couch. Of course, I'd insist on authorities getting involved by that point as well. Like hell should someone be afraid to stay in their own home.

Still, I couldn't help but worry for Indie. This was obsessive behaviour. How far would this guy go to get her back?

"Indie, have you considered getting a restraining order against Jeremy?"

She frowned, sitting up straighter. "No, why? Do you think he would hurt me?"

"I don't know the guy, so I can't answer that," I told her truthfully. "Only you can. He mightn't have hurt you before, but his obsessive behaviour has me concerned that maybe he might under the right circumstances. Plus, you've made it clear you're not interested anymore. He should be backing down and he's not. Blowing up your phone is one thing. Stalking you at work is another. It's not right and he knows it, or else he wouldn't have cornered you outside alone. It was an intentional move, Indie, and I can't help but be worried. I care for you. I don't like that he's doing this to you."

"Liv said the same thing," Indie said with a sigh, now playing with the ring on her finger. "He's always had a…possessive…streak when it's come to me. I thought my leaving him would end it, but it's only getting worse. The texts, the calls, now this... Honestly, I thought he'd even try to follow me home. It's getting out of hand."

Home. My apartment had become her home. I liked that. I liked that a bloody lot, in fact.

"I don't like feeling this way, either," she added, eyes flickering between me and her fingertips. "Truthfully, Xavier, I don't think he's going to stop until he knows I've moved on. Maybe then he'll be done with me once and for all. I won't be a shiny new toy that was only his, you know? Once someone else has had their turn, he won't want me anymore."

I shook my head in disgust. "You're not an *object*, Indie. You shouldn't be talking about yourself like that. Hell, he should've never made you feel like that. Your worth has nothing to do with...*sex*."

She shrugged sheepishly. "You may think so, but I doubt he sees it that way. He made some remark today about me being so in love with him I could never sleep with another guy, and...I may have told him I already have out of spite."

I froze. *Wait...* She was sleeping with other people already? I thought she wasn't ready to move on yet? I hadn't heard her bring any guys home, either... Was I okay with it if she had? I did tell her to make herself at home, after all. I mightn't have liked it, but I didn't really have a right to tell her not to, either. Just because I liked her as more than a friend didn't mean she'd reciprocated those feelings.

"I haven't," she clarified quickly. "But...I want to. Not for Jeremy, but for me. He was my first, and I don't want him to be my only...not anymore. We're done, and I think that'd feel more concrete if I solidified that by doing the deed, so to speak. Only...I've never really been good at doing hook-ups. Do— Do you think you could help me set something up on one of those apps?"

"Of course, if that's what you want," I answered evenly, swallowing my feelings about it. I wasn't sure why this was bothering me so much. Perhaps because I knew what the guys on the apps were like and thought she could do better. They'd lie to her, just like her ex. They'd do anything, say anything, if it meant getting into her pants. It's why I stopped using them. I didn't like being associated with such dickish behaviour.

"It is," she answered. "I trust your opinion on the matter. Plus, you know what guys find appealing and can help me customise my profile accordingly. The sooner I get this over with the better."

Oh trust me, she wasn't going to have any issue finding matches online. It'd come down to her taste in men and if any of them were appealing to her. A picture was worth a thousand words. I bet she wouldn't even need to fill out the profile with any prompts to have her inbox filling up with matches.

However, I also didn't want her jumping the first guy she matched with, either. If she was so eager to do this, she might land herself in hot water if she didn't properly vet the guy first. I was liking this idea less and less. In fact, it was really beginning to unsettle me.

"Indie..."

"Yes, Xavier?" she asked so soft, so sweetly. I could tell from those two words alone that she really wanted this. Nothing would change her mind. Telling her my concerns wouldn't stop her from trying. Still, I had to try something — anything — to make her reconsider.

I took her hand in mine, squeezing it as I said, "Are you sure about this? *Really* sure about it? As you said, you don't normally do hook-ups. I worry about how you'll feel afterwards if you're not one-hundred per cent sure about wanting one. I just don't want you to rush this and have any regrets. There's no going back once you do this."

She sighed softly. "Your concern is sweet, but I have to do this, Xavier. This is about putting the final nail in the coffin and extraditing Jeremy from my life once and for all. I don't know how to describe it to you, but it feels like I'm still connected to him and I need that connection severed so I can move on. I feel I can't do that until I've slept with someone else and put him in my past. Of course, I have no idea if this is the right way to go about it, but it's not like I can just walk up to a guy in a bar and say will you have sex with me? It seems just as risky, and it's not like I have many friends who can set me up. Sure, Liv has her boy toys, but I don't really like the idea of sleeping with someone my best friend has been with. I'm not left with many options, Xavier. This is the only way."

I hated that she felt this way. I hated that she felt she had to sleep with some bastard who'd use her for his pleasure and not give her what she deserved. It wasn't right, especially after everything she'd been through. She deserved to be worshipped. To know what it was like to have a man devoted to her pleasure and not his own. I doubted she'd find many guys on the app or take the time to find one. She was eager to have this done.

"Then let me do the honour," I found myself saying before I could stop myself.

Her eyes went wide. "W— What?"

I was taking a huge gamble right now, but I liked Indie. She was an incredible woman, and her ex didn't see that. Neither would those boys on the apps. She could reject my offer, but it made sense for us to do this together. She wanted the job done as soon as possible. I was here, willing and ready to please her. There was no account activation needed, no vetting or small talk conversations required. She knew me. She trusted me. So why hook up with some stranger when there was a safer option available?

I took a deep breath and said again, "Let me do the honour, Indie. I understand your desire to not have that bastard be your one and only, but I don't want you to be taken advantage of by another arsehole, either. You deserve so much better than what most of them are even capable of. Best of all, we're friends. You know I'm not going to dick you around. I like having you around too much to risk that. Plus, you know me, trust me, the same way I know and trust you. If you're wanting to move on like this...then let me do the honour."

Her lips parted slightly. "You'd do that for me?"

"I'd do anything for you, Indie."

Her brows furrowed. "Y— You're not worried it'd make things... awkward...between us afterwards? It's not like we can just walk away and pretend it never happened. We live together, Xavier."

I couldn't help but smile. I wasn't hearing a no, just concerns about how it could impact our friendship, which I took as a good sign that she didn't want to lose me, either. I was glad we were on the same page about that. It gave me hope we'd be just fine.

My smile shifted into a smirk. "Afraid you'll see me walking around the house and want to jump me, beautiful?"

She bit her lip cheekily. "Assuming the sex isn't bad? Perhaps..."

"Oh, the sex won't be bad, beautiful," I quipped confidently. "I happen to know my way around the female body."

She offered a small laugh. "No, actually I was more worried for you. I'm not sure I'm all that...good...in bed. I could never satisfy Jeremy, and I'm not really into anything all that...*kinky*. I think I'd disappoint you and most men."

That bastard. Did he really make her doubt her worth because they had different preferences when it came to the bedroom? If he wasn't willing to enjoy what she liked, then he should've walked away a hell of a lot sooner instead of stringing her along. There were plenty of guys out there who'd have treated her right given the chance.

Myself included.

"You could never disappoint me, beautiful," I promised her, resting a palm on her cheek. "I'd only be disappointed with *myself* if you didn't enjoy the experience as much as I did."

"Really?" she asked softly, relief palpable in her voice.

I nodded. "We'll only do what you're comfortable with. We can keep it simple. No need to overcomplicate it. Mind you, there is *nothing* wrong with vanilla sex. Vanilla is one of my favourite flavours, in fact..."

A blush crept over her beautiful porcelain skin. "You don't like...*kinky*...sex?"

I smirked. "Well, I didn't say that. But, sex is only enjoyable if both partners are having fun. What I want is to make this experience pleasurable for you, Indie. I want you to forget all about what's-his-face and focus only on the way *I* make you feel."

She bit her lip once more, this time anticipation clouding her eyes, not nerves. "And how's that?"

I crawled to my knees. "Let me show you, beautiful."

3

Indie

Xavier kneeled before me, causing my eyes to widen in shock. *Ah...*what was he doing? Was he about to go down on me? Here, on the couch, in the middle of the living room? You know, the place where his guests often sat and chatted over a glass of wine?

His strong hands answered my question for me as they parted my thighs, spreading them wide. My little black dress rose up toward my hips, giving him a glimpse at what I had on underneath. I had no doubt in my mind that he knew what he was doing too. From the ravenous look in his brown eyes, Xavier wasn't planning on keeping the scrape of lace on me for much longer anyway.

He leaned forward and gently kissed my inner thigh. "Is this okay, beautiful?"

"Yes," I replied breathlessly. Dear Lord, he'd barely touched me and I was already melting like putty. The anticipation of what else he could do to me had me well and truly wet and ready for him. I'd never felt so alive, so electric, from such a small gesture. I was excited to see what he did to me next.

"Good." His fingertips gently danced upon my skin, starting from my ankles and working their way up higher and higher, stopping as they approached my ass. His hands then gripped me tightly before they yanked me closer to him. A gasp of surprise fell from my lips. I'd never been touched like this before, and I was shocked by how much I liked it.

"*Hmm*...yes, much better," Xavier mused, a wicked grin on his face. "Now you can lay back and relax while I eat you out."

Lord Almighty, this man knew exactly what to say and how to say it to make my body crave him. I couldn't remember the last time I'd been so turned on from words alone. Hell, I couldn't remember the last time I'd felt so desired.

"Sh— Shouldn't we move to the bedroom?" I asked warily, not wanting to ruin the moment, but also wary of the space we occupied. If we made a mess on his couch...

Xavier gently kissed my inner thigh again. "Oh, don't you worry, beautiful. We're only just getting started. There's plenty of time for bedroom activities after foreplay. But if that'd make you more comfortable, I can certainly move us in there..."

Move us in there. It was almost comical, like he thought he could lift me and whisk me away like one of those heroines in a romance novel. But I didn't comment as such. Instead, I just shook my head. I liked that this was different from anything I'd experienced before. I liked that he had no quarrels about us getting down and dirty on his — quite possibly expensive — couch. It was surprisingly...hot.

He kissed my inner thigh once more, only this time, his mouth was much, much higher than before. His fingertips slid beneath my panties, causing him to groan. "Fuck, beautiful. You're so wet already."

He then slipped a finger into my core, eliciting a soft moan from my lips as my head tilted back in pleasure. Why did that feel so much better than my own inside of me? This man could quite possibly be my undoing. Was sex supposed to feel this good? It never had with Jeremy...

Xavier's heated gaze held mine as he slid his thick number in and out of my pussy, a wicked grin growing wide and wider on his lips each time I moaned in pleasure. *My oh my.* I liked that look. I liked it a freaking lot. This man was literally on his knees, looking up at me as if it were an honour to be there. As if it was his God-given duty to give me as many orgasms as he possibly could, and that it was a damn pleasure to do so. I don't think my ex had ever looked at me like that. Hell, I *know* he hadn't. He never went down on me, either. He made an excuse every single chance he could, yet expected me to happily sit there bobbing up and down, taking his cock like a good little girl.

Yuck. Why had I stayed with him for so long? This right here was just a casual, one-time thing, and yet I'd felt more pleasure in merely minutes with Xavier than I ever had in my entire relationship with Jeremy. Was this normal for a fling, or had Jeremy just not had a freaking clue what he was doing when it came to the bedroom?

Xavier withdrew his finger, causing me to whimper. He chuckled lightly, knowing I wanted more without asking. Apparently, I was a greedy girl this evening and I couldn't get enough of him. Before I could ask him to keep going, he took the finger that had been inside of me and sucked it clean.

Holy fuck... My jaw dropped in awe. I hadn't thought it possible to get even wetter than I already was and he'd just proven me wrong. Hell, Xavier was proving me wrong on all accounts tonight. I thought I'd experienced sex before...but this felt like something else entirely. Something I happened to like quite a lot.

"You taste so good, beautiful. Bet you'll taste just as good with my mouth."

"I bet I would," I remarked boldly. I had no idea where that came from, but it probably had something to do with how desperate I was to find out how much he enjoyed tasting me with his tongue. With how good he was making me feel, though, I wanted to return the favour. Xavier, however, had other plans. His hands tightened on my thighs, holding me in place when he sensed me preparing to reposition.

"Don't you dare move," he ordered. "I'm nowhere near done with you yet, beautiful."

I frowned in confusion. "You don't want me to go down on you? I thought all men liked it when a woman was on her knees..."

He clucked his tongue. "Well, you're not wrong, beautiful, but two things — first, I don't do tit for tat. I'm going down on you because I *want* to. Because I *enjoy* it. I don't expect you to do the same, especially not out of any misguided sense of obligation. If you ever take my cock in your mouth, I want it to be because you have an uncontrollable desire to do so. Nothing else, okay? Second, tonight is all about *your* pleasure, not mine. As such, you won't be servicing my cock. Instead, it's at your mercy, a slave to your beautiful pussy with only one objective — to pleasure you."

My oh my. This man. He continued to surprise me. Were most men this selfless in the bedroom, or was he an anomaly? I'd only ever read such talk in romance novels. I never expected this in reality.

"Now, if you don't mind, I'd like to get back to licking, sucking and teasing every inch of your beautiful body until you're coming hard of my cock and tongue."

I shivered with anticipation. *Yes, please.* I liked the sound of that a lot.

Xavier buried himself at the apex of my thighs, pushing my panties aside to access my pussy. Each touch felt absolutely divine, but it wasn't enough after his spicy words had set me alight. I wanted more. I *needed* more.

"Rip them off," I told him, surprising us both.

A wicked gleam shone in his eyes. "Really?"

I nodded. I mightn't have expected to say it, but I wanted it. I wanted him to rip my panties right off of me. Needed it in fact. *Craved it.* I wanted to experience what I never had before — giving into my desires, however naughty they may be.

"Maybe you're more kinky than you think, beautiful," he teased, kissing my pussy once more. Maybe he was right. Maybe I'd never felt comfortable enough with Jeremy to let myself want anything remotely unconventional. Aside from me going down on him, we only ever did it missionary. I had a feeling Xavier had something else in mind other than that position, though. Nothing too wild or crazy...unless maybe I begged him for it.

"I guess we'll find out," I mused, letting him know I was open to trying something a little...*dirtier*...than just plain old vanilla. Besides, he'd said we'd only do what I was comfortable with, which meant I was taking the lead on this one. If I didn't like something, I'd tell him and we'd stop. This could actually be a good opportunity for me to try new things out of my comfort zone. Things that I hadn't let myself explore before now.

Xavier tore my panties off as requested and threw the scrappy piece of material to the floor. It was just as hot as I'd imagined it would be. The lack of lace in his way gave him ample room to play with my pussy. Licking. Sucking. *Devouring*.

God, I needed more.

My hands buried themselves in the thick strands of his hair as he worked his magic on my body, making it shake with pleasure. The moment he added his fingers back inside me, it was over. The combination of him filling me whilst taking care of my clit sent me over the edge. I was pretty damn sure the neighbours heard me screaming his name.

"Holy shit," I whispered, coming down from my orgasm.

"And I'm only just getting started," he mused, rising to stand. Somehow, I followed suit, his muscled arms lifting me from the couch and carrying me to the bedroom, just like he'd promised. Xavier then laid me softly on the bed, lying beside me, letting his fingers play with the tendrils of my hair. "Tell me, how do you like it, beautiful? What gives you the most pleasure?"

I felt my cheeks heat with embarrassment. "I don't really know..."

"That's okay," he assured me with a sweet and gentle kiss on the forehead. "*Hmm*... Any fantasies on your mind that I can make a reality?"

I bit my lip and nodded, whispering a couple of ideas in his ear. From his playful grin, I knew he liked them. I guessed reading romance books after all these years was finally going to come in handy.

"Don't worry, beautiful. I can make those happen."

And he did. He really freaking did. Honestly, it was the best sex I'd ever had. Not that the bar was set too high by Jeremy, apparently, but I was now worried about the next man to cross my path. Would he treat me as well as Xavier did tonight? Would he care about my pleasure as much as he had? He'd spoilt me, I was sure. I mean, two orgasms in one night? I'm sure he'd have made it three if I asked.

Xavier kissed the crook of my neck, wrapping an arm around my waist. "Fuck, Indie, that was amazing. *You* are amazing."

I couldn't agree more. The man knew how to please a woman, that was for damn sure. That was hands down a night I'd never forget. However, afterward, as we were falling asleep in his bed, reality dawned on me.

I'd just slept with not only my friend, but my roommate...

The worst part of all? I *really* freaking loved it. More than I should've.

After all, this was a one-time thing. Xavier fucking me was simply a favour, not something he'd actually desired. It was best I remember that come morning when we'd inevitably pretend that this never happened.

The End...For Now

You can read more about Indie and Xavier's story in *Love Me, Love Me Not* where these two love birds make an appearance in her best friend's love story. Fear not, Indie and Xavier will be getting their own story very soon. Stay tuned xx

https://books2read.com/love-me-love-me-not

About the Author

Keighley Bradford is an Australian writer based in Newcastle, Australia. She has an undergraduate and postgraduate degree in Creative Industries (Writing, Publishing, and Marketing) as well as a background in arts administration, communication and media. She is also actively involved in her local writing and arts communities. While Keighley likes to dabble in many forms of creative writing, novels are her passion. She's been writing since she was thirteen and has since won several awards for her short-fiction pieces. *Once We Were* is her first published novel. When Keighley isn't stuck behind the computer working, you will often find her chilling out at the beach or binge-watching a new Netflix series.

www.keighleybradford.com.au

Making the Move

Amanda Shelley

1
Miles

My body jolts as the door clicks shut.

Holy shit, I fell asleep!

Yawning, I rub a hand down my face and process my situation.

This is *her* hotel room.

I vaguely remember her saying something about meeting with family today, but that's not for hours. Where could she possibly go this early?

As I look around the room, something feels off.

Wait... What the hell is happening?

The suitcase in the corner, her hairbrush in front of the mirror, and the extra pair of shoes, have all disappeared.

No. It can't be.

We lit the sheets on fire last night. I wrung multiple orgasms out of her, and she was down with wanting more. I'm positive I didn't misread things. I've never seen someone so responsive. It was one of the hottest nights of my fucking life.

Did she really just ghost me?

Jumping out of bed, I clench the sheet around my body and dart for the door. Maybe she's still at the elevator, and I can catch up. Flinging the door open, I look down the hall—only to find the elevator door close along with any hope I had of continuing whatever this is between us, sinking as the car zips downstairs.

When a woman gasps behind me with a twinkle in her eye, I'm brought back to my harsh reality.

I can't chase after Tori.

No—I'm the idiot standing in the hall without pants.

Yep. I'm that guy. Hopefully, no one recognizes me, or my publicist, not to mention my coach, will have my ass.

Fuck my life.

Thankfully, as the door nearly locks me out in the hall, I dart my hand out just in time to avoid this disaster in the making. I can just imagine the headlines. *Miles Matthews, the Rainier Renegades receiver was sighted wrangling with a sheet as he chased after a girl who ditched him.*

No—Not a chance. I stay clear from headlines like that.

Picking up my crumpled jeans from the floor, I shove my legs through them and find my shirt that we'd tossed over a chair. There's no sense in sticking around. It may be my day off, but I need to get a light workout in and then make sure my place is ready for my temporary roommate.

For the entire ride home, my adventurous night with Tori consumes my thoughts. She was the perfect combination of sweet and sexy. I'd noticed her the moment we'd walked into The Point. Not only was she a knockout—beautiful blue eyes, kissable lips, and dark-brown hair that flowed down her back in waves.

Nate Bellinger and I had stopped in to grab a few beers and catch up—something we do frequently in the off-season. We frequent The Point because it is a local sports bar, and the patrons, for the most part, leave us alone. With the final games of the season in play, and March Madness on the horizon, basketball was displayed on most screens throughout the bar.

Tori was seated at the table next to us. She caught my attention when the waitress stopped to deliver her drink. Tori practically predicted Columbia River's next moves. "Zander Williams will break away, bank to the right and at the last moment, switch things up by giving Jacobs one hell of an assist."

At the time, I'd thought it had been a lucky guess. But she immediately had both my and Nash's attention. Eventually, we invited her to join us. She was a riot, with her quick wit and endless stats. Before we knew it, the game was over. I wasn't ready for my time with her to end, so when Nash said he was meeting his brother for an early morning and excused himself, I took the opportunity to keep talking with Tori.

Eventually, I walked her down the street to her hotel. I'd only planned to get her number and ask to see her again. However, when she kissed me good night at the door, things escalated quickly and turned into one of the hottest nights of my life.

How could she walk away without a trace?

Fuck. I didn't even think to get her number when she said she'd be in town for a few months. *I'm such a fucking idiot.*

Who lets the girl just up and sneak off?

I guess karma's a bitch because I've done this exact thing—but they knew the stakes going in. Tori... well... she was different. Or at least I thought she was.

I guess I'll never know.

When I get home, I go through the motions of working out, showering, and changing the sheets in the guest room. As I struggle to get the damn fitted sheet to stay on the bed, I grumble, "Chance is lucky he's one of my best friends."

Chance Morgan was my roommate freshman year. We've gone through everything together. College dorms, championships, the Combine, and even managed to play on the same team as rookies. Though he was traded to the New York Mavericks, he's still one of my closest friends. There's nothing I wouldn't do for him.

Which is why I agreed to let his little sister stay with me for the next few months. Chance doesn't want Vicky dealing with being in a new city and hassling with a short-term lease. Besides, I've got plenty of room, so it's not a burden. With it being the off-season, I'll hardly be around.

Just as I'm double checking the closet and dresser to ensure Vicky has all the room she'll need, there's a knock at my door. Excited to see Chance, I rush to answer it.

"Matty... It's great to see you!" Chance bellows, greeting me with a handshake that quickly turns into a bro-hug.

With two hard thwacks on my back, we pull apart. "You, too, man. It's been way too long."

We both know life is crazy during the season, but I really should make a point to see him more. These last few years passed by like a blur, but it's no excuse. "Thanks again for keeping an eye on Vicky. I'll feel much better knowing that while she's in a new town, someone's watching out for her."

Someone clears their throat from behind him and grumbles, "I'm right here, you fool. I'm twenty-two, not twelve. I've lived in Chicago for crying out loud, I can certainly handle the burbs of Tacoma."

Holy shit, Vicky's a firecracker. I like this girl already.

Laughing at how easily she handles her brother, I finally turn my attention to Chance's sister, still standing on the porch. Suddenly, it feels as if a weight rack just landed in the center of my chest, and all the air catches in my throat.

Holy. Fucking. Shit.

This is not happening.

Knowing it must be a mirage, I blink a few times... but the image before me remains the same and scenes from last night fly through my thoroughly fucked brain.

I'm dead.

That's the only explanation because the moment Chance finds out about my night with his sister, I might as well be.

Her eyes widen, and I'm certain she's as shocked as I am, but somehow, she manages a deep breath as her features morph back into a passive expression. Then, she turns to her brother, who slaps his hand on my shoulder, and grins, "Matty... I want you to meet Vicky, my pain in the ass kid sister. Don't you let her bark fool you. *Apparently*... she thinks she's all grown up now and doesn't want anyone telling her what to do."

Oh, she's grown all right... She's smart, witty, independent, yet... I distinctly remember her dripping wet when I took control and bossed her around in bed... holy shit, that was a sight to see.

Fuck... stop thinking about last night.

That can't happen.

Ever. Again.

Somehow, my blood flow manages to return to the brain in my head, and something Chance says clicks in my brain... and I scrutinize her face. "Vicky?" comes out as a question, tilting my head to the side to get a better look.

As if she understands my real question, she quickly explains, "Victoria. Only family still call me Vicky. When this overprotective ass went away to college, I started going by Tori."

So many unspoken things pass between us, but the biggest of all is when she tilts her head toward her brother with a pleading look that clearly says, *keep last night between us.*

I'm not sure how long we stare wordlessly at one another, but Chance knocks me out of my stupor by placing a hand on her shoulder. "Yeah... old habits die hard, Vic. Not sure you'll ever be Tori to me."

Then as if he's completely oblivious to the tension in the room, he points to the driveway. "Let's get your crap from the rental, so I can catch the ferry and meet up with Coach Leighton later. I wanna make sure you're settled before leaving."

With a loud huff, Tori grumbles, "I told you—I'm perfectly fine getting myself settled. There was *zero* reason for you to traipse across the country to help me move in... but no... you wouldn't listen."

"You know I have business out here, and it's the least I can do. You've never met Matty, and thanks to me, you're living with him. I want you comfortable. This is also a great opportunity to visit my buddies from the team."

Suddenly, I'm in Tori's crosshairs as her brows draw in on me, "Matty?"

Clearly, that wasn't the name I'd given her last night.

"Yeah... Miles Matthews..." Chance cuts in before I can mutter a sound. "You know... my first college roommate?"

Tori's eyes go wide as recognition hits, then she closes them for a few heartbeats before heavily exhaling. "Miles Matthews joined the Rainier Renegades four years ago and has started every game since his rookie year. He averages over one-thousand yards a season, with his best being thirteen-oh-three in a single season, with a dozen touchdowns. According to the media guide, you're six-five..." She stops, and her eyes roam me from head to toe before smirking. "But we all know you're barely six-three." With her eyes sweeping across my chest, she adds, "Though you're certainly all ripped at 235 in what you're wearing today. You know they make bigger shirts, right? Even in your best year, you still dropped over forty passes. You may think you're great with your hands, but obviously, there's work to do."

Holy fucking shit, that's a lot to unpack – and did she really just go there? I recall using my hands quite well last night—she certainly didn't have any complaints.

Fuck, Matthews, stop thinking about last night. That's a one-way road to disaster.

Thinking through her string of facts, this girl doesn't just know basketball. Clearly, she knows football, too. Hell, I'm not even sure I could rattle off my stats like that.

Finally, my mouth catches up with my brain. "Uh... that's me," I admit, unsure what to think. It's equally impressive and terrifying to have her knowing such specific details about my game.

"We get it... He's a bad-ass receiver... Let's get your shit, Vic, so we can get started on the day."

Geez, Chance, what's the rush?

But I don't dare say anything in fear of drawing attention to the conundrum swirling in my head.

Chance walks outside, and Tori shakes her head—clearly piecing things together.

"How did I not make the connection before? God, you must think I'm an idiot. I had no idea you were *The Miles Matthews*. Chance always called you Matty... I thought you were Matt Holmes—the running back. Clearly, I didn't pay enough attention—and I certainly never made the connection to Miles last night. Hell, I never even considered you an athlete... wait... was that Nash Bellinger?"

Nodding slowly with unease, I admit, "Yeah. To be clear..." I pause, making sure she understands before continuing, "I never meant to hide anything. You knew my name was Miles..."

"Are you two coming?" Chance hollers from the driveway, interrupting us.

With a side-eye glancing my way and, in a voice only I can hear, she says, "Let's talk about this *after* Chance leaves."

Once we've placed Tori's suitcases in her bedroom, I show her where she can store her food in the pantry before giving her a tour of the house. It's not huge, compared to others on my team, but it works for me. Tori's excited to know I have my own personal gym with both cardio and free weights available.

I nearly choke on my tongue when Chance pipes in, "See... I told you; you don't need a gym membership or have to work out at the Renegades' facility. Matty's got you covered. Besides—you won't have any unwanted creeps hitting on you this way."

Cocking a brow at Chance, Tori asks, "Is that how you'd describe your former teammates? You do know I'm working with them for the next few months, right?"

"Victoria," Chance admonishes, "you know I'm only looking out for you. I can't be on my game if I'm worrying about guys taking advantage of you."

"Uh... you and I both know I'd never let that happen. So stop with your overprotective brother crap... Besides..." she glances in my direction before adding, "what if I *want* to be taken advantage of? That would be my business and my business alone. Again, Chance, I'm an adult. I make my own decisions."

"Victoria!" Chance booms. "Stay away from *everyone* on the team. Thank God Matty's here. He'll protect you, too. If things get out of hand, I'm only a flight away, and I'll kick the shit out of anyone who needs it."

Puffing her chest out to her brother, she glares. "You're not the boss of me, Chance."

"My former teammates know I'll kick the shit out of anyone who goes near you. You're off limits to them. Hell, you're only here a few months... maybe focus on the job and please, for the love of God, can we stop talking about you being with anyone? I'm here to relax."

In a much calmer voice than I expect, Tori places a hand on her brother's and gives it a squeeze. "Enough. You know how much I have riding on this internship. I doubt I'll be doing much of anything other than work and sleep in the foreseeable future." Then she turns her beautiful smile my way. "It's a good thing I've got Matty here to keep me company."

Holy shit. I am so fucked.

2
Tori

Of all the possible roommates Chance could choose for me—I get Miles Matthews.

My luck with men has been terrible lately. I finally have an out of this world experience, and it's with one of my brother's best friends. Why?

Why can't my new roommate be Matt Holmes?

Nope—Apparently, the universe is against me.

I've never experienced a night like last night. I don't do one-night stands. But that was... hot. It was fun, sexy, and ohmigod, that man did more things to my body than I've ever dreamed of. Just thinking about Miles has my body clenching in places I never knew existed. How is this possible?

It was hard leaving him this morning, but I'd promised myself I wouldn't wait around for an awkward goodbye. I mean, that's what a one-night stand is, right?

But now, he's my freaking roommate?

Apparently, I also suck at keeping no strings attached.

To avoid things getting awkward while Chance is here, I jump at the opportunity to get settled in my room. After all, I start my internship tomorrow, and I need to be prepared. As I put my things away, I can't stop wondering, *how the hell am I going to get through the next few months?*

It's bad enough I made the colossal mistake by assuming *Matty* was Holmes. I mean it's possible. How am I supposed to remember who my brother lived with when I was thirteen? I wasn't even allowed to visit Chance his first year because my family didn't have the money to send me across the country—and they certainly wouldn't let me sleep in his dorm if I had.

Now, I'm living with the man who brought all my fantasies to life merely hours ago. The one who will star in my dreams for the unforeseeable future because let's be real—he'll be a tough act to follow.

What the hell am I going to do?

I need this internship to work. This could potentially land me my dream job of being the team's statistician. My passion for sabermetrics could bring the Rainier Renegades to a whole new level of performance on the field. I've been able to predict their offensive and defensive trends for the last two seasons while studying in college. With a couple of tweaks, I could be even better.

I will not let my living situation get in the way of work.

Wait... Will things be too awkward between Miles and me, that I need to move?

Fuck, if I can't make this work, I'll have to explain to Chance *why it's not working*—And that's just not happening.

Nope – he doesn't need to know anything about my personal life.

I'm an adult. I can deal with this.

Hell, I haven't stopped thinking about Miles since forcing myself to leave the hotel. When I saw him standing there looking sexy as hell in his black fitted shirt and athletic shorts, I seriously thought I'd been stuck in my fantasy from this morning, and it took me a moment to compose myself.

Miles and I have a lot of things to talk about.

It's been hell waiting for my brother to leave, and I'm running out of things to organize. His dumb ass wanted to rush getting my things out of the car but abandoned me once the heavy lifting was done. Now, he and Miles are somewhere in the house, hanging out, and I'm left here stuck in my head.

Making the Move 73

When there's nothing left for me to organize, I force myself to venture out from the safety of my room. I find the guys talking in the game room. I can't quite hear what they're saying, but when I approach the doorway, I hear my brother ask, "So, Miles, have you been seeing anyone?"

Immediately, I freeze in place, however not undetected.

Miles darts his eyes to mine, and I feel my cheeks get warm as I vividly remember that same smirk from last night. To Chance, he says, "No one you'd want to hear about."

I swear my heart nearly thuds out of my chest as I await Chance's response.

My brother steps up to the table to take another shot with a laugh. "You always did like keeping your personal life private."

Needing their conversation to end, I clear my throat and do my best to pretend I didn't hear their exchange. "What are you guys up to?"

I dart my eyes to Miles, and I have so many questions that we can't discuss in front of my brother.

Fortunately, Chance breaks the tension between Miles and me when he asks, "Are you settled?"

Shrugging, I admit, "It's not like I brought much."

Miles pipes in, "I've got the car set for you with a fresh oil change and a full tank of gas. The keys are on the hook and after Chance leaves, why don't we go for a drive, so I can show you around the neighborhood and the quickest route to headquarters? Then we can grab something to eat."

Rocking back on my heels, I draw out, "Suurrrree."

Chance obliviously slaps Miles on the back and gushes, "That sounds like a great plan, Matty. I knew you were just the guy for her."

Miles visibly gulps and glances my way. "My pleasure."

Somehow, I manage to keep up with casual conversation for the rest of Chance's stay, though I rely on random trivia I've spent years storing in my wheelhouse to remain calm and collected. Miles and I clearly keep our distance, but the tension feels so tight, I might as well have a neon sign flashing "I slept with Miles... I slept with Miles..." hanging above my head.

We manage to play a few rounds of pool before Chance leaves to catch the Anderson Island ferry. It's torture pretending I'm not on pins and needles waiting for him to leave, especially as we go through the motions of saying goodbye.

"Tell Coach hello for me and that I'm sorry I can't make the boating trip. I'm travelling with my brother this week and wouldn't want to rush things," Miles says when Chance finally gets into his car.

"Thanks again for keeping an eye on my sister. I'll be back next week to visit before heading home. Vic, I'll let you know the details later."

I finally feel as if I can fully exhale when Chance pulls out of the driveway. Now, I can focus on the problem that's been plaguing me from the moment I arrived. At least the universe is on my side in one way. Somehow, Chance has left without being any the wiser of last night's activities.

The moment we're alone, Miles pins me with his golden-brown eyes, making my heart sputter out of control while he stares at me wordlessly.

Crap, maybe it was better with Chance as our buffer.

I can barely breathe as his lips flatten into a straight line, and he takes a step closer. The hairs on the back of my neck prickle as a shiver runs through my spine. In a voice that commands control, he simply says, "We need to talk."

3

Miles

While waiting for Tori to grab her purse, I contemplate our precarious situation. When she returns, a smile plays at my lips, and I mutter the famous lines from my mom's favorite Humphrey Bogart movie, "Of all the gin joints in all the towns in all the world, she walks into mine..."

I've never felt this quote stronger in my soul than now.

Of course, I wanted to see Tori again, but I never could've guessed it would be under these circumstances. I feel like the shittiest friend on Earth, especially since Chance insists I keep an eye on her. Fuck, if he only knew my actual thoughts, let alone what happened last night. I'd be deader than a doornail in two seconds flat.

It doesn't matter that she's the first woman I've felt a connection with in forever—it can never happen. I've promised Chance I'll watch out for her—and that includes keeping her from assholes like me.

As she walks toward me, my tongue sticks to the roof of my mouth. Even though I've merely seen her minutes before, now that we're alone, it takes everything I have not to reach out and touch her again. My body heats, and I'm drawn to her like a moth to a flame. I know without a doubt if I give into temptation, I'll never stop.

As I scoot back the stool I'd been waiting on, the screech of the legs against the hardwood floor is the harsh reminder I need to squelch all thoughts of anything happening in the future. I need to put last night behind me. Chance is my friend. I can't betray him like that—especially when he expects me to protect her.

When I find her staring at me expectantly, I realize I've been so lost in my thoughts that I've missed something. *Shit... what did she say?*

Brushing it off, I quickly stand and point to the garage door. "You ready? I leave the extra keys hanging inside this closet for both vehicles if you need them."

God, could I be more awkward?

Get your head on straight and figure out how to navigate this delicate situation. On one hand, she needs to know last night can't ever happen again, but on the other... my body hasn't gotten the message.

As if on cue with my thoughts, my hand instinctively reaches for her lower back, but the moment I realize what I'm doing, I immediately shove my hands into my pockets. Pockets are safe. Pockets will keep me from doing all the things I've fantasized about this entire morning. When we go into the garage, I'm certain I hear Tori gasp, which draws my eyes to hers in a heartbeat.

"What's wrong?"

Shaking her head, she mutters, "I wasn't sure what to expect. But I never thought you'd drive such reasonable vehicles. I've been afraid you'd be lending me a Bugatti or something ridiculously fast and expensive. Something I'd be afraid to sit in, let alone drive. But a Land Rover..." she draws out with a beautiful grin, and her eyes sparkle with delight, "now... I can handle that."

"Uh..." What the hell do I even say to that? "You're welcome?"

Shaking her head, she flashes a smile that could stop my heart. "Hell, I can even drive your F-250. I learned to drive our farm truck because that's the only thing that got me to school if I didn't want to ride the bus. Though I'm sure yours is much fancier than I'm used to. Are you sure you don't mind me borrowing this for a few months? I mean... I've got some savings..."

"I can only drive one vehicle at a time," I remind her.

According to Chance, she's extremely stubborn when it comes to doing things on her own. She didn't even want to room with me in the first place, but it's pointless to pay for a short-term lease when I know this is the first paying gig she's had since college. Hell, it's still an internship, so I'm certain it doesn't pay close to what she deserves if she can rattle off stats like she does.

Fuck... the way she bites on her lip as she gets stuck in her head is sexy as hell.

Nope... don't go there... friend zone.

She's gotta be in the friend zone for good, Matthews.

She. Is. Chance's sister.

And the woman you're living with for the next few months.

Holding up the keys, I ask, "You wanna drive... Or have me show you around first?"

"You can. I haven't seen much other than the shopping center near my hotel this morning and once I get a feel for things, I'm less likely to get lost."

Quickly, I open her door and wait for her to get settled into the passenger side of the Range Rover.

The moment I get settled behind the wheel, a thought that's been plaguing me pours from my lips. "Uh... why wasn't Chance with you last night?" As protective as he was this morning, I'm surprised he let his sister out of his sight.

Tori's cheeks darken as she pulls on her lower lip with her teeth. "He hung out at a friend's house for the night with a few buddies. I didn't feel like being in a crowd, so I booked a hotel instead. When I found myself too wound up, I thought a drink from the bar down the street might calm me. Besides, I could see the entrance from the hotel and with it being a sports bar, I knew I'd be entertained with the basketball game. I'd planned to catch CRU and head back to my hotel."

"Can you rattle off stats for all sports, or do you have your limits?"

"Oh, I started following Columbia River University's basketball team my sophomore year when my professor selected a basketball team at random for us to study and predict outcomes. However, on a side note, I'm certain they're taking the tournament this year with the way they've been playing."

"Is this something I should place bets on?" I tease. "After all, I'll be in Vegas with my brother this week." The woman was spot on with her predictions last night. I'm sure she'd kill it with the odds in Vegas.

When her face visibly blanches, I quickly sputter, "Relax, Tori. I'm joking. I'll be in Vegas, but we're not going anywhere near The Strip or gambling. In fact, we're renting a houseboat on Lake Mead and spending the week bass fishing."

Her expression is adorable as it morphs into disbelief. "You fish?"

"Uh, I'm a man of many talents." I feign offense, but when she squints her eyes in my direction, I lose my composure. "Well," I say on a laugh, "my brother Mason is. I'm treating him to a few days of fishing for his birthday. Ever since my parents took us on a road trip to the Hoover Dam when we were kids, we've always dreamed about renting a houseboat on Lake Mead." Shrugging, I explain, "Our schedules finally match up this week."

"Do you have other siblings?"

"Yeah, a younger sister, Nola, who's still in college. But Mason's been building his law practice, so he's been too busy to take a full week off until now. I'm really looking forward to it."

"That's great for you. Did you know that nearly fifty-three percent of Americans don't use their vacation time each year?"

I chuckle at her random factoid, as it completely catches me off guard. "No, I can't say that I did. But I'm *definitely* in the forty-seven percent. I work hard during the season and have zero guilt enjoying my time off. Speaking of facts..." I ask, hoping to segue back to satisfying my curiosity about her. "I know you're a statistician, and you've studied at CRU, but how did you get into knowing the depth of facts you do about sports and football in general?"

Taking a deep breath, she sighs, "Well, I've always been a fan of football. I'm sure Chance has something to do with that though. I think I grew up on a bleacher watching him play. But to answer your question, my mind stores information like a steel trap. Once I've read or heard it, I somehow never forget it. I've always rattled off useless information I've had stored. So in college, I put my skills to use. Eventually, I found I was quite good at it. I even created a reliable formula to make predictions based on players' past plays. Of course, the more I study a team as a unit and get to know the players on a personal level, the better I'm able to predict which players are a greater asset than others."

She takes a huge breath and beams. "It's a dream come true to work for a team of this caliber. I'm dying to learn more about the Renegades so I can put my theories into practice on a greater scale. I can't wait to help the management and coaches build the best team possible for this next season."

"I'm sure you'll kill it."

She practically squeals with excitement, and her face splits into a wide grin. "I think I'm more interested in the Combine than the potential players. I'm dying to watch it in person. Can you imagine how many records and stats will come out of this one competition alone?"

Laughing, I admit, "I've never thought of it like that."

Tori shakes her head as her eyes roll dramatically. Clearly, we're not on the same wavelength. During the Combine, I was so focused on keeping my head in the game and making sure I did my best to notice it from a global perspective like hers.

Ignoring my comment, Tori spits out facts about potential players she thinks will be a benefit to our team, and I find myself hanging on her every word. I'm so lost in her explanation that I barely notice we've arrived at the restaurant. In a matter of minutes, we're inside and have ordered, though I'm so focused on Tori, I merely picked the first thing I saw on the menu.

Tori is even more attractive than I found her last night. She's not only beautiful but wicked smart, funny, and intriguing. It takes everything in me not to reach for her hand when she lays it on the table in front of us.

If she wasn't Chance's sister, I know without a doubt, I'd pursue things further. The connection we have is unlike anything I've ever experienced. Maybe I'm still reeling from last night, but even when she's completely lost in her own world, spouting off more facts about the Renegades than I'd known as a member for the past four years, I find myself entranced. Every part of her intrigues me, and I need to walk a fine line moving forward if I'm to survive these next few months. I'm dying to satisfy my curiosity but need to keep my distance. I'm not sure I can trust myself otherwise.

Before I know it, we've finished our meal, and we're on the way to the Rainier Renegades' headquarters. I quickly show her how to get into the staff parking lot as well as my favorite places to shop along the way home. She spots a bookstore and a coffee shop she's eager to check out. I quickly learn that her chosen way to unwind from all the factoids as she calls it, is reading fiction.

When I pry further, her cheeks turn a beautiful shade of pink as she admits, "My go-to jam after a long day at working with stats is romantic suspense. Well, to be truthful, all romance works. But I love a great plot with lots of chemistry and action."

By the time we enter my driveway, it feels as if time stood still. I'm caught off guard when I glance at the clock and realize we've spent nearly three hours together. The more time I spend with this woman, the more I want to know about her.

We're so lost in conversation when I park inside the garage, neither of us seem eager to get out. Unbuckling, I turn to face her, and I truly can't believe how beautiful Tori is. Her expressive blue eyes are captivating as she prattles on about the benefits of reading.

I nearly lose it when she says, "Did you know that reading romance lowers the risk of heart attacks? I read somewhere that it not only lowers stress, but it can make your heart pound during suspenseful parts. It's also been known to inspire physical activity."

I'm certain my brows raise to my hairline, and I'm so flabbergasted by her unexpected comment, that I quite possibly mimic a goldfish with my mouth flapping as I try to come back with a witty response.

Holy shit. She really said that?

My body heats as memories from last night flash through my mind. However, I can tell the moment her brain sinks to the same level as mine when her amused expression morphs into mortification. "Ohmigod. I didn't mean it like that... Well, I *could* mean it like that... but that isn't my intention."

God, she's adorable.

I feel my traitorous lips pull into a grin, but somehow, I manage, "Reading is good for a lot of things."

Her beautiful laugh fills the air as she shakes her head and regains her composure. When her eyes meet mine, neither of us say anything for the longest time. So much so that I feel myself leaning closer to her, as she minutely inches toward me.

I am this close to saying fuck my righteous reasons from before, when she breaks the silence.

"Speaking of getting physical... I want to thank you for not telling Chance about last night."

Christ. She chooses this moment to finally address the elephant in the room.

But the mention of Chance is just the bucket of cold water I need to keep my convictions. Chance is my friend... but fuck my life. With my eyes locked onto hers, my chest constricts as I say what must be said. "First, it's none of his business, and I wouldn't betray you like that. But I think we need to talk. Chance *is* your brother, and *I've* made a promise..." Fuck. These words sound wrong, but I force out what needs to be said. Watching her face fall makes me wish she'd just kick me in the nuts and get it over with. Needing her to know how I feel, I struggle with words and admit a partial truth. "Tori..." Why does her name feel so right rolling off my lips?

Mustering the courage to spit out what needs to be said, I admit, "I really like you and think you're amazing, but we can't let anything happen again."

For the first time since I met her, I watch her face shift into a smile that isn't genuine; it doesn't reach her eyes, and my heart pangs. She exhales heavily, and her voice is strong as she nods in agreement. "I think that's the best idea. Besides, I've read somewhere that one-night stands hardly build into lasting relationships."

Wow. That stings, but I get it.

She's quiet for a long moment, then reaches for the handle to exit the car.

I can't let her leave like this.

"Look, I've really enjoyed spending time with you today. We're living together for the next few months. Do you think we can... at the very least... be friends?"

My body revolts at the idea, but what choice do I have?

I watch her mull over my words, and my heart nearly stops while waiting for her response. When her eyes finally lock onto mine, she reaches her hand across the console and needing to touch her, I stupidly grasp hers in mine. I feel a gentle squeeze as her tongue traces her bottom lip. Something I've quickly learned is her tell for formulating her thoughts. "Friends it is."

4

Miles

And the asshole of the year goes to... Miles Mathews.

Within minutes, she's in the house, making some excuse of needing a shower and getting ready for work in the morning. Before parting ways, I make sure we exchange numbers and give her the codes to the house.

Now, it's nearly three in the morning, and I'm tossing and turning. My once-comfortable bed might as well be a box of rocks for as relaxed as I feel. I swear, I've roamed over every inch of this king-sized bed and still can't find any peace.

I know I did the right thing by putting her in the friend zone, but why do I feel like I'm not only an ass, but I'm making a huge mistake? Every part of me wants to march down the hall and tell her I'm wrong. I'm dying to slip under her covers and continue what we started last night. I want her to wrap those long legs around me and worship her the way she deserves, until she forgives me.

God, what I would do to her body.

My dick hardens at the thought, and I push back my covers to give myself some relief. I've been perpetually turned on since she walked out of the hotel this morning, and the only way I'm getting any sleep is if I take care of this.

I allow memories from last night to trickle into my conscious thoughts. I'd played her body like it was made for me. I want to ravage every inch of her over and over until both of us are so consumed by bliss, we pass out.

My mouth waters at the thought of tasting her arousal on my lips when she came apart beneath me, and I loved the way she clenched around me like a vise as she came all over my dick as she rode me from above. Pumping my hand faster, I vividly recall the way her breasts bounced, how her eyes locked on mine when I took her from behind in front of the bathroom mirror.

Though my fantasies are nowhere near the real thing, they'll have to do. Memories of last night play on a loop as I pump my dick harder and faster. Soon, my balls tighten, and tingles bolt up my spine.

Squeezing the base of my dick and covering my tip with a tissue, all it takes is picturing Tori on her knees, sucking me off in the shower, to tip me over the edge. Before I know it, I'm grunting through an orgasm, wishing she were here with me.

I lie here panting and out of breath, hoping like hell she didn't hear me yell her name as I exploded with thoughts of her.

Eventually, I walk into my bathroom and clean up.

As I return to bed, a nagging thought hits me.

This is all I'll ever get.

Fantasies are both a blessing and a curse.

I'd give anything to touch her again.

Flipping my pillow, I pull up my comforter and find myself exhausted from the day. As I drift off to sleep, one final thought hits me, putting a nail in the coffin of any possible future with Tori... Chance would never forgive me. Besides, if I'm anything... I'm a man of my word.

Ding-Dong. Ding-Dong.

Fuck, that's my doorbell.

Glancing at my clock, I realize I've overslept, and my brother's going to kick my ass. I still need to pull a few things together. If I don't answer the freaking door, he's liable to take it off its hinges with the way he's suddenly pounding on it.

"Okay, okay. I'm here," I mutter, swinging the door wide.

His eyes are wide as he takes me in. "Bro, why aren't you ready? We're supposed to be at the airport in an hour."

"Chill out, Mason," I say on a yawn as I let him in. "People have been known to get to the airport less than two hours before their flight and survive. Besides, worse case, we take the next one. Go make me coffee while I get my things," I say, pointing to the kitchen while I return to my room.

As I walk past Tori's door, my body reacts to the smell of her and instantly, I'm turned on. Christ, I've only known her a few days. Why am I reacting this way? Before I can think about it further, Mason chooses this moment to shout, "Since when do you drink coffee creamer?"

Shaking my head, I rush to my room as I holler, "I don't! It's Tori's. She moved in yesterday."

I hear him respond, but I don't pay it any attention as I dash into my bathroom for the quickest shower of my life. Within a few minutes, I'm dressed and putting my toiletries into my travel bag. I throw in a few pairs of jeans, a couple of shorts, a few t-shirts, and a button-up in case we need anything fancier. Even though it's the off-season, I throw in my workout gear and my e-reader for good measure.

Before leaving my room, I spot a pad of paper and quickly jot a note to Tori, needing to let her know I'm thinking of her. Not allowing myself to worry over my words, I quickly spit out my thoughts and drop it on her bed, returning to my brother before I have a chance to think better of it.

As if Mason has a homing device on me, he meets me in the hall, cup in hand. "You ready yet?"

"Yeah, let's go," I say much more cheerfully than I feel as I gratefully take the cup from his hand. Glancing one last time at Tori's door, I wish more than anything things could be different between us. This trip is exactly what I need to get her off my mind. Thankfully, Mason is none the wiser of my little pit stop. If he even caught wind I had an interest in my new roommate, I'd never hear the end of it.

5
Tori

Being put in the friend zone sucks. There's no way around it. I know it's best given our situation and rationally, I know it's what should happen. Between being nervous about my new job and the fact that I'm living with Miles, I didn't get much sleep last night. I'd gotten up early for my first day at work and was literally the first one in the parking lot. As far as first days go, it was decent. I'm sure I'll fit in and get the hang of things quickly. I met nearly everyone in upper management and the coaching staff today during my first meeting. Maybe if I look at the website a few more times, I'll be able to put names to the faces I met.

The moment I get home from work, even though I don't feel like it, I force myself to change and work out. Then I grab my laptop and look over some potential players' stats for the upcoming Combine. Eventually, my eyes feel as if they're going to bug out of my head, so I take a shower and get ready for bed. It's not even eight, but with the way I tossed and turned last night, I'm exhausted.

As I pull back my covers, I notice a folded paper on my pillow.

My heart nearly stops as I read his words:

Tori,

Hope you had a great first day. I'm sure you killed it. I

wish I was here to celebrate your first day. Text me. Can't wait to hear all the details.

I meant to tell you, there's a soaking tub in my bathroom. Please make yourself at home and use anything you need. What's mine is yours.

Talk later – Miles

I reread that last sentence multiple times, wishing it could be true. I'd love nothing more than to make him mine, but that's just not in the cards for us. Besides, I'm sure he's just being a gracious host and wants me to feel comfortable, right? I mean, we're friends. That's what friends would do. Friends text about their day and use each other's things? Surely, that's what he means by this?

Knowing my overactive mind will overthink this if given the chance, I quickly pick up my phone and tap out a text.

Me: I got your note.

Shit. I hit send before I could add more to it. I quickly start to type the rest, but a message comes through before I can finish.

Miles: So... how was your first day? Did you kick ass? Did you make all the other statisticians quake in their boots? I can't wait to hear about it.

Laughing, I quickly reply.

Me: I'm sure there was no quaking. But I did meet everyone. And when I say everyone, I mean EVERYONE in upper management and on the coaching staff. We had a meeting, and I've got to figure out all their names pronto so I don't make an ass of myself the next time we meet.

Miles: You could never make an ass of yourself. You're the smartest person I know.

Me: (eye roll emoji) Please. I'm just better at remembering random facts. I'm sure I'm not the smartest person you know. There are many ways to be smart.

Miles: Not the point. Did you have a good day though? I know it's stressful starting over.

A smile plays at my lips as I swoon over his thoughtfulness. Even though I've only known him for a few days, this fits his character and was one of the things I liked about him at the bar. He's genuine when he asks questions.

Me: Yes. I had a good day. I'm glad to be a part of the team. How are things with your brother?

Miles: Good. We're on the boat and will fish more tomorrow. It's good to see him relax. We're officially boat bums.

An attachment shows up, and my heart skips a beat when I see Miles' beautiful smile light up the screen. It's a picture of him and his brother with the lake in the background at sunset. I can't help but zoom in and screenshot the picture with just him. His smile reminds me of the night we met. Damn, he is gorgeous.

Me: Does that mean you're giving up your day job?

Him: Haha, no. I'd miss the comforts of home and catching TDs for the team. Can't work out on the boat either.

Me: I'm sure that's a sacrifice worth making—to spend time with your brother.

Him: Mason has dinner ready. Gotta run. Let me know how tomorrow goes.

While Miles is gone, we get into the habit of texting. He sends pictures of his adventures with his brother, and I tell him what I've learned about the team. We talk about random things from our childhood, our favorite foods, and what we're currently reading.

I'm sitting down to lunch at my desk when a text pops up from him, and I nearly spit out my drink.

Miles: Are you still reading Brittney Sahin's latest book? (An image of the book cover downloads) **I started with the first book in the series because I can't handle reading out of order. But I'm hooked.**

Me: Seriously?

Miles: Well... if you're gonna talk about books as if

they're real people, I figure I should at least read them to know what you're talking about.

This man never ceases to amaze me. Last night, he'd texted to ask what I'd been up to. I jokingly replied—crying. He didn't even give me a chance to explain before my phone rang. His voice was immediately filled with concern. Of course, I quickly explained I'd been reading and was so emotionally attached to the characters in my book, I was stupidly crying. I assured him his worry was completely unnecessary. Then he made me explain the plot to him so he could understand. I never would have guessed he'd pick up the series and read it for himself. We talked for hours, and I couldn't believe it was nearly midnight when we'd hung up.

Me: If I'm invested in the story, I'm gonna talk like they're real people.

Miles: Makes sense. I'm only halfway through book one, but I've gotta know how it ends. Wait… do Asher and Luke's sister ever get together?

Me: Hahaha. I won't spoil it for you. So don't ask. But I'd bet you'll read book two immediately.

Miles: How's your day otherwise?

Me: Good. Meeting with the coaches this afternoon to give them my thoughts on some potential players going into the Combine.

Miles: You flying solo, or is there a team?

Me: Team. But I'm prepared if they ask my opinion.

Miles: (laughing emoji) Oh, to be a fly on that wall. I can just imagine what you'll say. But seriously. You'll do great. You've got this.

Miles: Gotta run. Talk soon.

After a simple text exchange, my stomach should definitely not be flipping, nor my pulse racing. He is my friend… And only my friend. I need to get this through my thick skull, so I don't make things awkward when he returns.

It's late, and I'm starving. I got home later than usual, worked out, then showered. I'm too tired to bother with clothes, so I grab a sleep tank and slip on a pair of my most comfortable undies before heading to the kitchen. Miles has extended his trip to meet up with a buddy in Los Angeles tomorrow, so I've got the place to myself.

Music blasts through the entire house, and I'm boppin' to the beat, belting out "Welcome to New York" by Taylor Swift as I cook my broccoli and chicken stir-fry. Spatula in hand, I'm killin' the vocals as I flip my food around the pan. When the song changes to "Blank Space", I sway to the beat as I turn off the stove and shimmy across the room to grab a plate from the cabinet. Just as I belt out the lyrics about boys only wanting love if it's torture, I hear a distinct sound of a throat clearing behind me.

Heart in my chest, I freeze. Then I slowly turn around, only to find a tall figure leaning against the door frame of the garage.

I scream.

Immediately, Miles bursts out laughing. "I'm so sorry," he says through gasps of air, closing the distance between us. My body tenses as his muscular arms wrap around me. "Hey now. I've got you. I never meant to scare you." His body quakes as he holds me close. "I thought for sure you heard the garage door open."

I try to push away, but the jackass holds me tighter. Now, I can feel him laughing at me. Just great. "I'll have you know..." I start, but I'm cut off by his words.

"Talk about torture..." His voice is thick, gravelly, and reminds me of our first night together. Then he clears it and pulls far enough away to look me in the eye. "Do you always have dance parties in your underwear? Is this something I should know about, or do you save these performances for when you're alone?"

"You... I... You... weren't supposed to be home for a few days," I finally sputter.

He shrugs impishly. "Plans changed."

"And you didn't think to call?" The words fly out of me before I can stop myself.

"It's late, and I thought you'd already be in bed. I didn't want to wake you. I jumped on a stand-by flight so I wasn't even sure I could get on board. Then by the time I landed, my phone was dead."

This is his house. He should be able to come and go as often as he wants. I'm clearly overreacting.

"Are you gonna answer the question?" The corner of his lips war with the rest of his facial features, and I can tell he's doing all he can to keep a straight face.

"What question?" I spit out defensively because all I can focus on is the fact he hasn't let go of me.

"Is dancing something you do every night?" His golden-brown eyes bore into mine as he darts his tongue out and wets his lower lip.

"I'll have you know, music and dancing are known to reduce anxiety and blood pressure. It also improves sleep quality and overall moods..." I stop when his finger presses against my mouth.

Cocking his head to the side, he raises a brow. "Still haven't answered the question."

What does he want me to say... I dance in my underwear like a raging lunatic on the regular? Of course, I don't do that. But instead of conceding to his point, I persist with mine. "Music also has the ability to reduce depression and..." When I take a breath to finish my point, his lips crash onto mine.

His tongue sweeps across my lower lip as I open to him. His strong hand at my hip pulls me close as the other slides up my back. He tastes divine. I could feast on him and never tire. His fervent kisses consume my body with need, and I want more.

Gripping the back of his neck, I run my fingers through his hair. As if he can read my mind, strong hands reach under my ass, lifting me to his height. Within seconds, my legs wrap around him, and we're moving. I'm too consumed with lust to care where he's taking me. I feel like a firecracker waiting to ignite. My senses are on overload, and I'm consumed by all things Miles.

"Need to see this gorgeous body of yours," he pants as he lays me down in the center of his bed. Kissing down my jaw, he practically growls with need, "You are so fucking beautiful, Tori. I swear you're better than every fantasy I could conjure while I was away. I've been trying to keep my distance, but you're like a fucking wet dream come to life." He pushes up my tank and trails kisses over each heaving breast, as he says, "You're smart..." He flicks his tongue around one nipple before sucking it into his mouth.

"Ohmigod," I rasp out as I arch into him as he slowly and tenderly removes my panties.

I love that Miles is a talker during sex. I'm so filled with need as he talks his way down my body. I think I might come with his voice alone.

"I'm dying... to lick and taste... every inch of you. I need to feel your dripping-wet pussy and know it's ready for me," Miles rasps out between kisses. Running his hand along my inner thigh, he touches me everywhere except where I need it most.

My body zings in anticipation as he drags his tongue along my lower belly. "You taste fucking incredible. Better than I remember..."

"Miles..." I practically beg, arching into his palm, and he kisses the base of my hip.

I can hear the smile in his voice when he reminds me of how vocal he likes it. "All you have to do is tell me what you want, Victoria... and it's yours."

"Umf..." I pant as I lift my hips to meet him. "Fuck me... with your tongue... make me come... then I wanna ride that cock of yours."

"Hmmm..." he moans, licking his tongue along my slit, swirls it around my clit, and I practically see stars. His fingers slide into me as he makes another pass with his tongue. Before he flicks my clit, he admits, "After watching you shake your sexy ass, I'm dying to take you from behind."

Instantly, my mind floods with memories of our last time together, and I nod profusely. "Yes... please, yes... Ohmigod. Right there. Please don't stop," I beg as he adds another finger and hits me in a place I never knew existed. I swear this man reads my body like no other. He has me speaking in tongues and on the edge of release faster than I ever thought possible. The moment I pulse around his fingers, he licks my slit once more before sucking my clit into his mouth. All I can do is hold on for dear life and ride out wave after wave of white-hot ecstasy.

Before I know it, he's flipped me over and enters me from behind. I'm dripping with pleasure, so he slides in with ease. Taking his time while I adjust to him, he slowly moves in and out, making me cry with need. He kisses at the small of my neck, across my shoulders, and down my back, all while telling me how amazing this feels. His strong hands feel heavenly on my hips as he guides our bodies together. Eventually, he leans forward, wrapping his body around mine, and kisses my neck as he groans into my ear, "I'm so glad to be home."

This is The End of this Novella...
But nowhere near the end of Miles and Tori's story.
Stay tuned for a full-length novel with much more to come.

A Note from Amanda Shelly

Thank you for reading *Making the Move*. If you're like me and can't wait for Miles and Tori's full story, be sure to join my newsletter so you won't miss its release. I can't wait to share how their story completely unfolds. *Making the Move* (the full-length novel) will become the second book in my Rainier Renegades Series and will release in 2025. To learn more about the Renegades, be sure to check out the coach's adventure in finding love where he least expected it, in *Making the Call*. You can read more about Luke Leighton as well as all my other books on my website: www.amandashelley.com

Newsletter: https://geni.us/AmandaShelleyNL

Amanda Shelley writes romantic stories you can escape into. Some are steamy, others are sweet but all have strong characters with a little bit of sass.

When not writing, Amanda enjoys time with her family, playing chauffeur, chef and being an enthusiastic fan for her children. Keeping up with them keeps her alert and grounded in reality. She enjoys long car rides, chai lattes and popping her SUV into four-wheel drive for adventures anywhere.

Amanda loves hearing from readers. Be sure to sign up for her newsletter and follow her on social media. Join her reader's group Amanda's Army of Readers to stay up to date on her latest information.

Readers group: https://www.facebook.com/groups/AmandasArmyofReaders/

Holly's Hero
Dania Voss

Blurb

Between her parent's disastrous marriage and her own awful taste in men, Holly Daniels has a low opinion of relationships. That is, until sexy army reservist Evan Hunter becomes her rommmate and her world turns upside down.

Evan jumped at the chance to move in with Holly despite the fact she'd only ever treated him as a friend. The gorgeous blonde with a heart of gold had captured his own, even if she didn't reciprocate his feelings.

Living in close quarters, things quickly get complicated as sparks fly between them. Their undeniable chemistry leads to a night of passion and a "roommates with benefits" arrangement that doesn't sit well with Evan. He wants more, but goes along anyway for fear of losing Holly.

Holly settles for their casual arrangement, believing she doesn't deserve a terrific guy like Evan, considering her history.

Can Evan convince Holly to explore what lies beneath the surface or will they be left miserable and alone, only to wonder what could have been?

1

Holly Daniels' eyes prickled with unshed tears as the last of her friend Aleesha Richards' things were carted out of her bedroom in Holly's house. Aleesha was getting married in two months and was moving in with her fiancé Brody Hunter.

Holly turned away when Aleesha kissed Brody in the doorway, unwilling to make a fool of herself. This was the natural next step for Aleesha and Holly was happy for her. Just sad for herself.

Her other good friend, Paige Ward wrapped a supportive arm around her shoulder. Holly welcomed Paige's comfort; grateful Paige was alive to give it. They'd almost lost Paige when they'd been eighteen and she'd gotten in a horrific car accident taking her younger sister Cassidy on a practice drive before getting her driver's license.

Paige had survived nearly burning to death in her car, but had sustained burn scars down the left side of her body and a very noticeable scar on her right cheek. Aleesha and Holly hadn't cared about the scarring. They hadn't considered Paige any different than they had before the accident, and loved her just the same.

Unfortunately, Paige's mother had been hard on Paige since the accident. Insisting on repeated surgeries as if Paige's scars would magically disappear. Thankfully Paige's father had stepped in and put a stop to the madness.

Aleesha joined her and Paige after Brody left. Her warm, buttery pecan brown skin was flushed and her soulful brown eyes were bright. "Don't be sad, Holly. You knew I'd move in with Brody eventually. It doesn't mean I don't love you anymore." She gathered her braids, arranged them into a neat bun and pinned them securely.

Holly sniffled, feeling foolish. The last thing she wanted to do was make Aleesha feel bad about moving in with her fiancé. "I'm surprised you didn't move in with him sooner, actually. You've been engaged for almost a year."

Aleesha rolled her eyes. "Grandmama Sadie Mae. It's not like she doesn't know Brody and I have sex. I'm thirty for Pete's sake."

A grin twitched at Holly's lips. Aleesha, the light skinned, biracial beauty had been raised by her loving, but strict Black grandmother after her parents had been killed in a tragic boating accident when she'd been eight years old.

Paige snickered and got to work cleaning the closet. Holly's stomach fluttered thinking about who was moving in as her new roommate in a little while. How had she agreed to this? Temporary insanity, most likely.

"She's looking out for you. Don't be too hard on her." Holly held Aleesha, now her *former* roommate, tight.

"I know." Aleesha sighed when they ended their embrace. "It's the end of an era, isn't it?"

It was, but it was also the beginning of a promising new one. Holly had purchased her small home in Lombard, Illinois five years ago for a steal and paid for it with half of the inheritance she'd been given when her grandmother had passed. She'd invested the other half to prepare for retirement. She'd never *needed* a roommate, but had enjoyed Aleesha's companionship.

Aleesha's soon-to-be in-laws owned the esteemed Hunter Homes and Renovations Company. Three years ago, at cost, they'd done an exceptional job updating Holly's place with new siding, windows, roof, beautiful natural stone countertops throughout, and hardwood flooring. Her home had a nice, updated look that fit in well with the many torn down and rebuilt homes on her block. They'd gone a step further and supervised the installation of a state-of-the-art alarm system and window security film.

"It's going to be great. You and Brody were meant to be together. I'm being silly and selfish. This is a happy day, not a sad one," Holly said, hoping she could convince herself of that fact, and ease Aleesha's mind.

"You're right. I can't wait to marry him, but I'm going to miss seeing you every day, that's all." Aleesha grabbed a Swiffer mop and got busy wiping down the floor.

"Not to mention, your new roommate Evan will be here soon. Hubba hubba." Paige teased with waggling brows as she emerged from the closet.

The mention of Brody's younger brother Evan, Holly's new roommate, made her pulse race and shiver with need. As if she stood a chance with the gorgeous blond-haired, green eyed former US Army Interior Electrician and current reservist.

Brody and Evan's parents were the poster children for a long and happy marriage. Whereas Holly's parents were a trainwreck. They'd divorced when she'd been seven due to her mother's infidelity and now, her parents could barely behave civilly toward each other when in the same room together.

Unlucky with relationships herself, Holly wouldn't dare to believe she and Evan could ever be more than they were: friends.

2

Evan Hunter wrapped the vacuum cord into place and tucked it into the closet in his now former basement bedroom in his older brother Brody's home. His meager belongings were packed along with Brody's nearly new seventy-five-inch flat screen TV, pool table with a removeable ping pong table top and a comfy couch set, and were ready for transport to his new place in town – Holly Daniels' place. A smile twitched at his lips at the thought of the stunning blonde who was waiting for him.

"You don't have to move out, you know? Aleesha has no problem with you staying. Neither do I," Brody said, leaning against the door frame, eyeing Evan suspiciously. "Between your reserve duty, your studies and the company jobs you're assigned, you're not around all that much."

Evan faced his brother, two years older than his thirty-four, with equal suspicion. Brody had always been a bit too bossy for Evan's liking. "Dude, your fiancée is moving in. It's time for me to leave and I'm so not moving in with Mom and Dad." He loved his parents dearly but the thought of moving in with them at his age made him cringe.

That brought a smile to Brody's much too serious expression. "I hear you. I just thought you'd move in with Dusty, not Holly, that's all."

Dustin Hunter, or Dusty as they all referred to him, was their first cousin and Evan's closest friend. They'd even gone through army basic training together. Dusty was also an enormous man whore.

"Really? With the revolving door of women he's got coming and going, I'd never get any studying done. I love the guy, but roommates? I don't think so. You got a problem with me moving in with Holly? I'd thought you'd be relieved. Or grateful that I'm keeping an eye on things over there with Aleesha moving out."

Both he and Brody had had their concerns about the women living alone. They were in a good neighborhood across town, but still. The security system and protective window film they'd insisted on after Brody and Aleesha became exclusive had calmed their anxieties somewhat, but you couldn't be too careful these days. Evan had six years left as a reservist and planned on having their construction company build him a custom home after his time concluded.

Evan's stomach roiled when Brody crossed his arms. Evan was an army veteran and reservist for fuck's sake and not in the mood to be lectured to by his brother. The golden child needed to keep his opinions to himself.

"I *am* relieved Holly's not going to be living alone. I *won't* be grateful if you cause problems over there. She's Aleesha's close friend. I don't need you sniffing around her and making problems for us. Am I clear?"

Evan cracked his neck from side to side and moved slowly, deliberately toward Brody, anger simmering through his veins. His six foot four, heavily muscled frame could easily take his brother down and Brody knew it.

"I'm a grown fucking man and I don't take orders from you. I won't cause problems for Holly or between you and Aleesha. Am *I* clear?" Moving out was the right thing to do, regardless of Aleesha. Brody had a chip on his shoulders Evan could barely tolerate any longer. If he and Holly didn't mix well as roommates, Evan would rent a studio apartment nearby until he had his home built later on.

Wisely, Brody took a step back, nodding slightly. "You are. I thought I sensed something between you two. It could get complicated for all of us is all I'm saying."

Evan nearly scoffed. What Brody may have sensed was Evan's attraction and affection toward Holly, not hers toward him. Painful as it was, Holly didn't appear to think of Evan as anything but a friend. Her lack of romantic interest in him stung, but he'd respect her boundaries. Brody hadn't needed to warn Evan off Holly. Evan knew where he stood with her.

"You don't need to worry. Trust me."

Two hours later, Holly's basement had been set to rights after moving in Evan's workout equipment, the pool table, flat screen television, and furniture. Evan, with Dusty's help, had assembled his bed frame.

Evan had just finished putting the bed linens on and was still pissed as fuck that Dusty had asked Holly out and she'd agreed. Evan had given Dusty an earful privately in his new bedroom, trying to protect Holly, but he hadn't settled yet.

"Hey man. I told you I'd leave her alone. I shouldn't have asked her out. You were right. Come outside. The pizzas just got here and the beers are cold," Dusty said as he reentered Evan's room. "Team up with her for lawn darts and have some fun."

Evan followed Dusty to the back yard. Everyone seemed to be enjoying themselves chowing down on pizza and beer. He grabbed a few slices of pepperoni pizza, a beer and took the empty seat beside Holly. Even devoid of makeup with her shiny blonde hair up in a pony tail, Holly was gorgeous. His heart skipped a beat just looking at her.

"I can't help but feel like I've completely taken over the basement with my workout gear and the entertainment area we set up. But don't worry, I won't throw any crazy parties. That's Dusty's area." Dusty's parties were more like near orgies and Evan would never subject Holly to something like that in her own home. Evan moaned; the pizza was so good. It was still warm and the pepperoni had a little kick to it.

Holly took a swig of her beer and shook her head. "Not at all. I think it'll be fun. I'm not that good at pool, but I'm pretty good at ping pong."

"I'm looking forward to seeing what you got." Shit. That had sounded sexual, not exactly what Evan had intended. Not that he'd mind seeing everything Holly had to offer. "I didn't mean - ."

A mischievous smile curved Holly's full, kissable lips. "I know what you meant and you're on."

3

Holly double checked her makeup in the bathroom mirror and applied a dab more color to her lips. She'd chosen a casual short sleeved, white scalloped V-neck dress with a pretty pink flowered print that ended just above the knee for the evening. Perfect for a warm July night.

Disappointed Dusty had never called to plan their date, a week after Evan moved in, Holly had decided she needed to get out of the house. The sexy reservist had proven to be too tempting.

So far, he'd been the perfect roommate, which made him all the more desirable. Evan picked up after himself and had surprised her with some delicious home cooked meals. He'd been considerate of Holly at every turn. It wasn't *his* fault she wanted to jump him.

Holly was only required to spend two days a month at one of the Kennison Healthcare facilities as part of her corporate responsibilities in finance, but she'd grown fond of the residents and staff at the Lombard active adult community and nursing home location.

And once a month families would join their loved ones for trivia game night. It was surprisingly competitive but also a lot of fun. She'd grab dinner with the residents at the facility's restaurant-style cafeteria and welcome the temporary reprieve from Evan.

If Elizabeth "Lizzy" Kennison was there, the VP of Senior Living, Holly might bend her ear about her conflicting feelings about Evan. Lizzy had become a sort of "second mother" to Holly over the six years she'd been working for Kennison Healthcare. Holly had shared things with Lizzy that she couldn't with her own mother. Sad but true.

On her way out the door she found Evan in the dining room. His laptop was open with text books and papers covering half of the table. Holly remembered those days. She admired him for pursuing his Bachelor of Business Administration online at UIC while working for his family and performing his reservist duties. It couldn't be easy to juggle so much, but somehow, he made it seem effortless. And another thing that made Evan so appealing.

Holly felt herself flush when Evan made slow work of looking her over, his sparkling green eyes intense as he studied her appearance.

"Where are you off to, Hols?" Evan's pet name for her, which Holly loved. "Big date with Dusty," Evan asked, his voice tight, almost seeming angry.

Why would Evan care? He and Dusty were as close as brothers. It was ridiculous to consider Evan might be jealous. Wasn't it?

"Um, no. I'm going to the Lombard Kennison retirement community for dinner and family trivia game night. I know it sounds dorky, but I've gotten to know the residents over the years." Holly shrugged. "Game and bingo nights are kind of fun." She hoped like hell Evan didn't see her as pathetic and unable to get a date. She'd turned down many potential match ups suggested by residents for their grandsons, sons and nephews.

Evan observed her carefully as if deciding on something. "Sounds fun. I could use a break from schoolwork. Up for some company? I can be ready in a few minutes."

Fifteen minutes later Holly was being escorted by Evan in his red Dodge Charger. He'd cleaned up nicely and coordinated with her dressed in light beige khaki pants and a pink polo shirt. He smelled delectable in his musky cologne. The evening was turning out to be the exact opposite of the Evan distraction she'd needed.

Feeling more like a date than an innocent outing, in her mind at least, Holly was apprehensive about how she and Evan would be received. She didn't want him to feel awkward or uncomfortable.

Although she'd introduced Evan as her *friend* and new roommate, Holly had received waggling brows, winks and silly teasing from the residents. Evan hadn't seemed bothered and had taken it all in stride, a warm smile never leaving his handsome face.

She'd introduced him to Carla, a staff LPN, Rebecca one of the staff counselors and were chatting up Mario the Executive Chef in the large professional kitchen. Mario beamed with pride as he gave Evan a tour of the operations.

"The food might be prepared a bit simply for your tastes, Evan. We have to account for food allergies, salt restrictions, and so forth. But I can make adjustments for your meal. We have herb roasted chicken, breaded pork tenderloin and salmon tonight with mixed grilled vegetables and a few starch options," Chef Mario said to Evan.

Evan clapped chef on the back. "Simply prepared sounds fine to me. Don't worry about making any adjustments on my account. Compared to the MREs I've had to eat over the years, I'm sure your food will be delicious."

"Some of the other male residents have mentioned MREs before. What is that exactly?" Holly hadn't wanted to ask and unintentionally offend someone.

"It stands for Meal, Ready to Eat. It's the military's prepacked meals. They're designed to withstand rough conditions and exposure to the elements," Evan said and winked at Chef Mario.

"Oh." Holly had no doubt Chef Mario's food was wonderful compared to packaged military meals.

With a few of the community's widows and widowers seated at her and Evan's table, they enjoyed their dinner and lively conversation. The men, some of them veterans themselves had been keen on exchanging "war stories" with Evan. Evan had been engaging, charming and personable. Holly wasn't sure what she'd expected of him, but her heart swelled with appreciation and affection. Evan didn't seem to realize how special he was.

"Son, you and Holly should be on opposite teams tonight."

Holly shook her head, laughing. "Told you game night was competitive."

Evan's eyes brimmed with desire, surprising her, and his lips curved into a mischievous grin. "I'm game if you are, Hols."

4

Evan enjoyed getting to know the facility residents and their families while everyone prepared for trivia night. He wasn't surprised everyone had wonderful things to say about "his girl" Holly. Apparently, she'd never brought anyone to game night before and she'd consistently resisted any matchmaking efforts from the residents.

He'd pushed aside the unexpected jealousy that had settled in his gut. Of course residents would want to set Holly up with their family members. She was bright, kind, big hearted and beautiful. Evan was selfishly relieved she'd refuted their efforts.

"All right everybody, you know the rules. Phones off and face down or put away." Nicole, the Life Enrichment / Activity Director warned everyone.

She waited patiently as the teams complied with her directive. Evan was ready to play for the win. He'd share whatever the prize was with Holly.

Nicole had selected interesting and entertaining questions. Evan could understand why trivia game night was so popular.

"Dogs are thought to be as smart as humans of what age?" Point to Holly's team.

"What does a "Geiger Counter" measure?" Point to Evan's team.

"Just like fingerprints, what other part of your body has a unique print on it?" Point to Holly's team.

"According to the National Science Foundation, what percentage of our thoughts are negative?" Point to Evan's team.

"One ostrich egg is equal in volume to roughly how many chicken eggs?" Point to Holly's team.

"Where did Dwayne Johnson play football?" Point to Evan's team.

"What famous line is the ending of Gone With the Wind?" Everyone groaned. Evan was confused, the question was much too easy. Everyone knew the answer.

"That's the freebie question," Nicole said wearing a warm smile. But the teams are tied so for the win - Cows produce 3% less milk when listening to what kind of music?"

Damn, Evan had no idea and both teams appeared stumped on the question. Shit.

Holly shyly raised her hand. "Is it country music? I know it's *my* least favorite."

They all waited with bated breath. "Yes! That's correct. Holly's team wins dinner at Weber Grill and a movie." Nicole announced.

"Oh, you have to let Holly bring her fella along, Nicole."

A pretty blush stained Holly's cheeks as all the women made a fuss about letting him tag along for dinner and the movie. Evan wasn't surprised when Nicole quickly agreed. The staff he'd met at Kennison were terrific. He could understand why Holly enjoyed working there and spent time at the facility outside of her job requirements.

After arrangements had been agreed upon for their prize, Evan and Holly said their goodbyes with promises to return the following month for a rematch, and invitations were made to visit on bingo night. It was so on.

"You really had a good time tonight?" Holly asked during the quick drive home.

Was she serious? "I did. The staff, residents, and their families were great. Dinner was delicious. I had a blast. And I can't wait for my team to beat yours next month."

Holly's angelic laugh made his cock twitch. The evening had felt intimate, like they were a real couple. For a little while Evan had acted as if they were.

"Fair enough. You know, Dusty was supposed to call me and to set up a date but he never did. He must have changed his mind." Holly shrugged as if she wasn't bothered.

Evan shoved the pang of guilt he felt aside as he led them into the house and to the living room. Warning Dusty away from Holly had been the right decision he assured himself.

"If Dusty ghosted you, then that's his loss and he's an ass," Evan said, meaning it wholeheartedly.

Holly's eyes lit up from his compliment. "That's nice of you to say. I didn't expect much. We all know how Dusty is. I was just looking to get out of the house and have a little fun."

Relieved with Holly's realistic expectations, Evan's guilt subsided. "I hope I did all right as a stand in tonight?" Evan closed the distance between them, unable to resist her loveliness and honesty. The scent of her sweet, sensuous perfume had lust warring with restraint inside him because of Brody's warning.

Holly stepped closer, her eyes dilated and gleaming, filling Evan with hope and causing his cock to stir again.

"You were wonderful," Holly said, glancing at his lips.

Brody's warnings cast aside, Evan gazed down at his lovely roommate and gently stroked her warm cheek with his thumb. "What am I going to do with you, Hols?" Evan knew what he *wanted* to do, but was hesitant, unsure about pressing his luck.

"I have an idea", Holly whispered, and to his surprise and delight, she brushed a feather light kiss against his lips.

She'd be the end of him, Evan thought. "I have a few ideas myself," Evan said as their mouths came together in a now hungry kiss. He drank in Holly's sweetness, immediately addicted, certain he'd never get enough of her.

When he led her to his room by the hand, Holly didn't resist, but once inside, Evan searched her gleaming, passion filled eyes for any hesitation or doubt.

She turned her back to him and glanced over her shoulder wearing a sexy grin. "Unzip me?"

Faster than Evan thought was possible, he had them both undressed and tumbling onto his bed in a tangle of limbs, their lips feeding on each other in a hot, desperate frenzy. He allowed himself a moment to nibble and suck on Holly's pebbled nipples and tease her slick slit and swollen clit with his eager tongue, nearly making her come, and she groaned in disappointment.

After he sheathed his hard, aching cock with trembling hands, Evan experienced a strange and unexpected awareness rush through him when he thrust into Holly's tight, warm pussy. The undeniable passion in her glimmering blue eyes ricocheted deep inside him.

Evan savored Holly's tight heat as he fucked her with purpose, his dream of claiming her finally realized, in *his* mind at least. She held him tight, writhing beneath him as he pistoned in and out of her snug pussy, moaning her pleasure.

Lust vibrated between them as they came together, shuddering in ecstasy. They lay silent for a beat while their breathing slowed before Evan disposed of his condom.

Evan gathered Holly in his arms, a sense of peace settling over him. Her soft, warm curves molded to him perfectly.

"You don't have to worry," Holly assured just as he was drifting off, "I won't make things weird. We can do a roommates with benefits kind of thing. No expectations or demands. Okay?"

Evan wanted to argue the point, but chose to wait. Holly was so much more than a no expectations or demands kind of woman. It hurt his heart that she didn't seem to think so. He'd go along. For now. "Sure. Of course."

5

Early Saturday morning two weeks later, Holly lay in Evan's bed, gloriously naked and deliciously sore. Damn but they were compatible in bed. And out, she'd learned over the course of their brief time living together. Unfortunately, she was alone in his bed as she watched him efficiently hustle to get his things together into his duffle for his drill training weekend.

Part of the 85th U.S. Army Support Command, Evan was due to report for his readiness muster at the Arlington Heights USAR Complex soon. Holly chastised herself for feeling down he wouldn't be around over the weekend until Sunday evening. They were just having fun, she reminded herself. No demands or expectations. They'd both agreed.

Holly didn't blame Evan for agreeing to a casual arrangement so easily, considering her parent's history, but she couldn't help but hope for more. Pointless as it was. He most likely didn't see her as a long-term proposition and Holly couldn't blame him for that either. He probably considered her a risky bet.

She'd have to enjoy their time together as long as it lasted with no regrets. Her heart would understand, wouldn't it?

Holly pulled the covers away exposing her nude flesh just as the air conditioning cycled on. Her nipples hardened in response to the cool air against her skin. Evan zipped up his duffle and turned toward her, his intense green eyes simmering with heat.

"Are you sure you have to leave now?" Holly nearly purred. She knew he did, but couldn't help herself.

With predatory grace he strode toward her and captured a tight nipple peak between his lips. Her senses spun and her skin felt as if it were on fire. He laved attention to the other peak before pulling away with determination.

"You know I do, Hols. I usually spend Friday and Saturday night in Arlington Heights so I'm not distracted and late for morning musters."

A satisfied smirk tugged at her lips and she sat up in bed, not bothering to cover up. Heat flared in Evan's eyes as he gazed at her intently.

"But you couldn't tear yourself away last night, could you?" Holly was playing with fire, she knew, but couldn't care less about getting burned.

"Damn straight. But tonight, I'll stay in Arlington Heights because I can't keep my hands off of you and I can't be late. You understand that, right?"

Holly nodded, enjoying the boost to her ego. She pulled the bedsheets up and covered herself. Playtime was over. She'd never forgive herself if she was responsible for making Evan late.

"Thanks, Hols. When I get back on Sunday, we'll go to dinner and continue from where we left off here. How does that sound?" Evan proceeded to the bedroom door and turned back toward her.

It sounded perfect to her. "It sounds like a great idea. Please be careful while you're gone, okay?" The training weekends weren't dangerous per se, but one never knew. Accidents happened.

Evan's gaze softened and a warm smile spread across his face. "Of course. Try and get some sleep. I'll be back before you know it." He winked at her and left as if not trusting himself to linger any longer.

Holly sighed when she heard the front door close, and then flopped back down onto the bed. She'd try getting more sleep, although she doubted she'd be able to. After two restless hours of tossing and turning, and a quick shower, she decided it would be best to keep herself busy until Evan got back on Sunday.

She texted Aleesha. Not surprisingly she had weekend plans with Evan's family and Grandma Sadie Mae. Holly immediately texted Paige, assuming she'd be free. Her jerk of a boyfriend Miles Beckett didn't seem to want to spend that much time with her outside of Paige's job at his family's Beckett Hotels chain headquartered in Chicago. To Holly's surprise, Paige had plans with Miles. Although Holly didn't care for Miles, she hoped he'd get his head out of his ass and treat Paige right.

Her house was miserably silent as Holly tidied up and did a load of laundry. How quickly she'd gotten used to and enjoyed Evan's company over the last several weeks. Aside from their combustible sexy time, they'd enjoyed home cooked meals together, played video games on the huge television in the basement and Evan had been teaching her how to play pool. Holly's game had improved significantly.

By lunch time, Holly had decided to drop by the Kennison Lombard facility, grab a bite, and see what activities were on the agenda for the day. She saw no reason to aimlessly ramble around her home alone.

Thirty minutes later, a scrumptious plate of steak tacos, rice, refried beans and more were placed in front of Holly on the table she shared in the restaurant / cafeteria with Lizzy Kennison and Marissa, one of the licensed staff counselors.

"I'll be honest. I never understood the whole 'friends with benefits' business," Lizzy said and sipped her iced tea.

Holly wasn't shocked at Lizzy's admission. Lizzy was in her early sixties and had been happily married for over thirty years.

"Jake and I started that way. Good friends from grade school first." Marissa offered with a wink. Marissa was in her late thirties, married nearly ten years now.

"But the real benefits come from the companionship, support, sharing memories. Not only the sex." Lizzy countered. "You've got so much to offer, dear. Evan would be crazy to keep things casual."

Holly wasn't so sure. She'd been experiencing those benefits with Evan but accepted their time together as only temporary. "But our families are so different. My parents are a complete shitshow. Evan's are amazing."

"You aren't your parents. You don't have to inherit their issues." Marissa asserted. Lizzy nodded in agreement.

Holly supposed Marissa was right, but she was conflicted. "I don't know. I don't think Evan wants anything more than casual." And she'd have to live with it, as heartbreaking as it would be.

She startled when her cell phone rang. Her cheeks burned when she noted Evan's name on the display. Both Lizzy and Marissa tossed her knowing glances as if to say, 'I told you so'.

"Hols. We just broke for lunch. I missed you so I wanted to give you a quick call."

Hope dared to bloom in Holly's heart and soul. Was there a chance Evan could want more than only something casual with her?

6

Now wearing his civilian clothing, Evan zipped up his duffle early Sunday evening, anxious to hit the road and get back to Holly. He'd decided to take her to Harry Caray's Italian Steakhouse in Lombard's Yorktown Mall for dinner, followed by dessert in his bed.

"Command Sergeant Major Lambert wants to see you, sir." Twenty-year-old Kyle Barnes informed him. Evan had taken the young man, who had just begun his electrician apprenticeship, under his wing during their drill weekend.

Kyle was bright, eager to learn, hardworking, and a team player. Exactly the kind of man their battalion needed.

Evan wondered why Sergeant Major wanted to see him. The weekend had gone off without a hitch. Their inspections, inventories, and preventive maintenance checks and services (PMCS) had been successful.

He nodded to Kyle and made to leave, hoping he wouldn't be delayed for very long.

"Thanks for everything this weekend, sir. I appreciate it. I hope I wasn't too much of a burden," Kyle said, glancing at the floor, seemingly embarrassed.

Evan was certain Kyle's confidence would increase with time. He was off to a great start. "You don't have to call me sir and you weren't a burden. You're an asset to our battalion. Don't think otherwise."

Kyle blushed. "Thank you. Evan."

They parted ways and Evan hustled to Sergeant Major Lambert's office. He was burning daylight and wanted to get back to Holly ASAP.

Evan wrapped on the door frame after reaching his superior's office. "You wanted to see me, sir? Nothing wrong I hope."

Still in his fatigues displaying his rank insignia; three chevrons, three rockers, and center star, he gestured for Evan to take a seat in front of his desk.

"Not at all. Kyle Barnes stopped by to let me know how much he appreciated your guidance and mentorship this weekend. Your efforts with him didn't go unnoticed. You did good by him and I wanted to thank you personally. Kyle's an excellent addition to our battalion, just needs a little time to build his confidence."

It was Evan's turn to blush. "Thank you, sir."

A few minutes later, he was on his way back home. To Holly. He couldn't get there fast enough but was mindful of the speed limit. Additional delays were not acceptable.

He sighed with relief when he pulled into the garage and parked next to Holly's car.

When he found Holly, all thoughts of going out to dinner fled. Damn but she was gorgeous. Evan's skin prickled with awareness at the sight of her. Her wavy golden locks cascaded over her shoulders and her form fitting lavender dress hugged her delicious curves. He ached to get his hands on her.

Lust burned in Evan's veins and he dropped his duffle. It hit the floor with a thunk. Holly's eyes smoldered with heat. They rushed toward each other and he captured her lips in a ravenous kiss that left him breathless and rock hard.

"What do you say to a little detour before dinner?" Evan didn't want to be a jerk. His interest in Holly went beyond the physical. If she wanted to grab dinner first, he'd be fine with that. They had all night.

With a gleam in her eyes, she grabbed him by the hand and led him to her bedroom. The sounds of zippers and rustling clothing mingled with their soft moans and heavy breathing as they made quick work of undressing each other..

"I missed you this weekend, Hols," Evan whispered as he gently tugged on one of Holly's pebbled nipples. "I missed you like crazy." It was the truth. The hours away from her had been torture.

Holly groaned and ran her fingers through his hair, tugging lightly. The sting heated every cell in his body.

"I missed you too. I'm glad you're back and safe."

Evan felt a sense of hope about their future, but would take his time, not wanting to spook Holly or scare her away.

"I'll always make my way back to you." It was the truth and Evan expected, in time, that Holly would believe him.

His stiff cock throbbed as he licked and teased the hard nub of Holly's clit. She lifted her hips, bringing his mouth closer to her drenched slit. His lips and tongue worked her pussy over until Holly called out his name as she came.

Beyond ready to claim her, Evan quickly sheathed himself, parted Holly's delicate folds with the tip of his cock and then plunged inside her welcoming tight, warm pussy. She stretched to accommodate him, gripping Evan snugly.

She wrapped her legs around his hips, while he fucked her with hard, rough strokes. Hands clasped, they moved together. Evan hammered in and out of her, the hot rush of pure need driving him.

Evan fucked her hard, savoring her welcoming tight heat. Fueled by their mutual desire, they came as one, both panting. His heart swelled with love for the woman of his dreams. He was deliriously happy but terrified of losing her at the same time.

About an hour later after a quick, sexy shower together and the short drive to the restaurant, their server placed delectable smelling Italian sausage toasted ravioli and calamari on their table. Evan was starved, having worked up an appetite back home.

They filled their plates and nibbled on their appetizers in companiable salience for a moment.

"So, you spent some time at Kennison's this weekend because the girls were busy?" A twinge of guilt nagged at him, knowing Holly had been alone all weekend since Paige and Aleesha both had plans. He'd need to get over it. Evan had commitments that were non-negotiable.

Holly nodded with a sweet smile on her face. At least she didn't seem upset, Evan mused.

"I had a nice lunch visit on Saturday afternoon with Lizzy and Marissa. And then on Sunday I won two hundred dollars against a few of the men at pool. I told you they're competitive over there. Your coaching really paid off, so to speak."

Evan was stunned, but proud. "That's my girl."

"I was wondering. Can you teach me to play poker," Holly asked with a mischievous glint in her eyes.

Evan tilted his head back and laughed, unable to help himself. Holly was precious and he'd do anything for her. "I think I've created a monster, but yes, I can teach you."

7

Anticipation vibrated through the room. Holly, Paige, and Aleesha were in one of the larger dressing rooms at the bridal salon. It was two weeks until Aleesha and Brody's wedding and this was their final dress fitting.

They'd begun with Aleesha. Her gorgeous wedding gown with a triangular back cutout and beautiful lace cutout cathedral train had fit her perfectly. No additional alterations needed.

Holly and Paige scrutinized their reflections in the wall of mirrors. Aleesha observed intently, wearing a blue satin robe with the salon's logo on the collar.

Their ink blue, A-line, V-neck chiffon floor length dress with hem ruffle was a perfect complement to Aleesha's gown. Holly loved the lace bodice, back cutout similar to Aleesha's and the flirty side split that began mid-thigh. The V-neck bodice offered a little sexy cleavage without being inappropriate for church, or Grandma Sadie Mae, God love her.

Holly wondered what Evan would think of her in the dress. They were standing up together – Holly as Maid of Honor and Evan as the Best Man. She was certain he'd look incredible in his black tuxedo suit with matching ink blue colored tie.

Holly frowned as Paige fussed with the three-quarter length sleeves of her dress. She and Aleesha exchanged a knowing glance.

"You know, Holly doesn't need to have longer sleeves like mine. She's not hiding scars like I am. There's nothing wrong with her having cap sleeves. There's plenty of time to make that simple alteration." Paige suggested, seemingly feeling guilty.

Holly's heart went out to her. She couldn't imagine what it must have been like to suffer as Paige had. Her physical scars had healed as best as they could, even with multiple surgeries, but her emotional scars remained.

"I love everything about the dress, including the sleeve length. Honestly." Aleesha tried to assure Paige.

Holly nodded in agreement. "A different sleeve length would completely change the look of the dress. Stop worrying. We look hot, right Aleesha?"

A smile twitched at Paige's lips.

"Absolutely. Wait until Evan sees you, Holly. He won't be able to keep his hands off you. Miles either, Paige," Aleesha said, waggling her brows.

Holly felt her face heat, but nearly scoffed. She doubted Miles would care what Paige wore. She hoped beyond hope that Paige would see the light and dump his ignorant ass, sooner rather than later. She deserved so much better. Paige shrugged, still scrutinizing her reflection.

"I don't know guys." Holly had shared her "relationship" in broad strokes with her best friends. "I feel all out of sorts where Evan is concerned. I suggested our "roommates with benefits" arrangement but…"

"You're in love with him." Aleesha and Paige announced in unison.

Holly nodded. Of course she was. Evan was a terrific guy. Although their personal relationship was casual, at her insistence, he treated her like gold. He opened doors for her, was considerate, seemed to enjoy spending time with her in and out of the bedroom and even enjoyed visits to Kennison's with her, and was well liked by the residents and staff alike.

"Yeah, I am," Holly admitted aloud, "But he hasn't pressed for anything more than our casual arrangement."

"Then you need to say something." Paige insisted.

"She's right," Aleesha said, "It's obvious to me that he cares about you. More than casually."

Holly wasn't so sure. Men were better at separating their feelings than women were. And did she want to risk scaring Evan away by pushing for something more?

Evan adjusted his blue tuxedo suit tie as he faced the mirror in the fitting room at Brody's tuxedo shop. The wedding was in two weeks and this was their final fitting. So far so good. The shop's tailors were exceptional and his, Brody's, their father's and Dusty's suits didn't require further alterations.

He and Brody had tried to get some idea of what the girls were wearing with little success. All they were told was Aleesha's dress was gorgeous and the bridesmaids dresses were the color of their ties and were sexy and flirty. Not much to go on.

It didn't really matter to Evan. Holly was beautiful regardless of what she wore – a flirty bridesmaid dress or faded jeans and t-shirt. Her beauty radiated from the inside out and didn't have much to do with her outward appearance. Damn, but he loved her.

His father looked them all over and nodded with satisfaction. "I think the women will be pleased, if I do say so myself."

"I think Holly will find you passable." Dusty snarked at Evan.

Brody immediately frowned and Evan's stomach churned. Fuck Brody and his holier than thou attitude.

Their father raised a brow.

Fuck it. "Brody tried to warn me against pursuing Hols. Like it's any of his damn business."

"I was worried about things going south and then causing problems for me and Aleesha. Forgive me for wanting to keep the peace." Brody explained.

"If your relationship with Aleesha is so fragile that it hinges on Evan and Holly's, then you should call things off right now," Their father said with a grim expression.

Brody's eyes grew wide. "No. Aleesha and I are solid. I promise you. It's just the girls are close and I wanted to avoid arguments and people taking sides."

"Son, you're all adults and you can't control everything, so give it a rest. Evan, it's obvious to me and your mother that you're in love with the girl. If you want a future beyond this stupid casual thing you've got going, you need to make your move. Now."

Evan knew his father was right. No one knew what the future held. As a reservist he could get called to active duty at any time and God forbid if something happened.

Evan knew he didn't want to continue with Holly the way things were for much longer. He also recognized he needed to do something, but would never forgive himself if he scared Holly into ending their relationship in the process.

8

Evan wiped his eyes *again*, as the pastor delivered the most romantic wedding ceremony he'd ever heard. He hadn't been the only one to shed tears. The entire wedding party and attendees had been just as emotional during the proceedings. Brody and Aleesha beamed with love and joy. And putting all the brotherly bullshit aside, Evan was truly happy for Brody.

"Love each other each and every day and live every day with full hearts and your bond will grow ever stronger with time. And so, by the power vested in me, I now pronounce you husband and wife. Brody, I invite you now to kiss your wife for the very first time. May there be many more to come."

Everyone applauded and cheered as Brody and Aleesha shared their first kiss as a married couple. Happy tears flowed in abundance.

Evan glanced at Holly in her sexy blue dress with the thigh high split. His heart swelled with love when she flashed him a sweet, dazzling smile.

Miles Beckett was a dick for how badly he treated Paige, but his family sure knew how to cater a wedding, Evan thought several hours later as he held Holly in his arms during a slow dance. He'd inhaled his scrumptious dinner, enjoyed feeding bites of decadent dessert to Holly and was now savoring the feel of her against him.

It had been the perfect day. Even Dusty had stepped up once he too realized Miles wasn't going to do right by Paige and had kept her engaged, entertained and dancing. Evan had been impressed. Could Dusty be reconsidering his cavalier lifestyle for something more meaningful?

Evan stood beside Dusty as the women positioned themselves for the bouquet toss. They'd managed to convince Grandma Sadie Mae to join in the "fun" as well.

"Who knew the women would be so competitive?" Dusty mused as some of the women elbowed each other to secure what they considered to be a better spot.

It was a silly superstition but Evan wanted Holly to catch it. He could admit he had imagined he and Holly in Brody and Aleesha's place today.

Once the shoving and shouting were over, by sheer accident it seemed, Holly had caught the bouquet to all the other women's disappointment. The look of sheer shock on Holly's face had been priceless. She'd glanced at him and shrugged.

"I'm gonna go for the garter," Evan heard himself say.

Dusty turned to him with determination and challenge in his eyes. "You'll have to fight me for it, man," he said before taking his place amongst the other men.

They eyed each other suspiciously waiting for Brody to make the toss. Evan had a split second to dart toward Dusty and leap up behind him when it looked as if Dusty might catch the garter. Evan nearly snatched it right out of Dusty's hand and held on tight, the garter charm digging into his palm.

It was a sign. Tonight, when he and Holly were alone, Evan would take a stand and plead his case for them. Win, lose or draw. Holly was worth the risk.

Holly lay gloriously naked and still damp with sweat on the luxurious king size bed in hers and Evan's suite at the Beckett hotel. It had been an incredible day. Love and fun had flowed in abundance. She couldn't believe Aleesha was now married and headed to Tahiti in the morning for her honeymoon.

She stretched out on the bed, deliciously sore while Evan took care of his condom. She groaned when she rolled her ankles and wiggled her toes. She'd ditched her shoes hours ago, but the heels were higher than she normally wore and her feet were killing her.

Evan exited the bathroom, still undressed himself, his muscular form on display. Holly's heart ached with desire, pulse quickening as her stomach flipped.

He sat at the end of the bed and took one of her feet in his large, capable hands, rubbing the pain away. She moaned in relief.

"Why did you wear shoes with such a high heel if they were going to hurt your feet so much, Hols?"

Holly sighed as Evan worked the tension from her other foot. "Because they matched my dress so perfectly. It's a girl thing. You wouldn't understand."

He chuckled and continued working on her sore feet. The serious look on his face had her stomach clench. Was he going to call off their arrangement? It hadn't been lost on her that she'd caught the bouquet and he'd caught the garter. She'd initially thought it was a sign and had planned on proposing they take their relationship to the next level. Now she wasn't so sure.

Evan focused his mesmerizing green eyes on hers. "I'm just going to come out and say it. I'm done with our roommates with benefits arrangement. I want something meaningful with you, not casual. I love you, Hols. So much."

Holly bolted up and sat against the headboard, pulling the sheets up against her, stunned and terrified. She wiped a tear that slid down her cheek. Evan took his place beside her and clasped her hand in his, his strength and warmth comforting her.

"I love you too, but I'm scared. My parent's marriage and relationship now are a wreck. Remember what happened when we invited everyone over for Labor Day?"

No one had expected her mother to bring a twenty-five-year-old as her "date". Her father had come alone. The woman had no shame. They'd been divorced for years, and there was no reason why her mother should continue to try to hurt her father.

Evan shrugged. "Well, there was that. But my dad and mom intercepted and we all had a decent time. This is about me and you. Not our parents. We're us and they're them. I believe we have a shot at something great. A real future together. Don't you?"

Holly wanted to. With all her heart and soul. "I want to. I'm nervous. I don't want to do anything to mess things up."

Evan kissed the palm of her hand, a spark of possessiveness in his bright green eyes. "Dad told us a few simple rules he and Mom follow to keep them on track when we had our final tuxedo fitting.

"Okay." Holly was all ears. She didn't want to lose him.

"Every day we sent each other a selfie. It doesn't have to be anything sexual. It's just a quick check in." Evan began.

That sounded simple enough to Holly.

"We don't go to sleep if we're angry with each other. We should never be afraid to ask each other questions. About anything."

So far so good, Holly thought.

"We have to be willing to trust each other and communicate our feelings clearly every day. And to me, the most important rule of all, we don't hesitate to tell each other we're uncomfortable with who we're with or where we're going."

Evan was right as far as Holly was concerned. Especially with his reservist duty. If these rules worked for Evan's parents, they could work for them too.

"So, what do you say? Do you Hols, vow to take a leap of faith with me Evan, for the amazing future we both deserve?"

The confidence of Evan's gaze pierced through all of Holly's defenses. Not that she had many where he was concerned. They deserved their shot at happiness. She honestly believed it now.

"I do."

About the Author

Int'l bestseller and award-winning author **Dania Voss** writes compelling, sexy romance with personality, heat, and heart. Born in Rome, Italy and raised in Chicagoland, she creates stories with authentic, engaging characters. She loves anything pink and is a huge fan of 80s hair bands.

A favorite with romance readers, her debut novel "On the Ropes," the first in her Windy City Nights series, became an international bestseller. Dania's books have won multiple awards, and her work has been highlighted on NBC, ABC, CBS, and FOX. She has been featured in the Chicago Tribune, Southern Writers Magazine, and Chicago Entrepreneurs Magazine (selected as the #8 Top Chicago Author in 2021).

When she's not writing, you can find Dania at a sporting event, a rock concert, or the movies (preferably a comedy).

Read More from Dania Voss
Dania Voss Books

Newsletter
Dania's Newsletter
Website
Dania's Website

All Spun Up
Laurel Wanrow

1

My summer at the old lodge had fallen into a pleasant, though exasperating, rhythm. I exchanged pleasantries, coffee duty and bathroom time with one of my housemates, Mrs. Windsor, from four a.m. to four thirty, at which time the retired art teacher left to capture another Rocky Mountain sunrise with her watercolors, and I finished my coffee, counting the seconds until the morning's Second Act. *Patience, Kenzie. It won't be long now.*

Craning to hear movement from upstairs, I held my breath. *Would he be jogging today?*

The sounds I lived for each morning filtered down: the creak of the door of the screened porch a floor above and his footsteps padding on the old floorboards.

Yes! I wiggled a dance, my heartbeat racing. *Stop it! Play it cool.*

I grabbed a yogurt and spoon and propped my rear against the red linoleum countertop to wait for Doctor Mac Dawson, veterinarian at Valley Animal Hospital.

I lived for this morning routine. *Sad, Kenzie, sad.*

Doubly sad I was stalking my housemate. My coffee shop job in downtown Estes Park provided free drinks. I could skip the coffee routine and be out the door in fifteen minutes. But that would mean missing Dr. Mac leaving for a jog, and he'd run the last eight days—not that I'd counted.

A shiver ran through me. Did he jog *every day* to run into me?

He crept downstairs, as I had. We'd never discussed it, but I was sure neither of us wanted to wake our other two housemates, a pair of college boys who bartended and kept the same late hours. I rarely talked to them, yet I joked with Dr. Mac every morning and chatted while preparing dinner if he wasn't on call. We'd traded everything from scrapes growing up to worst dates in college—which ended a month ago for me. I'd put myself through on the ten-year plan to earn my degree at twenty-eight. We discovered we'd overlapped at Colorado State. Now twenty-nine, he'd had gaps between earning his B.S. and completing vet school and internships.

Older than the students flocking to Estes for summer jobs, we'd hit it off. Yet, I hadn't suggested anything leading to more. Not even *let's have coffee sometime*.

As his lanky, bowlegged cowboy figure appeared in the doorframe, my body cried, *Why not?* His tanned freckles and tumble of brown curls were cute, but I seriously appreciated his biceps and muscular thighs, and especially that tight butt beneath his running shorts.

"Morning," he rumbled in his deep voice, and with a grin, he scanned my Morning Moose uniform: pink T-shirt sporting the cartoon moose with a bow on her antler, black capris and a fleece jacket to start the crisp morning. Nothing low-cut or alluring for the matronly sisters who ran the coffee shop. Then—as usual—his gaze darted to the breakfast nook, where he dropped his shoes on the booth seat and opened the casement window. With practiced ease, he plucked two hummingbird feeders from the antique cookstove and stepped onto the seat to hang out the window. As he stretched, his rear tightened, and biceps stretched his T-shirt sleeves. He deftly looped the feeder rings onto their hooks and swung back inside.

And that, I told my pleading body, *is why we aren't making moves on Dr. Mac*. He'd been hanging those feeders since he was six and could reach the hooks with a grandparent clutching his waist. His grandmother still owned this 1930s log lodge, and Mac had been charged with managing renters to cover expenses. I couldn't risk jeopardizing this setup.

I'd failed at scoring my dream job in Rocky Mountain National Park—"the Park," to the locals—as a seasonal researcher gathering plant data. My consolation prize was working *nearby* as a barista, with the awesome mountain views I'd enjoyed every summer vacation. Finding this rental—with views of Mac and real conversations—*almost* made up for not using my hard-earned degree.

Nope, my body answered. *Only one thing will make amends.*

I diverted my gaze to my yogurt as Mac hopped down and grabbed a glass from the cupboard, trailing a scent I couldn't name. Once he drank his water, his gravelly morning voice would disappear, leaving it only dreamy deep.

Oh yeah, I had our routine memorized.

As he ran the water, I cleared my throat to keep a high pitch from my voice. "Morning. You running far today?"

"Couple of miles. Got to. Old Doc Prichard is single-handedly keeping the Donut Haus in business. Brings in a dozen for snacking between morning appointments, then leaves the rest for Doc Cory and me."

I grinned. "You lucky dog! I love their doughnuts. I'd eat them every day if I could."

Mac wagged a finger. "Better not let the Morning Moose sisters hear that. Their Marvelous Moose Blintzes have a following, including my Gramma Louise."

I rolled my eyes. "Nothing compares to Donut Haus applesauce cake doughnuts."

"Ah, the wholesome appeal of the humble cake doughnuts compared to those fancy blintzes." He leaned a hip against the counter. "Are you saying you'd prefer a plain applesauce?"

I nodded and tucked a spoonful of yogurt into my mouth to keep it busy.

"It's like choosing trucks over hybrids," he said in complete deadpan.

Um, maybe we weren't still talking about doughnuts? Mac drove a truck, and the blond college bartenders drove a hybrid. I could play this game. "It's like choosing cowboys over computer geeks." Which both the bartenders were. And Mac's family ran a ranch on the plains outside of Loveland. When not jogging, he wore a cowboy hat with his western shirts and tight jeans.

He stared at me.

Oh crap…where had I gone with that one? I couldn't get involved with him. If it fell apart or became awkward in any way, I'd lose my affordable rent. For that, I could live with five of us sharing one bathroom, no air conditioning and window screens that let in the mayflies.

Mac gulped some water. "Applesauce cake is the special of the day tomorrow. Don't you have off? Want to split a half dozen?"

———

I clenched my glass while Kenzie's big brown eyes widened as if I'd offered her a steak…or a pie, or something that certainly wasn't doughnuts. Her tongue traced her bottom lip, and my thoughts dove south.

No! Not now, not in running shorts, and not when she hadn't even answered. In desperation, I ordered my thoughts to work—cats, dogs, the endless notes and files. I blurted, "I mean, I have the day off, so…"

Only because I'd wrangled a vacation day to match her days off two weeks ago.

"Yeah," she mumbled, her voice husky.

Thank you, Fate.

"That'd be nice. Fun." Kenzie scooped into her yogurt again, grinning. "You hit me in a weak area. As if I could say *no*."

"Nope." I laughed, mostly in relief she hadn't refused, as she had a casual pizza invite last week. "No way you could, not after that buildup." Good. I'd take her for doughnuts. Then I'd suggest a hike in the Park… Shoot! Park reservations. I snapped my fingers.

She looked up. "Something wrong?"

Already, Kenzie Cooper knew my habits. In vet training, I'd had to stop cursing—a common practice on the ranch, but unacceptable with paying clients—so I'd begun snapping my fingers instead. "Tough client expected today." I thought fast. "A cat. I like cats, mind you, but not teeth bared and swiping."

"Gotcha. I love cats." With a glance to her watch, she straightened and licked the spoon.

My mouth parted. I yearned to taste her lips.

I sat abruptly, snatched a running shoe and hoisted my foot onto the bench for distraction. *Stick to the conversation.* Kenzie was easy to talk to, hardworking and considerate of everyone. Over a couple of weeks, my appreciation of her cute looks had grown to liking her as a person... far beyond a hookup.

Kenzie washed her yogurt things, grabbed her pack, said, "Gotta run," and left before I'd even tied my laces.

I let my head fall back against the seat. "Bye," I whispered and blew her a kiss.

Maybe one day, my sorely out-of-practice lips would know what kissing felt like again. I smiled. *Kenzie said yes!*

I yanked off the shoe. Gathering both shoes, I turned out the light and light-footed it up the dark stairs, my plans forming.

Since the pandemic, the Park required entrance reservations. But if we left early, we could drive in before the restrictions. Would Kenzie want to spend her day off in the Park?

Damn, that's what I got for trying to make this seem not-like-a-date.

I closed the door to "my room" for the summer. I'd taken the screened sleeping porch to free a bedroom for another summer roommate. The cabin had five bedrooms between the three floors, but Gramma Louise hadn't wanted to risk damage to her parents' Victorian bedroom set in her second-floor room. We'd stuffed that room and the attic storage with everything precious and locked the doors.

I rolled onto the twin bed and pulled up my covers. Growing up, I'd slept here during cousin sleepovers. We lived the closest, so I was here the most and had laid claim to the attic bedroom.

Which was now Kenzie's room.

During the roommate interviews, I'd been surprised the cute brunette's name was the same as mine—Mackenzie, Gramma Louise's maiden name. That could've been awkward, but Kenzie had laughed. Staring at Mackenzie Cooper, I'd had to remind myself we'd be roommates. This wasn't a dating service. Gramma had made rules about female roommates not becoming hookups.

To live in the family cabin, I had to pay the utilities *and* taxes. Between student loans and the payment on my used truck, I needed roommates to build savings for my own place after this five-year deal ended. So…either rent to all guys—and police parties and drunken damage—or go co-ed and keep the house romance-free. Gramma had warned I wouldn't be able to find replacement roommates midsummer. And I didn't want to get a reputation, being the new vet in town.

Gramma Louise had firm ideas and liked to be right, things I was learning to work around.

I scrubbed my face. True, I hadn't had time for a girlfriend while in school. Classes, labs, clinic trials and *everything* had consumed my time. I'd wanted to be a vet since I was ten and saved one of the barn cats who'd been cornered by a coyote. I'd coerced my parents into putting a cat door into the shed to keep them safe. Then I got them vaccinated, spayed and neutered. Eventually, I'd offer at-cost vetting to ranches trying to do better by their strays and ferals.

The wind picked up, whooshing through the ponderosas surrounding the cabins along Mary's Lake Road. The magpies began squawking. I usually went back to sleep after seeing Kenzie—*but she'd said yes!* The same elation had spun me up when, smitten, I'd led Kenzie straight to my childhood room. She'd smiled, looking around, and said, "I like it."

I threw back the covers. A jog in the fifty-degree chill would cool me off. Or the shower I'd need before work.

Besides, Doc Prichard's daily box of doughnuts wasn't a lie, though he usually left us only one apiece.

2

Customers stormed Morning Moose, giving me little time to think about Mac while I pulled order after order. Hazelnut latte. Large red-eye. Vanilla latte, extra foam. As the other stores' opening times approached, their shopkeepers' orders became frantic. It never flustered the sisters, Sarah and Ruth, and as Sarah said, *I have no need to put out others' brushfires.*

How did Mac like his coffee? Would I ever know?

During the midmorning lull, I took out the trash. When the bear-proof dumpster lid clanged shut, a pitiful *meow* squeaked.

I peeked around the side. Two green eyes shone in the shadows. A longhaired black cat was wedged into a narrow fence gap. The sight of him took me back a decade with a gut punch. In high school, our last family cats had included a black longhaired. Drawing a breath, I shook off their memory.

"Good thing I'm not superstitious. Whatcha doing there, kitty cat?" I'd never seen a loose cat around town. Maybe Mac—vets must have connections—could help find the owner?

I crouched and extended my hand. "Kitty, kitty."

He peered at me through half-open eyes, which seemed odd. As I considered going inside to snitch a piece of egg as bait, he rose awkwardly—also odd. "That's it, kitty." It was hard to tell under that floof, but he looked rounded. Not a stray. "Do you need to find your way home? I'll help you, buddy."

Giving another tiny meow, he came to me in that coy way cats did, like I wasn't his goal. I kept my fingers at chin height, and once he'd had a sniff and a rub, I scratched him right where he wanted. He melted into my hand, gave a rumble of a purr and stumbled, leaning heavily.

I scooped him against me and rose. As I headed to the back door, reality set in. I couldn't keep a cat at work. But a vet could—another excellent excuse to see Mac.

"You've got to be cool with hanging out in a box," I told the cat. Fortunately, I hadn't flattened the recycling yet, and several cartons sat by the door. I lowered the cat into one, to his sharp protest.

"Sorry, buddy." My forearm still felt the warmth of his body, and as I closed the flaps, I glimpsed my jacket sleeve. Blood soaked it.

Oh no. Dismay bit at me. The cat actually *did* need to see a vet.

Holding the box, I eased into the coffee shop. Luck was with me. Sarah stepped through the swinging door. Swallowing, I explained about the injured cat. "Do you mind if I take him to the animal hospital?"

Sarah clucked. "Emergency calls are costly, dear, and likely he'll need stitches with that amount of blood. Perhaps you should turn him over to the shelter?"

"It's too much blood," I whispered. "Can I take him and count the time as my lunch?"

A hand on my shoulder, she turned me and held the door. "Go ahead, dear."

"Dr. Dawson, a woman with a bleeding cat is asking to see you. Says her name is Kenzie Cooper."

"Kenzie? Where'd she get a—never mind." I strode to the waiting area with our receptionist following.

The room was half full, but I zeroed in on Kenzie, perched on a chair's edge, a box on her lap. She pushed her hair behind her ear, a nervous habit I'd noted, but that'd disappeared recently.

Our gazes met. She rose and walked forward, her face pinched. "Can you check him even if I don't have an appointment?" she whispered. "He's injured, and all I thought of was bringing him to you."

Her first thought was me? My heart swelled, but she'd come about the cat. To my work, where I had to be professional. "From the look of your jacket, you made a good decision. Come with me." I lifted my arm, about to wrap it around her shoulders, but instead waved her into the back hallway.

"I've interrupted your appointments," she said, "but I couldn't leave him. Or wait. Not with the blood. I'm sorry to cause trouble—"

"Kenzie." I clasped her elbow and squeezed in what I hoped was a comforting, not overt I-want-you-closer way and let go. "Nothing to be sorry about. It's definitely an emergency. Judi," I called to a vet tech, "some help?"

The cat-savvy tech—a mom of college kids who'd worked for Doc Prichard for ten years—covered the surgery table with a towel as I opened the box. The cat crouched in the bottom, hunched in pain, eyes half lidded.

"Aw," said Judi. "Don't think he's going to give us any trouble." She gently wrapped him in another towel and lifted the cat, who uttered a weak meow.

While Judi supported him, I pushed aside fur. Blood matted the inner side of the right rear leg. I yanked on latex gloves. "Lacerations to the inner thigh." Bad enough for stitches. "Likely he tangled with a larger predator."

"Animal bites? He won't die, will he?" asked Kenzie.

"Well..." My gaze met Judi's frown. We knew how bad animal bites could be.

Judi nodded toward the kennels for animals scheduled for surgery. "Shall I settle him in?"

"Please. I'll sort the schedule to move him up." We only had neuters, nothing urgent. I turned back to find Kenzie repeatedly rehooking her hair at her ear. "Once he's under anesthesia, I'll check for other cuts and puncture wounds. We'll flush them before stitching and start antibiotics."

"Oh." She put a hand to her forehead. "Surgery. I...can't afford that."

"We'll scan for a microchip and contact the owners. But if no one turns up..."

Her tear-filled eyes lifted to mine and grabbed at my heart.

Fate, don't ever force me to choose my living expenses over saving an animal. How had this stray become so personal so fast for her? Removing my gloves, I fought an urge to hug her, Gramma's roommate rules ringing through my head. Yet I couldn't watch Kenzie lose hope. I leaned closer. "No charge for my time, just at-cost fees for other staff, meds and supplies."

"Oh. Thank you, Mac." Kenzie hugged me, letting out an unsteady breath against my chest.

Excitement filled me—nothing like what a vet should feel when comforting a client—and my arms tightened around her.

She mumbled, "I really appreciate it," and stepped back, face pink.

My heart raced, but beyond Kenzie, Judi watched us, her arms crossed.

I snapped my fingers. Three times.

Kenzie turned even redder, gaze shooting to me, then around.

I gestured toward the exit, my own face heating. "To fit in emergency surgery, I'll need to hustle." And maybe pacify grumbling clients. But I'd do it for Kenzie. "I can't promise anything until we have him under and shave this fur. There's a reason lost pets don't become strays in the Rockies—predators hunting for an easy meal. Coyote, bobcat, mountain lion."

She jerked up her head, her eyes wide.

I shrugged. "Living in mountains surrounded by federal lands, we're visitors. Disruptive, but predators still rule the night. Even we have to be careful."

"I've read the warnings." She hugged herself, and when her fingers brushed her bloody sleeve, she shook her head. "That poor kitty, alone at night, being stalked."

I put up a palm. "We'll fix him up like we have others."

Judi followed us and chimed in, "We'll call animal control and check local social media for lost cats."

"Thanks," Kenzie murmured. "I have to get back to work."

"I bet you do." Judi nodded to the pink shirt showing under Kenzie's bloodied jacket. "I worked for Sarah and Ruth before earning my tech license. They're picky. Or Ruth always was. Use our washroom to clean up," she advised.

The gregarious tech had hijacked our conversation, but Kenzie looked appreciative.

I opened the door to the waiting room. "I'll touch base when he comes out of anesthesia. I'm glad you brought him in." And I was. Not everyone would leave work to help a stray.

Kenzie squeezed my forearm. "Thanks for…everything. It's so kind of you." She smiled at me before heading for the restroom.

I stared after her. My work gave me many satisfying moments, but this was the best by far. I went to shuffle my schedule. When I returned to the surgery, Judi had set it up.

"The cat has no microchip," she said. "I caught Kenzie and told her."

Snapping my fingers, I huffed a curse. "Upset?"

"Resigned." Judi raised her brows. "Roommates, huh?"

I held up my hands. "Truth. I have four roommates, student loans and a truck payment."

"But you're gonna cover the surgery time?"

I ignored her unapproving look. "She drives a Subaru older than my truck, changes the subject every time family comes up and for some mysterious reason is treating herself to a summer in the mountains after not landing her dream job following graduation."

Judi wrinkled her nose. "Isn't she older than a new graduate?"

"She put herself through. No student loans."

"That's incredible. And here I'm footing the bill for my kids." Judi rolled her eyes.

"Let's start. I don't want to tell Kenzie her stray didn't make it."

3

Of course I hit traffic driving back to Morning Moose. I drummed the steering wheel. *Enjoy the view of the Rockies.* I should feel lucky I'd found the kitty and that he was in good hands. Mac's hands.

Mac, whom I'd hugged without thinking...*and* who had hugged me back. I was such a mess, and he'd been so kind... *Crap.* What was I going to do about it? Nothing? Something? I found myself smiling, then warming at thoughts of his hard-muscled chest. And his tangy pine scent. I navigated winding side streets, tilting toward the window to cool my face before I reached the coffee shop.

Just after noon, Mac's text came. *The cat is in recovery. Three lacerations, two punctures. He's resting fine.*

I sighed. Okay, not out of the woods yet, but the cat—whom I'd begun thinking of as Lucky—had made it so far. I texted back, *Thanks!*

When my shift ended midafternoon, I headed straight for the animal hospital. The waiting room was empty this time. At the desk, I said, "I'd like to see the cat I brought in." *And Mac, please.*

The receptionist shook her head. "Surgery patients don't go home until after six."

"Can someone tell me how he's doing?"

Another headshake. "They're in surgery, backed up because of your cat emergency and now a stomach pumping."

I turned as the restroom door opened. "Oh, hi, Sophie," I said to the sweetheart of a lady who ran the yarn shop. Her typical order—half chocolate and half mocha in her giant ceramic mug—ran through my head. Her long brown hair fell over an amber homespun sweater, one she'd made, from raising the goats to spinning their mohair yarn. When I'd admired it, she'd given me knitting lessons at her shop without making me purchase anything. "What are you doing here?"

Sophie groaned. "One of my goats ate something that's made him ill. You?"

"An injured stray." Had her goat eaten toxic plants? My mind flew over the possibilities.

"Sophie?" Mac emerged from the back.

My heartbeat sped up. Mac didn't look as good in scrubs as he did in running shorts, or with his curls covered by that cap, but the uniform of a man who saved cats could grow on me. I mouthed, "The cat?"

"I'll bring him home after my shift." Mac gave a thumbs-up before showing Sophie a tray of mucous-covered greenery. "I found one flower among plant leaves."

"Pasture plants all look alike to me," said Sophie. "Our partner Monica has the green thumb, but she's on a trip."

Mac pointed tweezers to one small smashed flower. "It's white. That narrows it down."

It certainly did. "May I?" I gestured to Mac's tweezers, and he handed them over. I teased open the sodden flower to expose four notched petals. I separated leaves, all slightly fuzzy and lance-shaped. "Yep. It's hoary alyssum, toxic to livestock, with the literature specifying horses, but I'd think goats would suffer, too." I shrugged.

"You know plants?" Sophie asked. "And you're working as a barista?"

I sighed. "I paid for college on barista tips. My independent study in ecological restoration focused on managing invasive plants. I'd planned to apply for the Park's resource section, but I got COVID and missed the deadline. I promised myself summer in the mountains as a consolation prize."

"If you know the genus-species name," Mac said, "we can better treat Sophie's goat."

"*Berteroa incana.*"

"Thanks. Move the other goats out of any pasture with white flowers," he said to Sophie and strode off.

"You busy?" Sophie asked, drawing my attention from Mac. "I'll pay you to help me find this plant."

After arriving at Sophie's place, a half mile from Mac's lodge, it wasn't hard to find the hoary alyssum in her back pasture. I explained if she removed the flowering plants before seeds set, she'd have it under control—in a few years—without spraying chemicals, which she was strongly against.

"These goats are our livelihood, and I can't risk their health. You studied ecological restoration?"

I nodded.

"I have to talk to my partners, but maybe we should hire you to develop a plan to manage the pastures."

I scanned her three overgrazed fields. Returning worn land to productive, native grasses and wildflowers made my heart happy. At the Park, I'd only have gathered plant data for another planner, but here I'd create the plan. "I'd love to, if you all agree."

"We'll talk. Meanwhile, I urgently need someone to do the grunt work of removing these toxic weeds. Would you like the job?" She named an hourly wage.

I grinned. "That'll sure offset my stray's vet bill."

Several hours and a half-dozen filled weed bags later, I'd cleared half of the smaller pasture. Sophie returned from the hardware store with more bags and a booklet describing the "ob-noxious" weeds in Estes Valley. She planned to spend her evening warning her ranching friends of the livestock risk.

"Could you continue weeding tomorrow?" asked Sophie.

I had the day off from the coffee shop. She was up early with the goats, so I could sleep an extra hour and arrive at dawn to avoid the day's heat. With Sophie's first payment transferred to my account, I climbed into my car, already plotting a management plan to convince them I knew my stuff.

Then it hit me. Mac and I were going for doughnuts tomorrow.

I'd have to cancel. I couldn't turn down this job and look him in the eye over doughnuts with no plan for paying the vet bill.

We couldn't be anything more than friends anyway. If Lucky's owner couldn't be found, I wanted to take him in. Which would bring more bills, so I needed to keep my cheap rent.

After an extra-long day in surgery and seeing clients, I finally pushed into my dark cabin, hauling the cat carrier and a bag containing a litter box, litter and food from the hospital. Judi had given me another look, but I couldn't stop at the store with a recovering cat in the car.

"Hello?" I called into the silence. Only Kenzie's car was parked in the driveway. If she was upstairs, and the door to my—*her*—room was closed, she'd never hear me. Gramma Louise would rail at me, but I'd love to knock on Kenzie's door.

I left the bag in the foyer, hung my hat and brought the carrier to the living room, where I flipped on a light.

"What?" someone huffed. A hand and Kenzie's brown hair appeared above the couch back.

"Aha! Caught you napping." I strode over, hiding the carrier behind the couch.

"Mm-hmm." She scrubbed her face. "Long day."

"Maybe you'd like a cat-napping buddy?" Grinning, I hefted the carrier.

Kenzie squealed.

While she talked to the cat, I set up his litter box and food in the kitchen. With the swinging door closed and a note warning our other roommates not to let him out, the room made a safe adjustment space.

Kenzie did the honors of opening the carrier. As I'd expected following surgery, the cat moved hesitantly. He inspected the litter and tasted the canned food. At my nod, Kenzie carefully lifted him and sat beside me on the booth seat.

The cat purred. She stroked him, the inches between us narrowing as the cat turned and settled.

"Are you this attached to all cats?" I asked gently.

After a pause, she shook her head. "Seeing this particular kind of cat brought back memories." She sighed. "While I was a freshman away at college, my family home caught fire in a gas explosion. No one survived. My mom, dad and my younger brother..." Her voice broke.

Oh damn... I'd suspected something had happened in her past, but nothing this devastating. What a louse I was for poking after she'd clearly been thrilled with the cat. Now Kenzie hunched into herself. Roommate rules be damned. I wrapped my arm around her shoulders and hugged her. "I'm so sorry."

Kenzie leaned into me and, after a moment, shakily said, "Thank you." Following a few breaths, she straightened and wiped her eyes, but didn't move away.

My hand felt natural on her shoulder, so I left it.

"Ten years later and it's still hard for me to talk about. I miss my family every day."

"And this cat?" I ventured. "Looks like yours did?"

She nodded. "We—I—also lost Shadow, a long-haired black cat, and Sunny, an orange tabby. Seeing either of those kinds of cats..."

"I bet," I murmured.

She turned, her large brown eyes meeting mine. "Having this cat might be—"

"Kenzie, don't," I whispered. "Owners can turn up weeks later looking for their lost pet."

She looked away. "Since finding him, I can't think of anything else."

I pushed a strand of hair behind her ear. "Maybe a change of scenery? We could go on a hike together—"

Kenzie froze.

That had come out without me thinking. Now I'd blown it. Before we'd even had our doughnut not-a-date, during which I'd hoped we could move forward.

She side-eyed me. "I've thought of that. Since the day I interviewed for the room."

I snapped my fingers. "Damn it all, Gramma."

"What?" Kenzie squinted. "She laid down a rule?"

I nodded. Maybe now wasn't the time, but... "If I lose a renter because a relationship fails, I make up the lost rent. I can't afford that."

Kenzie shifted back, her softly quizzical eyes hardening to something wary. "I'm sorry I hugged you at the animal hospital. I didn't mean to..." She pointed between us.

Da—I fisted my traitorous hand. *Okay, Fate, it's now or never.* "I'm not sorry."

"You aren't?"

"I like you."

She laughed, her eyes widening and softening again. "Are you always this easy? What about your grandma? And at work, your tech was watching."

"And she gave me grief about it. You owe me."

"About that." Kenzie put up a finger.

I wrapped it into my palm. "We are not discussing the vet bill. Not when you haven't told me if I have a chance."

She stared at my hand, and I held my breath. Her lips pressed together. Slowly, her gaze rose to mine. "I like you, too."

Our fingers laced, and Kenzie tugged me toward her. It felt like every time I'd dreamed of kissing her and stopped short. But this time, my lips met hers.

Thank you, Fate. I closed my eyes and savored the sweet and salty of the kettle corn she liked to snack on. Her tongue traced my lips. And we kissed. Long and hungry.

"I think," I finally said, my voice rough, "the cat is ready to sleep in his bed."

We settled the cat. Then, pulling her along, I closed the kitchen door and headed for the stairs. Her room would be the most private.

But Kenzie tugged on my hand to stop me. When I turned, she wrapped her arms around me, and my thoughts hazed into the smoothness of her lips on mine, the softness of her skin. *What I'd been missing!*

Kenzie scooped up my shirt first. Heck, I'd follow that lead. My fingers blazed a trail along her neckline. *Easy does it, Mac. Second kiss and all.* But my body had different ideas.

With a moan, she nipped my lip. Evidently, Kenzie had different ideas, too. She peeled off my shirt.

I fingered the hem of her shirt, but hesitated. Some women preferred to remove their own clothes.

My skin burned where her hands smoothed over my bare chest. Her sweet lips claimed my mouth. Then my hip pressed against the couch, my arms around her, no thought to where my hands stroked because all paths were good. We'd danced around each other for weeks, so it was like I knew her already. Soon, we danced around the couch and tumbled onto it.

She shed her shirt and pulled me over her. A sweet, peachy scent drifted from her. Stroking her curves took me deep beyond my fantasies. Yet no daydreams had prepared me for her hand shoving beneath my jeans to massage my ass.

I rose to unzip my fly—

The door lock clicked, followed by a heavy wooden creak. I dropped onto Kenzie's chest.

She gasped in protest, but I shushed her. "Someone's coming in."

The soft footsteps had to be Mrs. Windsor. I didn't dare look. As she tapped across the wooden floor, I groped for Kenzie's shirt. The bathroom light and fan came on. Water began running, with the door open.

"She's washing her hands," I whispered. "Quick." I rose onto my knees, retrieved Kenzie's shirt and shoved it to her.

She sat enough to pull it on, but settled back, gripping my shoulder. "She won't be long."

Kenzie was right. I settled my weight half on, half beside her. "Mrs. Windsor discovering us would be like Gramma finding us *necking*, as she'd say."

"You mean *napping* together on the couch?" Her brows lifted. "*If* she finds us."

I hadn't seen my shirt, so I yanked over the red plaid blanket to cover us. "Great disguise, a wool blanket in summer," I muttered.

"Close your eyes." She wiggled against me.

She didn't have a tense muscle in her. But I was my family's rental manager, imagining accusing looks and spreading gossip.

Mrs. Windsor stepped out of the bathroom, and I held my breath.

She crossed the foyer, approached the couch and...walked past. Her bedroom door closed.

"Home free," Kenzie said into my ear.

"She's not asleep yet," I whispered.

"Neither am I." The heat in her eyes melted my objections.

I leaned to Kenzie's lips, my hand sliding up her smooth waist. Her hand reentered my jeans, and my brain fogged.

The clothes stayed on, but the exploring reached maddening levels. The heat between us rose, and I tossed the blanket. I lost the focus of finding pure softness under her bra when Kenzie's tongue prodded deeper, then again as my strokes prompted her rough moan. I panted, trying to relieve the pressure, but Kenzie held my ass tight, grinding against me.

I was completely spun up. "We should go upstairs. If you want—"

Thunk!

Kenzie jerked. "What was that?"

The thump of hollow rubber sounded again.

"A trash can." I nuzzled her, followed by the tinkle of cans and glass, plastic and cardboard takeaway boxes clattering. I groaned. "A *bear* in a trash can."

People yelled. A car honked.

Kenzie pushed me back.

Snap. I wanted her, but we'd entered territory I hadn't anticipated *this* soon. How could I get around Gramma's no-dating-the-roommates rule? I got up, zipped my jeans and stumbled to the door, snatching the airhorn on the way. From the porch, I sorted the three-ring circus of the rental cottage vacationers trying to separate the bear from its feast by waving and yelling. I leaned over the railing, shouted, "Cover your ears," and blasted the airhorn.

The bear scampered.

"He'll be back," I called. "Clean it up and put it inside until the trash truck comes tomorrow morning." I turned to go inside.

Kenzie watched, wide-eyed, from the doorway.

4

I handed Mac his shirt. My body trembled for him, but my cleared head asked, *What? You jumped straight to groping him?* Still, the sight of his abs made me want to invite him upstairs. *Bad idea, Kenzie. You could end up homeless in a week.*

"Typical summer event with renters." Mac pulled on his shirt. "Hey." He nudged my arm. "I'd love to go somewhere more private, but also...maybe this is too fast?"

I toed the rug. "Yeah. The guys will be home soon. Plus, you didn't let me talk about the vet bill earlier. I can pay it. I got a second job. With Sophie."

"Identifying her toxic weed? That's great."

"Yeah, but...she needs them removed ASAP. I agreed on tomorrow, starting early to avoid the heat."

He leaned his head to mine. "Canceling doughnuts is disappointing, but my ego can handle it. You do your thing tomorrow."

Could he be more perfect? I kissed him, my body cheering—until I pulled back. "I like you. We'll talk." I forced myself up the stairs, and before I reached the landing, the shower started in the bathroom below.

. . .

I woke before my alarm rang, thinking of my canceled doughnut date. How could we make this work? Keep it secret? My room or his? Neither, and get a room somewhere? And if it didn't work out... Should I insist on some agreement guaranteeing my room through September?

Mac held a lot of cards.

And I had no doughnuts to console me. I ate my yogurt with Lucky. He didn't have any advice, but was happy to lick my spoon. Washing up, I felt...lost. Something was missing—Mac.

I drove through the quiet Mary's Lake area in the dim predawn light. As I left the car, Sophie emerged from the goat shed. We chatted before she headed inside to spin, and I started weeding.

Several filled bags later, a low whistle sounded. "That's a lot of weeds."

I straightened. Mac stood outside the pasture, cowboy hat shading his face, western shirt tucked into tight jeans. He held two coffees and a white bag. "Can you take a break?"

"I'm drooling already."

We sat shoulder-to-shoulder on a rock beneath the ponderosas. Mac handed me an applesauce cake.

"They're still warm!" I gushed.

"The perk of keeping these hours." He tipped his hat and took a bite of his doughnut.

That hat tip... Heat pooled low, and I squeezed so hard I mashed my doughnut. *Slow down. Talking comes first.*

I ate two and drank half my coffee before I attempted conversation. "If it doesn't work out"—I pointed back and forth between us—"I need to continue renting my room for the fall."

He paused mid-doughnut. "I'm praying fate is with us on this one, but *if* it doesn't work out, no way do I want my family knowing I broke the no-dating-the-roommates rule. You rent as long as you like, and we'll be two ships passing."

My body cried, *It'll work*, but I added, "*If* it doesn't work out, I'll find another place after tourist season ends." Probably impossible at the same rent.

"Deal." We shook on it.

"I should be done midafternoon. Want to go for that hike?"

Mac flashed me a grin and planted a kiss on my cheek, then left.

I watched his tight butt—him—climb into his truck and drive off. Footsteps sounded, and I turned toward Sophie. "You two?" she asked pointedly.

"Um, we're...housemates. We'd planned to get doughnuts this morning."

"Housemates don't bring you coffee and doughnuts when you've canceled a date."

"It wasn't a date," I insisted.

She crossed her arms. "After he patched up your stray." My face heated, and Sophie threw her hands in the air in exasperation. "You canceled on *him* to weed my goat pasture? The goats are safe in the weed-free corral and happy as long as I throw in more hay. Weeding could wait a few days. I'll hire you regardless."

"I...that would be great."

"So?" She looked at me expectantly.

I frowned. "Oh. I should go. For a hike."

"I hope not." Sophie laughed.

As I drove, clouds churned purple and blue, a mountain thunderstorm brewing. Would Mac be there... That was his truck, yes! I scrambled out, the wind whipping my hair. Heart pounding, I crossed the porch.

Inside, running water sounded from the open bathroom door. Mac stood over the sink, splashing water on his face, his western shirt unsnapped.

The floor creaked, and he looked up, mouth falling open.

"I didn't want to wait." My voice sounded strange.

We stared a long moment, then Mac slowly paced forward. "No chance of a hike now." His breath warmed my lips.

Our kiss took over.

When I gripped his firm glutes, he groaned against my mouth. "Do you..."

"Want to replay last night? Yes, with less clothes." We fell together again, heat burning between us. Mac tugged me by the hips toward the stairs. "But not in my room," I blurted.

His brows lifted.

"I'd like to keep that space mine. Just in case."

"My screened porch isn't private enough, but I have an idea." He led the way upstairs, stopping for a key and condoms.

I hesitated at the attic steps, but he passed my room to a locked door. The peaked-ceiling room was finished and clean, though stuffed with storage tubs.

"It's above the unused second-floor bedroom, so we'll have privacy. Anytime."

I squeezed past an old camp bed to the window, rubbing my arms against the chill and watching the rain fall. Was I risking my future? Raindrops sparkled on pine needles, creating a wonderland to close us in. "I feel so sneaky."

"We weren't sneaky last night?" Mac came up behind me. His fingers traced my arm, sending a shiver over me. "I think you like sneaky."

Yes! Say yes! my body demanded. I turned.

He brushed my chin, then stroked my hair. "You're perfect," he whispered against my lips. "Cute and a cat lover."

"You, too," I rasped. "Every morning, I've nearly blurted how much I admire these." I squeezed his biceps.

"Really? I'd have said you prefer my ass."

My breath hitched. "Caught." I molded my frustrated curves to Mac's hard ones and let our bodies continue talking...caressing...kissing. The scent of pine wafted between us. After a month of chatting, Mac's warm fingers were finally on my skin. My head muddled. His muscles rippled under his open shirt as I skimmed them. His tongue teased mine, then my earlobes and neck and left a moist path over my tightening breasts. One of those incredible thighs slid between mine. The room warmed until I was on fire, hungrily groping his muscular butt.

Knees weak and light-headed, I broke from Mac's lips.

Groaning, he clasped my hips, pinning me close. "You want more?"

"All of it." My hands fumbled over the hard front of his jeans and unzipped them.

"Thank you, Fate," he mumbled and tried to toe off his boots, nearly toppling both of us.

I tugged him to the bed, and we helped each other into less clothing. Mac's lips sampled me until I shuddered with aching for him. He donned protection, and we shifted, placing Mac where I needed him. His slow thrust sent pleasure blossoming, piquing my urgency to have more. More of *him*. Mac's rhythm quickened. Heat flushed at my center. I held tight, eyes rolling back, and lost myself to him.

———

I'd promised myself to meet Kenzie's pace, but from the moment she'd stripped her exquisite body for me, I was gone. Heart banging in my chest, I endured the sweet torture of her spasms and low moans. I wanted to give her a moment, but in her fever, she clung to my ass, and my staying power evaporated. I pushed harder, drove higher—

She. Felt. Perfect.

I gasped my release, keeping my seat through the bite of her fingernails. Afterward, we collapsed, both panting under the drum of rain on the metal roof.

My ass would be tender tonight, but I wouldn't have traded that for anything. I curled around her. "You okay?"

"Mmm, *so* okay."

I puffed out my chest. "My ego. It's heating up."

"We'll see how well your ego does in a bit."

She made it my best day off in years.

———

Over the next weeks, sneaking upstairs became as routine as cuddles with Lucky while waiting for Mac on the living room couch. The animal hospital had put out a "found cat" post with a photo, but no one had come forward to claim the black cat. After a month, even Judi said it'd been enough time. I could consider Lucky mine.

"Which makes you twice as lucky," I cooed to the purring feline as I put down his dinner.

Mac pulled into the driveway, followed by a smaller truck.

I watched out the window as he closed the driver's side door for a spry, older woman. I hesitated. Could this be Lucky's owner? Curiosity got me. I opened the door for them, and Mac introduced me to his bright-eyed Gramma Louise.

Crap, now I had to worry about her rules.

"She came up on the spur of the moment, wanting to see where I work. It was slow enough at the clinic I could leave, but next time"—he turned to her—"please call first."

Yeah, in case *we* were busy. I avoided Mac's gaze. His grandma looked past me and gasped.

She spun to Mac. "You said you weren't getting a cat."

My stomach dropped as everyone watched Lucky circling my ankles.

"He's Kenzie's cat, actually." Mac patted her arm in a placating gesture.

Throwing me under the bus, huh? If the lodge owner said no pets, it didn't matter what Mac said. My mind hurtled to boarding Lucky while I looked for another rental. Despite how much I'd fallen for Mac, I'd give up a new boyfriend before my cat.

Gramma Louise pointed at Lucky. "You claimed a new vet has no time for pets."

"I did say that." Mac looked at me and shrugged.

I didn't know quite what to think. Was I homeless?

His grandma harrumphed.

Crap. I was homeless for sure.

"Told him the mice are wicked clever about getting in, but he wouldn't have me setting traps. I always bring my kitties when we visit, and they take care of it." She nodded firmly. "You're sneaking around me." She poked Mac's chest.

My breath caught. Was she still talking about cats, or had she guessed Mac and I were sneaking around in other ways?

"I didn't mean to." Mac patted her shoulder again. "I forgot to tell you. I've been...busy."

Had he ever said having a cat was okay? I couldn't remember now, because finding Lucky was all tangled up with finding out Mac and I felt the same way. But he'd *implied* it was okay.

Mac hung up his hat. "I know what you say, Gramma, and you're right. Best solution is to keep a predator's scent around."

Gramma Louise followed Lucky as he jumped onto the couch.

Coming up behind me, Mac whispered, "She has to believe it's her idea."

My muscles eased.

"Kenzie's smart for seeing the cabin needs a cat before fall arrives." She smiled at me and petted Lucky. "Pretty girl."

"Lucky is a boy."

"Handsome boy," she corrected without missing a beat. "You're the lucky one."

She'd complimented me? Face heating, I smiled back.

Over her head, Mac winked. "Hey, what about me? I'm lucky Kenzie picked our cabin. How about we get to know her and Lucky better over dinner?" And as Gramma Louise headed for the kitchen with Lucky following, Mac hugged my shoulders. "I bet you a kiss behind her back that before she leaves, she tells us we ought to date."

I raised my brows. "And she'll be right."

"Of course she will."

About the Author

Passionate about nature since she was young, Laurel Wanrow writes stories about living close to the land, falling in love, and the magic in both. She's the author of *The Luminated Threads* series, a Victorian historical fantasy mixing witches and shapeshifters, and *The Windborne*, a nature-focused YA cozy fantasy series. When not writing, she loves to camp, hike, garden with native plants and dream about building out a camper van to explore North America.

Learn more about Laurel's books and sign up for her newsletter at www.laurelwanrow.com

Sharing a Bed with Someone Like Him

Susanna Eastman

1

Full tank of gas. Check.

Two water bottles. Check.

One divorce decree signed by a judge. Check, check, check.

Rachel kept one hand on the steering wheel and patted the backpack on the seat beside her. She'd read the legal paperwork more than a dozen times. Ending a marriage to a serial cheater should have been a no-brainer. But, damn, it still hurt.

He'd wanted a blonde, so she'd dyed her brown hair. Brown eyes didn't sparkle enough, so she'd purchased blue contacts. When he'd brought home brochures from a plastic surgeon about enhancing her breasts, she'd said no, and he'd been pissed.

She'd never been enough for him.

But Jeff had done a turnabout as soon as she'd contacted a lawyer. Suddenly, he wanted her back. He wanted her and only her. Ha! What a joke. Thank God he hadn't given her any diseases—the gift that kept on giving.

For so long she'd felt paralyzed, unsure of herself and every decision she made. He'd knocked her off balance, and she was about to get her equilibrium back. Safe, sane, responsible Rachel needed to shake up her life, and this weekend at the Fantasy resort would be the start of a new beginning. She could clear her head and take care of a needy itch. Oh to feel good in her own skin again.

But before she arrived at Fantasy for 60 hours of decadent fun, she needed to make a stop.

She grinned, probably her first real grin in ages, as Hopewell House came into view at the end of the quiet country road. Hopewell was one of a dozen antebellum mansions dotting the foothills of the Allegheny Mountains near White Sulfur Springs, West Virginia. Since the late 18th century, the well-to-do had visited Hopewell and other similar grand houses and estates for the healing waters. Today, most of the houses had been turned into posh bed and breakfasts.

Hopewell was a little different. Even though it boasted a dozen rooms for overnight guests, it also contained an extravagant Cold War fallout shelter built for high-ranking government officials and their families in the event of a nuclear attack. The once-secret bunker, built into the hill at the rear of the building in the early 1960s, still housed most of the original furnishings.

A burst of nervous excitement bubbled up inside her. Rachel's family had a long history with Hopewell House, and if all went well that history would continue for a long time. If only it weren't costing her every penny she owned—and more.

No, she shook her head and pushed away those worrisome thoughts. She wouldn't think about the money—all her money—she'd sunk into the property. It was a risk she'd had to take. She owed her grandfather that and much more.

So, a quick stop to check on things, then she'd be on her way to a weekend of debauchery.

Once inside the Greek Revival-style building, Rachel passed through a series of rooms decorated with bold and dramatic florals and plaids. While the look was far from subtle, it worked, staying true to the House's more than 200-year-old roots.

An elderly man in a crisp navy blazer, a fixture for years at Hopewell, sat at a small desk outside the entrance to the bunker. A neat stack of pamphlets discussing the history of Hopewell and the bunker lay beside his fingertips.

"Hello, Mr. Hopper."

"Miss Westman." He rose from his desk and extended his hand. "How wonderful to see you today. Your brother didn't mention you'd be coming by."

"Oh." She blinked with surprise, then her lips tugged into a smile. For years, Steven had flitted from job to job, never happy anywhere, but all that changed six months ago. He'd joined a company he liked, and they liked him. On top of that, he'd stepped up in a big way with Grandpa John and the work she'd started at Hopewell House. What a huge help that was! "He must be meeting with some of the contractors."

Mr. Hopper shrugged. "He's in the green room with some men in suits."

Her smile widened. Steven stepping up again. Ah! One less meeting for her. "When you see him, please let him know I'm down in the bunker."

The older man nodded then glanced down at his watch. "I usually close at 5 p.m., and I need to leave promptly today. Would you mind shutting the door on your way out?"

"No, I wouldn't mind at all," Rachel gushed. The heavy, wide steel door was 20-inches thick and weighed more than 20 tons. A little architectural and engineering magic let it open and close with only 40 pounds of pressure. The eight-year-old Rachel would have been thrilled beyond reason with the task to close the door. The 30-year-old Rachel was almost as pleased.

Rachel scooted through the door and hurried down the four flights of cement stairs. Finally, she stepped into the ante room of the bunker. Once this space served as a greeting room for guests, but now it functioned as a place for bunker memorabilia, the thick walls—two feet of reinforced concrete, according to Grandpa John—covered with framed documents, news articles and photographs about the bunker.

Like she did most times she visited, Rachel skimmed over the news articles then strode to the back wall of the room to the series of photographs. Her heart melted a bit. There was Grandpa John, young and handsome, shaking hands with the governor of West Virginia.

She loved looking at these old photos, but there was more to do before getting back on the road.

Stepping into the main room, a storage space that once contained 50 dorm-style bunk beds, she headed to the rear of the shelter to see the well-preserved—at least semi well-preserved—cafeteria, medical area and the governor's suite.

Like always, she gravitated to the medical area and its large glass cabinet with dated medicines. A box with neatly folded straitjackets was wedged in the corner. She leaned over and touched the crisp off-white material.

"Not a good place for a nervous breakdown, is it?"

Startled by the deep male voice, Rachel spun around and pressed her back against the wall. Her eyes fixed on a man—dark hair, darker eyes and a good foot taller than her—standing only inches behind her.

Thankfully, he also possessed a warm, welcoming smile.

He reached for her arm to steady her. "Sorry. I didn't mean to startle you."

Rachel pulled in a deep breath and swallowed hard. "I didn't hear you come in."

"Guess I have silent sneakers." He offered a lopsided grin. "I'll try to clump around and make as much noise as possible."

"Actually, that won't do much good here," she explained with a smile. Even though this man and his long, *long* legs looked like he could do plenty of clumping. "The floors were designed to absorb sound."

"I didn't know that."

She nodded, always happy to play tour guide here. "They wanted to create a space that was quiet and calm. They even brought kids down here to make as much racket as possible in the toy room."

"There's a toy room here?"

"A playroom." She grinned again. "If they'd had to use the bunker for real, they wanted an area that would keep children busy." She pointed her hand toward the back of the shelter then took a step toward the doorway. "I can show you."

Rachel picked up her step as she strode into the kids' play area. Boxes of board games, wooden building blocks, train sets, dolls, two dollhouses and hula hoops were piled high against a wall. "I used to be a killer at Yahtzee."

He smiled down at her. "It was Sorry for me."

"You look like a Monopoly man."

"Do I?" He pressed his lips together to hold back a bigger grin. "I did okay."

Rachel nodded as she studied him. Tall, dark and handsome. Even though the man wore faded jeans and a casual polo, she could picture him in a sharp navy pinstripe. Yup, a Monopoly man.

She forced herself to stop staring and lifted her hand toward the doorway again. "The coolest space is hidden in the governor's suite. I can show you that too, if you'd like."

He walked beside her, his arm almost brushing hers, as they strode into the suite with well-made mahogany furniture and a king-sized bed with a canopy. "This is nice." He glanced around. "Fancier than I would have expected for a fallout shelter."

"I think the governor's wife wasn't one to rough it—even in a catastrophe. She used to have clothes in the wardrobe—including two evening gowns—just in case." Rachel laughed at the memory. "Under the bed there's a trapdoor to a kind of bunker within the bunker. The ceiling is lead-enforced to keep the room safe—safer—from radiation."

The man kneeled and looked beneath the bed. "I can see the handle for the trapdoor, but I can't reach it from here."

Rachel smirked at that. "I once crawled under there, but the door was too heavy for me to lift."

"You seem to know the place well."

"Yes, my family—" She cut herself off—he was just asking to make polite conversation—then glanced at her watch. Oh, no. Time had whizzed by. "Hey, I'm afraid I need to leave, and I promised to lock up."

"Okay." He lifted his hand in a friendly salute. "I've seen more than I expected thanks to you. I'm ready to go."

They climbed up the four flights of stairs. When they reached the top, Rachel stopped moving and frowned at the exit. "That's weird. The door's already closed."

She grabbed the bar-style handle, and it wouldn't budge. That was even weirder. "Hello!" she called out, raising her voice, then she got even louder. "Hello. We're still here." She knocked on the thick metal door. "Hello!"

She turned toward the man beside her. "I told Mr. Hopper, the man at the desk, that I would lock up." She opened her handbag and reached for her cell. Ugh! No bars.

The man also checked his cell phone—no luck either—then plucked his folded-up brochure from his back pocket. "This says they open up at 8 a.m."

"8 a.m.? No, no, no. I have to get out of here."

"I don't think we're going anywhere." He checked his cell again. "Still no bars."

"But I have somewhere to go, somewhere important," she cried, slamming the side of her fist against the door again.

"I understand. I have plans too." He reached for her shoulder. "Don't hurt yourself."

"I'm fine." She shook out her hand and moaned then crumbled onto the floor. "This weekend was supposed to be my new start. And my new start doesn't start here." She rolled her eyes and tossed her head back. "Ow." She rubbed the back of her head. "Two feet of reinforced concrete is damned hard."

"It is." He extended a hand to help her up. "Why don't we go back down and see if there's any communication devices down there? There used to be broadcast capabilities."

She took a step onto the stairs, but her shoulders sank. "I'm pretty sure that stuff was ripped out years ago."

"Let's look just in case." He paused then gave her his hand again. "I'm Matt."

She met his eyes and took his offered grip. "I'm Rachel."

2

Twenty minutes later, they'd checked all the nooks and crannies of the bunker. She'd been right. No broadcast or communications remained.

"For emergencies, there should be some way to reach the outside world." Rachel groaned with exasperation as they stood in the ante room again.

"I don't think anyone expected something like this."

"I'm sure no one did," she huffed, resisting the urge to stomp her feet, her gaze fixed on her wrist. "God, it's almost 6 p.m."

"You should stop looking at your watch."

"I can't help it." She groaned again. "You don't understand. I've been in this super sucky marriage."

He turned and faced her. "Then we have something else in common. I was also in a super sucky marriage."

"You were?" She blinked up at him. Sometimes she forgot she wasn't the only one with a crappy marital past. "I'm sorry. How long were you married?"

"Too long. Six years."

"Wow. Me too." And she felt the weight of each of those years. "I'm sorry we have that in common." Then the craziest thought occurred to her. "My ex would laugh hysterically if he knew I was trapped in here. He hated the place."

"Really? Why?"

"Oh ... I don't think I mentioned it earlier." Rachel rolled her eyes. They'd talked all about Hopewell but not about this. "I know so much about Hopewell and the bunker because my family—my grandfather—has owned it for decades. He was the architect that designed the bunker."

"So you're John Westman's ... granddaughter?"

"I am," she said, proud of her grandfather and his accomplishments. "He loves this place, and especially the bunker. I became an architect because of him, and now I'm renovating—"

"You're renovating?" His eyes narrowed as if confused. "You mean to get it ready for sale?"

"Oh, God, no." She scrunched her face and shook her head. Selling was the last thing they wanted to do. "We get offers for Hopewell all the time but always reject them. My grandfather would hate that. He hopes we'll keep it in the family forever."

"He does?"

"I know it looks like a mess down here, but we're expanding the excavated but unfinished section of the bunker in the back. We're maintaining the historic parts of the place and creating a half dozen 1960-style guest suites. It took all my savings and a big, fat loan, but it will be worth it."

"You've been doing this on your own?"

"Yes, well, at least the money part." She took a deep breath. "Early on, my ex pretended to want to help, but his goals were a whole lot different than mine. I realized I couldn't trust anybody else with this."

"That's too bad."

"It is." Some days the stress and fear of it all overwhelmed her. She'd put so much—everything—into this. But when it was done, it would be perfect. Grandpa would be thrilled his special achievement would live on. "Grandpa John, he's been struggling for a while—Alzheimer's, but he still has great ideas and loves talking about the renovation." She smiled, remembering how excited he'd been looking through her last round of renderings. He still had such an eye for details. "Also, my brother's recently jumped in. Grandpa's medical appointments and scheduling meetings with some of the contractors. He's new to all this, but he's become interested in the project."

"Working with family can get tricky," he said, his tone suddenly a little off.

"Yes, but he's great. Best brother in the world. I'm organized, but sometimes another set of hands helps." She shook her head, annoyed at herself for prattling on. "Sorry for all that TMI rambling about my family."

"That's okay. Are they going to worry about you tonight?"

"No, they think I'm visiting some college friends this weekend."

He raised a brow. "And you're not?"

"No, I'm doing something else." Her cell phone chimed again, and she winced. "But someone is going to wonder what happened to me. This woman will likely try to reach me." She stared at the notification that popped up on her phone and groaned under her breath. "Oh, Stephanie, I hope you don't worry."

"Stephanie?"

Rachel turned off her phone and shoved it back in her purse. "It's nothing." Why couldn't she stop talking? "Just someone—"

"I was meeting a Stephanie tonight too."

A chill ran up her spine. "You were?"

He tilted his head toward hers. "At the Fantasy resort."

"Oh my God." Her mouth dropped open as she stared up at him. "You were going there too?"

3

Rachel gasped. *Oh my God. He was headed to Fantasy tonight.*

"No, I can't believe—" She started to back up and spun around. God, there was nowhere to go. She was trapped down here with a man she didn't know, a man headed to a sex club resort. The fact that she was headed there too didn't matter. "Don't get any ideas."

His palms lifted in protest. "I have no ideas."

"I don't want you to think I regularly frequent places like that."

"Rachel, I get it." He released a long sigh as his shoulder sagged. "Like you, I'm out of a crappy marriage. We met in college, and I fell hard. Now I have no idea how to date, how to talk to women, how to be with women …."

"I wonder if this weekend is for people like us?" Rachel blurted, and then she shook her head. People like us? Matt was gorgeous, and he seemed so … normal. His ex had to be nuts. "Sorry. That was a dumb question. I'm sure you're not a mess like me."

"I don't know." His eyes were suddenly lighter than before. "I've certainly felt like a mess. I thought we were fine. But then she cheated—more than once."

"More than once?" Rachel shuddered. "I'm sorry … really sorry."

"Bottom line is that she didn't want to be with me. Whatever it was, I wasn't enough."

"I know the feeling—so much." *Too much.*

"You shouldn't." He opened his mouth as if to say more, then pressed his lips together. "You really shouldn't know that feeling."

"That's nice of you to say," she replied, then a strange sound echoed through the room. Her stomach was making itself heard.

"A little hungry?"

Her cheeks warmed as her stomach growled again. "A lot hungry. I skipped lunch today so I could get on the road sooner."

"Well, I believe I noticed a choice of canned soup and more canned soup in the kitchen. Chicken noodle, chicken dumpling, chicken and rice."

She shrugged. Why not? "Sounds yummy."

Because of Mr. Hopper and members of the Hopewell staff, the kitchen was fully stocked with pots and pans and an eight-burner stove with power. Matt dumped three cans of the chicken noodle into a small Dutch oven, and soon the room smelled of warm, chicken-y goodness.

Rachel checked the cupboards beside the stove and found two white bowls and a ladle. "I can't believe we have a ladle to serve soup and no emergency button to get out of here."

Matt held up the empty soup cans. "At least the expiration dates aren't until next year."

"I guess that's something," she said with a grin. Matt was a nice guy, a decent guy. A soup dinner with him might be the best meal she'd had in a long time.

He brought the steaming bowls to the nearest dining table and stood, waiting for her to join him. "When we're done, why don't you show me the unfinished, excavated areas and explain what will go where." He sat down when she did and picked up his spoon. The steam from the chicken soup wafted around them. "After that, do you want to play a game?"

"Yahtzee," Rachel yelled and almost shot up from her seat on the small sofa in the toy room. They'd been playing for hours, and he'd beaten her soundly at Sorry and Clue. But she still had it when it came to Yahtzee.

He rolled four of the five dice in his hand. "You've got quite the competitive streak."

She smiled back. "I guess I do." It had been a while since she'd had an evening like this. Most nights she brought home work or did research for future projects. Even when she'd lived with Jeff, she'd done the same thing. And he'd been glued to his laptop.

This was nice.

Really nice.

Matt grinned at her, then carefully leaned back in the child-sized chair he sat in. She'd offered to take the mini seat, but he'd insisted she have the sofa. In his scrunched-up position, his long legs practically pushed his knees to his shoulders. With such a tall body and wide shoulders, he made the miniature chair even more miniature.

Rachel lifted a hand to her mouth and yawned. She'd been up early, needing to get work done before leaving on her trip.

"It's getting late," he commented and yawned in return.

She nodded and stretched. It had to be close to midnight. Eight a.m. would be here soon.

She pressed her lips together. The only place to sleep in the bunker was the glamorous bed for the governor and his wife. All the bunk beds were gone. She twisted to face the door opening. "You can take the bed, of course."

"No." He waved off her suggestion with a flick of his finger. "I can sleep right there." He nodded to the sofa she sat on. "I'll be fine."

Rachel made a face. "It's tiny. I don't think one of your shoulders will fit on this thing."

"I'll be okay."

"No you won't." He would be miserable. She gnawed on her lower lip as a thought occurred to her. "It's a big bed. We could share."

"I don't want to make you uncomfortable."

"You won't. And I'd feel terrible being in that big bed with you in here."

He pressed back a smile. "Well, I'd hate for you to feel terrible."

Rachel glanced down at her clothes—a coral-colored knit top and faded blue jeans—and sighed. Jeans were the worst to sleep in. "It's been ages since I've gone to bed in regular clothes, but I'll manage."

"Did you see that box of Hopewell t-shirts?" He lifted a hand and pointed toward the open doorway. "They were in that box next to the straitjackets you like so much."

She pursed her lips and reared back her head. "Who says I like them?"

"Well, you seemed *interested* in them."

"Just the idea of them used to scare me."

"Then ignore those and just check the tees. Some must be large enough for a sleep shirt for you."

Rachel stood up and sprinted out of the room, heading for the medical supply area. When she found the box of tees, she riffled through them looking for the larger sizes. She picked up an extra, extra large and held it up to her body. Thankfully, the bottom hung to her knees.

"Hey," she called out. "This will work."

Before she could say more, Matt appeared in the doorway. He eyed the garment in her hands. "Any more like that?"

Rachel nodded, her gaze fixed on her companion, then reached in the box for another. While still oversized, the shirt wouldn't hang like a sack on him. She wet her lips and stared, unable to look away. No, with his broad shoulders and sizable biceps, he'd fill it out in a whole different way.

If they'd made it to Fantasy, maybe she would have been matched with someone like him tonight. Tall, dark and handsome and nice too. He'd be good in bed—she just knew it.

Too bad they were here.

Rachel shifted in place, clutching the tee in her hand a little tighter. "Um ... I'll go change," she said and headed toward the bathroom adjacent to the toy room.

"Wow, I look ridiculous." Rachel stared at herself in the tall bathroom mirror and groaned. The stupid shirt really hung on her like a sack. Not that she'd expected to look sexy, but she'd hoped for ... cute. She rolled her eyes. Nope, she missed that mark.

4

Rachel's heart pounded as she entered the bedroom. Matt was already in bed, his back against a stack of pillows covering the headboard. Suddenly the king-size didn't seem so king-sized anymore. "I've never shared a bed with anyone but my ex before."

He nodded, understanding emanating from his warm dark eyes. "I had a pretty wild first year at college, but then I met Cheryl my sophomore year. And that was it."

Rachel pressed her lips together. *And that was it*. She knew that feeling—so content, so perfect—and then it was yanked away.

Trusting someone that much was truly a bad idea.

"Thankfully, they've replaced the bedding over the years. I don't think this is a 1960 mattress." Matt pulled back the covers to what would be her side of the bed. "It's comfortable."

"That's good." She continued to stand feet away from the bed.

"I'm wearing the tee shirt and my boxers. If you want, we can put a wall of pillows between us." His eyes glimmered as he teased her. "I saw that in a movie once."

She grinned, enjoying his playful expression, and her heart stopped racing. Nothing about Matt set off her safety radar, and he'd already been vetted by Fantasy. "No, not necessary." She darted to her side of the bed and slipped in, pulling the covers to her waist. "I used to imagine what it would be like to stay here and sleep in this bed."

"Does it meet your expectations?"

"It does." She sat up and turned to him. "Thanks for making this so much less weird than it could be."

"We get to sleep in the governor's suite. That's not a bad deal. What you've done here, what you're doing ... it's impressive."

"We're a part of history." Her chest puffed up.

"It's good, really good."

She blushed. How wonderful to hear those words. "Are you disappointed you're not at Fantasy tonight?" she asked, her throat a little tight.

"Not really."

"I wonder if Stephanie or any of the staff at Fantasy are wondering about us."

"I'm sure they've tried to contact us. It's a well-run organization."

"You know a lot about it?"

"No." He rolled his eyes and laughed. "I have a friend who said the weekend retreat would help me get back in the saddle again."

"The saddle?"

He rolled his eyes once more. "What he really meant was stop pretending I'm now a monk."

"And a sex resort is the best place to do that?"

"I don't know. When I spoke to Stephanie, I got the feeling it could be whatever I needed it to be."

Rachel pulled the blanket a little closer and smoothed down the sheets covering her lap. Yes, she'd gotten the same feeling.

Months ago, she'd learned about Fantasy from her good friend Anna Wakefield. Anna had met the love of her life at Fantasy, the uber private sex club specializing in safe, consensual and anonymous fun. The organization had clubs in several major cities as well as beach resorts for week-long stays and mountain retreats for weekend getaways. She and Matt had been headed to one of the newest weekend retreats abutting the Greenbrier Mountains. To participate in any Fantasy experience, guests had to be thoroughly vetted. On top of that, women had to be using contraceptive implants, and all had to be tested for sexually transmitted diseases.

He was safe and so was she.

"I've enjoyed our evening together so far." Rachel's voice thickened.

"Me too."

She closed her eyes and blurted out the only thought on her mind. "You know, if we'd made it to Fantasy, we might be together in a bed like this right now."

"We might."

"Um ...."

"Do you want to imagine we're at Fantasy?"

Rachel released her tight grip on the bedding and slowly turned to face him. She tipped her chin down. "I'd like that."

Matt leaned toward her and murmured, "Me too."

She released the breath she'd been holding. That was good. They were on the same page.

Thank God.

She liked Matt, liked his smile and his laugh and the way he listened when she talked. She wanted this, wanted him, for this first time. But first times were hard. "I'm ...."

"Can I kiss you?" he asked, his gaze darting from her eyes to her lips.

"Yes," she answered, and his lips brushed against hers. Soft, sweet, perfect.

Rachel froze. *Oh, God, what if* ....

Matt's eyes narrowed with concern. "Was that okay?"

"Yes, but it's been a long time. I'm having trouble getting out of my head."

"You mean getting *him* out of your head?"

Rachel winced, hating she sounded so pathetic. "Sorry. There were things he said that made me feel inadequate. I thought at Fantasy, if I didn't really know someone ... not that I know you, but I wouldn't care."

"Tell me what he said."

"Matt, I'm not sure that will help."

"I'm excited—very excited"—he glanced down at his lap for emphasis—"to be here with you like this. I never imagined meeting someone like you at Fantasy." He stopped and leaned closer. "Nothing he said, nothing you think, is going to make me any less excited. Let's move past him."

Rachel nodded. Of course she agreed, but years of disappointing Jeff had left its mark.

"We can sit here talking if you want. We don't have to do anything."

"But I don't want to sit."

"Rachel, I think you're beautiful and sexy and ...."

"He said my breasts were too small to be truly ... enjoyable," she blurted, unable to hold back the hurtful words.

Matt blinked, and then his eyes narrowed. His gaze didn't leave her face. "Seriously?"

"Regularly. He said that regularly. And he complained—" She shook her head. While it felt good sharing, her stomach started to turn. "During sex, I usually have a hard time ... finishing, and he said women should ...."

"I can imagine what he said." His lips twisted with disgust. "I'm thinking your ex was a nasty piece of work as well as stupid. Let's get him out of your head for good."

Rachel nodded, wanting that more than she could say.

"Let's take these off now." Matt pulled his oversized tee over his head and tossed it onto the floor.

Her eyes widened as her gaze drifted over his body. Her chest tightened. Of course, he had six-pack abs. "You look ... good."

"And you're going to look good to me." One of his hands reached for her shoulder and squeezed then slowly slid over her collarbone before gently cupping the underside of her breast. "I promise."

Rachel stared down at his large hand, huge against her small form. For the first time in a long time, she didn't feel like hiding.

Matt leaned forward and brushed his lips over hers again. At the same time, his hand skimmed down her torso and gripped the hem of her tee. "Do you want some help?" He kissed her once more. "Let's do it together."

The heavy bed curtains and dim overhead lights couldn't make the room dark enough. Rachel released a breath, slow and long. But she'd planned this weekend to move forward, and Matt seemed like the perfect person.

Rachel placed a hand beside his, and together they lifted the tee over her head. Immediately, the tips of her breasts puckered as a chill spread across her exposed skin. Without really thinking, she lifted her hands to cover herself, but Matt caught them in midair.

"Let me look.

"Baby, the guy is insane. These are damned pretty." He shifted and cupped both her breasts in his palms. "Please believe me."

"They're small," she murmured.

"They're perfect." His thumbs slid up to her nipples, and the tight tips hardened even more under his touch.

Matt smiled as Rachel whimpered and clenched her legs together.

"Scoot down a bit." He moved the pillows behind her back and nudged her down so she lay flat on the comfy bed. "I like this." He leaned over, half covering her with his body. The smile on his face widened.

Rachel shivered. She liked it too, his weight on her, his touch. And the way he looked at her—as if he couldn't look away.

She wrapped one arm around his neck and slid the other to his bicep. The man was hard muscle everywhere, including the shaft pressing into her hip. He wanted her, wanted her as much as she wanted him. She breathed in, the tight feeling between her legs turning into a needy ache.

She tipped her chin up and kissed him, pressing her lips to his. His soft lips and sweet taste made her tremble inside. "I was nervous about this weekend. I almost backed out."

"I don't know the best way forward for a fresh start, but I'm glad you didn't back out—for both of us." His arms around her tightened, and then he cupped the back of her head. "You're exactly—exactly—who I want to be with right now."

"I feel the same way."

. . .

Matt smiled, a smile that made her melt inside. "Hold on a sec." He shifted again and moved between her thighs, his hard cock making its presence known. His mouth captured hers once more, soft and gentle, almost teasing.

And that only made her want more.

"We'll go slow," he murmured in her ear, his warm breath skimming over her cheek. "Whatever feels good to you."

"It all feels good to me."

Matt lifted his head and cuffed the back of her neck, kissing her mouth then brushing his lips across her lower lip. "I'm going to keep going."

Rachel nodded, not exactly sure what he meant, but didn't care. Whatever he wanted to do was fine with her.

"I want to know your body." His tongue slicked over her skin, making goosebumps pop in his wake. He kissed her collarbone then gently covered her breasts with his hands. He brushed his fingertips over her nipples. "Tell me, Rachel."

"Ahh ... I think you know," she whimpered as his lips skimmed over the tips of her breasts, and a little cry escaped from her throat. She arched her back, pushing her needy flesh further into his mouth. "You're certainly figuring it out."

"I love these," he said and sucked. Then he lifted his head and grinned up at her. "And I love how much you like this too."

Rachel's throat tightened. When had she ever felt this way before? "You make me feel so ... so ...."

"Good. You deserve this and so do I." His dark eyes heated as his gaze darted down her body. "And we both want this."

Before Rachel could take in a full breath, Matt shifted and yanked her panties down her legs and tossed it onto the growing pile of clothes on the floor. She gasped, the cool air hitting her newly exposed skin. That was fast.

Matt kissed the inside of her thighs and spread her legs wide. "You're so wet for me." He ran a thick finger down the seam of her sex, and his voice deepened. He stroked her clit, and she jerked in place. Oh, his touch was perfect. *More, please.* That smile of his widened—could he read her mind?—and he lowered his head. "This is going to be fun."

Oh, God! Rachel groaned as his tongue swept over her slick flesh. She arched her back and thankfully he held on. It seemed his mouth and his hands were everywhere.

And then the pleasure coursing through her exploded, and her body took flight. Rachel collapsed on the fluffy bed, panting like she'd never panted before. How ... how?

She never came that fast—never.

Matt wiped at his mouth and stood at the foot of the bed, shucking off his boxers. He was big, thick and hard, but she was ready. So ready. He climbed up her body, and she couldn't wait to feel him on hers again.

He kissed her mouth and groaned, a tight expression on his handsome face, settling between legs that she might never close again. At least not tonight.

Rachel gasped as Matt's eyes shut and jaw clenched, and he slowly entered her body, pressing in, stopping, then pressing in again.

He was big, and she was nervous, but the care he showed her .... Her heart melted again.

This was what she imagined great sex could be. He'd made her worry and lack of confidence fade away. Wasn't that something a man—a good man—would do?

She didn't want to ever settle for something missing again.

Matt's hand wove between their bodies, and his fingers found her clit. "Let's go for number two."

Hours later—*had they really been doing this for hours?*—Rachel cuddled beside him, loving the feel of his warm, strong body.

"Do you still want to go to Fantasy?" he asked.

"I do, but only if you—" She flinched. It was insane to think he'd want to spend all his time at Fantasy with her. At Fantasy, he could explore his desires and have his choice of companions.

"Rachel, I can't imagine being there with anybody but you."

Her heart thumped as she nodded, tipping her chin into his chest. This night, this moment with him, could be her fresh start.

5

"Good morning." Matt sat in the lounge chair beside the bed. Fully dressed. *Damn.*

Rachel wiped at her eyes. "Is it morning?"

"I'm afraid so."

"I had a nice time last night ... this morning." She added the last bit since they'd still been at it for hours after midnight.

"So did I."

For a long moment, they stared at each other, and then her gaze darted to her watch. Oh, no! It was two minutes to eight. "They open in a few minutes. I don't want to be naked." She jumped from the bed and scurried to pick up clothes she'd discarded last night.

"Don't worry. I'm sure we'll hear them coming down those cement steps."

She pulled up her jeans and fumbled with the zipper and button. "I want to be ready."

"Listen, Rachel, there's something I need to tell you—"

She froze then turned her head toward the front of the bunker. "I think I hear something."

"We still have a few—"

"I don't want anyone to think we were in bed together." She gripped the sheets and pulled them to the top of the bed and then did the same with the comforter. "I never understood the idea of making a bed with military corners, but I think this looks okay." She plumped up the pillows—that looked right—and smoothed down the bedding with her hands. No wrinkles anywhere. "As good as new."

"No one's going to care."

"I will." She scanned the room again. Okay, nothing out of place.

"All right, but—"

Rachel glanced down at her clothes, her shirt and pants pulled into place and all buttons buttoned, and sighed.

"Ms. Westman?" a male voice, a little shaky sounding, called out. "Ms. Westman?"

Rachel clasped her hands together and held them in front of her.

"Ms. Westman? I noticed your car still in the lot." Felix, a senior member of her contractor team, jogged into the room. His gaze darted from Rachel to Matt. "Oh, you're here with Mr. Carr."

"Yes, somehow we both got stuck down here last evening."

Felix frowned and scratched at the back of his head. "I saw your brother close it late yesterday, but I assumed he'd checked …."

"We're fine." Rachel offered a weak smile.

"I guess I'm surprised to see you and Mr. Carr together." Felix's eyes narrowed, and he shook his head. "Mr. Westman—your brother, Ma'am—said we should stop working and pick up our supplies this morning."

"Steven did what? What are you talking about, Felix?"

"After he sold Hopewell House to Mr. Carr's company, he said we should pack our stuff and go." He shook his head again. "He wasn't very nice about it, either."

"Steven sold Hopewell House?" Rachel pressed her fingertips into her temples. No, no, no. This didn't make sense.

"Your brother sold Hopewell House to my company yesterday. We signed the papers, he walked me out to my car, but then I decided to go down and look at the bunker one more time." Matt stuck his hands in the front pockets of his pants. "I don't think he knew I went back into the house."

"But Steven has no authority to sell, to—"

"He possesses your grandfather's power of attorney."

Her eyes widened, and her heart skipped a beat. "Oh God. I've had Grandpa's POA for years. A month ago, Steven asked if I could add him, that it might help him with some of Gramp's paperwork ... the easy stuff."

"Rachel—"

"You knew—" Air trapped in her lungs. "You didn't say a thing."

"I wanted to explain."

Her mouth fell open, and all she could do was stare at him. "Yes, you should have." She stood stick straight. Then while she still had the ability to talk, she turned to Felix. "Don't pick up your equipment and supplies yet. I need to figure this out."

Without glancing at Matt again, she grabbed her purse and dashed from the room.

Oh, she was stupid, so stupid. Rachel moved as quickly as she could up the cement steps, getting away from this, from him, as soon as possible.

Matt—head of mega-big Carr Properties, Inc.—wasn't the nice, decent guy he pretended to be. Members of the Carr group had been trying to get Hopewell House for years—years. He knew who she was—*he knew*—and he hadn't said a word.

Maybe all men, at least the men she met, were deceptive assholes. God, could she pick 'em?

Her hands shook as she pulled open the wide, stately doors at the entrance to Hopewell House then dashed through the pretty front yard garden and headed for the parking lot at the side of the building. A moment later, she dug into her purse, hunting for her car keys. Where were the damn things?

"Rachel!" Matt's deep, loud voice echoed in the parking lot. She didn't need to look up to know he was coming toward her, his long legs on the pebbled lot getting closer by the second.

No, she would not turn her head.

"Don't go," he called out. "Let me explain."

She changed her mind and faced him, glaring. "How could you not tell me who you are after I shared so much with you, Mr. Carr?"

"I wanted to, but I needed to—"

Rachel pursed her lips together and shook her head from side to side. "I don't want to hear what you want or need. Argh!" She groaned low in her throat. "I can't believe I was starting to fall for you."

"I'm falling for you too."

"No!" She shook her head even harder. How could he say that now? "I was with a man for years who said he cared about me, but he didn't, he really didn't."

"I know. And that's the last thing I want to do."

Rachel rolled her eyes. Last night, for the first time in a long time, many things felt possible. She was not going to go back now. "I'm going to contact a lawyer, I'm going to stop you and your company." Her jaw clenched as she faced him. "I know you know I've wrapped all my money in this—and you have lots of money to fight me—but I won't be brushed off. I've stood aside too many times. This is important to me, to my grandfather."

"Good. You should trust yourself before you trust anyone else."

She breathed in, her chest heaving. "Matt, don't pretend you're on my side."

He tore a hand through his hair. "When we were stuck in the bunker, we had no connection to the outside world. I know how you feel about your brother, how happy you were that he'd been helping you. I didn't want to say something, upset you, when I wasn't sure. But it looks like he locked you down there so you wouldn't stumble into his meeting with my staff." He paused and caught his breath. "Rachel, sweetheart, I didn't want to hurt you."

"Please. Look at this." He tapped at his cell phone and held the screen up for her to read. "I wrote this late last night."

Phil,

I've become acquainted with Steven Westman's sister, Rachel. She's an architect, skilled and has invested a great deal of money—her money—into Hopewell House. I like what she's doing—a lot. Also, I like her—a lot.

I believe Steven Westman has misrepresented his position and authority with Hopewell. While he does possess a power of attorney, I'm concerned he may have committed fraud or at least a severe dereliction of fiduciary responsibilities. I don't want to make accusations at this time—his sister cares about him, and I care about her—so we need to proceed with caution. So contact Steven Westman's attorney and settlement agent immediately and void the contract. Whatever you do, act with discretion. Rachel Westman MATTERS to me.

I'll be in touch Monday morning.

-Matt

Rachel shook her head but couldn't stop staring at his cell phone screen. That didn't make sense. "Carr doesn't help with projects like this. You tear down and rebuild new and shiny."

"We used to do that—we still do when it makes sense—but we'd never tear down a place like Hopewell House." He reached for her then stood back as she pressed against the door of her car. "Do you think I was faking last night?"

She swallowed hard. "I don't know what to believe."

"Yes, you do." He stepped closer, and she didn't shift away this time. "I tried to handle this the best way possible. I needed information and couldn't get it down there. But I like you Rachel. I feel lucky that if I had to get trapped in a bunker, it was with you."

Rachel pressed her lips together and nodded, her gaze moving from his cell phone to the earnest expression on his handsome face. *Void the contract. Act with discretion. Rachel Westman MATTERS to me.* Her heart clutched. While she'd been sleeping last night, he'd been working to protect her. "You're right. It's not your fault Steven did this. And ... I like you too."

"Rachel, sweetheart, I'd like to help with Hopewell House."

"No, I can do this on my own."

"It sounds like you've been doing a lot on your own lately." He reached her side and took her hand in his. "Maybe you can benefit from an advisor? This is a big project, and you don't want to waste money, resources." He quirked a brow. "I have access to a lot of resources, but I'll only step where you want me."

The tightness in her chest eased. He was offering so much, but she could still take baby steps. "Thank you. We can talk about it?"

"Yes, let's do that."

"What am I going to do about Steven?" She squeezed his hand. "What are *you* going to do? I'm furious with him, but—"

"We need to unravel the illegal versus the unethical parts of his actions. But I'll do whatever you want. However, I don't want to think about it until Monday morning."

"Monday morning?"

His eyes gleamed down at her. "Because I hope we still have plans this weekend."

Her breath caught, remembering those hands of his. Truly magic. "I think we do."

His brow shot up again. "And maybe we have plans next weekend and the weekend after that?"

She nodded, happier than she'd been a long time. "I hope so."

THE END

About the Author

I was a public relations writer before I turned to romantic fiction. While I enjoyed working in the corporate world, it was more fun to write about the sexy characters in my head.

I was fortunate to meet my personal romance hero during college. We met at a fraternity party my freshman year at school and became fast friends. One night I was eating dinner at his fraternity, and my future husband suavely sat on an empty table beside me to chat. Unfortunately, that table was missing a leg and it collapsed on my arm. When he called the next day to check on me, I had to tell him my arm was broken. (It was!) Devastated but still gallant, he asked me out on a date. We've now been married more than a few decades and have two teenage sons.

Note: Hopewell House is based on the Greenbrier resort in White Sulphur Springs, West Virginia. The Greenbrier was the location of a real life secret Cold War fallout shelter for U.S. Congress members, built in the early 1960s. I've toured the bunker and so can you.

Please sign up for Susanna Eastman's newsletter for information on new releases, sales and other book news

www.susannaeastman.com

Read More from Susanna Eastman

https://books2read.com/b/38PgQd

The Unicorn
Denise Wells

1

Blake

Seven is my limit.

I'm done.

Ready to admit defeat.

Tonight marks the seventh disastrous date in almost as many weeks. But it took that many to realize I've lost my touch with women.

It's gone.

The Casanova of my youth is nowhere to be found. Not that I'm old at thirty-two, even though it sure as fuck feels like it sometimes. It's been two years since I broke off my engagement with my sociopathic, pregnancy-faking, fanatical control freak of a fiancée Taylor, and I'm no closer to getting back on the proverbial horse now than I was then.

I pull my car in the garage and park next to my Harley, then head into the house. It's completely dark except for the light the TV gives off. Darby is in the living room watching some movie that's making her cry. Either that or she's just crying and plans to use the movie as an excuse.

"Hey, Darbs," I call out as I head down the hall to my room so I can change into shorts and a t-shirt.

"Hey," she calls back shakily. Darby is my little sister's best friend.

She recently went through a messy and hurtful breakup and had been living with the guy. When I heard they broke up, and Darby was sleeping on their couch while he brought other women home to the bedroom, my *knight-in-shining-armor* complex jumped to attention like it was spring activated.

The next day, we moved her into my spare room.

I didn't even need a roommate. I *like* living alone. But I'm not doing much with the house yet anyway, and I have a few spare rooms. I bought it because it was a fixer in a good neighborhood—close to my best friend Wyatt and his wife Bristol, aka, my little sister—and the price was right.

Plus, I need the tax deductions. My income has gone up significantly in the past year thanks to my latest video game design being picked up by a huge manufacturer whose name rhymes with *bike-row-loft*. Then, they gave me a huge advance to design the follow-up. I live simply, so I'm set with money for a while if I keep my current standard of living mostly the same.

I change my clothes, grab a beer from the kitchen, and join Darby in the living room.

"What are you watching?" I ask, taking a seat on the other side of the couch from her.

She sniffs and tells me the name of the movie, which doesn't help at all since I've never heard of it.

"Is it sad?" I ask dumbly.

She turns toward me and nods. Her big, blue eyes are red rimmed, and her chin is quivering.

Fuck.

I set my beer on the coffee table, scoot to her side, and pull her in my arms. "It's going to get better, sweetheart. I promise."

She burrows into my embrace, half on my lap. I kiss the top of her head and try not to breathe in the scent of her shampoo. Like many things about Darby that I've discovered since she moved in over a month ago, her shampoo turns me on.

I silently recite C++ commands in my mind to distract my dick since he doesn't care that Darby is off limits. Even if she wasn't just out of a serious relationship and still hung up on the guy, Darby is my sister's best friend, practically a member of our family. She's also my new roommate, and you don't shit where you sleep, so to speak.

I rub her back while she blows her nose and collects herself. She starts to tell me about the characters appearing on the screen, and when something happens that she likes, she sighs and relaxes against my chest. Which ordinarily would be fine; I'm a grown man, I can hold myself back from a woman I'm attracted to. Except her butt cheek is pressing against the aforementioned oblivious dick who just wants to get laid. He and I have been virtually celibate since Taylor.

So, I've lost my touch with women. I have a roommate I don't need. I've spent the last two years having sex with myself. My beer is out of reach. The woman I'm lusting after is an emotional wreck who sees me as a security blanket she can cuddle with on the couch. And her nice, round, perfect peach of an ass is pressing against my dick, who, in turn, is excited to let her know he's there.

"This is nice," Darby whispers.

I grunt in response.

I've never had an issue with women before her. If anything, the problem has been deciding which woman I wanted amongst those who wanted me. Relationships have been easy and fun; we've always ended on good terms. When my career took off, women took more seriously. I wasn't a fresh-out-of-college software designer living in my parents' basement any longer.

Enter Taylor. Exit Taylor.

And here I am.

2

Darby – Three Weeks Later

I'm just pouring myself a cup of coffee as Blake blows into the kitchen like a category-five hurricane, disrupting everything in his path with his very solid, very sweaty, and very manly presence.

I can't believe he does this every morning when it's all I can do to make the trek down the hallway to the kitchen for coffee. He has so much energy in the morning. I turn and lean against the edge of the center island in the kitchen, needing to drink him in as much as I do my coffee. His shirt is off, and he's wiping the sweat from his face with it.

He hasn't seen me yet, and it's only a matter of seconds before he does, so until then, I take my fill and mentally file it away to be brought out later. There are only so many times a girl can see a guy dressed only in shorts, boxers, a towel, or swim trunks before she must either tear said coverings from his body and take her fill or slink off to some dark corner and rub one out.

Unfortunately for me, sometime in the last couple of weeks, I've realized that Blake is a man. Yes, he's my bestie's older brother and someone I've known since childhood, but he's also six feet of sinewy, well-proportioned, muscular magnificence. With a chiseled jaw, piercing green eyes, sexy smile, and great hair. How I didn't notice before is baffling.

I shift slightly, rubbing my thighs together to stem the rush of heat between them. His chest glistens with sweat, highlighting the definition in his pecs and the ridges in his abdomen. Blake's shorts ride low on his hips, showcasing those crazy fucking v-muscle things on both sides that I'm convinced exist for the sole purpose of driving women crazy. A faint trail of dark hair pulls my eyes further down his front to the impressive bulge in his shorts.

Fuuuuuck.

I wipe my chin in case I'm drooling over him, then close my eyes against the visual onslaught of masculine virility in front of me and try to appear unaffected and disinterested. Not easy to do when his very existence commands the room, making it hard to breathe.

"Mornin', Darbs," he says. His low, husky voice sends shockwaves through my nether regions. My thighs want to open wide, give him their best come-hither invitation, and welcome him inside.

But I won't let them.

Damaged goods like me don't get the guys like Blake.

"Sleep okay?" he asks.

I keep my eyes closed and try to look natural. Natural but sleepy. And not like the lascivious harlot I am. Then nod in response to his question. If my ex taught me anything, it's that I'm not the kind of girl guys want to love and stay faithful to. He said I belong on the '*Go Backs*' shelf.

I have no reason not to believe him. He was the only guy to stop the rotating door of relationships I'd grown accustomed to. So, obviously, he saw something in me he thought was worthy in the beginning, only to realize it was a façade.

Blake passes through the kitchen, stopping next to me to grab a bottled water from the fridge. The scent of man sweat drifts by—the good kind that's clean and a little soapy—not the gross, grungy, dirty clothes kind. His arm brushes against mine as he opens the bottle, and a shiver of desire runs through me. I want to roll my eyes at myself with how pathetic I'm acting. But this is Blake.

My best friend's brother.

One of the most decent guys I've ever met.

Not to mention one of the hottest guys I've ever seen.

He's not the type to shop from the 'Go Backs' shelf.

"You awake, babe?" Blake trails a finger up my neck, stopping under my chin to tilt my head slightly. Every muscle in my body tenses. My breath catches. I clutch my coffee tighter to my chest and let my eyes flutter open. He's standing so close, the scant hair on his abdomen tickles my knuckles. My gaze travels lazily up his sculpted body, past the broad shoulders, up the oh-so-lickable neck, along that movie star jawline, to those deep-green eyes I want to drown in. The color is so similar to Bristol's, but the heat in his hold is like nothing I've seen before.

His gaze drops to my lips, making me wet them with my tongue nervously, but my mouth is dry. If I could remember how to move, I'd take a sip of coffee to wet it. The sizzle of chemistry is so palpable between us, I feel caged in.

"I'm awake," I croak.

A half smile graces his face as he nods once, then takes a step back. The heat of his body goes with him, jolting me like a jump from the hot tub into the pool. If I didn't know any better, I'd swear we hadn't just had a sexually charged interaction based on how quickly he's able to school any emotion on his face. He brings the water bottle to his lips and drains half of it quickly. I watch his Adam's apple bob as he swallows, mesmerized, and wonder if it's possible to lust after an Adam's apple.

"I'm going to grab a shower. I reek. I'll see you later."

I want to tell him there's no need, that he smells good, like a walking sex-vertisement, but I'm pretty sure my voice has left the vicinity of my body. Instead, I watch his ass as he disappears down the hall toward his bedroom, whistling a tune I don't recognize.

He must do squats.

No one is born with an ass that nice.

I slap myself to shock me out of my lust-filled stupor, refill my coffee cup, and head for the guest room I temporarily call home. Where I should really hole myself in until I'm over this infatuation with Blake Moore, or I die—whichever comes first.

3

Blake

My best friend Wyatt and I are on mile three of our usual five-mile run. He knows how I feel about Darby, but he's not useful in helping me get over it. He thinks Darby wants me as much as I want her. But I already know that's not true.

"I didn't offer her my spare room just so I could jump her bones," I say.

"No one says jump her bones anymore."

"Really, dude," I huff. "Is that the point here?"

Wyatt laughs.

"What do we say?" I ask, wincing. Because no way should Wyatt be hipper than me. He's a dad now for fuck's sake.

"Tap. Bang. Fuck." He turns and jogs backward in front of me.

Show off.

"Nail. Boink." He picks up the pace a bit. "If she'd been with me, the word would be satisfied." He thumps his chest twice with his fists, then throws his arms up in the air in victory as he turns back to face front and increases his speed again. I dig in to catch up with him.

"You're married. You can't talk about sex with other women."

"I was referring to my wife."

"Aaah!" I cover my ears. "That's gross. Your wife is my sister. I don't need to know these things." I swallow down the bile threatening to make its way up my throat.

We're silent for a few hundred feet before I say anything more. "Fine, I didn't offer my spare room so I could fuck her."

"But you want to."

"So bad," I groan.

"Want me to ask Bristol if she thinks Darby would be open to some roommates-with-benefits action?"

"No," I huff. "Brie will blow it way out of proportion, naming our babies and shit." An image of Darby pregnant with my baby pops into the forefront of my mind, and I don't hate it.

What the fuck?

Christ, I need to get laid.

He speeds up again because he's a sadistic asshole, and it takes all my concentration to keep up with him and not let him know it hurts to do so. As a result, we're mostly silent for the remainder of our run.

"You'll be there tomorrow, right?" he asks about our weekly Sunday football-watching party with a group of friends.

"Yeah, why? You guys wanna carpool?" I ask, assuming Brie and my nephew Nico are going with him.

"No," he says and then surprises me with a follow-up question. "Do you like Darby, or do you just want to fuck her?"

An image of her face pops into my head, and a smile threatens to break my face. "I like her."

"Then invite her to go with you tomorrow."

"Like, a date?" I look at him quizzically.

"Or, you know, just a friendly get-together with a group of people to watch the game. Feel out the situation. It's low pressure. Bristol will be there, and you can use Nico to run interference if you need it."

It's not a bad idea. But I also feel like I'm being called to task. He must see the hesitation on my face because he says, "You know you haven't lost your mojo, right?"

"Dude," I protest because he's wrong.

"You just went through a rough patch, man. You're out of it and stronger for it."

I wait to see if he'll say anything else, not wanting to admit to him or myself that I kind of need to hear this.

"You're a good-looking guy," he says. "You're physically fit, financially stable—"

I scoff.

"I'm not done," Wyatt continues. "You're funny, charming, open to commitment—"

"Well, shit," I interrupt. "I guess I'm just the mother-fucking unicorn of single men, then."

"Yes!" He claps his hands and jumps in place like he's on a pogo stick. "You're the mother fucking unicorn of single men!" He turns and heads in the direction of his house before calling back to me, "Now own it!"

I head towards home feeling pumped up. I can do this. Yes, Darby is emotionally fragile, and I don't want to take advantage of that. But we are friends, and there's nothing wrong with two friends going to a party.

4

Darby

I'm going with Blake to a football-watching party, and I haven't been out in a social situation with a group in over two months. I'm not sure if I remember how to act, dress, or even have a conversation.

I hate that I'm so insecure lately. Logically, I know my ex fucked with my head. And my heart. But that didn't stop the words from penetrating deep into my psyche. I tried to make it work with him, harder than I've ever worked at anything before. But it was clear after a while that I wasn't successful. Then he cheated. Er, I discovered him cheating. He claimed it was the first time, but I have my doubts looking back. Still, I'm convinced we had love for one another in the beginning. We must have. It was just a love that turned toxic the longer we stayed together.

Anymore, most of my friends are married and already have kids or are pregnant. What used to feel like I had the upper hand in still being single with nothing tying me down, now feels like I'm the odd one out who can't relate to any of the things my friends are experiencing. I wanted to fit in and moving in with my ex seemed like the first step to that.

Now, I'm back to square one. Maybe even square zero if such a thing exists, because I don't know how to get myself off the '*Go Backs*' shelf and onto the one that guys shop at first.

I'm dressed in a light-blue, short-sleeved romper that's shirred and fitted on the top with tiered flowy layers on the bottom, which make it look more like a dress. Shoes are a no-brainer. I'm a Dr. Martens fiend and love pairing combat-style boots with feminine-looking clothing. The combination makes me feel fierce but still sexy.

I'm just surveying myself in the full-length mirror when Blake knocks on my door.

"Hey, Darbs," he calls. "You decent?"

Not usually, I think, but say, "Yeah, come on in."

His large body fills my doorway and wow, he's beautiful. How did I never notice his smile before? It's gorgeous, transforming his entire face from stoically handsome to '*Can I please have your babies, you beautiful man, you.*' His well-worn jeans are just snug enough on his hips and thighs to show everything to its best advantage. I wish I could see his butt in them at the same time. A vintage concert t-shirt stretches tight on his chest and biceps, I can practically see the ridges of his muscles outlined in the cotton cover. And he's looking at me like he's starving, and I'm the meal. I feel emboldened by the look on his face, and any insecurity I may have felt vanishes.

5

Blake

I poke my head into her room, she's standing in front of the window, backlit by the sun shining in. Her blond hair falls over her shoulders like liquid gold. She's wearing a sundress that shows every delicious part to the best advantage. The top hugs her perky tits with a tantalizing glimpse of cleavage in between. My dick stirs in my jeans. She's so picture-perfect pretty I forget what I came in here for.

"Hey," she says, sounding almost shy.

I clear my throat. "Wow. You look great."

"Yeah?" She looks down at herself, then back up at me.

"Really good."

She smiles. I do the same, unable to stop myself.

"What's up?" she asks.

"Oh, yeah," I run my hand through my thick hair, trying to remember. "I was thinking of leaving a little early and taking Jenny on a ride around the bay. You up for that?"

"Jenny?" she asks, a look crosses her face that I can't quite identify, but it's not happy.

"My Harley's name is Jenny."

She looks relieved when I say that. Was she worried I would bring another girl? "You're my only date today." I take a chance.

"Is this a date?" she asks, looking down at her feet so I can't tell what she's thinking.

"A friendly date," I hedge.

A look of dread combined with excitement fills her face in equal parts. "I'm a safe driver, I swear. But if you're more comfortable taking the truck, we can."

"No." A big smile splits her face. "I'm good on a bike."

"Great," I say in relief, my smile matches hers. "Let me know when you're ready."

"I'm ready."

I hold out my hand toward her. "Shall we?"

She grasps my hand in hers, and a jolt of excitement surges through me at her touch.

Calm down, Blake.

If I get this worked up about holding her hand, what the fuck am I going to do when she's got her arms around my waist, and her legs are straddling my hips from the back of my bike?

"That's a gorgeous bike," Darby enthuses. Jenny is a Harley Davidson Road Glide CVO. I've had her a little over a year, and she was a splurge.

"You're smart to compliment her at the start," I tell Darby with a hint of a smile.

She looks at me, puzzled.

"She's never had to share me with another woman." I look at her as I unlock my helmet from the clip and wink.

Darby laughs. "Are you saying I'm your first?"

I straighten as my body heats at the implication and for a moment, I find myself tongue-tied at how sexy she is. I mentally shake my head to clear it and move toward her with the spare helmet I'd set out earlier.

"Let's see how this fits that sassy head of yours." I gather her hair in one hand to move it away from her face and behind her shoulders. I want to run my fingers through the silky strands. An image of me holding it while fucking her pops into my head; it's so visceral that I inadvertently tug. She gasps as her head tilts back, and our eyes meet; her pupils are wide.

"Did I hurt you?" I ask softly, my voice hoarse.

She shakes her head slowly.

Fuuuck.

She looks up at me with her big blue eyes, and I feel like I can do anything. Conquer the fucking world? No problem. Make her mine forever? Absofuckinglutely. I release her hair and run the backs of my fingers across her cheek to smooth an imaginary stray piece back. It's just an excuse to touch her. She shivers despite the warmth of the day, making me hope I affect her as much as she does me.

I get her helmet secured and make sure the fit is snug.

"Feel good?" I ask.

She nods.

I let my hand trail from under her chin, across her clavicle, and down the outside of her arm. When I reach her hand, I hook one finger with hers and tug her toward me a step. What I want to do is throw her over my shoulder, march back inside, and fuck her until neither of us can see straight.

Instead, I let her finger go and show her how to use the intercom between the helmets. Then I rearrange my near-hard cock in what I hope is a subtle manner and get on the bike. I start the ignition, secure my helmet, and hold out a hand to help Darby get on the back.

"Don't be afraid to scoot close and hang on tight."

"Unlike you," she says, "this isn't my first time."

I laugh, even as a surge of jealousy shoots through me.

Who has she been on a bike with before?

Not that it's any of my business.

But who?

She tucks her pelvis tight against me and wraps her arms around my waist like it's the most natural thing in the world to do. I force myself to relax.

I have no right to be jealous.

"I'm excited," she says.

I cover her clasped hands with one of mine and squeeze in acknowledgment.

By the time we reach the end of the street, it's clear she's comfortable on the back of a bike, so I try to ignore how much I like her on the back of mine.

6

Darby

I like that I'm the first girl to ride on the back of Blake's bike. I'm not going to lie, part of me wants to be the last too. Blake handles the bike well; his confidence is apparent when he drives. There's something about a man secure in himself, at home in his body and his actions, that makes me want to drop my panties and beg to be fulfilled. Or just filled.

We slow at a stoplight. Blake puts his hand on my thigh and squeezes lightly. "Doing okay?" he asks. His thumb runs back and forth on my inner thigh, sending bolts of desire rushing through me. It's bad enough being this close to him with the vibrations of the bike under us. I'm also wrapped around him like a monkey and can feel every ridge of his hard, muscular body.

The thin material of my romper does nothing to shield my lady parts from his ass in those jeans. Every shift of his body moves the rough denim across the already sensitive skin. Now, he's touching my thigh, and the rough-edged callouses on his hand feels so good on my skin, I want to combust.

I'm so turned on right now.

"Mmm, so good," I moan. The muscles under my hands jump,

making me wonder if he heard the sex I hadn't meant to let infuse my voice. I'm glad he can't see the flush that heats my face.

"That good, huh?" he teases.

I respond with what I hope is a non-sexual sound of agreement, still not able to form actual words.

"Fuuuck, Darbs. The sounds you make do things to a guy."

I guess not.

We turn a corner around a berm, and the water comes into view. It's beautiful, and I tell him so. The hard plane of his abdomen vibrates as he chuckles, making me want to leave my hands there all the time just to keep feeling him. I take a deep breath and let it out slowly.

Did I mention how good he smells? Like pine or maybe sandalwood, and a hint of fabric softener. Then something else that's uniquely him. It causes some kind of Pavlovian response in me. Smell Blake, go wet between my legs. I've got an entire freaking immersive sensory experience going on here. Feeling the sun, touching the muscles, smelling the man, seeing the water.

He slows so we can better enjoy the scenic route. There aren't many people out considering how beautiful the day is. It makes me feel reckless. The tips of my fingers slip under the waistband of his jeans where the skin is warmer. Hot even. Just enough to feel the muscles contract at my touch, my new favorite thing.

"You trying to make us crash?" His voice is husky.

"Oh, is that distracting?" I ask, with pretend innocence.

"You want to switch places and find out?"

"No," I say.

And then, "Yes," after I think on it a moment.

To my surprise, he pulls over to the side of the near-deserted road and stops the bike, engine idling. I climb off the back with a *whoop* that makes him laugh. He scoots back to the seat I vacated and motions for me to get on in front of him. Blake situates me on the seat like I'm a rag doll who weighs nothing, and then he gets close. Really close. Like, I can feel his dick pressing against my tailbone kind of close.

He leans over me to take the controls and rests his chin on my shoulder. I feel insulated and protected in a way I haven't experienced in a long time, if ever, with a man. His breath is hot against my neck, and a flash of him sucking on the sensitive skin flits through my mind. Followed by the thought of him naked above me, entering me, making me come.

"It's a good thing you're so small; I can see right over you," he says, interrupting my thoughts. His voice washes over me like silk on my naked skin. I want him to keep talking. He tells me where to put my hands and feet, does a few things with the controls, and then, we're moving again. This time, the pace is much slower, on cruise control. Even with the low speed, it's a much different experience in the front of the bike, like riding in the first car on a rollercoaster.

I lean my head back against his shoulder and close my eyes, letting the sun beat down on my face, feeling content. Blake rests his hand on my thigh. High on my thigh with his fingers spread, making me gasp. Like before, his thumb runs lazily back and forth. The blunt edge of his nail lightly scratches my skin like a sugar scrub; the sensation is excruciatingly sensual.

Blake hums along with some song coming through the helmets like he hasn't a care in the world. All the while, his fingers inch closer to my clit, making it impossible for me to focus. I take a deep breath and release it slowly to relax my racing pulse. Which is a joke, because really, who can relax in a situation like this? His thumb grazes the hem of my romper leg, catching the material so it moves with him. It tickles in a *holy-shit-this-is-turning-me-on-even-more* kind of way.

"Is that distracting?" Blake asks in a low, devilish tone.

I nod shakily. "You know it is."

"Breathe, baby," he coaxes.

I release my breath with a whoosh—again—and try to regulate my intake and outflow. It doesn't work. His hand is too present, too distracting, creeping ever higher on my thigh. I close my eyes against the onslaught of desire that courses through me and shift my ass on the seat. "Mmmm."

"Christ, you sound sexy as fuck," he rasps.

At least Blake sounds as out of breath as I feel.

"Can I touch you?"

I nod. His hand slides easily into the leg of my romper, and the pads of his fingers skim the barely-there covering over my sex. A small cry escapes my lips. I knew I was wet. Now he does too. Blake pushes the panel of my panties to the side and slides his fingers through my folds.

My left hand grabs at his knee and squeezes. "Oh, god!"

"So hot, Darby." His voice is husky. "You're killing me, babe." One finger rubs my clit as another breaches my entrance.

"Ohmigod!" My right hand grips the handlebar so tight, the skin has turned white. My thighs clench around the seat. This is insane. I'm about to come on a moving motorcycle, and we haven't even kissed.

"Weneedtopullover. Weneedtopullover," I chant, trying to appear normal. I'm convinced anyone looking at us knows exactly what's going on.

His fingers keep moving. In and out. Around and around. Everywhere at once. It feels so fucking good.

"Ah!" I cry out as he hits the perfect spot.

Fuck it.

My eyes close, and my head lolls back. I don't care anymore that we're moving or if anyone can see. I'm in imminent orgasmic bliss, and it's the best thing I've ever felt. "Oh, god, Blake. Don't stop!"

"Not stopping, babe."

And he doesn't. He keeps stroking and finger fucking me like it's his job. "You feel so good, Darby. You're so wet, baby. Fuuuck."

It's the drawn-out fuck in his deep, husky voice that sends me over the edge. "Oh!" I scream as the world's fastest orgasm drills through me like a freight train.

"Ohgodfuckohgod. Ohgodfuckohgod." I'm pretty sure it's just nonsense leaving my mouth as I ride through the torrent of sensation disrupting the normal orchestrations of my body.

Blake whispers sweet nothings and compliments in my ear, telling me I'm a good girl in that sexy baritone of his which does crazy, wicked things to my insides all over again.

My brain tries to wrap itself around what just happened as I finally come back down from the most insane high I've ever experienced. As good as I feel from that, I'm sad it's over already. That I came so soon.

"Baby, that was fucking beautiful," Blake says as he pulls his fingers from inside me, making me whimper from the loss. "Don't worry. I'm just pulling over. I got you."

7

Blake

I pull over behind a big oak tree in a relatively secluded spot overgrown with seagrass and shrubbery. I barely have the bike stopped and the engine killed when Darby slips under my arm and is off the bike. She yanks her helmet off and screeches, "You just made me come on a moving motorcycle, Blake Moore!"

"I know." I pull off my helmet, and a lazy smile grows on my face. "I want to do it again."

"We could have died!"

"Doubtful, but I probably won't do it again while driving," I concede.

"Someone could have seen." Her voice is still amplified.

"No one's around, babe." I gesture with my arm as she walks toward me. "Fuck, you're hot," I say.

She reaches the bike that I'm still straddling. "C'mere." I crook a finger at her.

"I'm right here," she says, much softer this time. I grab her around the waist and pull her closer, searching her face for any signs of reluctance and seeing none. Her cheeks are flushed, and her eyes look a little dazed. She looks like she just had her world rocked, and I can't wait to do it again.

I dismount and hang our helmets on the bike, "I have an idea," I say. There's a blanket in my side storage that will be perfect. I disappear behind the tree we parked next to and spread it out in a small clearing surrounded by seagrass.

"Oh!" I hear from behind me and turn, I hadn't realized Darby had followed me.

"We don't have to do anything," I blurt, suddenly feeling foolishly presumptuous. "I thought it might be nice to hang out for a little bit."

"It will be," she says, moving closer until we're toe to toe. Her hands come up to rest on my chest a moment before snaking up and around my shoulders to join behind my neck.

My arms band around her waist, and I pull her flush against me so she can feel her effect on my cock, on me.

"Hi," I whisper, rubbing the tip of her nose with my own.

"Hi," she says.

I'm about to ask if I can kiss her when she leans in and presses her lips to mine in a soft and barely there kiss.

I guess that's my answer.

I bury a hand in her hair and take over the kiss. My tongue seeks hers, and she meets me in the middle, giving as good as she gets. I can't help the groan that escapes my chest. She feels amazing. Better than I'd imagined if that's even possible. I pull her thigh up my leg to the side of my waist, trying to get closer. She raises the other one and locks her feet together at my lower back.

"Fuck, Darby. You're going to be the death of me."

She tilts her hips and grinds against me, releasing little moans that send shockwaves through my system. My knees weaken. I lean to the side to try to reach the ground so I can sit us down. It's awkward as hell, and we end up tumbling down. I twist at the last second so Darby lands on me and not the other way around. She erupts with laughter.

I close my eyes as my face heats, embarrassed I couldn't keep it together.

"Ohmigod, thank you for not falling on me," she gasps.

I look at her, brow furrowed, unsure if I'm being laughed at. She laughs harder.

"You made my knees weak, woman," I growl, but there's no force behind it since I can't help but laugh with her.

"Stop laughing," she cries. "Your stomach moves and bounces me, making me laugh even harder." She's stretched over me, our faces mere inches apart, and I'm struck (again) by how beautiful she is. So, I tell her so as I tuck her hair behind her ear so it's out of her face.

Her laughter slows. "Is it weird that I feel beautiful when I'm with you?" Her cheeks flush lightly.

"That's not weird at all," I say. "It means I'm doing my job right."

"You're job?" She cocks her head.

I debate how to respond, then decide to just play my hand and let the cards fall where they may.

"I like you, Darby." My voice is raspy, but clearing my throat doesn't help. "A lot." My chest feels tight. "As more than a friend."

"I would hope so," she says. "You had your fingers inside me moments ago." Her smile holds a hint of mischief. She traces her fingers across my face, along my cheekbones and eyebrows, down around my jaw and over my chin, a look of wonder on her face.

"I want to do it again." I cup her cheek with my hand and pull her lips closer to mine. I like her touch, but I have other things in mind. She places her hand against my chest to slow her descent, forcing me to let her take the lead.

Her head lowers, and her tongue peeks from between her lips to trace mine; my body vibrates with restraint. She brushes her lips back and forth on mine; the contact is so soft, it barely registers. But still, my cock is hard as steel from her touch. My fists clench against her back and ass as I hold myself back.

"I want you to do it again," she says against my lips.

Which I take as an invitation. I flip us so she's on her back, and I'm above her with my weight braced on my forearms. I cradle her face in my hands and kiss her. Hard. There's nothing slow or soft about it. My tongue plunges in her mouth, and my lips press against hers as fierce as they are passionate.

"Mmm," she moans and wraps her legs around my waist, pulling my cock against her center.

"Jesus," I pant. My hands leave her face to explore her body. Her waist and hips, her thighs and ass. Oh god, that ass. One hand fills with those luscious globes of rounded flesh as the other travels to her breasts. I can't get enough. Each tit is a perfectly formed twin mound that fits in the palm of my hand. Needing to see them, I pull at her stretchy top to bare them. Her nipples are hard and pebbled, and my lips automatically leave hers and travel down to pull one into my mouth with a long, hard draw. She arches with a long moan.

I want to watch that beautiful face when she comes this time. I grind my hips against her, trying to find a groove she likes. Her needy whimpers join the sounds of tiny waves casting on the sand.

"Ohmigod," she breathes. "I think I could come like this."

I'm dying to fuck her. Instead, I squeeze an arm between us to work my fingers between her legs, seeking out that wet, hot paradise that resides there.

"I can help with that." I pull her shorts and panties to the side, revealing trim curls and a beautiful, glistening pussy. "Fuck. Look at you, beautiful, sexy girl." My voice is gravelly with need.

"Oh god!" she cries out as I bury two fingers in her. "Holy shit, that feels good."

I use my thumb to rub her juices around her clit as my fingers pump in and out of her. She's so wet, I can hear it, which drives me fucking crazy with desire.

"Blake," she pleads.

"Yeah, baby?" My lips travel to her neck, biting and sucking on the sensitive skin, feeling her pussy clench when I do something she likes.

"Blake," she breathes. "Blake. God. Blake," she repeats, like a mantra, until her body stiffens, and her muscles clamp down around my fingers. I raise my head to see. Fuck, she's gorgeous when she comes. Her head arches back, the veins in her neck thrum, and her hands form a death grip on my biceps as the waves of pleasure roll through her.

She is fucking exquisite. I could watch her do this forever.

"Mmm." She opens her eyes after a moment, but they stay at half-mast. "Wow." Her cheeks are flushed, and a loopy post-orgasmic smile covers her face. She grips my face in her hands and pulls me down to capture my mouth with hers. "You are my favorite person in the whole world," she says before kissing me again.

I smile back, but it's strained. My dick is raging hard against the confines of my jeans. I was *this close* to getting off by getting her off. "I've never wanted anything as much as I want you, Darby."

Her hands move to the button on my jeans to unfasten them. "Have me."

Fuck, yes!

I help her get them lower on my ass and before I can blink, she's got my dick out of my boxers and in her grip.

I nearly black out.

My body spasms. I clench my jaw, trying with all my might not to come. "Oh fuck. Darby. Baby. Fuck. Stop. Don't move." I don't want this to be over before it begins.

She pushes at me to roll over, then straddles my hips and kisses her way along my jaw to my neck. Her tongue slowly draws up to my ear. "I want to make you feel good," she whispers and bites the lobe gently.

"You make me feel good just being here."

"Aw, that's sweet," she says cheekily. "Now, fuck me."

Goddammit!

"I don't have any condoms," I groan.

"I'm on birth control," she says.

I hesitate, knowing her ex cheated on her. "I got tested right after I moved out," she says as though reading my mind. "First thing." She rises to her knees, my dick back in her hands, and her pussy hovering over my tip. "Please, Blake."

"I'm not lasting long bare," I warn as she sinks down on me.

Oh. My. Fucking. God.

This time, I'm pretty sure I do black out.

Someone lets out a long, shuddering moan—it may have been me—as I bottom out inside her. My hands dig in at her hips to keep her still. "Don't move, baby. Give me one second." My eyes squeeze shut. Never mind moving. If I breathe, I'm going to come.

"Blake." Her voice is a low whimper.

Fuck it.

I'm as much in control as I'll ever get. If I come, I'll make it up to her.

She quickly finds a rhythm she likes. Up and down. Back and forth. Her hips cast a spell over my cock that I don't think I'll ever get out from under. She feels decadent around me.

"Oh, Blake. You feel so... wow," she cries. Her breasts bounce as she undulates her body over me, hypnotizing me with her moves. I grab one and tweak the nipple; her low, guttural moan almost does me in.

"Sorry, baby." I switch our positions so she's on her back and fuck her with a fury I can't contain.

Savage, brutal thrusts.

My hips piston at a ruthless pace.

I'm feral.

Out of control.

I can't get enough. Not deep enough, not fast enough, not hard enough.

The blanket bunches and moves as I drive into her again and again. I'm out of my mind with lust and so fucking close to coming, my head spins. She bites down on my shoulder to smother her cries as she peaks again.

It's so hot.

So wet.

So.

Fucking.

Good.

This time, she brings me with her.

I bury my face between her breasts as I come with a roar. Violent and uncontained. My body shudders uncontrollably, and my hips continue to pump. Once. Twice. Three times before stilling. I let it all go inside her. Everything I have.

I'm spent. Done.

I roll to the side and bring her with me, my cock still inside her. Her body drapes over mine listlessly as we try to catch our breath. My arms lock around her small frame like she's the life raft, and I'm drowning.

I have never.

Ever.

Come so hard in my life.

It takes minutes, multiple minutes, to catch my breath. "That... was..." I struggle to think of the right word.

"Mind blowing," Darby finishes.

I smile and lean in to kiss her softly. "Yes."

We lie on the blanket, wrapped in each other's arms, listening to the slaps of the tiny bay waves on the sand as they compete with the calls of the seagulls circling above.

I can't think of a more perfect moment than right now.

After a bit longer, she pushes off me gingerly, wincing slightly.

"Did I hurt you?"

"Only in the absolute best way," she says. "But I'm not sure I'm party appropriate any longer." She stands and gestures at her outfit; it's utterly destroyed. The crotch of her shorts/dress thing is wet and twisted, drooping between her thighs. The elastic stretchy top has lost its stretch in places where I ripped the seams. Her hair is a tangled mess from both my hands and the blanket, and her eye makeup has pooled under her eyes.

"You look absolutely beautiful," I say, standing and tucking myself back in my jeans.

She shakes one leg to the side and laughs as our combined juices run down her thigh. "I don't know about that."

"I do." I cup her cheek and plant a soft kiss on her lips. "Wait right here."

I get the wipes from my bike and turn back. She's shaking the blanket, preparing to fold it. I take it from her and toss it to the side. Then I kneel and use the wipes to clean her as best I can, planting small, reverent kisses along her abdomen and thighs as I go.

This woman owns me now. Body and soul.

She has tears in her eyes when I stand.

"Are you okay?" I cradle her chin in my palm; my brow furrows in concern. "Did I do something?"

"No." She shakes her head and smiles. "You're amazing. That"—she gestures to where we were lying—"was amazing."

I run my thumb along the smooth skin of her cheekbone. "You're amazing," I say truthfully.

She rolls her eyes.

"Look at me." My voice is harsher than I intend, but I need her to hear me on this.

Her eyes meet mine.

"You are everything." I plant small kisses on her face to punctuate my words. "Smart, funny, drop-dead gorgeous, sexy as hell, and fucking amazing."

She pulls back and searches my face. "Okay, fine," she says with a valley girl-like drawl. "We're both ah-mazing, and we have, like, totally ah-mazing sex."

We laugh, and I feel happier than I have a right to.

"You wanna head out?" I ask.

She nods.

"You, uh, wouldn't want to skip the party, would you?" I hedge, as we walk hand in hand back to the bike.

"Ohmigod, yes," she groans. "Is that okay?"

"It was my idea," I say. "I'm happy to have you to myself for the rest of the day."

"Me too," she says, smiling.

We're almost home, and I offer to make us lunch when we get there —I've worked up an appetite.

"Make sure it's protein packed," she says, sounding coy.

"Why?" I chuckle.

"So, we're ready for round two." She gives my waist a quick squeeze for emphasis.

My chest tightens with emotion, and I can't stop the smile that fills my face. I will do

everything in my power to make sure this woman feels loved and appreciated every day.

I have to.

Because if round two is anything like round one, I'm never letting her go.

8

Darby

Round two was even better.

And it just keeps going with each new day surpassing the one before it. Not just the sex, but everything about the two of us together. It's weird because Blake thinks *he's* the lucky one. But I know the truth.

Somehow, I got my unicorn.

And he's a sexy, generous, loyal unicorn endowed with a long, thick, girthy horn that I get to ride on the regular. And my life couldn't get any better.

About the Author

Denise has been reading since before she could talk. And to this day, escaping into a book is her go-to activity before anything else.

She likes to write about sassy women and semi-flawed alpha-esque men (hard on the outside and just a little soft on the inside.) Denise's female characters always have strong friendships, potty mouths, and like to drink—a lot.

Denise is loyal to a fault, a bit too sarcastic, blindingly optimistic, and pretty freakin' happy with life overall. If she couldn't be a writer, she'd be a singer in a classic rock band. Right after she learned to carry a tune. She has more purses than days in the month, an obsession with colored ink pens, and a slightly unhealthy bracelet habit.

Home is in the Pacific Northwest where she lives with six special needs Siberian Huskies and a husband (BW) who has the patience and tolerance of a saint. And, lest she forget, Denise also lives with too many to count characters inside her head, who will eventually have their stories told.

For more about Denise visit her website at: www.DeniseWells.com
Or follow her on any of the social media sites below:
facebook.com/denisewellsauthor
instagram.com/denisewellsauthor
bookbub.com/authors/denise-wells
goodreads.com/denisewells
pinterest.com/denisewellsauthor
tiktok.com/@denisewellsauthor
patreon.com/DeniseWells

Frenching My Flatmate

Skye Knight

1

Day One

Man nipples greeted Izzy's first step into her new Parisian townhouse. There was a lot to take in with the open format of the space, but the nipples belonged to a ridiculously hot specimen of a man and captivated her attention despite her resolve to remain focused on her studies.

Clad only in shorts, the man sat cross-legged on the floor of the kitchen. His hands rested palm-up on his knees, his eyes were shut, and there was no tension in his trim body.

Gripped between envy and attraction at his relaxed state, Izzy dismissed it as an option for her.

"Ahh, enfin! Coucou ma chérie et bienvenue chez nous!" The French chatter broke her from her contemplation, and a smile erupted across her face as she kissed the cheeks of her new French flatmates.

"We cannot wait for you to experience all Paris has to offer!" Roxane said with a big grin.

"I'm sorry it's just me, and Avery couldn't come," Izzy said.

Camille arched an eyebrow. "No apologies. You are la crème de la crème, a future brilliant neurosurgeon after you graduate from Paris Descartes." She leaned close and whispered, "And Julien isn't so bad on the eyes, non?"

"Or ears, it appears," Izzy added, lifting her hands in a shrug and gesturing toward him, slightly perturbed that he hadn't acknowledged her presence.

"Don't let him bother you, Isabel. He's cordial once he breaks his meditative state," Camille said.

Her bestie, Avery, had sworn that since she couldn't move to Paris with her, her cousin Julien would help Izzy stay chill. Izzy wasn't so sure about that with the way his shirtlessness had made her hot already.

"Come, let's get you and your stuff settled in your room. Julien already carried the boxes you had delivered there for you."

Hustling while lugging her bags, she followed her cheerful leaders. Julien didn't flinch a muscle as they banged into furniture and made a racket.

Distracted, she clipped the corner of the kitchen table with her rolling bag. Atop a blue-and-white porcelain bowl mounded high with superfluous apples, a single red one wobbled, thumped down the pile, and tumbled across the table to fall to the floor by Julien's knee.

Roxane and Camille giggled as they ducked into the bedroom. Julien remained still as a marble-cut statue.

"What's up with the apples?" The quantity was absurd.

Roxane called back, "He eats a lot but super clean. It's a Julien thing."

Izzy rolled her eyes. As an aspiring doctor, she supported healthy choices, but there was no way to eat that many apples before they went bad. Releasing her bag and squatting next to him, she grasped the fruit. Best to toss it since it would be too bruised to enjoy after its adventure from mountain to man.

She paused when rising to admire the man's gorgeous lips. His dark scruff highlighted their softness. Wondering what they might feel like against hers came as a shock.

Kissing hadn't crossed her mind in years since she'd been focused on caring for her mother and studying. Before her mom got sick, Izzy had been a social butterfly in high school—cheerleading, going to parties, kissing cute boys. But she didn't move to Paris in pursuit of the light fun of a teen. So why were these lips making her stop and stare?

It was as though he was emitting some kind of weird energy with his aura.

She shook her head, chucked the apple in the trash, and pushed into the small room.

Attacking the bags and boxes, she and the girls chatted as they worked seamlessly. Izzy was grateful for their help, since she'd flown in early and had only the weekend to get settled before her first day of classes.

She'd packed lightly, knowing that the space would be negligible. All she needed were clothes and books. After her mom had passed, she went through probate to handle her mother's debts and affairs. Izzy had chosen to let go of most things that just carried sad memories. That included the US and the home she once had.

The girls were hanging her clothing and remarking, not unkindly, how they'd have to help her adopt a more Parisian style. To be fair, she tended to favor the American college student aesthetic of oversized sweats and little shirts. Cute and comfy, yes, but lacking any sort of sophistication.

Trying to find places to stack all the heavy textbooks she'd preordered from the university, Izzy came across her sentimental box. Her heart squeezed at the sight of the unopened letter within it, but it wasn't time to deal with that yet. There wasn't much else in the box other than a few items to display on the wall over her desk.

First, a pic of her and Avery at twelve, gangly, with matching smiles full of braces.

Avery was one of the few who'd known her before she became a big ball of stress. Ignored by her own parents, Izzy's mom had folded Avery into their household like a second daughter. Which meant they were more than friends for life. They were sisters.

Next, a picture of Izzy on top of a pyramid of cheerleaders, a reminder of lighter times when she hadn't carried the weight of the world.

Last, a photo of beloved Mama. Smiling as she hung that one, she stroked it with reverence.

That's when she became aware of the stillness of her flatmates watching her.

"Elle est très charmante," Camille said as she moved closer to look.

"Merci. She's why I'm here. My mother died of a brain tumor a little less than a year ago. She got sick, and that's when I decided to become a neurosurgeon. She was a single mom and my best friend." Grief swept through her. "I'd do anything to bring her back."

Roxane rested a hand on Izzy's shoulder, and Izzy sank to the bed. She wasn't one to let people in and liked to retain her hard shell, but with her nerves frayed from all the change and their warm acceptance, she just gave in and wept.

The liberation of those tightly wrought feelings was as if someone had sliced through ropes to release a prisoner. Maybe she'd find a new way here.

2

Day Two

Slinging her keys on the console table and dropping her bookbag on the floor, Izzy released a sigh and ran her hands over her face. She could visualize Marcel's sneer as he said, "You know they'll never give the best rotations to a non-native French speaker."

Prick.

Crunch. Spinning on her heel toward the open room, she found Julien's pretty eyes contemplating her as he bit into an apple.

"Oh, hi." She smiled and waved a little, then tucked her arms behind her back. "I thought I was the only one here."

"Clairemente." He gestured to the seat across from him at the kitchen table and took another bite of la pomme.

No bisous? It was silly to resent that he didn't give her the traditional French greeting, yet she was contemplating his lips again. She almost envied the apple, and she bet he also tasted sweet. But was he sweet? To be determined. At least he was wearing a T-shirt today.

Sliding into the seat, she tucked her hair behind her ear. "I'm Izzy. Nice to meet you."

"Enchantée. Sorry I wasn't able to introduce myself yesterday. I am very fond of Avery. She raves about you."

He sat straight but relaxed, hands resting in his lap.

"What took you so long to get home?" he asked, his focus making her self-conscious.

"How do you know my schedule?"

"The girls—Rox and Cami—who hate when I call them that, by the way," he said with a grin, "insisted that I wait here for your return since it was your first time out in France by yourself."

"OMG. That is so embarrassing. You did *not* need to do that. I'm a big girl," she said, flushing.

"No worries. I don't have appointments with my clients on the weekends. I graduated from Ecole Européene d'Acupuncture a year ago, so I understand your situation."

He lifted the apple for another bite. Chewing slowly, his eyes closed like he was savoring the tart flavors.

Enthralled, she watched his mouth and throat work. His neck was slender but muscular. As Mr. Healthy, she wondered how he moved and built such a body.

"I was a little upset." She shrugged.

"I gathered," he said with a chuckle.

"Yeah. I was assigned to collaborate with a group of classmates for the quarter, and we agreed to meet before the school week started, but this prick of a Frenchman—" She winced, worrying he might take offense.

"Don't worry, I'm French-Tunisian," he interjected with a smile. It was adorable, and his teeth were nice.

He wasn't a horse. Why was she inspecting and admiring his teeth?

"Oh, totally different then?" she teased, hoping he hadn't noticed her gazing at his mouth.

"Trust me, it is. You'll learn."

"Gotcha. Well, prickface didn't like my American ways and was dismissive of me. It's not how I dreamed anyone would treat me in front of my new classmates. And now I feel like I have to prove myself even more."

"He's threatened by you."

"Regardless, I'm already so anxious with my desire to succeed over here, and he piled on my pressure party, so I wandered to the Curie

Museum, hoping to be inspired and reminded of the goodness in what I'm doing. But that museum is closed on Sundays, so I wandered the Jardin de Luxembourg. A band played music, children were navigating little boats in the pond, people of all ages dueled in chess—" She cut off her self-conscious babbling.

"It was good to allow yourself to wander without destination."

"I mean, the destination was still here. I was just lost in my thoughts."

"But you were present enough to notice your surroundings." He nodded his approval.

A thrill of pleasure shot down her core. That was all it took with her current desperation for validation. She'd come to see him as the guru of finding peace already.

"May I have your hand?"

Heck, she'd give him her lips if he'd asked. Why was he so compelling?

"You Americans all 'live to work' rather than 'work to live'—and care so much," he said. "Chinese pulse diagnosis. Do you mind?"

It was true about most Americans as compared to the rest of the world. His warm, strong hands held hers, his calm steadiness undeniably appealing. She attempted to moderate her breathing and relax. She would give anything to present his kind of self-assurance and control without holding on so tightly.

Using three fingers, he moved along her wrist, applying steady pressure. His touch was so sure, she wondered how much he could perceive about her. An edginess overtook her body, a mix of tension that verged on arousal.

She imagined those three fingers elsewhere: pressing, feeling, probing.

Eyes shooting to his, she was met with heat. Releasing her wrist and withdrawing, he licked his lips again.

She didn't think it was because of the apple this time.

"Your pulse is strong." He cleared his throat. "Not unexpected with your stress. You need to find ways to alleviate the pressure with sleep, breathing, diet, exercise, acupuncture."

He didn't say sex, but was he thinking it like she was?

"I'm fascinated by your practice." She was, but she needed to escape his powerful chi or she might do something embarrassing. Giving his lips one last look in spite of herself, she stood. "I'll let you know if I need more direction."

Those lips quirked. "It'd be my pleasure."

3

Day Three

His lips pressed against hers, hard and warm. She'd forgotten how good it was to be kissed. He was rubbing them softly back and forth when she heard applause. What in the hell?

Izzy, hella turned on, flickered her bleary eyes open. She was studying a laborious text, and the exhaustion from her first day of classes had walloped her. She'd meant to lie down for only a few minutes to rest—what time was it now?

The red numbers on her analog clock blinked 17:00. Her roomies were watching a TV show featuring an audience. In its resting state, her brain had dreamed of making out with Julien. With the background noise, she might be able to get away with burning off more stress. Trying to focus on her lessons without fulfilling the ache would be fruitless.

After riffling through her nightstand to pull out her trusty suction vibrator, she grazed it over her nipples, once again imagining his lush lips before centering it over her nub that was tight with longing. Releasing a sigh, she thanked the toy's makers for the quiet design and prayed the old walls of the place weren't too thin.

Usually, as her pleasure climbed, her mind would go blank. She wasn't much for fantasy and didn't need visuals to get herself there. She handled the fundamental release her body needed and moved on, having little use for crushes or men, remaining focused on her more significant goals.

And yet, this time, Julien's image didn't whisk away. In her mind's eye, Izzy saw his wiry form, making slow and methodical choices in how he teased out her wishes until he had her fantasy self begging. What was it about his steady nature and dry humor reflecting in that twinkle of his eyes that made her want to relinquish the tension in her body to him?

Since he had aimed to know the body intimately and what alleviated its pain, she bet he was a selfless and thoughtful lover. Regardless, imaginary Julien was fucking hot in a way that she hadn't found any man until now. The idea of giving herself over to him heightened her arousal, and she crescendoed at the thought of his mouth over her very center, sucking the stress out.

A low moan accompanied a single shake of her legs, and Izzy let herself lie loose-limbed, mind blank for a peaceful moment.

Awareness checking back in, she hoped her bliss had gone unnoticed. Shoving her little friend back into his hiding place, Izzy sprang out of bed. She had much to do to avoid falling behind in her course load. Time to use the facilities and get some fuel.

Stepping out of her room, hair mussed and clothes wrinkled, she glanced over at Camille and Roxane reclining on the couch, watching tennis on classic red clay courts. Oh, to be able to embrace their c'est la vie. They still had school and work but didn't let it keep them from relaxing.

She slipped into the shared petit coin to relieve herself before going to the refrigerator.

Bending over to dig through the drawers, she located the fromage and backed out only to bump against a hard, warm body. It was also damp.

"Whoa there." Two hands landed on her hips to steady her, which she didn't need but wouldn't complain about.

Straightening and shutting the fridge, she pivoted toward Julien. When his hands fell away, their absence was noticeable. They'd conveyed energy, soothing while stirring.

"Um, I know it's a small kitchen, but did you have to stand so close?" Why was he sweaty and shirtless? Again, with the man nipples!

"I was curious what you were going to get." Shrugging, his cute smile slipped across his face.

It melted her, drawing her stare to his lips again. She had to say something.

"Where are you coming from?" She forced her eyes to meet his, holding the cheese in front of her chest as though the Comté were a shield.

Taking it from her, Julien set it on a small platter. He turned to the sink and washed and dried his hands before unwrapping the cheese. The silence stretched out as he utilized deft strokes to slice it super thin.

"My bedroom," he said at last, raising his eyes to give her a knowing look.

She went stock still.

"After my long, tension-relieving run, my shirt was soaked with sweat. I went to toss it in my hamper because it was making me cold. From what I heard, it sounded like you found a way to release your stress, too."

He punctuated his comment with a wink and stuck a piece of cheese into his mouth.

Fffff me. Waves of mortification mixed with shocks of arousal sliced through her body, flushing her face and spreading heat farther south.

Her expression caused the languid spread of a wry smile across his face.

"What, you think I haven't wanked one when you're here?"

To me? Because mine was definitely to you.

She shoved a slice in her trap before she said something she'd regret. They stood there, chewing, watching each other. The amusement in his eyes made smiling back unavoidable.

"Shut up. If it's gouda for you, it's gouda for me."

His responding chuckle lightened her, reminding her of the last time she and Avery had shared some hilarity, laughing until they cried.

"Julien—isn't this your famous ex?" Camille called from the sitting area.

Storm clouds formed, and his brows drew together. Sliding past Izzy, he went to join their flatmates, and she followed.

On the screen, a slender woman, elegant with long ash-blond hair in a ponytail, smiled and answered the interviewer's questions. She leaned on a tall man in tennis whites with a ball cap, her hand resting on his shoulder.

When she said she gave all the credit to her coach beside her, Julien used the TV remote to snap it off.

"Ce que c'est que ce bordel? We were watching the match!" Roxane exclaimed.

He turned and prowled from the living room to his bedroom, clicking the door shut behind him.

4
Day Four

Izzy directed the taxi to the once-artsy neighborhood of Hemingway. She'd enjoyed her new favorite dish—prosciutto with melon—with Camille and Roxane, venting about her second day of classes with that asshole Marcel. He continued to hassle her, implying that she was deficient both as an American and a woman.

But her flatmates would stay at that sidewalk café for who knew how long, and that was not in her ability, no matter how much conceptually she admired the culture.

Izzy had things to do.

Especially since she was driven to prove Marcel wrong. Despite needing to save money, she'd taken a taxi home because she was desperate to maximize her studying time.

Climbing out of the cab, her laptop bag weighed down with books almost brought her to her knees as she slung it over her shoulder.

Turning her head caused pain to shoot down her neck. After moving it and deciding she was not paralyzed, she shut the door and thanked the driver with a "merci!"

Holy hell, what had she done? She slipped the strap over her other shoulder, and inched toward the steps, rolling her neck to loosen it.

Entering the apartment and shutting the door, she turned, and there was Julien, as if on cue.

Why was he always wet and shirtless?

Rubbing a towel brusquely over his dark hair, he scattered droplets over defined shoulders and pecs. He didn't seem real, more like something out of a movie. Looking around to see if this perfect male specimen was on display for someone else, another shock of pain jolted her, making her wince.

"Isabel? Ca va?"

He tossed the towel over a kitchen chair and then was beside her, hands on either side of her face, looking into her eyes. The absentminded intimacy of holding her face almost made her eyes tear up. Her neck hurt so damn bad, though she didn't want to admit it. She knew there was no shame in doing so, and that admitting she hurt was an essential factor in a medical evaluation.

But having someone care about her without really knowing her, when she was alone without her mama or best friend, was a comfort.

"I'm all right! It's like I'm an old woman instead of a first-year med student. I somehow tweaked my neck getting out of the cab with my bag."

"Let me take that." Removing the bag from her shoulders, he cast her an admonishing look. He curled her bookbag, bicep bulging. "Is this a joke? I'd use this for lifting if I was into that sort of thing."

While he did super marathon runs and bodyweight workouts, she didn't know how he wasn't lifting with arms like that. If she weren't in such pain, she'd salivate.

Something must be wrong with her; she did *not* have time to notice boys.

"I don't really need the books for class, but it's the first week. I want to make a good impression, and I don't want to be caught unprepared." She could only imagine the snide remark Marcel would make if the American girl was the one who didn't have what she needed.

Tears filled her eyes for the second time since her arrival. She must be strung too tight.

"I have to study, there's so much to do, and I left Camille and

Roxane to do it, but then I went and debilitated myself. I may as well pack up and go home."

"This is your home now. And I get the impression you're a fighter. You're not about to give up." He ran his hand up and down her arm to soothe her while keeping space between them.

Her eyes slid to watch the muscles flex in his forearms. "This is so humiliating. I don't know what's wrong with me. I'm just so—"

"Overwhelmed?"

"That's part of it."

"Would you let me help you?"

"Whatever it takes to be able to study again." Shrugging forced another wince from her.

"Fire cupping and acupuncture would relieve a lot of the stress and tension you're carrying, plus I can try to get that trigger point ailing you to release. We can work on the upper half of your back, with just a few needles in other places to tap into your parasympathetic nerve system."

"I don't know much about Eastern medicine, though I'm willing to give it a shot. But I need to study now," Izzy said. Going to his clinic would be a huge delay.

"I can treat you in my room. I have everything for home visits."

Stepping back, he looked at her. Unlike some, needles never creeped her out, and she knew he was certified and had put in the hours.

She was hesitant to be vulnerable but conceded. "Okay, let's do it."

Flushing at her word choice, she dipped her head and gestured for him to lead.

"You'll get a lot of relief, Izzy," he said.

Entering his room, he pulled on a soft crew shirt and lit incense, dimmed the lights, and turned on instrumental music. He popped open the massage table and covered it with sheets.

He handed her a hospital gown. "You can lose everything but the underwear if you're comfortable with that. Lie face down, and just drape this over your rear."

She tried to focus on what he was saying and not on his lips' beautiful shape. He was a medical professional giving her a treatment that he was trained to administer. That was all this was. As she reached for the gown, the pain reminded her of her purpose.

When he stepped out of the room, she removed all but her thong, thankful it was just a plain black pair and nothing embarrassing, though he wouldn't see it with the gown covering. Despite the intensity of his gaze in the past, she didn't think he'd be checking her out.

Settling on the table, she tugged the gown over her backside but didn't unfold it as much as she could have, stopping herself from overthinking her motivations.

In-two-three-four. Holding for four, exhaling for four, and holding again. She prayed the box breathing would calm her nerves. Though wasn't that what the acupuncture was for?

His feet padded across his rug, and she heard glass clinking.

"You ready?"

She nodded her assent, not trusting her voice. At least her face was hidden. Oh God, he could probably read her body even better.

He laid his hand on her upper spine, letting her get used to his touch so she wouldn't jump. With expertise, he moved his hand along her back, rubbing and squeezing to identify the areas of tension.

"We'll start with the cups, and then I will apply the first set of needles around them." He told her what he was doing before he did it. No surprises.

A match was struck, and she smelled smoke. The pulling sensation as the first cup pressed to her back was relieving. A pressure inverse from her shoulders drawing taut.

"Can you explain what fire cupping is exactly?" she asked, trying to take her mind off him touching her body. While it was relaxing, the Julien factor created a different tension.

"Sure. So, I soak the cotton balls in alcohol and light them. I hold that in the cup to evenly heat the air inside and then place the cup on the skin. That's what creates the suction."

"Oh, cool." Izzy probably should know these things.

"Some clinicians use plastic cups, likely because they don't want fire in their offices and use vacuum pumps instead, but they don't work as well."

After he'd applied eight cups alongside her spine, he said, "Okay, now for the needles."

He started at the top of her neck below the skull, measuring the distance from her spine and adding a needle to each side. With a quick twist here and there, he tuned her like a guitar.

When he hit a particular spot in her trap, right where the pain was centralized and shot up into her neck, he delivered extra turns and wiggles that hurt a bit, but she tried to breathe and relax into it. She trusted him, she realized.

Continuing, he applied a few more needles to her back and some to the outsides of her hands, ankles, upper calves, and ears. It was such a strange sensation.

Wheeling over a heat lamp, he switched it on. "I'll leave you for a little while, and then I'll come back to remove the cups and add needles in their place. Are you all right?"

Though aware of the devices sucking and poking her back, she wasn't uncomfortable. The lamp's warmth was lovely.

"No, I'm good."

He left. Izzy tried to ease into stillness, but her mind kept jumping around. His caretaking was so sweet. Maybe a relationship could supplement her life and goals rather than impede them. That was a nice thought.

The next thing she knew, he was back, and she wondered whether she'd been drooling.

The cups were coming off, and already the pain was less. What was this magic?

"I had a sensation like a thread was running between the needles," she said, surprised at the huskiness of her voice.

"Yes, that's the energy. There's not physically a thread, but they're all connected with your nervous system."

Now, he was applying more needles along her spine, one to two inches on either side. It was an exacting science as to where to put them. Some he twisted more than others; some hit a nerve, yet sometimes it was stimulating. He was an expert musician, and her body, the instrument. She studied the human body, but his connection to her physicality and energy was stunning.

When he left again, the darkness consumed her, and random muscles shuddered their release, out of her control. She held on so tight she had to be prodded and needled to let go, but God, it was so necessary, so needed, so right.

Time was lost to her, but when he returned, the needles slipped away quicker than she was ready. Then, his hands were on her, solid and warm. Testing for tension.

"Better? How do you feel?" His voice was deep, care in his questions.

She didn't want him to stop touching her. His touch was so soothing after all her energy had been trained to the tune he'd set. The song had ended, but she wasn't prepared for the quiet. He was entirely professional, yet as the strain left her, she wanted a different release from him.

"Much." It was all she could manage without giving away her thoughts.

"You will likely be a little sore, and there may be some bruising and swelling in the morning, but I hope the crick has released enough for you to get done what you need to tonight."

How did he know she needed him? Realization hit her with a wave. Her studying! That was what he was referring to her needing. How had he expunged that stress from her mind?

"Thank you. I really appreciate it. Sorry to put you to work at home."

"Got to take care of yourself, Doc. Happy to help."

He left her to dress. As she pulled on her clothes, she was amazed at how much looser her muscles were and that she was able to move her neck again. But while her physical pain had been alleviated, she still had so much to do, and now, she was strapped with even more distracting thoughts of Julien to impede her progress.

5

Day Five

Drizzle fell as Izzy walked along the Seine. Disappointment hung over her like a cloud ever since she'd discovered most of the over 900 bouquinistes of Paris were closed, their green metal boxes pulled shut to protect the used books.

Truthfully, a cloud had hung over her since she'd stumbled across Julien in the kitchen—finally shirted to go into his office—and he'd inspected her healing. While he was rubbing the back of her neck as she faced the counter, she looked down at his cell in front of her and was surprised to see his ex on his lock screen.

Why did he still have a picture of her on his phone?

It shouldn't bug her. But it did.

Then at school, Marcel had made snarky comments about her need for self-care and her high-stress nature when he glimpsed red circles peeking out of her shirt.

Earlier that morning, when she'd looked in the mirror and realized Julien had marked her, she was surprised by her strange attachment to the spots.

She'd attempted to shut Marcel up, stating that she'd have more knowledge of all medical practices than he ever would, but he just laughed at her. Asshole.

So, on her route home she'd decided to take a detour to play tourist and visit a literary landmark of the city, since she and her mother had shared a love of books.

Failure and rain turned her mood gloomy, but her phone buzzed in her back pocket, and when she saw Avery's name on the screen, a ray of sunshine found its way in.

"Bonjour!"

"Oh, stop! Now you're making me jealous! How's the first week?"

"Well, as I texted, there's this asshole in my class—"

"Assholes are everywhere."

"True enough. The workload is already overwhelming, and it's raining."

"All right, Eeyore. At least you like your flatmates and apartment."

"Thanks to you! I am grateful for your cuz. He's helped me manage my stress."

"Please tell me you didn't let him poke you."

"Ha! Not like that! As I'm sure you know." But damn, Izzy did want him to.

"As much as I'd like you to have that kind of fun, it's for the best. I don't know if Julien's healed from the breakup that caused him to move."

Avery's words confirmed her fears and affirmed that she shouldn't be tempted to let a man distract her from her goals.

"It sucks not having you here. But I'm glad Julien was able to take your room. He does model good energy. Maybe someday I'll figure out how to slow down."

Then the sky opened.

"Shit! It's pouring! I gotta run and grab a cab."

"All right, babe. Keep breathing and taking time for yourself. You're in the City of Light, so find ways to lighten up!"

"Yeah, well, tell that to the rain clouds. Laters," she said and snorted.

"Later! Tell Julien bonjour for me!"

In earlier delusional moments, she'd contemplated whether Paris was also the city of love. Resolved now, Izzy wouldn't fantasize about such things.

6
Day Six

Izzy couldn't believe she had a test the first week of school, but she was determined to score higher than assface Marcel.

Last night, on the living room couch, zoned out with her earbuds in, Julien had rested his hands on her neck to check her over.

"Would you stop pushing and prodding me? I don't have time for this!" She'd slammed her laptop shut and stormed to her room.

The pressure to do well on the test, her muddled feelings about Julien after her conversation with Avery, and then his distracting presence made her combustible, but Julien didn't deserve her bad mood.

Izzy had continued studying after her outburst, even falling asleep on her textbook, but she hoped she'd absorbed some of its content via osmosis.

Today, she'd been studying nonstop since class ended, but now she was spent. She knew the content backward and forward, and studying more was inconceivable.

An alarm popped up on her phone, reminding her that it had been a year since her mom had passed. Not like she'd forgotten. Avery had been texting and calling incessantly. Izzy had just tersely replied that she was fine and had an exam to study for.

The truth was that she was delaying opening the letter her mother had left her to read on this milestone.

Izzy hadn't been willing to read it until she was confident she'd reviewed everything because she knew it would wring her emotions and she had to prioritize the test.

The alarm had been going off every hour on the hour, but it was time.

Digging through her sentimental box, she found the envelope, flowers wrapping the edges and Izzy's name across the front in her mother's unmistakable looping cursive.

Her mother was a magnificent letter-writer.

My dearest Isabel,

You filled the last years of my life with your love and light.

I am honored my sickness fueled your passion for preserving and prolonging life. We only had each other, but while my gratitude is eternal, you refused to relinquish the caretaking role for even a second.

If you don't live your life, though, what are you preserving? I know you wouldn't trade your years by my side for anything and that our shared love was enough.

But love, honey, is what makes the world go round. I hope as you pursue the passion of your career, you also find the passion in your heart.

I lost your father young, but as Tennyson said, " 'tis better to have loved and lost than never to have loved at all."

To the light of my life, may you find yours.

You have all my love forever.

Mama

The quiet tears running down Izzy's face were cleansing. It was like her mother was by her side. Like she saw Izzy, as she always did. Her mama knew that Izzy had wanted to control everything and would never let go long enough to love.

A kitchen cabinet shut. Julien.

She needed to apologize.

After quickly rubbing some lotion over her face to brighten it and erase the tearstains, she hurried to catch him.

He was pacing in gray sweats and a white T-shirt, lips pursed like he didn't know what he wanted.

Such pretty lips. Gosh, would she ever not want to kiss him? Only one way to find out.

Walking toward him, she trailed her hand along the kitchen table. He paused his stalking to look at her with hesitation in his eyes.

Might as well get on with it.

"I'm sorry, Julien. I know you were only trying to help yesterday. And what you did worked. I just—no excuses. My first exam is tomorrow, and I'm not regulating my emotions well."

"I appreciate your self-knowledge. Apology accepted. Is there anything I can do? I don't like feeling helpless when I see someone in need."

"Well, honestly, I was wondering—" She shifted her weight between her feet, casting her eyes down, embarrassed.

"Yes?"

"The um, girl on your phone? That's your ex, right? Are you not over her?"

The quizzical expression on his face was almost humorous. "The what?" He pulled his phone out and glanced at it. "Ugh. I didn't even realize that was still there, to be honest. I'm pretty anti-technology, and she saved her own photo on it. I don't even know how to get it off."

She giggled, but that didn't explain the other day. "What about when you turned the TV off when she was on?"

"I was annoyed because Rox and Cami said that she was famous, but she's like French-famous. No one outside our country would know her. Also, she gives all the credit to her coach, but he's the very reason I had to treat her, because he didn't allow enough recovery time post-injury. The interview reminded me that I can't help someone who refuses to help themself."

He shrugged. "I wish her the best, but trust me, I am so over her."

Izzy didn't mean to pry, but him being pissed about that made sense. Salt in the wound. "Do you want me to fix your phone?"

"That would be amazing." He unlocked it and handed it over.

"What do you want me to replace, uh, her with?" She grinned at him.

"I couldn't care less."

"Um, okay." She snapped a quick photo of the bowl of shiny apples. Kinda like a still life. Maybe he'd see it as Zen. She set it as the new wallpaper, then held it out to him.

As he took it from her, he put his hands around hers. Their warm energy encapsulated her, and her eyes connected to his. A vibration akin to the needles flowed between them.

Neither released the phone as they stood together.

"How can I return the favor and help you?" he asked.

Her eyes dipped to his lips. God, she wanted to feel them. But she wasn't quite sure how to express what she needed.

"Rub my neck a little? I know you're not a masseuse, but I'd really enjoy it."

"Happy to." Releasing Izzy's hands, Julien placed his phone on the table. He walked behind her and kneaded at the tension in her muscles. Within moments, she let a moan slip out. Embarrassing. But his heavenly touch drew her to wriggle closer.

"Feel good?" he whispered close to her ear, his breath causing her hair to flutter, tickling her skin.

She gave a little nod, eyes squeezed shut as she clenched the kitchen chair in front of her.

"You know—" He kissed the hairline on the back of her neck, and goose bumps lit up her whole body. He massaged her forearm, trying to get her muscles to relax. "Sex not only helps relieve stress but also can make you perform better the next day on tests and in athletic competitions."

"Is that so?" Her breath hitched on her reply, but she couldn't help the small smile sneaking onto her face.

"Mm-hmm," he said, kissing the corresponding spot on the other side of her neck.

Wow. Julien's lips shot energy right down to her clit. She was lit up, so turned on every fiber of her being vibrated.

She wanted this. She needed this release now, no matter what tomorrow might bring.

"Well, if it's for the test," she whispered back, and snuggled her rear into him, feeling his hardness between her cheeks. Oh damn. That was some chi.

He chuckled and pressed her hips to him. "I meant to help with my race training tomorrow, not for your exam."

She was grinning now. "Yeah, right."

Pivoting, she grasped his length through his sweats. Then, releasing him, she reached behind his neck, weaving her fingers into his silky hair, intending to bring those lush lips down to meet hers.

But he was quicker, and his mouth found where her neck met her shoulders, her weakness.

Those kisses shot straight to her core, making her a mass of quaking desire. Her head fell back, and she released his hair to rub her palms along his firm chest and then around his back, to pull him to her, arching her small breasts against him.

"Isabel," he uttered. "You have so much light penned up that needs to be let out."

"Yesss." It was all she managed as she ground herself on him through all the layers. "Let it out."

She wasn't sure if she meant her light or his cock, or her light via his cock, but whatever.

Her hands had a mind of their own and shoved his waistband down, freeing his erection, and she grabbed it greedily. She gasped at the hard velvet texture of him. "Oh, now, please."

A responding grin took over his face.

"How do you want it?"

"Maybe on this table?" She gave him a mischievous smile.

Decision made; he thrust the chair aside and started to lift her.

"No. Like this." She turned, leaning over the table, her smile turning shy as she looked at him over her shoulder.

"How very carnal, Doc." After putting on protection, he moved gently, pushing her flannel pants and panties down until they pooled on the floor. He slipped one hand around her hip to her abdomen and down to stroke her essence, then readjusted his grip back to her hip.

Slowly, he gave himself to her, and she saw lights, like occipital flares, but brought on by pleasure. She wasn't a virgin by any means, but her sexual encounters had been more about medical curiosity than soul-deep need.

This was different. Julien understood her body, her mind, and treated her with tenderness. She'd been caring for someone else for so long that it was mind-blowing to have Julien putting her needs as his whole focus.

With each thrust an apple toppled off the table, tumbling to the floor. They were both panting, working together, riding the wave of their mutual desire, and in any other moment, she would have collapsed in giggles, but the voracity of pleasure was mounting so high her vision blurred. She closed her eyes to the distraction and just let herself feel, let herself be absorbed to the point where their auras might merge.

They might have outshone the City of Light when their energies imploded as one.

When they finished, he led her to his room, guiding her by hand. She followed, at a loss for words. He pulled her onto his bed and tucked her into his arms, spooning her. She'd never had his lips on hers. But she was too exhausted to remedy the matter.

His face was buried in her hair at the nape of her neck, and she was on the verge of falling asleep when she remembered to set an alarm to wake her in the morning for her exam. Sated, she was ready to slip into peaceful slumber when she heard his soft words.

"Just don't leave me when I've helped you achieve your goals. I couldn't take that again."

She snuggled her butt against him in recognition of the confession as reassurance. She hoped it was enough. Her energy was depleted, but it was so good to have let go.

7
Day Seven

Her heart might burst with joy. Not only had Izzy aced the exam—it had been administered electronically and their grades spat out at the end, so there was no wait—but karma had caught up with Marcel. He'd made an untoward offer to one of the female professors in hopes of advancement, and she saw him dismissed. The woman was a badass and took no prisoners.

She'd awakened to Julien's absence, but to start the day on the right foot, he'd brewed the coffee—which he didn't drink—and left Izzy one of his homemade breakfast bars on the counter. A note had instructions for her to complement it with yogurt to fuel herself for the exam, which he assured her she would slay.

He also wrote, *Around when I finish my training run (50 km this time!), you should be getting home. I hope you'll want to hang out again even once you've realized you don't need me to succeed.*

He was obsessed with these ultramarathons. But even as he teased, she heard the insecurity behind his words. She'd lost the person she'd loved most in the world. Love was never in anyone's control. Now, she was willing to be present, take risks, and let go of her tightly held reins. Or at least try with Julien's tutoring.

She needed to show him he had nothing to fear.

Looking around, she spotted the pile of apples. They were in a neat stack this morning. Roxane and Camille were still asleep from an apparent bender, so it had to be Julien who'd restacked his treasure.

The devil took her, and she grabbed the trash can, chucking the fruit with glee.

The door swung open, and there he was, again soaking wet, but his shirt and hair were plastered down from rain this time. His eyebrows rose, and she froze.

"What are you doing?"

She laughed. Julien must think she was an unpredictable time bomb of emotion.

"I'm showing you I won't leave just because I succeeded. They say an apple a day keeps the doctor away, but I'd like you to keep me around. So, you won't be needing these. Plus, they're all bruised anyhow."

"Congrats on your success then, I presume?"

When she nodded, he shut the door, stripped his shirt off, and approached her, tossing the soaked cotton into the sink. He shook his hair out of his eyes, scattering her with droplets.

"Well, Doctor, I got to poke you, but where's my examination?"

Smiling, she ran her fingers along his collarbone, tracing. "Hmm, let me see." She flattened her palm against him and stroked down to find his Adonis belt. "Cool to the touch, but appears to be a healthy male in prime condition."

She pulled back.

"As much as I enjoy this doctor role-playing and love looking to the future, I opened a letter from my mom yesterday, and she reminded me to focus on the present. So what I really want is to try frenching my flatmate." She raised one fingertip to press against the center of his lower lip.

"Well, you know, while kissing gives a metabolic boost, we should be careful. It also releases oxytocin, and you know what they call that, don't you?" He waggled his eyebrows at her.

"I can't remember!" She tried racking her brain, but everything was fuzzy when she was so close to tasting him.

"The love hormone. Might stir up affection or attachment." He grinned down at her and tapped her nose.

"In the City of Love? Heaven forbid." She wrapped her arms around him and pressed her lips to his.

The warmth of his lips filled her with heat, his tongue opening and invading her mouth. This time, she wasn't shocked by the electricity.

The sun broke through the rain clouds outside, and the City of Light shone through the windows to bathe them in sunbeams.

At any other time, she might have been grateful for the vitamin D, but right now, she was only aware of being in the present moment with an open heart.

The End... for now.

About the Author

Skye Knight writes stories about scrappy heroines fighting falling in love. Prior to achieving her dream of being a full-time writer, she worked for 15 years as a TV executive. She lives in Washington, D.C. with her husband (and college sweetheart), her two spunky elementary school-aged daughters, and her dogs: mini sheepadoodle Huxley and labradoodle rescue Sasha.

She hails from South Carolina, y'all (but was born in New Hampshire), and escapes to her happy place in Kiawah Island, SC, as much as possible. To stress-bust, she plays tennis and takes Pilates reformer classes. Also, she's been known to pick up a paintbrush and dabbles in watercolor, acrylic, and oil.

If you want to learn more about Skye, please visit her website to subscribe to her newsletter at www.skye-knight.com and find easy links to her social presence on all the usual suspects. Generally, her handle is @skyeknightwriter.

Authors need your love and support! Here is how to show yours:

- Leave a rating, or better, a review of our books on your preferred platform—they don't have to be long
- Post about our books on social media (or engage with ours: subscribe, follow, heart, share, bookmark)
- Request our books at your local library
- Tell others about our books
- Recommend our books for book club
- Add our books to your "want to read" or "read" shelf on Goodreads
- And if you're up to spending your dollars, please preorder

Thank you for enjoying my story! Readers are writers' lifeblood.

Level Up

Julie Halperson

This story would not exist without the community of writers in my morning writing group hosted by fellow author Keely Thrall. This group has been my place to roost and grow while learning the facets of writing and publishing.

My family has always been my steadfast cheering team and source of encouragement. My parents always supported our reading whatever we wanted, and my siblings and I share books, movies, and all forms of art. Thank you, family!

1

"Lucy, something's got to change." Erica sat cross-legged on Lucy Stock's bedroom floor, stroking the purring cat. Jazz was lapping up all the attention. Lucy, not so much.

"How long have you been mooning after this guy? The so-called other half of the balanced portfolio?" Erica shook her head. "You've been putting your assets into storage." Looking up, she frowned, critically. "No, not that shade of eye shadow. You need to bring out the blue of the Guardian robes." Reaching over, she pulled out a blue that called to mind a deep mountain lake with a bit of sparkle. And then stroked Lucy's dark-brown hair, just like she'd stroked Jazz's.

"It's time to level up."

They were in the midst of packing, clothes and cosplay strewn over her bedroom, obscuring the utilitarian furniture. Erica helped her curate the collection every year, to pick who she wanted to be this time.

Level up. Lucy did not need this right now. Her head was full of convention plans, cosplay combinations, travel arrangements. And Harry. Harry Bond, the other half of the balanced portfolio. Balanced, because her last name was Stock and his was Bond.

They'd been meeting at this same convention, this same weekend— the third weekend in May— for five years. She was not local to the Con.

It was far enough away that it made sense to fly in every year. If she drove, it would tack on an extra day at either end. He was close to Philadelphia, and she was in the wilds of Illinois. And the Con was her antidote to an antiseptic job in the front office of a dental practice, hidden behind the same uniform tunic that everyone wore.

Erica was right. Her own love life was on hold because of Harry. And truthfully, not just her love life. This weekend was like Christmas. The year revolved around it.

"What else do you know about him? Is he seeing anyone? Does he live with his parents? Does he even have a job?" Erica started to go through Lucy's cosplay, accessorizing.

Lucy started to laugh. "Erica, of course he has a job. He moved to Springfield for a new job five years ago, and then we met afterward." But then, she'd been dating Mike, who had played her and then dumped her.

She trusted Harry. He made her smile. But more than that, she felt… cherished when she was with Harry.

Could she risk losing that? By leveling up, making that move, testing those uncharted waters?

Erica pulled out a suitcase and began packing.

"Yes, it's a risk." Erica was mind-reading again. "But do you want more? I think sometimes that mess up with Mike destroyed any chance of another relationship."

Lucy slumped into her bedroom chair. "Yes, I guess I want more. But I love what Harry and I have. And I'm terrified that I will miss the signals again and go into another crash." She hadn't paid attention to the signals of the missed calls and the sudden emergencies when she was with Mike, signs he was focusing on someone who was not her. Lucy swiped away the tear from her cheek. "And then I will lose Harry and the Con at the same time."

"But think what you could gain." Erica carefully wrapped the angel's wings, then sandwiched them between two pieces of cardboard. She clipped the delicate package to a hanger, then slipped it into the garment bag. Tilting her head, she asked, "Bubble wrap?"

But Lucy was thinking about what she could gain. More than one weekend a year. A chance to build on what she and Harry already had?

"Lucy. I am not saying you need to move to Springfield, into his apartment. Let's start small. Maybe have sex? See how you both like it?" Erica zipped the garment bag shut. "A spent soldier. I want some proof that you are moving forward." She went to her backpack, pulled out three foil-wrapped packets, and slipped them into the front pocket of the backpack. "Bring one back, and I'll make your next cosplay for you." She smiled. "It needs to be spent! No fair if it's still wrapped."

Erica was always prepared. Instead of one condom in her backpack, she had three. At least. And Erica's sewing and design skills were amazing. But would bringing home that spent condom be worth the risk? Lucy tried to look over that cliff of no Harry, no convention.

But... If she didn't make this move, she would lose Harry anyway, eventually. He was too nice a guy to be single for long—unless he wanted to be.

That was another cliff to look over. The result was the same. No Harry. No Con to look forward to.

Lucy shook her head to clear it. Too many possible paths to track. There was only one path to concentrate on. Level up. Undiscovered Country. Maybe... Uncovered Country? Her cheeks warmed.

"Deal." Lucy tried to embrace that shiver in her belly. Erica was right. Time to make a move. Even if it was terrifying.

Erica smiled, then said, "I already know what that next cosplay is going to be." She leaned forward. "And have fun! Just think, you finally have Trace Clark, Jane Houston, and Harry! An action-packed weekend." She pushed the backpack toward Lucy. "Trace Clark, movie star. Jane Houston, famous author. And Harry. All at once."

Lucy groaned and burrowed deeper into the chair.

2

Harry Bond stared at the desk clerk at the conference hotel, filtering out the noise of the chitter-chatter in various galactic languages around him.

"What do you mean that my room isn't available?" The same room he'd had for the past five years.

The clerk sighed and rubbed his forehead. "It was part of the block assigned to one of the VIPs and their party." He glanced down at the reservation screen. "There is always the possibility that a certain room will not be available. However"—he tapped at another section of the screen—"we can place you in one of our suites. That reservation was just cancelled."

Harry sighed. It would cost him more, but he would not give up this one weekend. "How much more?"

"Same cost, as you've been such a good customer, Mr. Bond."

Maybe his convention luck had started. "And I can keep it for the entire weekend?"

The clerk smiled. "Yes, we can even give you a later checkout time."

Excellent, Harry thought.

"Tell me, has Lucy Stock checked in yet?" He could text her, but that would mean pulling out his phone.

"Yes, Ms. Stock has checked in."

More excellence.

He collected his key and went off to find his suite. Zigzagging his way through the clumps of intergalactic visitors still waiting for rooms, withstanding squeals of excitement, and barely avoiding a misplaced footstep on the gold cape of a pint-sized superhero, he sighed when he made it to the elevator bank. And pressed Up.

Let's see. First, dump stuff. Then, text Lucy. Then... He reminded himself of the goal.

Harry had discovered this Con quite by chance. He was new in town, driving around, getting his bearings. The hotel sign read Welcome SpringCon! The garish sign board electronically flipped through pictures of large groups of conference goers dressed in cosplay, rooms filled with tables piled high with gear, smiling groups of people arm in arm. But what caught his attention was the cosplay of a group dressed in the uniforms from his favorite game. He had to find out more.

He registered. And he had a signing bonus from his new job, so he sprang for a hotel room. That way—fingers crossed—he would find somebody to have a beer with and wouldn't have to drive home on unfamiliar streets.

And he met Lucy Stock.

Her dimples caught his attention. He was entranced by them. They weren't normal dimples. They extended from the sides of her mouth all the way through her cheeks almost to her ears. And her deep-brown eyes sparkled. She was the epitome of happiness when she smiled. She was also the perfect height, her head coming to just under his chin. And she was always dressed in beautiful cosplay, several versions over the weekend. He stayed away from cosplay himself. His creative imagination went blank when trying to imagine himself as anyone other than his boring self.

She was waiting in line for the autograph of an actor from a popular action-hero franchise. She looked approachable and would probably answer a question. Or two.

And she did.

He asked about the autographs, the costume parades, the vendor tables, the giveaways. The best place for lunch and dinner and a beer.

He made some sort of lame dad joke about their names—Stocks and

Bonds, can't go wrong with a portfolio like that, right? She groaned, then asked if he did finances.

"No, I'm a developer. I work for Zylon up the street."

They moved up in the line.

He had to know. "Are you local?"

She shook her head. "No, just a superfan of the Avenging Devils. I'm pretty much a groupie and see them whenever I can."

The person in charge of line split them up. Damn him! "Hope to see you around."

And they caught up with each other at the bar.

And that had been the first Con with Lucy.

They had met up the next year, laughing when they found themselves in the same line again. And that year, he decided to count how many times he caught her smiling with those dimples. And because he was learning about performance improvement at his job, he decided to up the count each year, with bonus points if he caused the smile.

And somewhere after the fourth year, he had realized he was in love with Lucy Stock.

3

Lucy pulled her suitcase from the hotel shuttle, plans whirling through her head. So many things she wanted to do and only a weekend to accomplish them. Cosplay to show off. Trace Watkins to swoon over. Maybe Jane Houston would be there. Her social media indicated she might be.

But for sure, Harry would be there. The other half of the balanced portfolio. She couldn't help smiling.

Harry Bond was the reason she snagged this weekend for vacation every year. The reason she paid the early bird fee once registration opened.

Did he realize how she felt about him?

And those three foil-wrapped packets were linked to her by some sort of invisible tether. She knew they were there, even though they were insulated by layers of backpack. Was she really ready to level up this balanced portfolio? Like an omen, the glass door in front of her slid open, filling her senses with color and sound. The Con was in full swing.

She had confirmed her room reservation and bypassed the desk. She needed a luggage rack to carry the garment bag and her conference wardrobe. Wrestling it through the crowd, she spun the luggage rack onto the elevator. She asked for the same room every year. Hmm. If she wanted things to change, should she have asked for a larger room? Too late. By this time, all the larger rooms had been taken. And she was never in her room on a conference weekend anyway.

Opening her case, she started to unpack the cosplay. Today, she planned to wear the Angel's cosplay. If she were lucky, she would find Trace Clark and he would recognize it. The Finder's Universe Guardian robe for tomorrow. Looking at it critically, she thought she had gotten the colors right. The swirling blue and brown with the insignia of the River Clan. With enough time, she might be able to put the blue highlights in her hair. She only had a description in a book. There was no movie, manga, or comic authorized by Jane Houston to guide her. Not even another person's ideas posted on a blog.

And then Sunday was usually kind of chill. Lots of people bailed early because of travel and work. Some true-hearted folks stayed over until Monday, squeezing in the last minutes. It was like a family reunion.

And her bio family just didn't get it.

Her phone buzzed with a text from Harry, all checked in and ready to go. *Meet at registration?*

Her fingers trembled a little when she texted back. *YES.*

She slipped her phone into her backpack, where those foil packets were still attached with that invisible cord. She turned and took one last look at her bed. Going out the door was the first step into leveling up—or so she told herself.

She hoped this weekend would be Thanksgiving, Fourth of July, and Christmas, all rolled into one.

4

And then all of Lucy's plans started to fall apart.

Not because of Harry. He had given her that special Harry grin, a little lopsided, a little toothy. His hair was a bit longer, his eyes still that warm hazel shot with gold. And she got a Harry hug. He was so tall, he had to stoop a little so her head fit into his neck. He had already registered, so he waited beside her in line.

The volunteer rifled through her registration packet. "Two meals. Check. Special session with Larry Price. Check. Here you go."

"Wait. What about Trace Clark?" She'd been waiting to attend a session with him for months, ever since the guests of honor had been posted.

Lucy pulled up the confirmation email on her phone, pointing at the entry. "See. One for Trace Clark." Harry craned his head to see the confirmation.

The clerk checked the registration packet again, shook her head, then called over another person. "Did we oversell the Clark registrations?"

The two clerks looked at each other. "We did have that ransomware issue a few months ago." The looks on their faces did not bode well. "The problem is, Mr. Clark set very firm restrictions on how many could be in his session." She handed a sheet of paper to Lucy. "Leave your phone number. Maybe someone will cancel, or we can slip you in somehow."

Lucy couldn't help it. She ducked her head, not wanting anyone to see her frustrated tears, staring at the geometric patterns in the carpet until her eyes could focus again. She'd looked forward to seeing Trace Clark in person for months and to hearing him talk about being on set of the Earthwalker Saga. A hand landed on her shoulder. Harry. He drew her to his side.

"Thanks," Lucy said, both to the clerk and to Harry.

Harry, ever so gently, turned her around to leave the registration line. "I'm pretty sure he'll be here all weekend. We can find a way."

Sighing, she looked for a place to sit. Harry, with his additional ten inches of height, spied a free table and led them to it.

"Let's compare schedules, okay?"

This was part of their annual routine. It had started in their second year, when both of them had searched the other out. She remembered wondering if he would be here.

Sigh. Still, she had wanted to see Trace Clark for months. She shook her head. *Focus, Lucy. Focus.*

Harry's schedule was only half full. "Why?" she asked him. Hers had every minute packed, except for the hole left by the session with Trace.

He shrugged. "Nothing really caught my eye." He cocked his head, considering. "Maybe this is the year I level up."

"How?" She stiffened at the phrase. What was the universe telling her?

He tapped his fingers over the unfilled slots. "I've been coming here for five years, right?"

She nodded.

"Maybe, since I'm local, I should think about getting more involved." He pulled out his phone. "I wonder if they still need gophers." He shrugged. "Or something else." He tapped out the number listed on the program, showing her the text.

She nodded.

And... level up?

So funny he'd said that. Erica's words were already an earworm, and now Harry's added to the chorus.

Would they level up? Could they?

She'd not been dating anyone beyond the few times she'd been on blind dates set up by friends at home. She didn't think Harry had been seeing anyone. Wouldn't he have told her? Mentioned a name? His social-media relationship status still showed a big round question mark. As did hers. His texts were devoid of the mention of any regular dates.

Well, there had been someone in his life. And in hers. But her romantic life had been a wasteland for the past couple of years. Maybe because she'd been falling for Harry. She sighed.

"Don't worry," Harry said. How sweet. He'd caught her sigh and not realized that he had been the cause. He'd been texting with the conference team. "I think I can get on the setup team. Meet me at Trace Clark's session. I think I can smuggle you in." He looked her up and down. "Although you're pretty eye-catching in that angel cosplay."

Her heart lifted, and she smiled. And then Harry smiled, his gaze on her mouth. Maybe, just maybe.

"Level up," she said, considering.

"Yes, leveling up."

5

Harry tried to keep all the instructions in his head. Listen to the GOH. That was the Guest of Honor, the volunteer coordinator had told him to make sure he knew. Put on the badge. Phone on vibrate. The command room was always staffed. Did he have the number to text if there was a problem?

And, the coordinator said, always remember this—We want our guest speakers to have a wonderful time, splash us all over their social media, and be eager to come back next year.

The coordinator looked him straight in the eyes. "Any questions?"

Harry took a deep breath and expelled it. "No, not any different than my regular job."

Finally, a smile broke out, throwing the coordinator's face paint into interesting patterns. He wanted to ask her about it, but she was already back on her phone, checking a new text.

"One thing," he started.

"Yes?" Her eyes were still on her phone.

"Your name?"

"Sheila McMasters." She looked up at him and smiled. "I'm part of the local group. Look us up online if you want to volunteer next year."

"Great. I live nearby. Looking forward to getting more involved."

"I've seen you around. You're a friend of Lucy's, yes?"

Startled, he nodded.

"She's good people. Been coming here for years."

A potential ally.

"Can I handle the Trace Clark show?"

Sheila drew back and looked at him square on. "Do you want to? He's rumored to be demanding."

"Yeah, I've heard about the strict limit on the audience size. Lucy really wants to get in. There was some snafu at the registration, and she's on the waiting list." He paused. "If I take on Trace, can I slip her in?"

"Don't tell me." She winked. "But you can have an assistant." She paused. "To take registration tickets or something like that."

She turned to go. "But remember, I don't know anything about it."

Great. He was part of the inner circle, privy to secrets and work-arounds.

"Will you take on another one?"

He nodded. Now that Lucy was taken care of, he owed Sheila.

"We have an author, Jane Houston. She just broke out and has a bestseller. More people than we projected want to see her. Can you help with crowd control in the readers lounge? See if she needs anything?"

He'd heard of Jane Houston. Lucy had raved about her books, talking about space-faring Guardians, Speakers, Finders, and whatnot. If Jane Houston had just had a bestseller, maybe there was really something there. "Of course, on my way."

Sheila gifted him another wink and strode off to deal with the next questioning volunteer.

6

Lucy found Harry standing at the bar in their usual spot. Close enough to get the bartender's attention and far enough out of the way that they could actually hear each other speak. He was about to order their standards, but she stopped him. First step in shaking things up.

"I think I'd like a dirty martini."

"Lucy? Is that you?"

She chuckled. "Yeah, just thought I'd try something new."

"If you like olives that much, we should go to the Italian restaurant up the street." He had ordered his standard draft. The bartender delivered both drinks.

Truth be told, Lucy had never had a dirty martini, and she didn't really like olives that much, but this was the weekend for stepping out of her comfort zone. Her dirty martini was cloudy with a garnish of three olives.

Damn, she should have googled it before ordering. It had sounded like something that she would never try, therefore perfect for leveling up. Well, maybe... The first whiff of the drink caused her to crinkle her nose.

"Lucy, you're not smiling."

That made her smile. She did like looking at him. He always seemed to be at ease in his skin, like he knew exactly how much space he filled, and at the same time, he knew how to navigate around others, respecting their space. The Con was perpetually crowded, but she always felt safe with him. Protected.

He leaned back, and the overhead bar light lit his hair but shadowed his hazel eyes. But she knew that they were green with brown flecks, and she was envious of his long black lashes. *Sigh*. And her own brown eyes were not swoon worthy. Oh well.

"Do you really want that drink? Or maybe you'd like to try another experiment?"

It was true. She was not a dirty-martini type of girl. She caught a snatch of conversation as somebody else ordered a cocktail. Something about an Italian Surfer. That sounded like a different type of experience. She ordered one.

The bartender set down her Surfer and a bowl of pretzels. Ah, that was more like it. The drink reminded her of a sunrise and had a maraschino cherry as a garnish. She pulled over the bar menu. She wanted something more substantial than pretzels. Harry also found a menu, and they ordered fried mozzarella sticks to start with.

"How was day one?" Harry asked.

"Day one? I went through the art show. And some people asked me about my cosplay. And some talked about the movie it's based on. Pretty good, I'd say. Erica will be happy."

"Oh, did Erica help you with that?" Harry gestured at her cosplay,

Lucy nodded. This Italian surfer went down very easily. It contained amaretto and something else. She loved amaretto. She would order this for the rest of her life but with a pretzel to cut the sweetness. She asked the bartender for another Surfer and a glass of ice water.

"How was your day?" she asked.

Harry shook his head. "I'm not sure I leveled up. It seems all I did was direct traffic." The mozzarella sticks arrived, and he dipped one in the tomato sauce, then bit into it. He nodded in approval. "Hits the spot. I guess I was hungrier than I realized."

"Direct traffic?"

"Yeah, at the authors room. Jane Houston…"

"You *met* her?"

Harry stopped the second bite of the fried cheese stick and cocked his head. "Yeah, you knew she was going to be here, right? Sheila asked me to help out."

Lucy sighed. Today had seemed like one missed opportunity after another. First no Trace session. Then, she'd missed a chance to meet Jane Houston in person while Harry was there.

"Oh, I wish I'd known that you... that she..." *Sigh.*

Harry reached over to take her hand. "I'm sorry, Lucy." He looked around the bar. "Let me see if I can find her. I'm sure she'll love to meet you." He tugged at his gopher armband. "This should be worth something."

"No, Harry, it's all right." She spied Sheila walking toward them, with business written all over her face. Behind her was Trace. She held her breath and nodded at Harry. "I think Sheila is walking this way." She gripped Harry's hand a little tighter. "And she's got Trace with her."

Harry felt his back stiffen at the excitement in Lucy's voice and the increased pressure in Lucy's grasp. Slowly, he twisted in the chair and met Sheila's gaze. He stood, leaning over to catch her words.

"Harry, I wanted you to meet Trace Clark before his session tomorrow." She turned to the man standing behind her, who was almost leering at Lucy. Harry's gut clenched. It actually did. He thought that only happened in books. Lucy stood, resplendent in her beautiful cosplay. looking like an angel, even with folded wings. He sighed and smiled at Sheila. He'd asked for this gopher job. Damn, leveling up could be painful.

"Great to have you here, Mr. Clark. I'm looking forward to working with you tomorrow."

The man stuck out his hand, and Harry automatically gripped it. And looked his rival over. His gut sank.

Trace Clark had the kind of looks that caught attention. It wasn't surprising that he made his life in front of a camera. He was as tall as Harry. His hair was blonde, damn it. And he wore clothes that showed off a toned physique. And this... thespian... had zeroed in on Lucy.

People at the surrounding tables were gawking. He had to get them out of here.

"Why don't we go and look at the—"

Sheila introduced Lucy before he could finish his sentence. "This is Lucy Stock. She'll be working with Harry tomorrow, taking tickets."

Damn it, he hadn't had a chance to even tell Lucy yet.

Lucy, the wonderful woman she was, didn't even look surprised. "Yes, isn't it wonderful, Mr. Clark?"

"Wonderful cosplay," he said, nodding at her costume.

She blushed, and her cheeks dimpled. "Thank you." Then, "You recognize it?"

"Of course. It's from the movie 'Darkness Becomes Her.' One of my personal favorites."

Harry felt his gut reach floor level.

"Trace, why don't we go and take a look at the meeting space?" he interjected. He had to get this man away from Lucy.

"Great idea," Sheila said. "I'll go with you. Lucy, do you want to come too?"

Lucy, now all smiles and dimples, threw money on the table to pay for the drinks. "Let's go!"

Nothing was going according to plan. He had to trust in the balanced portfolio. Or was it at risk of becoming unbalanced?

Opening the door to his spacious suite with the king-sized bed, Harry felt incredibly lonely. Trace Clark had directed all his charisma and good looks at Lucy. The results were predictable. He'd won her over.

They had returned to the bar, where she ordered another Italian Surfer—he suspected Clark had asked the bartender to make it a double—and started to discuss his oeuvre. The man actually used the word *oeuvre* to discuss his own body of work.

Harry couldn't blame Lucy. She'd dreamed about seeing Trace in person for months.

He couldn't even blame Clark. Lucy was Lucy. When she focused those large brown eyes on you and flashed those deep dimples, who could resist? Add to that the form-fitting cosplay from a movie from Trace's own fucking oeuvre. *Fuck. Fuckity, fuckity fuck.*

Harry called room service and ordered a six-pack of beer and the appetizer sampling plate. The beer would put him to sleep. The food meant he could drink more.

He switched off his phone and turned on the late news. The financial news of the day flashed along the crawl bar. Of course, the topic of discussion was the balanced portfolio. The analyst said the current market conditions did not recommend it.

Fuckity, fuckity fuck.

7

On Saturday, Lucy fought her way through the crowds in the lobby to the central fountain, the place where she and Harry always met. The robe of her Finders Universe Guardian cosplay trailed behind her. Where was he? He had texted her to meet him there. He had left the bar early, and she'd continued to sit and talk with Trace.

That had been... wearisome. She got tired of asking conversational questions. His attention had been flattering but without substance.

She needed her world back in balance.

She could hear Harry. Not so much what he said but his sweet western Pennsylvania accent, with the last syllables sometimes clipped off. She shook her head. *Lucy, Lucy. You've lost your head over him.* The last text from Erica was seared in her brain. *Update? It's day two.*

Erica was right. Lucy needed to Do Something. Where was he?

Harry was standing near the hotel concierge's area. He was easy to locate, wearing the fluorescent armband of the Con crew but no cosplay. She had to love him for his *normalness*. He towered over most of the others by at least two inches. Who was he talking to? Oh, Sheila. He was handing her something. It looked like his room key. What the hell was happening?

They turned toward the elevators. She must be wrong. Not Harry.

Lucy turned away from the elevator bank and made her way back to the fountain. Sitting down, she reached into her backpack and pulled out a water bottle. Looking at it, she wondered if she should pour it over her head. Had she been such a fool again? Missing the signs?

She smelled Harry before he sat down beside her, his body warmth comforting but strange. Harry just sat, like he was waiting for… something. For Sheila? For Lucy to talk? She snuck a look over at him. No, he was looking at his phone. He sighed and palmed it.

"What's next for you, Lucy?"

She'd been asking herself that same question. But he was inquiring about her schedule, not her entire future. Looking at the schedule app on her phone, she confirmed she had a reading by Jane Houston on tap. Maybe that was what she needed. A distraction. Someone to take her mind off Harry. She was wearing the Guardian cosplay. Maybe she could ask the author herself if she had gotten it right.

She told Harry her plans, and he said he needed to check with Sheila about where he was needed next. Of course he did. Harry's actions where becoming too much like that bastard Mike's had been. Her world was tilting.

The reading room was full, and thankfully, quiet. She was able to slip into a seat between two others in Guardian cosplay and felt like she was with her people. Finally.

Lucy was slightly disappointed that, when the author entered the room, she was in standard business attire. Shouldn't Jane Houston have made the effort?

Jane fiddled with the microphone and started talking. "How wonderful to see all of you today. This is the first time I was invited to a Con as an author, and I wasn't sure who I should be in cosplay! I love seeing how so many of you are interpreting people from my books."

Now this is more like it. It was more interesting to hear Jane talk as herself instead of listening to a reading. As if she were psychic, the author asked, "Would you like this to be more of a chat instead of a reading?" A smile twitched over her lips. "How about a vote? Raise hands for chat, reading, or both?"

Lucy wanted it all. She wanted to put Harry far back in her mind, to give herself an oasis until she had to make the next decision.

The room monitor counted the votes. The Both option carried the room.

"Great! Let's start with the reading. Not too long so we have time for the chat. The monitor will keep us on track."

The monitor nodded, raising a card.

"Yes, she'll let us know when we're getting close to the end."

"How about we start with some exciting news? I was approached just before I got on the plane about an option for a TV pilot based on my character Fyfe!" She leaned forward. "This is something I've always dreamed of. Let's blue sky a little. Who do you think could play him?"

Lucy knew there was only one person who could play Fyfe. She'd known it the minute she'd read *The Fyfe Cycle*, the intrepid Fixer.

She raised her hand. "Have you considered Trace Clark?"

Others around her murmured in agreement.

"Yeah, he was great in 'Death Becomes Her.'"

"Yeah, and that Earthwalker series was hot!"

"He's here, right?" Jane asked. "Maybe I can meet him."

Lucy raised her hand. "I think I can help with that."

"Stop by at the end of the session," the author suggested. "That's it for my big news. Let's continue with the reading, then take questions."

Lucy sat back, satisfied, feeling like something finally had gone right. But her mind's eye kept circling back to watching Harry give Sheila what appeared to be his room key. If Harry had really given Sheila his room key, better to find it out now instead of making a fool of herself. But that wasn't fair. She and Harry had five years of friendship. She would not walk away without asking him about that damn key. If she had to get Harry to her hotel room to thrash this out, she would do it. Level up, be damned.

This was beyond leveling up. It was regaining the balance.

8

Harry couldn't believe his eyes. Lucy, standing there in her Guardian cosplay, next to Trace Clark, smiling up at him. And she looked so damn comfortable. He couldn't add that smile to his tracker. It didn't count.

Why had he given up his room for that… thespian? That thespian did not deserve Lucy. That thespian was an ego-bloated grasping… freeloader. Trading on roles created by someone else, grasping for and at all the wonderful things around him.

Harry's ears were hot. Was there steam pouring out of them?

Sheila walked up to join Lucy and the thespian. Harry stepped a little close. He must hear the exchange.

"Mr. Clark, the holder of that suite agreed to let you have it, as you are one of our special guests this weekend." Sheila turned and gestured to Harry to come over.

The carpet seemed strewn with boulders bruising his feet as he joined the little group. "Yes?" he forced out.

"Harry, I was mentioning to Trace that you were kind enough to give up your suite for him." Sheila smiled brightly, kindly ignoring the scowl on Harry's face. Lucy's smile faltered, then froze. Her gaze tracked from Harry to Trace to Sheila.

There was little point in trashing the mood, Harry thought. "Happy to do it, Trace," he lied through his teeth. "We want to keep our guests happy." He knew Lucy would want Trace to have a good time, but no. He would fight for Lucy with his dying breath. The abyss floated at Harry's feet. He moved closer to her side.

But she didn't lean into him as she usually did. *Crap*. Things were falling apart in front of him.

"Excuse me." He had to get out of there. He spied the circular wall in the lobby and saw a free spot. Perfect.

So much noise was around him that he was surprised when Lucy sat down next to him. She was rummaging in her carryall—amazing that it matched the blue of her cosplay—and pulled out a chocolate meal bar. Breaking it in two, she handed him half. "Hungry?"

His stomach did growl, on cue. Maybe he was hungry. No, it was more than that. The abyss called at him. For all her kindness, he was losing Lucy.

"Harry, is something wrong?" Her hand touched his arm, bringing a bit of warmth, quieting the call of the abyss.

He shook his head, and then he nodded. He—calm, quiet Harry—was dissolving.

"Here, come with me." Lucy led him through the obstacle course in the lobby to the elevator bank. She pressed a button and stood quietly, still holding his hand. Anchoring him.

The walk from the elevator to the door of her room was short. Her room was small, her cosplay hung up on doors, neatly organized, complete with accessories, and labeled. Saturday Morning. Saturday Night.

She put him in the chair and cracked open one of the water bottles on the desk, handing it to him. She sat on the bed and leaned forward, with her elbows on her knees. "Now, can you tell me what is wrong?"

Harry could only see concern on her face. It was a now-or-never moment. The abyss yawned on either side of him. To stay on the edge, he had to speak.

"Lucy, I think I'm in love with you." And then he dove into the abyss. It was a now moment. Never had passed.

Gulping a swig of water, he said, "I only want you to be happy. And if that means you would be happier with that... thespian..." His limited linguistic talents failed him.

Lucy blinked, then reached her hands forward to grasp his arm and shook it. "Trace? Harry, why would you think that?"

"I don't have a good track record with relationships. My last one ended because she said I didn't make her happy."

Lucy straightened. "Harry, why did you give Sheila a room key?"

"Sheila said it was important that our special guests have a good time so..."

"So our Con would get favorable feedback on social media." Lucy completed the sentence.

Harry nodded. She was so smart. "And I thought if he was happy, you'd be happy. You were so excited that he was here."

She settled on the carpet at his feet. "But Harry, all you've been doing these weekends is making people happy." She ticked it off her fingers. "One, through your actions, I got to meet Chase. Two, you were Jane Houston's personal assistant at her signing. Three, you *gave* Chase your suite to make him happy, and you did it for the Con. Harry, you are the reason I walk around her smiling year after year. "

Harry reached up to touch her mouth. "I love your dimples. They radiate from your mouth to almost your ears." He pulled out his phone, tabbed open his note tracker. It was another now-or-never moment. Deep breath in, release. She just sat there, waiting.

"You see, I have a goal for myself. Every year, I want to see you smile more than last year." He held out his phone.

"L plus one?"

"Lucy plus one." Oh, yeah, he had to explain his shorthand. "Lucy plus one year."

"And what's this number?"

He felt his cheeks getting warm. "The number of times I saw you smile." He pulled back to see all of her face. "Lucy, you're not smiling."

In fact, there were tears in her eyes. She pulled him close, nestling her head under his chin. She was the perfect height. He'd known that for years.

"Harry"—she leaned back and took a deep breath—"since you gave up your room, do you have a place to sleep tonight?"

Another deep breath. "Lucy, are you saying what I think you're saying? Or I can set something up with a blanket on the floor...."

"I'm saying what you think I'm saying."

He laughed and then had to say, "This might imbalance our balanced portfolio. I'll be honest, I've thought about it. I've worried that I won't make you happy."

"Harry, I've thought about it too. I've been worried that I am holding on to something that has no future beyond an annual meetup here at Con." Holding his hand, she led him to the bed. They sat.

"All week, I've looked over that cliff." Twisting, she reached over to her backpack and pulled out three condoms.

"My best friend, Erica, gave these to me before I left, challenging me to level up." She shook her head. "Everywhere I turn this weekend, people say Level Up. It's a message from the cosmos."

Holding the three packets in her hand, she continued. "I think we will always be friends." Tilting her head, she continued, "But I want more. I want to see you more than one weekend a year. Maybe several weekends a year? And maybe, eventually, every day." And then she gulped, looking surprised.

"I think that's the first time I've ever admitted that to myself." Swallowing again, she continued, "If you want to continue as we are, I am okay with that. But others will come into our lives, and we will have to share space with them." Looking at him, she asked, "Shall we, um, level up, Harry?"

Harry was lost. The last fifteen minutes had completely shifted his paradigm. He had only wanted Lucy to be happy, to smile, to see those amazing dimples.

And here she was, smiling. Offering more occasions for him to see those dimples. His heart opened.

She pulled off his shirt, and the movement of her arms lifted the shirt of her beautiful blue Guardian cosplay. He could see her belly button and the edge of her bra, and then he lost it.

Those dimples... His mouth found hers, then his tongue sought the corners. He was rewarded with a chuckle. He could feel her tremble under his hands as he unhooked her bra.

Then he was lying flat on his back, and the pillow was behind his head, and gravity was playing with her hair. He blew at it, just to prove that physics still worked and he was really on earth. Success.

Physiology was in play, too, as his body started to react to Lucy's nearness.

The room was silent. Slowly, the outside sounds filtered in. He could hear the traffic outside and a snatch of a song, sounding like the theme song from... His eyes closed as he savored this slice of time.

"Lucy."

"Uh huh?"

"Lucy, I need to tell you something."

The bed creaked, and she moved away. He turned to his side, and Lucy was in self-protective mode, arms wrapped around her knees, waiting. She had also taken off her cosplay tunic, and he could see the white straps of her loosened bra against her creamy skin.

He twisted to sit upright. "What's wrong?"

She shrugged. "That particular phrase usually means bad news."

He held out his arms. "Come here." Then, "If you want to."

She unfolded herself and climbed over to him. He felt naked, uncovered. The abyss was now all around him. He resisted the urge to clasp a pillow to his chest.

The abyss was fading into the distance. "Can I kiss you?"

A chuckle. "Please."

Her lips were warm. Her cheeks were still damp. Grabbing the sheet, he wiped them dry.

"Harry, do you ever think of yourself?"

He leaned back to look at her. He took her hand and moved it to his crotch. "I don't want to rush this, but yeah, I'm thinking of myself." He kissed her. "And you." Her fingers, her amazing fingers, were adding their warmth to his erection. He groaned. He looked at her. She nodded. And smiled.

He reached behind her and took off her bra the rest of the way. Her breasts released were inviting, and he kissed them, filling his hands with them. She pulled at his jeans. He tugged at her pants. "I really do like this cosplay."

"When you meet Erica, you can thank her." Her chuckle was lost in his neck.

That thought chased around in his head, but then it went straight to another. "Erica, the giver of the condoms?"

"The same."

She found the foil packet. Their hands fumbled as they opened it together, and they started laughing.

"Harry, I'm in love with you." She kissed him. "I've never told you, but you're the reason I make my hotel reservation for next year when I'm on my way home."

Both of them sat back on the bed, the condom still compacted, the foil glinting in the afternoon sunlight.

He didn't know what to say, except to make a joke. "I guess we're in the right place, then."

"I guess so."

And then, both were naked, and the condom somehow had found its purpose, and now he was just holding on. He wanted—*needed*—to feel her release. She was riding him, and his hands slid from her hips up to her breasts. Her gasp of pleasure kept his hands there, his thumbs circling her nipples. Her head reared back, her legs gripped his hips, and she spasmed. And collapsed on his chest.

"Harry."

He grunted.

"Harry, don't start counting my orgasms."

"Don't put that idea in my head." His hand went to the nape of her neck, and he gently stroked her hair. "Lucy?"

"Um, yeah?" She turned so she was nestled in his favorite place, somewhere in the crook of his neck.

"Does that mean you want to have... multiple orgasms?"

The laughter gurgled in her throat. "Oh yeah."

He glanced at the clock on the nightstand and at the sun slanting through the room window. He thought about dinner and room service. He thought about schedules, and then... having a warm, willing Lucy and a soft bed, with no one asking him to organize anything. He kissed her. Slow and deep. Her body began to respond again. This time, they took their time. And together they found completion.

He mentally counted two. Level up, indeed.

About the Author

Julie Halperson is proud to be a native of Washington, D. C. and proud that it's her home base. She's always loved to read, ranging from World Book encyclopedias and Nancy Drews to wherever her friends and libraries lead her. She also loves to explore the real world: by car, by cruise ship, and plane. When she's not writing and traveling, she enjoys spending time with her family and friends, practicing fiber arts, and of course, exploring other story worlds.

Sign up for her mailing list to hear about future releases: subscribepage.io/SRzsSw

My Roommate Confession

Ilyse Hartt

1
Alice

I have a confession. I have the hots for my roommate.

And it's all kinds of wrong.

The front door slams shut, rattling the large windows of Wade's condo, startling me.

"Hey, Alice. You here?"

Seriously? He couldn't have hit a few red lights. Maybe stopped to for a beer with his hot friends or buddy cops. Talk about a mood spoiler, even if he is the inspiration for my wet dreams. What the hell is he doing home so early anyway?

Let's be honest—Wade Mercer has been the star of my fantasies since the day Mom brought him home. Even at the tender age of eleven, I knew this one had something special. Then, I hit my teens, and saw him in a different light. He started factoring into my dreams at night, and not as a father-figure. My friends gushed over his sexy good looks. My teachers swooned every time he picked me up. Mom and Wade's relationship started to crumble around that time.

The day he moved out, I honestly couldn't say if I was more upset that I wouldn't have a step-in dad or that my secret poster boy had left the building. Mom gave two shits about my needs and moved on to the next man to light up her world.

I had no idea Wade lived in Chicago until I moved here for school. I didn't expect to live with my ex-stepdaddy while attending chiropractic school. It's not like I'm his real daughter. He owes me nothing. But I'm sure Mom he offered his spare room at Mom's urging.

Initially, I declined his offer, but when my would-be roommate, and rent partner, decided at the last minute to drop out of school to marry her high-school boyfriend, I called Wade to see if his spare room might still be available.

At first, I thought it would be a great idea. Afterall, I'm living in the heart of The Loop, in downtown Chicago, with its iconic skyscrapers and lively atmosphere. The skyline view from his living room is stunning. I wouldn't think he could afford it on a cop's salary. But Mom once mentioned his family has money—hence her desire to rush him to the alter. Apparently, he had no intention of sharing the wealth, thus the divorce.

When he opened his front door that first day in early September, the man who once held my young heart in the palm of his hand—I think my panties incinerated on the spot.

My teenage crush had moved on to flat-out craving my extremely handsome ex-stepfather, now roommate, and I've been pampering my pussy ever since.

Living under his roof, eating at this dining table, sharing air with him—it's my back-when-I-was-a-teenager-wish come true. We even spent the holidays together because Mom took a vacation with her new boyfriend. That's when he exposed me to poker night with his sexy besties. There should be a rule limiting the number of handsome older hunks allowed to occupy the same space simultaneously.

Pulling my hand from between my legs, I slip two fingers into my mouth and lick them clean. All I need is Officer Mercer discovering how I spend any spare moment I can find mouthing his name while I make myself come.

I slip off the mattress and yank my underwear up my freshly shaved legs and snatch up the leggings that I'd left lying on the floor where I dropped them when the urge to finger fuck myself came upon me. I'd been imagining myself handcuffed and naked in the backseat of Wade's police car.

"Alice?" I can hear my sexy-as fuck, hotter than any man has a right to be, roomie rummaging through the fridge. Bottles clank as they smack together. I imagine him shoving aside take-out containers as he searches for a beer. A cold brew to quench the fire burning inside me would be good right now.

Hopping on one foot and then the other, I haul my leggings up over my wide hips. Pausing in front of my full-length mirror, my expression sours as my gaze roams over my curves, the extra fifteen pounds I can't seem to shed, my dull brown hair, lackluster hazel eyes, and too-large boobs.

Definitely not Wade's type. He dates women who look like Mom—high-maintenance arm candy. I take after my late father's side of the family—soccer mom, who's eaten too many chocolate chip cookies. I teeter on three-inch wedge heels, whereas Mom moves in stilettos as though she were born wearing them.

I find him in the living room, loosening his tie. "You're home early." Picture the hottest guy you can imagine. Dressed up, dressed down, undressed, he's fucking gorgeous all the time, especially in uniform. But when he's in a shirt and tie like he is today... Yum.

He brushes a hand lazily down his broad chest. I'm envious of that dress shirt. "Had to do a presentation today."

"I hate doing those. I get all tongue-tied." I plop down in the chair opposite him. There's something about how he leans back on the couch, one arm draped over the backrest and the other cupping the beer bottle between his firm thighs encased in black creased trousers, that makes my heart beat faster. His thick biceps flex beneath the white cotton as he takes a sip of cold ale, and I can't help but stare at the movement of his muscles, imagining what it would feel like to have those hands on my body.

He chuckles. "I'm sure you do just fine. How was your day?" he asks as he swallows another mouthful of beer, giving me a delightful opportunity to watch his Adam's apple move up and down the long column of his throat.

"Class in the morning, and then I did a short shift at the bakery." I have big plans to open my own chiropractic clinic when I graduate.

Initially, I envisioned that happening in the Big Apple. But Chicago has become very appealing.

"So, you've just been hanging out around the house the rest of the day."

My mind jumps to my earlier activities. "Made some cookies and then read for bit."

They got married the year I turned twelve. My father passed away while I was a baby, so while Mom and Wade's marriage only lasted a few years, I actually experienced family life for a little while, and it wasn't too bad. I looked up to him like a love-struck puppy. He treated me like his wife's young daughter. Meaning he tolerated me but was nice about it.

When I hit my teens, I had to fight off my friends for his attention. He attended one school event, and suddenly, I had a rash of self-invited sleepovers scheduled. I'd never been so popular.

Then he got tired of Mom harping about his money, and he left. But he continued to appear in my dreams. To this day, I notice everything about him. Like the way his dark hair curls messily around his forehead when he's relaxed, the stubble along his jawline that's always in some state of growth, and the way his sky-blue eyes crinkle at the corners when he smiles.

Makes me wet as fuck.

"Any plans for dinner?" he asks.

2
Alice

I'm in the kitchen making a sandwich when I feel Wade's gaze on me. The sizzle of awareness is intense. It's like the pads of his fingers are tap dancing a path from the base of my neck down my spine to my ass. I look up, and my stomach flip-flops when our eyes connect. I try to ignore the heat that spreads through my body.

He wanders into the kitchen, fresh from a shower, and walks to the fridge. Retrieving a beer, he cracks it open. I notice a drop of sweat drip down his forehead. What would he do if I walked over, rolled to the tips of my toes, and licked it off?

My heart races when he turns and walks to me, so close I feel his body heat.

"Hey," he murmurs, his voice low and rough.

I swallow hard, unable to look away from those blue eyes.

"Want one?"

I nod, unable to form words.

He reaches around me to place his untouched drink on the counter, and the side of his arm brushes against my shoulder.

My chest rises and falls heavily. My nipples turn to hard aching points under my sweater. The pine-fresh scent of his bodywash fills my nose, and my eyes drift closed, snapping open again when he steps away and moves back to the fridge.

Returning with a second beer, he removes the cap, hands it over, and then reaches for his. This time he's so close, a piece of paper couldn't slip between us.

Swallowing becomes complicated, and I'm not sure where to look. Our breaths mingle, and I bite my bottom lip to keep from moaning. I can smell the mint of toothpaste on his breath. My head is spinning. I want to wrap myself around him.

Risking it, I glance up, and his gaze drops to my lips before lazily returning to meet mine. We stare at each other in silent anticipation.

Or maybe that's just me.

Wade shifts his large muscular body, his chest pressing against me, making my nipples tingle with excitement. Then his fingers are roughly brushing against my jawline.

My lips part.

At first, the kiss is slow and gentle, but it escalates quickly.

His hands are in my hair, pulling me closer as he deepens the connection. Our tongues dance together wildly, as my hands find their way up his thick arms.

A whimper escapes into his mouth. This has been my secret fantasy for so long—to feel his touch, to taste him. To have him taste me.

He breaks the kiss abruptly, breathing heavily, his forehead pressed tight to mine. "Holy shit," he mutters, his voice ragged. "We shouldn't be doing this."

My eyes flutter open, sadness falling over me, knowing he's right. He was married to my mother. He's older than me by at least ten years.

Wade releases me and stumbles back. "I'm sorry. I've obviously had too much to drink," he says gruffly, brushing one hand over his face before spinning on his heel, and leaving.

I watch him go, my heart pounding in my chest. Taking a deep breath, I try to calm myself, but I can't shake the desire that's burning hotter than a wildfire inside me. When he's out of sight, I drop into a chair at the kitchen table, closing my eyes on the welling tears, my legs shaking beneath me.

What the hell was I thinking?

All I know is that he's left me desperate for his touch.

Instinctively, I spread my legs a bit and move my hands down to my sleep shorts, shoving aside the soft material at the crotch to bare the skin I'd shaved that morning, letting my figures skip across the silky smoothness. My flesh is hot, wet, needy, and it comes alive at the slightest contact.

A warm hand lands on my knee, and I gasp, my eyes springing open.

Wade is on his knees in front of me, naked from the waist up.

"I can't walk away." His gently squeezes my leg. "Let me?"

I simply nod, but shivers race down my spine.

He slides his hand up my inner thigh. I suck in a ragged breath when he slips his fingers beneath the fabric of my shorts and brushes mine aside. His rough fingertips find my smooth pussy, and I bite down on my lip to stop from moaning out loud.

"Wade." My voice is thick with desire as my hips buck.

He starts to circle my clit, the pad of his finger teasing it maddeningly slow. "You're so wet, baby girl," he murmurs as he our gazes stay locked on one another.

I close my eyes, savoring the emotions swirling over me.

"Do you want my cock, Alice? Do you want my big cock in your mouth? Or deep inside your tight young pussy?"

It sounds so dirty. And so good. I bite my lip. Should I tell him the truth? I decide to take the risk. "I want you everywhere. On me. In me." I've never been so needy, so hungry for anybody.

I whimper when he slides a thick finger inside. Tossing my head back, my lips part in awe. He thrusts in and out slowly, causing me to tremble and groan, my whole body on fire with pleasure.

"Wade, please."

He adds a second finger, opening me wider, stretching me the way his cock would. The burn is real. I've only had a couple of boyfriends, and neither had anything overly exciting between their legs. But I have a feeling Wade's will definitely cause some discomfort.

"I'm going to make you suck my cock one day and watch as you take every ounce of my cum down your throat. But right now, I want you to come for me. Do it, Alice. Come all over my fingers."

"Oh!"

He pumps those fingers fast, and I shudder against him, my thighs clamping tight against his hand as the walls of my vagina clench at his fingers driving into me at a pace that takes my breath away.

He rises and slams his mouth over mine, swallowing the cry that escapes my throat, his own rough groan making my pussy squeeze and quiver even harder.

I'm helpless to do anything but sit in his kitchen chair, trembling through my orgasm.

When it's over, without warning, he pulls away, leaving me empty and panting, aching for more.

"Enough for now, sweet girl," he says, a wicked grin on his face as he shoves his fingers into his mouth and licks them clean. Then he stands, moving back a few steps. His hard length is bulging against his zipper. He adjusts it, looks at me, and nods in satisfaction. Then he walks away, leaving me shattered.

I wake up, my eyes staring at the ceiling of my bedroom. The skyline's glow seeps through the opening in my blinds. Rising slightly, I look at the time on my phone—three am.

What kind of person dreams about their mother's ex-husband like that?

I'm his roommate.

I'm his ex-stepdaughter.

I roll to one side, burying my face into my pillow. *But I want to be his lover.*

3
Wade

I'm the worst kind of asshole.

Rain pelts against the windshield like a thousand tiny drummers, each droplet creating a cacophony in my ears, antagonizing the headache pounding behind my eyes.

As I sit in an unmarked police cruiser on a Friday night, staring at a dimly lit warehouse, a bead of sweat slips down my temple despite the cool February air outside the car.

"Wade, you see that?" My partner Rick whispers, nodding toward a black sedan pulling up to the warehouse we've been sitting on for hours. "That's our guy."

"Wait for money to change hands," I remind him. My eyes lock on two shady figures emerging from the sedan and another two from the warehouse. They meet partway, greeting each other with firm handshakes.

The tension in the car is palpable; every second that ticks by feeling like an eternity.

"Money's exchanged," Rick announces.

"Alright, let's move!" I shout into the radio, signaling the team to swoop in. The instant the words leave my lips, lights flash, sirens blare, and tires screech as we descend on the scene like hawks going in for the kill. The suspects scramble like drowned rats, looking for an escape route. In minutes, the men we've been after for months are handcuffed and led to waiting cars.

And now that it's done, of course, thoughts of Alice pop right back into my brain.

I moved back to Chicago after my divorce from her mother, accepting a detective's position with the transfer I requested. I enjoyed being a beat cop in New York but missed my family and friends. After the breakup, I needed a place to start over, and returning to where I grew up, where I had a trusted circle, seemed the right thing to do. Connie had no interest in the things I did or craved. All she wanted was my money.

Alice isn't like her mother.

Back at the office, I stare at the mountain of paperwork that awaits me to close out this collar. I gifted my partner with the night off, letting him head home to his family, promising I'd do the dirty work. Going home myself doesn't hold much appeal, not after what happened the other night. Alice wouldn't even look at me the following day before she ran out the door to catch the bus. She's been scarce since, spending all her time in her room or at the bakery when she's not at school.

Shame sours my gut. For Christ's sake, she's twelve years younger than me. She was my stepdaughter. When I split with Connie, Alice was about seventeen. I always thought her mom was hard on her—joking about her weight or tomboyish looks. Her father died when she was just a baby, so initially I felt obligated to give her some attention. She was a good kid. I didn't mind her being around.

When Connie called, I didn't hesitate to offer her daughter a place to stay while she attended school. But I didn't expect the beautiful, vibrant young woman who turned up on my doorstep. Gone was the little girl with long brown hair and hazel eyes. In her place, I discovered a curvy brunette with eyes more green than brown and tits a man could bury his face, or his cock, between and die a happy man.

I try to shake off those images, but they refuse to budge. The way she smiles when she's genuinely happy, laughter that lights up a room, and her ever-growing confidence as she nails tests and assignments at school. All these things would make me proud as her stepfather.

But I'm not her stepfather anymore.

Now, she's technically just my roommate.

Tell that to her mother.

"Get it together," I shake my head. I have to stamp down my attraction for the sake of my relationship with Alice, and my sanity.

The memory of her tanned legs, showcased by those barely-there shorts she loves to wear around the condo, invades my thoughts. My heart races with guilt and excitement as I recall how I've resorted to relieving myself in the shower since she moved in.

A couple of months ago, I caught her walking from the bathroom back to her room after she'd taken a shower. She'd been naked, only a towel wrapped around her hair and headphones on her ears. She didn't see or hear me.

Then her towel loosened and fell to the floor. I stood stock still, my back flat against the wall, as she bent over to pick it up, her back to me. I vividly recall the shape of her curved back, her perfect ass ripe like a peach, a glimpse of a freshly shaved and glistening pussy peeking out between her legs, and tits hanging low and heavy in front of her.

"Damn it." My hand tightens around the mouse as my cock twitches in my pants. I can't keep lying to myself about how my roommate affects me. Not after the other night.

I'd come home early from work, dressed for the business meeting I'd attended. Her eyes devoured me, and I ate it up, the pig that I am. I sat there, sucking back my beer, rubbing my hand down my chest, watching her pupils grow big and black and her breath hitch. Her nipples peaked beneath her shirt, and the way she wiggled around on the sofa left no doubt that if I'd had the balls to slip my fingers between her legs, I'd find her nice and wet and ready for me.

We'd warmed up leftovers for dinner and watched a movie. But she kept glancing in my direction all evening. Finally, she said she had a class the following day and called it a night.

On my way to bed a couple of hours later, I passed her bedroom and heard a noise. Leaning my ear to the door, I caught it again. A moan. Or a groan. Worried she might be hurt or in pain, I twisted the doorknob and slowly eased the door open, thinking I'd just check to make sure she was alright.

Oh, she'd been just fine. Fine and primed, with the blankets thrown back, her legs bent at the knees and spread wide enough that I could stand in her doorway and watch while she drove two fingers in and out of her hole. Wet, squishy sounds filled the room, competing with her heavy pants.

My cock sprang to attention, wanting to get in on the game.

Then she reached up to her breasts with her free hand and started tugging on her rosy nipples. Down lower, she pulled her fingers free and started furiously rubbing her clit.

Saliva filled my mouth as the need to taste her overwhelmed me, and I actually took a step forward before catching myself. Clenching my fists, feet rooted to the floor, I waited until her back arched, and she came, crying out my name.

I backed out of her room and closed the door as quietly as possible. Then I walked straight into an ice fucking cold shower and rubbed one out, one hand splayed flat against the tile, the other choking my cock, her name spilling from my lips as cum forcefully splattered against the wall.

Smoothing a hand down my face, I sigh deeply. I need to get out of here. If I can't have Alice, I need something to quench this thirst before I face her again.

4
Wade

"Wade, what's up fucker?"

Beckett Kingsley can never just say 'hello' when he answers his phone. Filthy-rich, the man oozes power and confidence from his pores. And he'll give you every dollar in his wallet and the shirt off his back if he thinks you need it.

"Hey, Beckett."

"Did you catch the bad guys today?"

"I did."

"Good for you."

Beckett and I roomed together at college and bonded over contract law and our passion for poker and women.

"I wondered if you wanted to hit up a club tonight," I ask, glancing at the time, realizing I probably should have called earlier.

"Need to burn off some energy?" I sense his smile, and his deep chuckle soon follows.

An image of Alice strumming her clit pops into my brain. "Yeah, something like that."

"I'm in. Let's text the guys and see who's available. You reach out to the Jagger and Jamie, and I'll connect with Connor and Slade. I hear there's a pop-up down by the river near Wrigley. Why don't we check it out?"

"I'll meet you in about sixty minutes."

"See you then." Beckett ends the call, and I quickly text the guys to see if they're available.

The police report needs a few final tweaks but can wait until Monday. I shut everything down and head to the locker room to shower and change into the spare set of clothes I keep on-site. In record time, I'm climbing from the Uber to find Jagger waiting and Slade strolling up the street, hands tucked into the pockets of his leather coat.

"Wade, my man. How's it hanging, dude?"

Jagger and I glance at him. "How's it hanging, dude?" I ask.

Slade shrugs. "Just testing it out."

"You sound like a twenty-year-old from the eighties." Jagger laughs.

"Do you have time in your calendar next week to adjust my back?" Slade asks Jagger. "I pulled something when I was fucking this broad the other night."

I can't stop the snort. "Now you sound like your father." Slade is a great guy and a good friend, but he comes from a family rumored to be involved with organized crime. He's never acknowledged the speculation, but he's never denied the accusations either.

He only looks slightly put out. "Well?"

Jagger looks like he's fighting to control his laughter. "I'm sure I can squeeze you in. Call the office and tell them I said to find the time."

"Thanks." Slade turns to greet Jamie and Connor as they join us, and we stand sharing our days while we wait for Beckett. When he finally arrives, we follow him down the street to the location of the pop-up club. Beckett once joked we should open our own place. With his money, I'm not so sure it was a joke.

From outside, I can hear the music thumping, and when Beckett pulls the door wide, it spills out onto the street. The five of us stroll behind Beckett as he leads us past a bustling bar and packed dance floor to a door in the back corner where there's a very large man dressed in a suit and tie standing guard. He seems to recognize Beckett and steps aside to press a button on a panel. The door swings open.

"Enjoy yourselves, gentlemen," he says, giving a slight head nod as we walk past.

As soon as I step into the back room, the energy shifts. I close my eyes and inhale the scent of oils, wax, and sex. *Yes.* This is what I need tonight.

Beckett turns to face us. "Meet up in," he checks his watch, "three hours."

Everyone disperses, leaving us alone.

He leans in but focuses on what's happening around us. "You okay?"

I can hear the concern in his voice. I see it in his eyes when his gaze shifts my way.

"Yeah." I sweep mine over the room, taking in the people and the stations, looking to see who might be available and what's empty. Since it's a pop-up there's limited options.

"Anything to do with Alice?"

My head snaps back around. "Why would you ask that?"

He shrugs. "You haven't said much about her since she moved in."

"Nothing to talk about."

"How old is she now?"

I squint my eyes at him. "Twenty-four."

"Have you heard from Connie?"

"Not since she called and asked if Alice could stay with me. Why the questions?"

He shakes his head. "Just curious. Let me know when you're ready to leave." He spins on his heel and walks away, probably searching for somebody to bind to a St. Andrew's cross.

I stroll through the room, occasionally stopping to watch a scene play out. A young woman wearing nothing but a blood-red velvet corset, matching thong, and black knee-high, laced-up, platform boots struts by, pausing and slowly giving me a once over with apparent interest.

"Are you looking for something special tonight?" Her blond ponytail swings as she tilts her head, her red lips in a seductive pout. She's young. Not as young as Alice, but younger than me.

"No thank you." I keep going.

Stopping at a spanking bench, I observe an older man set up a punishing rhythm with a paddle, leaving bright red blotches on his partner's jiggling ass cheeks. She cries out and counts each strike. Moisture drips down her inner thighs, and she dips her back to arch her butt higher.

Everywhere I look, I picture what Alice would look like in each situation. How her eyes would widen in arousal. She'd be stunning buckled to a cross or tied down on a bench while I dripped hot wax on her sensitized skin. I want to bring her to a place like this and do all sorts of dirty things to her nubile body. Sometimes in private. Sometimes, while others watched.

Glancing around the room, I see Jagger is already pounding into a woman who's on her hands and knees in front of him. Jamie is playing with a flogger and a set of twins. Slade and Connor are watching a woman service two men. They've each got a girl in their arms.

"You sure you don't want company?" The blonde is back, and she has one hand hovering near my crotch. She batts her lashes and smiles, her tongue coming out to lick along her upper lip. She leans close and lowers her voice. "I give good head." She shows me her tongue piercing.

All I can think about is my roommate and what she looked like crying out my name as she made herself come. "I'm sure you do, but no thank you. I was just leaving."

I turn and walk back to the entrance. On the way, I spot Beckett talking to a few men in the corner. He raises his head when he sees me. I point to the door, indicating I'm not sticking around.

I catch the furrow of his brows, but he nods and returns to his conversation.

I need to go home. I need to figure out how to live with a woman that I'm craving with every fiber of my being.

And I need to do it without laying my hands on her. Because God help me, if I touch her, there won't be any turning back.

5
Alice

I need to find another place to live. I can't stop thinking of Wade as just my roommate any longer. I want more. I want him. And, if I were to hazard a guess, I'd say he's probably regretting his offer to let me stay here.

The last few weeks have been strained whenever we're together. It's like we're suddenly strangers. After that dream I had, there was no way I could face him, so I'd hightailed it out the following day, saying I had class and would grab breakfast on campus. Since that morning, I've used varied excuses to keep my distance.

He's been acting strange too, putting in extra hours, most nights not coming home until I'm already in bed for the night.

Every time I'm near him, my dirty dream flashes behind my eyes, and I'm filled with embarrassment.

Wade left a note saying he'd be working late again, so it's the perfect time to indulge in a steam shower and an all-over shave before I nuke some leftovers for dinner and then hide away in my room before he arrives home.

With my playlist blasting, I open the glass door and step inside under the hot stream of water, instantly feeling the tension drain away to swirl down the drain along with the suds. As I scrub my favorite tangerine shampoo into my hair, lazily scratching my scalp, I close my eyes and sink into my dilemma.

I've got enough money saved to cover the cost of first and last months' rent at the cheapest place possible. And I've already talked to the bakery owner about extra hours. I'll figure out how to cover the expenses of the next school term later.

Turning the water off, I reach for a fluffy white towel to wrap around my body after towel drying my hair. Of course, the damn thing doesn't fit and leaves a generous gap. Tucking the edges over my breasts as best I can, I hurry down the hallway, casting a quick glance toward the floor-to-ceiling windows at the spectacular view as I pass. I didn't turn any lights on when I got home, so the room is mostly dark, and I can just start to make out my reflection in the glass. Moving through the spacious condo mechanically, I cross the open living room toward the kitchen area, my bare feet slapping against the hardwood.

I'm halfway across the room when I hear a sound, a scrape, and I pause, listening. Not hearing it again, I keep going, my mind on dinner and getting back to my room.

There's that noise again, only it sounds like... a painful moan? I spin around but don't see anything. On this floor, the traffic and street lights don't reach this far. Only the ambient light from outside illuminates a small portion of the room, leaving the rest in shadows.

The silence is broken by a faint tinkling, like ice in a glass.

"Is somebody there?"

I peer into the darkness, ready to run like a gazelle to lock myself in my room and call Wade—I mean the police. *Fuck.*

And then I spot him. Sitting in the dark, an empty glass dangling from his fingers.

"Wade? What are you doing here?"

A choked sound precedes his response. "I live here." The rumble of words is rough like they're scratching his throat.

"I thought you were working late." I can't see the features of his face, but I hear a heavy sigh leave his mouth. He rises, and suddenly he's prowling toward me, emerging from the shadows.

I take a step back. Two.

He's got a glass in one hand and a half-empty bottle of whiskey in the other. Dressed in all black, his shirt is pulled out from his jeans, unbuttoned, and rumpled, splayed open, baring his muscular upper body, covered by a tight cotton shirt. His jeans are unzipped and hanging low on his hips. His feet are bare. The heavy stubble on his jawline makes him look gruff and untamed. He's a walking sex god with a stark expression of raw desire on his face.

My heart skips a beat as our eyes meet, both of us freezing momentarily.

He looks away first, then takes a long swig from the bottle, the amber liquid disappearing down his throat before he sets it down on a side table, harder than necessary.

"Are you okay?"

He lifts his head slowly, his eyes traveling up my body, setting it on fire every inch of the way. Raising his right arm, he gestures toward me. "Do you think you could put some clothes on?" His words sound strangled.

Glancing down, I see what he sees, and heat blazes up my cheeks, but I don't move a muscle to cover myself. From somewhere a sense of confidence appears, and I raise my head and stare back at him.

But his eyes are glued to the gap that exposes my pussy.

I widen my stance.

He groans a raspy sound like he's fighting, restraining himself.

I thrust out my chest, knowing full well that the way I've tucked the edges of the towel to hold it in place is precarious at best. A little shimmy... thrust... oops.

It lands at my feet.

A growl rumbles in his throat.

And then, without warning, Wade rushes me. He yanks me into his arms, his mouth crashing down on mine. The smoky taste of whiskey mixes with desire as the kiss lingers and goes deeper. His hands roam up my bare back, possessive and hungry, as he pulls me tight to his body. My nipples dig into his shirt. I can feel his cock straining for release as he brings our hips together. A glorious feeling rushes through me, realizing that he is as hot and hungry for me as I've been for him.

I curl one hand around his neck, and with a desperate moan, melt into him, returning his kiss with an intensity that mirrors his own.

My heart races as his lips leave mine to trail a fiery path down my neck. My nipples harden, and I can't wait to feel his lips around them.

Surprising me, Wade sweeps me into his arms and stalks down the hall to his bedroom, where he lays me on the bed. His eyes are bright, and his jaw tense. "Tell me to stop, Alice. Please."

I don't say a word. I don't move. I hardly breathe.

"Alice." An order, not a request.

Swallowing past the lump of excitement quickly building, I shake my head slowly.

He makes a deep, guttural sound before he yanks his shirt off and strips away the t-shirt underneath, then pushes his jeans down his legs, baring his beautiful body.

His cock is pointing right at me, big, thick, red, with a drop of moisture beaded at the tip.

Gulp.

Then he falls over me, placing his hands on either side of my shoulders as he leans down and takes one of my engorged nipples into his mouth, swirling his tongue around and around before clamping his lips around it.

I gasp. *God yes.* This is precisely what I wanted. My eyes drift close as a soft moan escapes.

Balancing on one forearm, he reaches down, finding my slick folds.

"More. I want you inside me, Daddy."

He pauses, his head snapping up, his eyes dark and full of some emotion I can't explain.

"What did you call me?"

My eyes pop open. "Daddy." It just slipped out, but somehow, it feels right. And not in a fatherly way.

6
Wade

"Daddy," Alice gasps, her eyes bright, her cheeks flushed.

I heard the shower running when I arrived home. I should have poured my whiskey and taken it to my room. But I didn't want to risk walking past the bathroom when she opened the door. So, I hid in a dark corner, waiting until she was tucked away safely for the night.

She'd surprised me when she walked out wearing nothing but a damn towel and smelling like oranges. At first, I held my breath, hoping she'd do her thing and head straight back to her bedroom. But I must have made a sound because she turned. And I discovered that the towel didn't cover her completely. My drink nearly slipped from my fingers.

And then the little vixen pushed out those gorgeous tits and let the towel fall to the floor.

I've never been one for daddy kink and usually reserve dirty talk for the clubs, but when she called me Daddy, my gut knotted, and coming in my pants became a very real possibility.

I swear to God I never thought of her in any way other than my ex-wife's daughter.

Until she showed up at my door, all grown up.

I swallow, gazing at her through heavy lids while I taste the sweet pearl of her nipple against my tongue, her hot pussy squeezing my finger as I slowly pump it in and out.

"Daddy, make me come," she whispers.

I add a second finger and pick up the pace, curling them a bit to rub that special sweet spot.

Alice starts to tremble right before she explodes, her back arching, her fingers clawing at the covers.

My breath is hot over her skin as I murmur in her ear. "Are you Daddy's dirty little girl, Alice? Is that it?" I press deep, filling her as she convulses around me, like I've fantasized about so many times since that night a few weeks ago.

Her hips jerk in response. "Yes, Daddy. I'm your dirty girl. Only yours."

"Have you been playing with yourself at night, Alice? Has my poor little girl been alone, needing her daddy's cock?" The words flowing naturally, making her shudder long and hard as I bend to her nipple again.

"Yes, I need it so much." Her admission spills out on an excited breath, and my gut clenches with anticipation.

"Touch me, Alice. Reach down and take it in your hand and feel it. You know you shouldn't, you know it's what bad girls do, playing with their daddy's cocks. But I'll let you, if you really want to," I whisper against her breast before clamping my lips down on the other one and sucking at it so hard I hope she come, while I use my thumb to tease her clit.

My breath catches when slides one hand down along my chest and past my waist. Her fingers play along my length as though measuring before she shyly wraps them around me.

My eyes roll back. This has got to be heaven.

"You're so big and thick. I don't think I can take it."

I stop, body going still. "Alice, are you a virgin?" She can't be. I've got two fingers inside her, and while she's tight, she doesn't seem to be in any pain.

"No, Daddy." She turns her head away. "I'm sorry."

Relief rolls over me. I force her face back to mine with a finger to her chin. "It's okay, baby. I'm glad you're not. I won't have to be extra gentle."

Alice's eyes and voice become clear as she looks straight at me. "I don't want you to be gentle, Wade. While we may play around, and I might call you Daddy because somehow it just feels right in this moment, I'm not a little girl."

"Oh fuck, Alice." I smash my mouth over hers again and kiss her like there's no tomorrow. Like I'll wake up in the chair in my living room with my hand in my pants after passing out from drinking too much whisky.

Dragging my lips away, giving her space to breath, I peer down at her. "This isn't right."

"We're both consenting adults."

"What will people—"

She puts a finger over my lips. "I don't care."

"Your—"

"She's my mother. Not my keeper."

"Are you—"

"Wade, just fuck me. Please."

7

Alice

"If we do this, you're mine, Alice," he growls, using a knee to nudge my legs wide.

"And if we do this, you're mine, Wade."

He gazes at me through tormented eyes. "Why? Why me when you could have so many men your own age?"

"Because I don't want them."

I can see his struggle. He wants to argue. He wants to try to convince me, but I've made up my mind. I knew it a long time ago. I know it now.

I reach up and place my hand over his heart. "I want you, Wade."

He shakes his head slightly but reaches into the drawer of his bedside table and retrieves a condom. Covering himself, he settles in the space he created, pulling my legs up around his waist.

I cross my ankles at the small of his back.

His cock nudges at my opening, and my exhilaration is muddled with a moment of fear that I won't live up to his expectations.

"Are you ready for this?" he asks, eyes dark with lust and perhaps a little fear that I'll ask him to stop.

I nod, too far gone to speak. I watch as he pushes the thick head of his cock inside of me, and I pant as, with each inch, my body stretches to adjust around him.

We're both breathing shakily. There's a flash of doubt in his eyes.

"Do you want this, Alice?" he demands. "Do you really want Daddy's cock? Because I'm not stopping until I'm balls deep. It's now or never. Are you sure?"

I respect that he's giving me plenty of opportunity to stop this. Even if my mother disowns me. I've wanted Wade since the day I met him. I just never wanted him as a father.

I nod, eyes on his, hips already moving to take more of him.

Daddy isn't gentle. He grips my waist and thrusts into me roughly. I feel every inch as he plunges deep. A sense of completeness overwhelms me, bringing tears to my eyes.

Wade groans before he pulls out just enough to look down at where we're joined, and then drives into me again.

I can't breathe. I can't think. It's all so strange, yet at the same time, so right. It feels so good.

He thrusts in and out, pleasure replacing any discomfort as he moves with confidence.

"Let Daddy show you how to fuck, Alice. Give me your hands."

Wade pins my wrists above my head with one hand and our hips move together, creating a rhythm then makes me hot, and that heat spreading out to my limbs. My daddy is fucking me for the very first time, and it's perfect. I'm quickly lost in the sensation, in the sounds, in the smells as he moves hard and fast, then slow and sensual.

"You take Daddy's cock like a good girl, Alice," he growls into my ear. "Fuck, you're so tight I'm going to come. Your pussy is perfect, made just for Daddy, isn't it?"

Wade reaches down and strums his thumb against my clit, distracting me from his hard strokes as he pounds into me.

"Come with me, baby girl."

He pumps faster, his thumb and his cock working in unison until I'm clawing at his hand that holds mine over my head. I drop my mouth to his shoulder, biting down. My back arches as my climax rips through me and stars appear behind my closed lids.

"Fuck," he cries, his hips jerking with the force of his release.

Afterward, Wade slips off the bed, returning a few moments later with a warm cloth. He uses it to clean me up, his touch gentle, while I'm nothing more than a limp noodle sprawled on the bed.

"This changes everything, doesn't it?" he says quietly when we're settled under the sheets, his arms protectively wrapped around me.

"Do you want me to leave?"

He stays silent for a long moment, and I swallow the fear that this one time is all I'll have with Wade.

"God help me, I should be saying yes, but I can't, Alice."

Although I can hear the difficulty of that admission in his voice, I can't contain the relief coursing through me. I turn more fully into his embrace, throwing one leg over his, letting the palm of my hand smooth over his bare chest. "I've always wanted you, Wade."

He scoffs. "You were a kid when we met."

"Maybe, but I knew something special had just walked into my life."

"Your mother will kill me."

"My mother has no say."

"I want you so much," he groans, his hand slowly trailing down to cup my ass cheek.

Our tongues tangle together in a slow erotic dance that leaves us panting. Without any warning, he rolls, taking me with him until I'm under him again.

"I need you, Alice. Again, right now," he whispers against my neck as he enters me slowly and steadily.

8
Wade

The little girl I once knew is a lovely memory. The young woman sharing my bed is a fantasy come true. Connie only wanted access to my family's money, always pressuring me to dig into my trust fund. When I refused one too many times, she became an enraged bitch.

But with Alice, I want her to have anything she wants. I want to spoil her.

When we're not at work or school, we're in bed, fucking, talking, and fucking some more. I can't get enough of her. I want her scent all over me and mine all over her.

Since we've been eating take-out in bed all week, I decided to surprise her and cook tonight. The apartment buzzer rings, and I head to the intercom, thinking she forgot her key. I buzz her in and stroll back to the kitchen.

The door opens and closes while I'm stirring the sauce, and I hear footsteps behind me.

"I thought we'd have a home-cooked meal tonight. How was class, sweetheart?"

"Sweetheart?"

I drop the spoon I'm holding into the pot, sending tomato sauce splattering over the stovetop, and spin around. "Connie. What are you doing here?"

Alice's mother is striking. Tall, killer body with long salon-dyed blonde hair, perfectly waxed brows, and lash extensions. We'd met in a bar—she approached me, coming on strong from that first night. We dated a few months before she suggested marriage.

She glances around the empty condo. "Is Alice here?"

"She's not home from school yet."

Connie nods absently as she prowls toward me, dropping her handbag on a kitchen chair before sauntering around the island to join me. She drags a long-painted fingernail along the marble countertop. "How's my little girl doing?"

The image of *'my little girl'* waking up with my head between her thighs comes to mind.

"She's fine. She should be home any minute."

Connie closes the distance and wraps her fingers around my arms, sliding her hands to my biceps. "How are you, Wade?" she coos. "I've missed you."

Stepping out of her grasp and away from the stove, I shove my hands into the pockets of my sweatpants. "What are you doing here?" To my knowledge, the woman hasn't even called her daughter since Alice moved in.

She sighs dramatically. "I came to see you. And Alice, of course. I regret the way things ended. We were good together, weren't we?"

No. We were never good together. We had sex. We lived in the same house when she wasn't out and about.

"I've been remembering all the fun things we did—the long drives in your car. Remember our honeymoon, sweetheart? You couldn't take your eyes off me the entire two weeks we were in Fiji." She runs her hands down her body. "You loved seeing me naked on the beach."

"Things have been over for a long time, Connie. We've both moved on."

She approaches again, but I put the island between us.

"I haven't," she says. "Oh, I tried to forget you, but nobody else compares. I thought, since Alice is an adult now and has her own life, maybe you and I could try again, without her around to interfere in our relationship."

"Interfere? Is that how you see me, Mom? An interference?"

Connie and I both spin around to see Alice standing there. I didn't hear her come in. The expression on her face pains me—anger, hurt, betrayal.

She looks my way, something flashing in her eyes before her gaze swings back to her mother.

"Of course not, honey." Connie attempts to approach Alice, but she throws up a hand.

"Don't. I'm so tired of your crap, Mom. What happened to, what's his name? Gerry? Gerald? George?"

"Grant. And he's not the man I thought he was, so I ended it."

"You mean he wouldn't give you money?"

Connie's gaze spits fire. "Don't you speak to me like that, young lady. I'm your mother."

"Please. Mothers spend time with their kids, take care of them, cook for them, play games, help with homework, go to school events."

"I was..."

"Too busy with your friends, being seen, or finding a new boytoy to keep you occupied so you wouldn't have to spend time with me."

"Wade was not a boytoy."

Alice glances at me, her voice softening. "No. He was different."

"I came here to see you, Alice. To see how you're doing."

"You came to see if you could get Wade back."

At a loss for words, Connie stands staring at her daughter, who's staring at me.

My gut twists.

"You can't have him, Mom."

"What?"

Alice turns back to Connie. "I said, you can't have him."

"Have who?" Connie is perplexed.

"Wade. He belongs to me. I love him. And I hope he loves me."

Connie chokes. "Excuse me?"

I take a tentative step forward. "Alice?"

"What are you talking about?" Connie shrieks, but we tune her out.

"I love you, Wade. I want to spend the rest of my life with you."

Finally, we're toe to toe and I'm cupping her face. I can see her pulse pounding in her neck. I can see the nervous twitch of her lips as she tips her head back to look at me.

"I love you too, Alice."

"What the hell is going on here? You're way too old for her. She's just a child. Oh my God, I can't believe I brought you into my home. Did you touch her back then? Did you—I'm calling the cops." She scrambles for her purse, but Alice grabs it and jerks it out of her grasp.

"I would never," I yell.

"Stop it," Alice yells over both me and her mother. "Just stop it. No, he did not."

"But—"

"I am an adult, Mother. And I can fall in love with whomever I choose. You and Wade split a long time ago."

"Not that long ago," Connie sputters.

"Long enough," Alice snaps.

"He's too old—"

"I'm fairly certain you've dated enough older men to not use that argument."

"But—"

"You can be happy for me, for us, or you can leave."

"Alice, honey."

"I mean it, Mom."

Connie's gaze swings between us, her eyes falling to where I have a protective arm around Alice's shoulders, her side tucked tight against mine."

"I don't know if I can accept this."

"I don't expect you to."

Connie reaches for her purse, and Alice hands it over. "You're making a mistake. Are you willing to live on a cop's salary?"

"I don't care what his job is. I love him, not his money."

I never plan to let this woman go.

"Good-bye, Mom."

Connie gives us one last look and leaves, the door slamming behind her.

I squeeze Alice close. "I'm sorry."

She shakes her head. "Don't be. My mother and I have co-existed, but we've never been close."

"Did you mean it?" I ask, curious if she'll change her mind now that her mother's left. It would rip my heart out, but I would find a way to survive.

"I meant every word. Did you?"

With my hands buried in her hair, I stare into her beautiful green eyes. "I love you more than anything, little girl."

She smiles, and her eyes shine. "I love you, too, Daddy."

<<<<>>>>

Would you like to see where Alice and Wade's confession takes them next?
https://geni.us/IlyseHartt_MRCEpilogue

About the Author

Ilyse Hartt loves to read and create sexy, dirty, stories—sinful confessions saved for when nobody's around. Those secret fantasies you *only* tell your best friend or most trusted confidant.
By day she's a wife and mother.
By night she's spinning tales of desire, lust, and naughty pleasures.
Grab a glass of your favorite beverage and find a private nook where you won't be interrupted.
What's *your* sinful confession?
Maybe Ilsye has a story just for you.

Follow Ilsye Hartt on Facebook: https://geni.us/IlyseHarttFBPage
Sign up for Ilyse Hartt's newsletter: https://geni.us/IlyseHarttNLSignup
Subscribe to Sinful Confessions: https://reamstories.com/ilysehartt

No More Waiting

ALEXIS R. CRAIG

1

Josh Matthews. What can I say about him that doesn't sound like a cliché description of an ex-high school jock? Nothing, because that's exactly what he is. He's six feet, four inches of muscle in all the right places. Well, that and he's also been my best friend since the sixth grade, and that he is now my roommate of sorts.

How did I manage not to notice how sexy he really is? I find myself watching him as if he's a stranger that I just met. I guess, in a way, that's exactly what he is. I mean, sure we've known each other for a long time. But most of that time after high school, we have been on different sides of the country. I moved out of small-town North Carolina to big city New York. Josh moved all the way to Oregon to live with his older brother. Now, ten years out of high school, here we are, sharing a two-bedroom apartment after not seeing each other for almost two years. Don't get me wrong, we have talked almost daily; facetiming each other with our news of our latest conquests, heartbreaks, job offers, whatever. But, damn, two years of facetiming didn't prepare me for up-close and personal Josh Matthews.

Three weeks ago, Josh called me up and asked if he could come out and see me. I was ecstatic that I would get to see my best-friend and hang out like old times. Two weeks ago, Josh knocks on my door, saying "surprise!" when I open said door. Boy, surprised was an understatement. The last time I saw him two years ago, he looked more like my old best-friend. The Josh standing at my door with a sheepish smile was a whole different person.

Of course, I hugged him and then told him to come in. We ordered a pizza and the rest, up until now, as they say, is history. He's been here for two weeks, and I still don't have a clue how long he's planning on staying. I hate to ask the inevitable question, but I would sort of like to know what his plans are.

Looking over the book I was pretending to read, I watch Josh as he fixes dinner in the kitchen. He looks at home wearing the apron with "kiss the chef" printed across the front. He had sent me the apron as a birthday gift a year ago. I never wore it, but it sure looked delicious on him. I shake my head at my crazy thoughts. He's your best-friend, Susie, stop with the crazy thoughts, I mentally scolded myself.

Me shaking my head caught Josh's attention. "You okay, Suzie-Q?"

"Hmmm?" I hummed as if I was so engrossed in the book I wasn't reading that I hadn't heard his question, or notice that he called me by the nickname he had used since grade school.

"What's up? What are you reading that is so enticing that you're shaking your head at it?" He laughed as he came over and sat in the chair across from me.

I put the book down as if I lost interest in it and smiled over at him. "It's just one of those smutty romance books. I've read it before, just got bored and thought I'd read it again."

"Right." He didn't believe me, but he didn't question me further about it.

"Whatever you're fixing, it sure smells good." I glanced past him into the kitchen.

"Oh, just you wait. It will make your toes curl, it's so good." He laughed.

"I can't wait." I said, smiling at him. "Do I have time to take a quick shower before dinner?"

"Absolutely, Suzie-Q. Off with you and your stinky self. Dinner will be on the table waiting when you come out."

I jumped up from the sofa and headed to my room to grab my shower essentials, stopping a moment to look back at him and smile at the man standing once again in my kitchen. Lord help me and my sinful mind.

2

Dinner was well worth the wait, and the creamy sauce on top of the pasta just about did curl my toes. Josh was an awesome cook. I hated to bring up the whole "how long are you staying" conversation, but I would like to know what's going on with him. I haven't seen him make any calls or work from his laptop since he's been here the last two weeks. I work from home, so I think I would notice those things.

"Thank you for dinner, Joshie. It was absolutely, toe-curling delicious."

"You are so very welcome, Suzie-Q. Only the best for my bestie." He clinked his wine glass against mine with a smile.

"Did you just use the word bestie?" I asked with a pretend shocked look.

"Yes, I think I did." He put his hand to his chest like he was shocked with himself.

We both laughed and clinked our glasses once more and took a sip of the wine.

"Let's go sit in the living room, shall we?" I said as I stood and moved to the big sofa that took up the space in the open floor plan apartment.

"Sure thing, bestie." He said, emphasizing the word bestie.

"Oh, please, stop." I laughed.

Once seated, he sat next to me, his arm along the back of the sofa, and twirled a loose ringlet of my dark hair in his fingers.

"I have missed you so much, you know that?" Josh said in a low tone, his gaze watching his fingers as they twirled my hair.

"What's wrong, Josh?"

"What do you mean? I missed you. I needed to see you." He still didn't look at me.

"Josh?" I put my hand on his, stopping his fingers from the twirling. When he finally looked at me, I knew something wasn't right. "What's wrong?" I asked again.

"You always had a way with knowing when something is wrong." He said.

"Well, you've been here for two weeks, Josh. I haven't seen you do any work or heard you on the phone with anyone. You have me worried. Spill."

"Are you tired of me already?" He tried to look hurt, but I knew he was deflecting from the original question.

"Josh." I gave him a look that let him know that I wasn't kidding anymore.

"Okay, okay." He put both hands in the air like he was saying he gave up. "I'll tell you everything, but I need to get that bottle of wine over there first. You and I both are going to need it."

Josh stood up and moved into the kitchen, grabbed both of our glasses in his left hand, and the open bottle of wine in his right. He brought them over, handing my glass to me, filling it up once more, then filling his glass, taking a huge sip, and filled it once more, before sitting back down on the sofa next to me.

"What is going on with you?" I asked, eyeing him with concern.

"I wasn't lying when I said I missed you. I just want you to know that up front."

"Okay, I missed you too, now for the real reason you're acting like you've done something and you're afraid of being found out." I said.

"You know me so well, Suze." He looked into his glass as he took a deep breath, then continued. "You know that I was seeing someone…"

"Yes, Chelsea? Or was it Kelly?" I couldn't keep up with his girlfriends.

"Sherry." He shot me a look of exasperation. "Kelly was before Chelsea. Chelsea was before Sherry."

"Well, I had their names right." I said. "Go on, what about Sherry?"

"She broke up with me." He took a gulp of his wine.

I waited, thinking there was something else, but he didn't continue.

"Okay?"

"I asked her to marry me, Suze." He didn't look up from his wine this time.

"You what?" I asked in disbelief. My Josh asked a girl to marry him? Why did he not tell me he cared that much about someone? He always told me important thing, or at least I thought he had.

"I asked her to marry me, and she turned me down."

"Oh." Was all I could manage.

3

"Oh? I tell you I asked another woman to marry me and all you can say is oh?" He almost looked mad at me.

"What am I supposed to say, Josh?" I shot back. "I didn't even know you liked this girl that much, let alone enough to marry her."

"Exactly!" He said with a huff.

"What?" Now, I was completely confused.

"Why do you think you didn't know?" He asked.

"Because you didn't tell me?" Duh.

Josh took in a long, deep breath before he calmly set his wine glass down onto the coffee table. He took another deep breath before he turned to me and took my hands.

"Suzie, I need a place to stay. Can I please stay here until I can get my transfer in place with the company I work for?"

"Transfer? You're moving here?" I sounded like an idiot, I know, but he had me so confused I had no idea what was happening.

"Sherry and I were living together. When she said no, I took time off from work, don't worry, I have plenty of built-up time." He stopped me before I could ask about his time off. "I just need a place to stay until I can find my own. I emailed my boss and he said he could transfer me to the New York division with no problem."

"Of course you can stay here. You know that. But why didn't you tell me all of this before?" I shot him a look of hurt. "I thought we told each other everything."

"I don't know why I didn't tell you. I don't even know why I asked her to marry me."

"Well, I suppose it was because you loved her?" I kind of said it in a question.

"I suppose. No, I don't think it was that. I think it was because I thought she expected me to propose, but when I did, well..." he trailed off with a wave of his hand.

I reached over and put my arms around his neck and hugged him. "It's going to be okay, Joshie. You can stay here as long as you like." Josh put his arms around me and pulled me tighter against him, and we hugged each other for a long time before he finally pulled back and kissed me on the forehead.

"Thank you, Suze. You mean the world to me." He said as he kissed me on the forehead once again before pulling me to my feet as he stood up.

"Yeah, what are best friends for?" I said.

"Right, best friends till the end." Replied Josh.

"Till the end." I replied back.

Letting me go, Josh picked up the wine glasses and the empty bottle and headed towards the kitchen. I watched him as he rinsed the glasses, and I thought to myself 'how in the world am I going to share an apartment with this man' before turning and picking up the book I had laid aside earlier in the evening.

"Hey, I'm going to go read before I turn in." I moved towards the hallway that led to my bedroom.

"Okay, Suze." He smiled over at me. "Oh, and Suze?"

"Yes?" I turned to glance back at him questioningly.

"Thank you, again." He said quietly.

"No need to thank me, Josh. That's what best-friends do." I blew him a kiss as I winked at him. "Goodnight."

"Goodnight." I heard Josh say as I shut my bedroom door.

4

Josh started his position with the advertising company a little over four months ago. It took his boss a week to get the transfer through, and he took a weekend and went back to Oregon to get most of his things. So, it's been almost six months in total that he's been living here. Three months of watching him in all stages of dress, and undress, move across our apartment. Three agonizing months of going to sleep with him across the hall, wishing he was in bed with me.

What in the hell was going on with me? I never thought of Josh like that. At least, not before he showed up at my door three months ago. It's like a switch was flipped and all my girlie senses are at attention whenever he's near me. Either he doesn't notice how awkward I act around him, or he does notice and thinks it's cute. I don't know which would be worse.

"Suze?" I heard Josh's voice as he opened the door to the apartment.

"In here." I called back.

"Hey, beautiful." He said as he poked his head through my bedroom door. Since Josh moved in, I moved my 'office' into my bedroom so that I had more privacy when he was home.

"Hey, how was your day?" I asked.

"Long." He replied. "How much longer do you need to work?"

I looked at my watch, it was almost six o'clock. "I can wrap up in about thirty minutes, why? What's up?"

"It's Friday." Was his only reply.

"Okay. It's Friday. And that means?" I laughed.

"I thought we could go to dinner at Rudolph's." He smiled.

Rudolph's was a swanky Italian restaurant on the other side of town. It was hard to get reservations six weeks out, much less on short notice.

"Rudolph's? You do realize that it's extremely hard to get reservations there?" I asked.

"Yes, Rudolph's. And, yes, I do realize how hard it is to get reservations there. But, what you don't realize is that I just finished up the advertising campaign for the owner and he has gifted me a dinner reservation for tonight." He said with a big smile on his face.

"Really?!?" I was closing down my laptop as I asked the question.

"Really. Now, get to moving. Our reservations are for seven-thirty, does that give you enough time to get ready?"

"I'll make it work." I jumped up and ran over to him and hugged his neck, giggling like a schoolgirl.

"Go!" Josh laughed as he patted my ass as I ran past him to the bathroom to take a shower.

―――

Forty-five minutes later we were getting into a cab heading to Rudolph's. I had rushed through a shower, blow dried my hair just to pull it up in a loose twist, keeping it in place with one of my fancy hair combs, applied just enough makeup, and spritzed on some of my expensive perfume that I only use for special occasions. I was so excited about the reservations that I had forgotten to grab my clothes on my way to the bathroom, so I had to walk back to my bedroom in only a towel. Josh's back had been to me when I came out, I was relieved. I don't think I could have faced him if he had seen me in a towel.

Sitting in the back of the cab, I placed my hand over Josh's and gave his a squeeze. He gave my hand a squeeze back.

"Thank you for asking me to go with you." I said to him.

"Of course. Who else would I ask?" He replied.

"I'm sure you could have asked anyone from work to go with you..." I started.

"I didn't want to take anyone else, Suze. I wanted you." He smiled that slow crooked smile he does when he gets serious. I couldn't help but smile back, wishing he meant those last three words in a totally different way.

"Well, thank you." I said, not know what else to say.

"You look beautiful, by the way." He pulled a tendril of my hair loose to hang along my neck.

"You look pretty dapper yourself, Mr. Matthews." I replied, meaning it. He had put on a dark blue suit with a bay blue tie that had dark blue paisleys on it.

"I prefer the towel, but this dress looks pretty damn good on you as well." He smirked.

"Oh. I didn't think you saw me." I placed both of my hands over my face, wishing I could melt back into the seat.

"Oh, I saw alright." He chuckled.

"Josh, stop." I groaned.

"Never." He chuckled again, pulling one of my hands to his lips and kissing it. "I love it when you blush like that, Suzy-Q."

I groaned again. He laughed a little more.

5

Dinner had been beyond delicious. The owner came out and welcomed us in person, thanking Josh profusely for the advertising he had done for his restaurant. Josh had apparently completely rebranded the look of the restaurant and tonight was the soft re-opening with the new look. Everything was very elegant, with crystal wine glasses and gold tableware. I almost felt underdressed for the occasion, but Josh assured me that I looked perfect. When we were finished and Josh asked for the check, the waiter told him that our bill was taken care of, courtesy of the owner. We thanked him and left the restaurant.

The ride back to our apartment was quiet. Not an uncomfortable type of quiet, but a quiet that was perfect for the end of a dinner date. Date? Had this been a date? No. He just asked me because we were friends. Right, we were friends.

The cab stopped outside of our apartment and Josh came around to open my door for me, then paid the driver. Taking my hand, he pulled me in a dancing twirl, then pulled me to him and dipped me backwards before pulling me slowly back to him. I was laughing as he pulled me from the dip; so was he. It had been a perfect evening. But as I came up from the dip, my hands moved from his arms to his chest. He was holding me so close that I knew he had to feel my heartbeat.

Our laughter dwindled until we were just standing there, our eyes meeting each other's gaze. I looked away first, pulling out of his embrace. We were best-friends, I told myself. We were just friends, and roommates. I have to stop thinking that there ever could be more between us.

"Suze?" Josh said softly.

"You ready to go up?" I asked as I started for the door to the apartment building.

"Suze?" Josh started again.

"I'm going on up. I have to pee." I have to pee? Well, if that didn't put out any burning desires, nothing would.

"Okay. I'll be up in a few. I think I'm going to walk off some of this dinner." He patted his stomach and smiled at me.

"Sure. Okay. I'll see you upstairs, then." I turned and walked into the building before I could stammer anything else out that would sound just as stupid as I have to pee.

I'm not sure how long Josh had stayed out. I had gone upstairs and washed my face, brushed my hair and put on my pajamas before he had returned. I had just turned out my bedroom light when I heard the front door open and close. I held my breath as I heard Josh walk through the apartment, wondering where he had gone, and what he had done when he had taken his walk.

A soft knock on my door startled me. I didn't know whether to pretend I was asleep or answer him. Josh opened the door before I could make either decision.

"Suze, can I come in?"

"Sure, Josh. What's up?" I tried to sound like I had been asleep.

"I just need to talk to you about something." He came in and set at the edge of my bed. When I started to turn the bedside lamp on, he stopped me. "No, leave it off. It's easier to say this in the dark." He said with a little laugh.

"Say what, Josh? Is something wrong?" I sat up, pulling my blanket up with me.

"No, not really. I just think I owe you the truth." He said softly.

"The truth? About what?" This man could confuse me to no end.

"About the real reason Sherry turned down my proposal."

Sherry was the last person I wanted to hear about, but something in his tone told me I needed to listen to him.

"Okay." I said. "I'm not sure what this is about, but go ahead, I'm listening."

"It was because of you, Suze."

"Me? But I never met her. I never even talked to her. Why would she not marry you because of me?" I was completely and utterly confused and frustrated at this. The woman didn't even know me.

"She said that all I talked about was you. That no woman was ever going to replace you, and I realized she was right. And I told her so. You have always been the one I turned to when I wanted to share something big, or even something small. It's always been you that I wanted to talk to late at night, so your voice was the last thing I heard before going to bed." At this, he looked up and I saw the longing in his eyes, and I believed him. I felt the same way, but I just realized it myself as he was saying the words.

"Josh?" I felt a tear drop from my eye and trail down my cheek. I didn't know what to say. I was afraid that this was just a dream, and that Josh was still out walking.

"I love you, Suzie-Q. I have always loved you. I don't know why I didn't tell you sooner."

I didn't wait for him to say anything else. I raised myself up and put my arms around his neck and claimed his mouth with my own. Josh didn't react at first, but then I felt his arms wrap around me as he pulled me into his lap, his mouth opening hungrily to accept my kiss.

My fingers wrapped themselves in Josh's golden curls as I kissed his mouth with such hunger, such need, that I didn't realize he had pulled me under him until I felt the bed against my back.

"I want you." I breathed into his mouth. My words seem to breath fire into him as he ran his hands over my breasts as he lifted my top over my head. Before I could move my hands down to remove his shirt, his warm mouth was sucking my nipple. A gasp wrenched itself from me as he moved his mouth to my other nipple, his tongue slowly licking around it, arousing it until it was achingly hard between his lips. My hands moved back up to his hair, once again wrapping my fingers in his curls, pulling his head down against me.

Josh raised himself above me, pulling my hands down to his shirt, he guided me to unbutton the first button, then the second, I took it from there by ripping his shirt open, popping the last few buttons into the air. He pulled his shirt from his body as I began to undo his pants. Josh pushed me back against the bed with his body as I moaned at having to relinquish the goods before I could set them free.

My body ached with a need that had been growing over the last few months. Another gasp came from me as I felt Josh's hands move down my body and into my panties. His fingers caressed my folds until they found my wetness, then, without pause, two fingers were inside me. My body arched up to meet his rhythm, wanting him to finish me before I exploded. Just as I was about to orgasm, his fingers left me. I opened my eyes to see him pulling his pants off, his erection straining to full hardness.

I licked my lips but before I could pull him to me, Josh pulled my legs so that I was on the edge of the bed, then he dropped down between my legs and his tongue found my wetness. The jolt of pure pleasure that went through me almost sent me over the edge.

"God, you taste so good." He murmured against my skin, licking slowly through my center until he reached my clit, running his tongue around that spot, then sucking it in, making me catch my breath. He would then run his tongue back through my wetness, dipping his tongue into me, then back up to my clit. I was about to go into convulsions if he didn't fuck me now.

"Josh..." I whimpered.

"Shhh." He whispered against my skin as his mouth moved up to my belly, then to my nipples, before capturing my mouth in a slow, hungry kiss. I moaned into his mouth as I could taste myself on his tongue. Just as the kiss deepened into a need that I didn't think I could handle; he buried his cock deep inside me in one maddingly slow stroke. I yelled out with so much pleasure that I know the neighbors could hear me. But I didn't care. Josh rocked into me faster and harder until my orgasm waved into a second orgasm before his own orgasm stilled his body deep inside me.

After a few moments of ragged breathing, Josh raised his body above mine and kissed me tenderly, then he kissed the tears from my cheeks, tears I didn't even know were there until I felt his lip on them. Turning over and pulling me with him to lay on his chest, he brushed my hair out of my face before asking if I was okay.

"I'm better than okay." I replied shakily.

"Then why are you crying? Did I hurt you?" He asked, hugging me closer.

"No, you didn't hurt me." I said softly.

"Suze, I would never hurt you. I love you."

"That's why I'm crying, Josh." I raised myself up to look into his eyes.

"I don't understand." He said softly.

"I love you too. I always have." I whispered.

"Good God, woman, but you sure know how to make a man wait." He laughed.

6

"When did you know you loved me?" I asked Josh the next morning.

"You really want to know?" He asked teasingly.

"Yes, I really want to know." I laughed, toying with a curl right behind his ear.

"I knew in the sixth grade when I met you. You were sitting by yourself on one of the swings, just barely pushing yourself with your foot to move the swing back and forth. I saw you and I knew that I had to have you for myself." He chuckled.

"Really?" I said with a little sarcasm.

"Really. That's when I walked over to you and asked if you wanted me to push you, remember?"

"I do remember that." I did remember, because that's when I knew that I wanted him to be mine. I meant as my friend. Maybe, I just meant mine.

"When did you know that you loved me?" He questioned back.

"You really want to know?" I teased.

"Yes, I really want to know." He tapped the end of my nose.

"I don't know." I said honestly. "I think I have always loved you, I just don't think that I knew it at the time. But that day you showed up at my door, I knew it then."

"Good God, woman, but you sure do know how to make a man wait." He growled against my mouth as he rolled over on top of me.

"No more waiting." I whispered back as I let his mouth take mine in his kiss.

THE END ... For Now

About the Author

Alexis R. Craig was born and raised in rural Indiana and then uprooted to the mountains of West Virginia. It is there that she learned, at an early age, to love the art of writing. She now lives in North Carolina with her soulmate and best friend... her husband.

She is a self-professed romantic, in love with the idea of love, romance, poetry, and, of course, a good wine.

Writing a good love story that defies all the rules and boundaries has become her addiction; an addiction that has become her passion, one that she loves to share with anyone that reads her words.

facebook.com/TheAlexisCraig
instagram.com/thealexiscraig
goodreads.com/Alexis_R_Craig

ON FIRE

A Short Story from Piñon Ridge

Sutton Bishop

1

Billie

Piñon Ridge, Mid-August, seven-thirty in the morning ...

Fresh out of a relaxing shower and back in her room, Billie hummed along to the country song coming from of the Bluetooth speaker and pulled the towel from her head. She finger-combed the heavy tendrils, mentally reviewing the day ahead of her. It was going to be another great one. After working a couple of hours at the Chamber of Commerce, she was hiking the rigorous Wicked Sister—a six-miler that would test her. There would be plenty of time to complete it and freshen up ahead of tonight's bartending shift at the Hazy Rebel's Deck.

The backpack containing her hiking shoes, snacks, and water was in the truck, a practice she committed to long ago. It allowed her to take impromptu hikes when a window of time was available. Her goal was to be hired by Intrepid Adventures, the premier wilderness guided-tours and -trips business of Peaks County. Working for owners Kenna Ambrose and Cori Wainsom was considered a plum job. The women were fair, the pay good, and the work steady. And then there was the scenery. God's country. It filled her with awe. At an elevation of 9600 feet, the small bohemian town was embraced by the soaring Taurus Range to the west. The Ruston River meandered through the area, adding more charm.

Something other than the fresh citrus shampoo and conditioner shifted her attention. Still bent over, she reached for the mousse in the same scent, applying it sparingly, then flipped her long hair back and straightened in one movement, gently squeezing to disperse the product and coax the waves into tighter curls as much as possible.

There it was again. Nothing like what she was using. Her humming ceased and she checked the window. Closed.

Maybe Lissa was up and using who knew what products to get ready. A surprise given that she had a tough time rising and was usually late for work. In the span of several weeks, she had discovered that Lissa had a penchant for "appearance is everything" whereas Billie preferred the less-is-more approach.

The cost of living in Piñon Ridge was considerable, and rentals scarce. So, at the age of twenty-eight Billie was again in a communal situation, unless she wanted to dip into her savings and investments, which she did not. Having a roommate after living on her own was a disappointment but a necessary sacrifice to succeed in her long-term plans. She counted herself lucky that it was only her and Lissa and not multiple roommates, like many single people who resided here. The shared single bathroom overflowed with a frightening assortment of face, hair, body products, and gadgets. After Lissa generously sampled some of her shower gel and lotion, Billie resorted to keeping her toiletries in a plastic tote, carrying it back and forth between her bedroom and the bathroom, as she had in college. No amount of talking had brought ditsy Lissa around to leaving Billie's personal items alone.

Billie pulled her damp hair into a loose knot and slipped her phone into the breast pocket of the threadbare butter-yellow robe—closing it where it gaped and retying the sash. The smell was still there. Chemical-like. Curious, she stepped into the hall. The odor was more pungent. *What the hell?*

Lissa's door was shut. The bathroom was as Billie had left it—the door ajar and exhaust fan on. Her head whipped in the opposite direction as crackling, spitting, and hissing captured her attention. She fell against the door jamb and about fainted.

Flames shot out of the kitchen closet that housed the stackable washer and dryer. The alarm started shrieking. *Shit! What to do first? This can't be happening.* Her hand shook as it closed around her phone. With difficulty, she made the call.

"9-1-1. What is the nature of your emergency?"

"Our laundry room is on fire." Near tears, her voice wobbled. "I think it's the dryer."

"Address please."

Billie's voice broke as she recited the address. Her heart pounded, making it hard to breathe. Acrid smoke billowed, causing her nostrils to sting and eyes to water. She wiped at tears spilling onto her cheeks and gulped down the fear, then covered her face with the collar of the robe and sprinted to Lissa's room. She opened the door with such force that the doorknob lodged in the wall and held the door open. "Lissa, get up!"

The dispatch woman spoke louder, but calmly. "Name?"

"Billie Gerit." Trembling made her words breathy and broken. She inhaled carefully and deeply through the thin fabric, trying to control the tremors, to not give into the panic gnawing at her. "It's growing, ma'am." *Hurry. Hurry.*

"Can you get outdoors?"

"Yes." *Hurry. Please ... Hurry.*

"Move to safety. Immediately, Ms. Gerit. Keep away from the building but stay in the vicinity. EMTs will perform assessments you and firefighters will need to speak with you."

"I've got to get my roommate out." She stomped to the side of her roommate's bed. "Lissa!" Then to dispatch. "I'm sorry, ma'am."

"You're all right, miss. Try to remain calm. Firefighters are on their way. Is anyone else in the residence other than you and your roommate? Pets?"

No, ma'am. No pets either." Lissa's boyfriend never stayed over during the week. Thank God. The last time she had seen Hud, it was *all* of him."

"Be safe."

"Thank you." Billie disconnected the call.

Sirens blared in the distance. Lissa's blinds were pulled up. *To keep her from oversleeping? Right,* Billie scoffed in her head. Sunlight streamed in through the window. A beautiful day and a fire. Unimaginable, and yet it was fact.

"Just a few more minutes," Lissa said groggily, eyes still shut. Her hand reached out, fingers tapping the screen of the phone on her nightstand. "Damned alarm."

"Get up! FIRE!"

Lissa jolted to a sitting position, eyes wide with panic, mouth round, the covers pooling at her hips, revealing what little she had on—a sheer camisole and matching bottoms. "What?"

"FIRE!" Billie ripped the white summer-weight blanket from the bed and cocooned Lissa in it. "Let's go or we'll have to get on the balcony."

The sirens were louder.

"My things!" Lissa wailed, panic evident in the pitch of her voice.

"Leave them. Get your purse and phone. NOW!" Billie led Lissa toward the front door, snatching her own purse and keys from the entry table.

Lissa froze—openmouthed and wide-eyed, terrified by the flames licking the kitchen walls, ceiling, and cabinets.

Billie clapped her hands in front of Lissa's face. "Snap out of it!" She grabbed her hand and jerked her toward the door, ripping it open.

Smoke-free air and firefighters greeted them. Billie lowered the shawl collar and rearranged her robe, feeling exposed. Faced with no time to slip on a bra and panties, she was forced to go commando. Given the situation, it was the least of her worries. Across the way, neighbors— a young married couple with one child and another due soon—were being escorted out of their condo. Dressed in sleepwear, they looked half-asleep and harried.

"You both all right?" The firefighter's respirator distorted his words.

"Yes. The fire is in the kitchen. I think it's the dryer."

He nodded slowly.

Billie couldn't see the details of his face through the full mask, but she sensed and heard the unruffled calm in his voice. "Confirming no other occupants or pets, correct?"

"Correct."

"Escort." He called over the commotion, then addressed both of them. "Watch the hoses, ladies."

A fireman on the landing waved Billie and Lissa toward him. "Got them, Captain."

As soon as they cleared the doorway, firefighters entered their condo. The women were taken to the parking lot where they were assessed by EMTs and released.

Three o'clock ...

The adrenaline coursing through Billie had worn off, but now waves of trembling washed over her without warning. Efforts to quiet herself were unsuccessful, making her feel sapped and chilled. On top of that, a ravenous appetite emerged. She wolfed down two turkey Reuben sandwiches and drained four glasses of iced lemon tea. She had never consumed so much at a sitting. Still feeling hollow, and realizing her system was overtaxed, she stopped eating and drinking and fixated on the magnificent Taurus Range.

Immediately she felt better.

The fire was merely a setback. Not for one minute did she regret her decision to move to Piñon Ridge. There was never a bad day in her new hometown's high alpine climate. How could there be when most days were sunny, and the scenery was stunning? Regardless of the weather or the hour, the view was panoramic and breathtaking. The residents and tourists, friendly for the most part.

When the firefighters were sure the building was safe to reenter, she, Lissa, and others were escorted back inside to get what they could. A smoky chemical stench permeated the condo. Everything was wet. Her gym shoes grew soaked as she slogged through the saturated cream carpeting, intent on packing her stuff into trash bags and bins. She heaved those into the bed of her pickup, grateful she had given away so much before moving only three weeks earlier. What furniture she had—rented—could be dealt with later.

At the laundromat, she started multiple loads. And after everything was dry and folded, she left it in the care of the launderette, promising to return within a few hours. She bought more bins to hold the freshly laundered clothing and linens. *What a flippin' mess.*

Hiking never happened. Neither had her shift at the Chamber of Commerce. On this beautiful afternoon, no one lingered on the Deck—where she was—or inside the Hazy Rebel. The restaurant had closed at two o'clock and would not reopen until five-thirty. Her bartending shift began in an hour-and-a-half, at four thirty.

Nick, one of the owners of the restaurant, plopped onto the stool to her left. "For someone who doesn't seem to have an ounce of extra on her, you sure put a lot away."

"Hey." She greeted her boss. "Thanks for letting me store all of those bins in your office. I think this morning did a number on me. I can't seem to fill up."

He offered a consoling smile. "Glad I could help in some small way. A fire would unnerve anyone. You're scheduled for tonight?"

"Yep."

"Why don't you skip your shift? We'll manage."

"The thought occurred to me, but working will keep my head clear. I already missed my shift at the Chamber. Do you know of anywhere I can stay tonight? I've called around. There aren't any vacancies. I can sleep in the truck but would prefer not to."

"You need a place to lay your head down, Billie. I can offer you a place tonight, offer you our place, but then we have family in town. That's the good and the bad of living in a tourist town that has everything to offer, right? Ask Owen. His girlfriend lives with him, but he might have a room or a couch for a night or two. I'm not sure how he and Tess have things set up."

She crossed the fingers that had been shredding a napkin in her lap. "I will, thanks."

———

After graduating college in New Mexico mid-year, Billie slope-hopped, skiing many of the ranges in the West through the next season. Wanting to settle somewhere within a few hours of fabulous skiing, she moved to

Denver and dedicated more than full-time hours to her remote position for four years. The demanding tech job took its toll on her dating life, which was mediocre at best, so she gave it up.

A year later, still single, and highly successful in her occupation but burned out, she joined a hiking community. The activity filled her in a way nothing else had. Hooked, she hiked at every opportunity and took classes to fine-tune pacing and learn safety protocols and navigation. Billie also participated in excursions to improve her knowledge about primitive camping and hone her climbing skills for a variety of terrain and challenging conditions. The club offered opportunities most weekends, and sometimes during the week.

It was the eight-day trip through the Taurus Range and time spent in Piñon Ridge that had her yearning to become an area resident. Committed, she relocated as soon as her lease was up. Against dipping into her healthy savings, she found someone to live with, quit her job, and secured part-time positions at the Chamber and the Hazy Rebel within days, covering her rent. She felt lighter immediately. The anxiety that had dogged her for years evaporated like the gauzy clouds breaking over the summit.

Billie was certain she had made the right decision.

Four days later ...

Her body was sore from couch surfing—the first night at Nick's and the second and third at Owen's. Even though she appreciated her bosses' generosity, sleeping at their places and doing laundry in their homes was awkward.

This morning, she witnessed Owen's girlfriend Tess's narrowed glare, twisted lips, and hands on hips when taking in the sight of Billie's panties and bras hanging on the drying rack in the laundry room. The floor creaked as her weight shifted.

Tess whipped around, a smile pasted on her face, and although her voice was light, the question was pointed. "How much longer are you staying?"

Billie was a third wheel. "Just tonight," she said, making it fact.

Tess nodded. "Sorry about the fire. It must be awful to have nowhere to go for now."

"It is. I keep asking around, but no luck. I'm seriously considering sleeping in my truck. The entire county doesn't have a vacancy. The management said it would be two months or longer until I could move back into my condo."

"How many units in your building?"

"Six. In addition to the fire destruction in our unit, there was extensive smoke and water damage throughout entire the building. If I sign a new lease, that's what they're offering even though there was eleven months left on mine, I've still got to find someone to share the rent. Lissa up and moved to Prescott to live with her boyfriend." She shrugged and mumbled under her breath. "I guess the timing worked."

"Finding a roommate shouldn't be an issue."

"I know, but finding someone I can live with might be more difficult."

"Right." Tess frowned thoughtfully. "You know, you could camp. The weather is fairly reliable right now. Do you have a tent?"

"I lost it in the fire."

It had been stored with her other camping equipment in the laundry room closet. Destroyed. Hopefully her renters insurance would replace most of it. She had already submitted photos and the dated receipts.

What Billie wanted was somewhere to land and reorganize her churned-up life until the condo was move-back-in ready. The idea of living where she had had a fire did not appeal to her, but the rental market was beyond tight and would be more so with ski season approaching. The reality was that the management was giving her two weeks to decide on renewing the lease, even though the unit wasn't available. If she wished to remain in Piñon Ridge, she had to act soon *and* find a roommate, with the understanding that the move-in date was fluid. Grrr ... What a pain in the ass, like she had time to vet candidates. Overwhelmed, she threw her arms up, laced her hands, and pressed down on the top of her head. *Shit.*

"Elevation Outfitters could help you out." Tess suggested.

Buying new camping equipment wasn't at the top of Billie's list right now. "If it's months before I can move back in, I'd be subject to some weather. Fall is around the corner."

"My brother camps regardless of conditions so he has all the equipment and then some. Maybe he can lend you—" Tess snapped her fingers, and a grin spread over her face. "Hey ... Lee's out of town training right now. I might have a solution. He has extra room and a schedule that would give you some personal space. I'll call and ask. You might have met him."

Billie shook her head. "I haven't met anyone by the name of Lee since I moved here."

"Given the situation, he might not have introduced himself. Lee's a firefighter."

"Yeah, no one introduced themselves. It was chaos. And I was wigged-out."

"I can only imagine." Tess wrapped her arms around Billie and squeezed. "I'll call him this morning and get back to you."

Hope bloomed in Billie's chest, and she blinked rapidly to clear the threatening tears. "I appreciate it, Tess."

Billie drove through dappled sunlight on the way to her temporary digs. The road grew steep and changed to one of rutted packed dirt and detritus hemmed in closely by dense forest. Needing more traction, Billie switched to four-wheel drive, climbing slowly, her head on a swivel as the truck moved forward, prepared to halt if she saw movement. Wildlife was abundant.

Only minutes out of the village, she felt transported to another place, as she often did when hiking in the mountains. Mid-afternoon brightened as the trees thinned, indicating she was close. Billie turned onto the drive, which dipped and then crested. Up ahead, she saw the clearing.

As Tess had promised, no one appeared to be home. Billie parked and took a few moments to absorb where she would be living temporarily. The house was truly what people would call mountain living—simple and charming. Four red Adirondack chairs circled a contained fire pit, with several buckets close by. Cords of wood were stacked a safe distance away. The front door, also red, was situated under a pitched roof—a welcoming pop of color contrasting with the otherwise dark-brown siding.

A heavy-duty snow shovel hung from the wide ski rack next to the door. No skis, but there were several fishing poles. Two blue single-person kayaks were attached to the front side of the house and several sets of ski poles filled a large zinc cylinder. Apparently, Lee enjoyed other activities in addition to camping.

On either side of the large front stoop, large river rocks bordered gardens that cried for attention. *There's something I can help with.* Tess had shared that Lee asked that Billie just keep things neat. At a minimum she would address the gardens' sorry appearance.

She approached the front door with only her purse, inserted the key given to her by Tess, and was greeted by a pleasant soapy scent when the door swung open. After slipping off her sandals, she padded through the small vestibule and into the great room. Abundant light slanted through the bank of large windows at the back of the home.

What a pleasant surprise. The space was warm and welcoming—not what she would consider a bachelor pad, but a masculine home. Tasteful furnishings with an occasional pop of color. She considered the wrought iron spiral staircase. Upstairs was where she was staying. *Ugh. Should be fun lugging my bags up there. Might as well check it out first.*

More surprises. Two unmade built-in bunks and a cute reading nook by another large window. She stepped closer and peered out. The view was spectacular. Aside from the fact that she was going to be sleeping in a twin bed and driving to work instead of walking, Lee's home was much nicer than her impersonal condo.

2

Lee

A week later ...

It was as dark as pitch when Lee arrived home. He dropped the large duffle bag on the mudroom bench and started toeing off his boots, pausing as new scents infiltrated his brain. His home smelled of a pleasant light citrus mixed with something that made his empty stomach growl.

The woman he was helping out short-term was in his home. Billie somebody. He was a softy when Tess asked for something, more so since their sister Nell died in a car accident with her husband. Tess's request was a favor on behalf of her boyfriend Owen, who employed the woman. Pulled from his training session by her call, he listened with half an ear to his sister, missing why interim housing was so damned important.

He dispensed with the other boot and entered the kitchen. The light over the sink glowed softly, illuminating the space. His guest had certainly made herself at home during his time away. The counters, usually stacked with snacks and clean dishes, because what was the point in putting them away when they were going to be reused? were bare, except for a loosely covered pie on the island.

He pulled back the aluminum foil. Butter, cooked apples, cinnamon, and sugar assaulted his senses. Apple pie, with a caramelized crumble topping. His absolute favorite. Homemade, and still warm. Damn. His mouth watered and the growling in his stomach increased. *Okay, maybe this situation isn't going to be so miserable ...*

A sliver was gone.

Considering that an invitation, and without looking away from the dessert, he took a plate from the cabinet, a serving spoon from a drawer, and scooped out a quarter of the pie. Ice cream would be the perfect addition, so he made his way to the freezer, hoping some had miraculously appeared. He had finished the vanilla bean after drowning it in caramel and chocolate sauce the night before leaving on his trip. Late night snacking was a bad habit, among others.

Low and behold. A pint of vanilla bean—the high-end shit—was at eye-level in the freezer, among the organized-and-full-of-new-food-options. His temporary live-in had been busy. Containers of soups. Freezer-wrapped coconut, zucchini, and banana breads. All were labeled and dated, including several containers of mystery green cubes—until he saw the tape on the side: PESTO. Double damn. He loved pesto.

In danger of drooling, he topped the pie with half of the pint, and took a bite, his appreciation audible in the empty room. He was spooning a larger amount into his mouth when the pendants over the island came on, nearly blinding him. Eyes narrowed, his head snapped up, and his mouth opened. Some of the pie and ice cream seeped out, coating his lips, and dripping down his chin.

Her expression—a stare-down. Arched brows lifted. Eyes focused on the mess on his face. Hands on hips. "You're Lee?"

Lord. Fuck me. The woman was even more tantalizing than what was in his mouth. Wearing threadbare baggy sweatpants and a clingy tee on her athletic frame. Seemingly oblivious that he could see the contours of her lovely ripe breasts. Her long tawny hair was wild. Just-been-fucked-good hair. *Down boy*, he silently ordered his cock.

His fingers ached to explore the tendrils. Was the bumper crop of waves as silky as they looked? He cleared his throat, licked his lips, and placed the plate on the island, which was, thankfully, between them. His erection had not subsided. Neither had his pulse. He wiped the back of his hand across his mouth, trying not to smear the food into the week-long scruff. His guest felt familiar, but then who in Piñon Ridge didn't?

"Good evening. Yes. I'm Lee Carpenter. Tess's brother, and your host."

She flashed a brief smile. "Billie Gerit."

"Nice to meet you. Welcome to my humble abode, Billie. Thanks for the pie. It's incredible."

She rolled her lips and nodded curtly. "Thank you for giving me a room until I can move back into my condo."

"Happy to help. Why do you need a place to stay? I don't remember what my sister told me."

"Fire. Our damned dryer."

It was *her*. He had been impressed in more ways than one that morning. She had remained calm even though she had to have been rattled as hell, comforting her roommate and the other condo occupants, while also extending kindness and patience with his crew and the other first responders. Then there was that worn yellow robe. Translucent when she had briefly been in full sunlight. Damn ...

His cock had been the happy recipient of more than a few collaborative sessions of his hand and imagination when what that robe teased played on a loop in his mind. A naughty smirk escaped before he could capture it.

"Seriously? You find a fire amusing?"

The heat in her voice and the disbelief written on her face made him feel like a jerk, but hell, he was a hot-blooded man.

"Billie—" He liked the feel of her name on his tongue, and he was certain he would enjoy the taste of her even more. "Fire and amusing don't belong in the same sentence. But you in that robe ..." He shook his head, fighting a grin. "Hard to forget."

She paled and crossed her arms over her breasts. "Oh ... ohmigod ..."

Her eyes dove for the floor and stayed there for a few beats, then flipped back to his. "You were there?"

Billie was arrestingly beautiful. Hazel eyes. Full lips. A light dusting of freckles on her tanned skin.

"Yup. In bunker gear. Met you and your roomie at your door. Later, we had a conversation in the parking lot while you were being cleared by the EMTs." He licked the serving spoon clean, then pointed it at her. "You might consider replacing that robe with something less evocative." He shook his head, unable to look away from her as his smile grew.

Billie shot him a scathing expression. "You might consider not being such a pig. Good night." She snapped, throwing ice water on his arousal.

She spun on her heel and marched out of the kitchen. The spiral staircase thrummed from her angry footfalls as she climbed toward the second floor. A resounding click carried into the kitchen after the bunk room door shut. He had forgotten there was a lock on it.

"That went well, you ass." He muttered under his breath.

―――

Normally Lee slept like the dead, but the thought of Billie upstairs in his bunkroom and erotic images of them tangled up in his sheets kept him awake. After fisting himself for the last time, he rolled over and checked the clock on the nightstand—a retro gift from Tess. Its glowing face displayed the hands at six o'clock. He might as well strip his bed, clean up, and start the day.

Instead of bounding into the kitchen naked or in briefs, he slipped on joggers and stepped quietly. He tossed the sheets on the laundry room floor as he passed, then entered the kitchen, sliding the dimmer switch to its lowest before turning on the pendants, intent on brewing coffee.

He opened the cabinet and stepped back. "What the hell?" he muttered. Everything associated with his morning ritual had been reordered. Some of it had been put into baskets.

While coffee brewed, he opened other cabinets. What else had Billie been up to while he was out of town training?

A lot.

Spices, including new offerings, were alphabetized. The few items kept as staples had been added to and were organized.

The bottom shelf of the pantry was filled with paper towels and *cloth* napkins. On other shelves, baking items filled new canisters. Marshmallows, graham crackers, and chocolate in others; for s'mores, he assumed. All labeled. New roasting tongs hung from the inside wall. He peered closer. Nope. They were his, just scrubbed to sparkling. He inspected the drawer where towels and hot pads were kept. His stained and ratty assortment had been replaced and were arranged by color and pattern. Did she bring them or buy them?

Lee went to the mudroom and investigated the lockers and cabinets. Everything had been cleaned and reorganized. His beloved worn and dirty boots looked offensive against the tile floor, which had been scrubbed. A brand-new mat lay just inside the door. Tired from an intense week and a long drive, he hadn't noticed any of it last night. He moved the boots next to her hiking shoes, which were neatly set in the large rubber tray—also a new addition, then took the duffle to the laundry and emptied it, sorting by color. He decided to do a load of lights with his sheets. It was obvious Billie had been in here too, but he didn't check. The aroma of coffee was beckoning him.

Lee popped back into the kitchen, poured a full mug, and ventured into the great room. It was cleaner than he had left it. The fireplace had a new screen. He examined it more closely. No; it was his, with a fresh coat of black. Had she thought to use high-heat paint? He surveyed the rest of the space. The windows sparkled. Fat candlesticks, again, not his, adorned the mantel, the pillars already used. Pillows were fluffed and blankets folded and stacked. Books were dusted and reshelved—alphabetically and by genre. *Damn.*

He was in a quandary. Grudgingly, he appreciated the changes. They were nice. Thoughtful even. But another part of him was less than pleased. This was *his* house. Billie had made herself just a little too much at home. Without asking, she had taken it upon herself to clean and reorder his life. He raked a free hand through bed-hair that was overdue for a cut. Was she a neat freak or was this her way of thanking him for giving her a place to stay rent-free?

Emboldened by her intrusion into his space, he crept upstairs to pay it forward. The light citrus scent he had noticed last night was stronger, melding with a fresh clean smell. Fluffy white towels and a flowered bathmat graced the bathroom. Again, hers or new? He looked inside the vanity. It was stocked full of a brand of toilet paper he never bought, and vinegar—for cleaning he assumed. At one side of the double sink was a tote of woman-stuff. Unable to help himself, he continued to snoop and opened a bottle.

Lee was inhaling the shampoo, eyes closed, when he sensed a presence behind him. He'd been quiet. Was she an early riser, too? He secured the top and turned slowly, not sure what he would be facing.

Billie leaned against the door jamb, lean muscled legs extending from black hiking shorts, her arms crossed over an unzipped lightweight, long-sleeved red hoodie with a light gray tee underneath, emblazoned with QUEEN in white.

He groaned inwardly. *Like I needed a reminder.* "Morning."

"Did you run out of shampoo, Lee?" She tilted her head and fixed him with a frank expression.

He set the shampoo on the counter. "Just taking stock of all the changes since you moved in."

Her eyes traveled his naked torso, lingering on the happy trail disappearing into the low-slung joggers. His cock stirred and roused. Her reaction was a slight flush and flared nostrils. A shiver passed through her so quickly, he wondered if he had imagined it.

She sucked in a shaky breath and fixed those stunning eyes on him. "It's my stuff. As are the towels, hot pads, and napkins in the kitchen. I laundered your things and stored them in the cabinets in laundry room, by the way. I also cleaned but stayed out of your bedroom." Her face flushed deeper. Interesting. "I didn't throw out anything, although it was tempting. I also left your junk drawers alone."

Lee hadn't opened the junk drawers and would check out the laundry another time. "Uh-huh." He bobbed his head slowly, processing that she might be as attracted to him as he was to her. "What about all of those canisters? The new spices? The food in the fridge and freezer?"

"The canisters were the solution to how you store your baking supplies. Just about everything was outdated." Her nose scrunched up and underscored her disgust. "I replaced it all before making the pie, so what you ate last night was safe. The canisters will extend the shelf life of what you buy in the future. I'll leave them when I move out. As for the food ... I like to have things on hand after a long day. Cooking and baking make me happy."

"I see. And you've done all of this to thank me?"

"Yes. I'm grateful for a place to stay, rent-free."

He wasn't about to accept money from someone down on their luck. "And you alphabetized my spices because?"

"Easier to find when I'm cooking and baking, and it's another way for me to repay you for your kindness."

"That's fair. Are you a good cook?"

"You inhaled the apple pie."

"That's baking. Cooking is different."

"I'm competent in the kitchen and a whiz with the grill. I've used yours. You'll notice that the next time you use it."

He shifted his weight to the other leg when she raised those lovely brows again and shot him a look that expressed the grill wasn't as clean as it should have been.

"As far as my cooking talent, you can discover it tonight if you want. Dinner is at seven, unless you're occupied?"

Drinks and dinner with some of his crew had been discussed but not confirmed. Lee would drop a message in their group chat just in case, say that he was going to hang at home and turn in early. It was true enough. They would understand, knowing he had been out of town all week.

Her boldness and confidence intrigued him, as did the character she had shown during and after the fire. And, if her cooking was anything close to the magical pie he had devoured, he was in for a real treat. "No plans. What're you making?"

"Show up and find out."

Bossy little thing. "I will."

"Do you have any food allergies or aversions, Lee?"

"No allergies. But organ meats and lima beans will put me on a hunger strike."

"Same here, so don't worry. Just checking. What I have planned will be fine then."

"I'll contribute something to drink."

"That would be appreciated." She regarded him for a beat before smiling softly. Her eyes held a challenge. "A Pinot would pair nicely."

He growled internally. Wine was not his thing. Whiskey was. He'd drop by Intrepid and get some guidance from Kenna and Cori before stopping at Camby's liquor store; they enjoyed wine.

———

It was early afternoon when Lee entered Intrepid Adventures. The business was quiet. "Hey, Cori. How's it going?"

"Lee! Wonderful."

"Got a minute? If you don't, maybe Kenna does? I need advice."

"She's leading a group through Duke's pass." Cori rose from the seat behind her desk and stretched, then approached and squeezed his forearm. "How can I help?"

"I've been directed to buy wine. A Pinot."

"I see. Is this a date?"

"No." Realizing his tone held an edge of protest, he paused before continuing neutrally. "My temporary guest is making dinner, but she wouldn't tell me what." *Because you didn't push it.*

"Dinner," Cori said slowly. "I'd buy a nice Pinot *Noir*. There's a number of them, Lee. Anyone at Camby's will steer you right."

"Thanks."

"Billie Gerit?" As usual, little escaped Cori.

"Uh-huh."

"We've talked. Once at the Chamber and a few times at the Rebel."

Lee rocked back on his heels as he filed that tidbit of information on Billie. "I knew about the Rebel but not the Chamber. "Busy."

"She is, like many of us. Tough going for a new resident. She's quite accomplished. Lovely too, but then, I've got to think you've noticed."

I'd have to be dead not to. Lee averted his eyes from Cori's bright blue ones, which were watching him carefully, and scanned the poster-size photos covering the walls before settling on the massive monitor highlighting an array of moments and videos from Intrepid's tours, trips, and other offerings. He had taken a number of them while out with clients.

He enjoyed helping Cori and Kenna with their booming business when he could. "I miss going out."

"Where are you at in your schedule? We're swamped and could use you."

"I'm starting a twenty-four late tomorrow night, then I'm off for forty-eight. Rinse and repeat."

"Can you do an assessment? I have someone we're considering bringing on. Well-qualified." Cori's grin took on an impish edge.

"Sure, if it's on the early side."

"I'm thinking ten o'clock. For about four hours. Will that give you enough sleep after a twenty-four?"

"Send me the details and I'll see what I can do and when." He beamed a smile at Cori. "Where will we be headed?"

"Wicked Sister. I heard about the fire. What happened?"

Her not-so-subtle way to steer the conversation back to his roommate—the first one he had ever had in Piñon Ridge—had him on alert. He liked to keep his personal life private. Cori, a diehard romantic and happily married, had been vocal about finding someone special for him, as had a number of his crew. The thing was, he wasn't looking for a relationship.

"Their dryer locked, overheated, and ..." He threw his hands in the air to mimic and explosion. "Ignition."

"Nice of you to offer Billie a place to stay."

"She and her roommate had to re-home due to the fire. Tess asked me to take her in. My sister wants her boyfriend to herself."

"Tess has nothing to worry about. Owen is crazy about her. Nice of you to help your sister and Billie out. You're a good man, Lee." She squeezed his forearm again. "Oh, and thanks for taking her out when you have time."

"Who's *her*?"

"Billie."

Lee mashed his lips together, twisting them, and nodded, tucking that nugget away. Sure, Billie had hiking shoes, but just about everyone in Piñon Ridge did. The fact that she was an outdoors-loving woman on top of everything else he was learning about her excited him. He was a sucker for an adventure.

"Uh-huh." Cori smiled like she had a secret.

Maybe it was stupid, but when reaching his property, he parked the truck at the end of the drive, before it crested, remaining hidden from view unless Billie was upstairs or not home. He had no idea where she was. It wasn't his business.

Lee turned off the truck, closed his eyes, and massaged the bridge of his nose. How on earth was he going to manage having her around and keep it platonic when what he really wanted was her in his bed.

The decision to buy Billie flowers was the right one, a thoughtful gesture, thanking her for the things she had done to make his house homier. But would the message be misconstrued? Did he care if it was? *You don't. You're interested. So is she.*

He restarted the truck and put it in Drive, slowing when he saw the vision in front of his home. Billie worked one of the two beds in front of the house wearing a bikini, long gloves, and his muck boots. Her wild hair was tucked haphazardly under a ball cap. Dirt streaked her skin and she appeared to be singing her heart out. She stood up, turned, and rhythmically shook her body, dancing with abandon, unaware that he watched. Sexy as all get-out.

He lowered the window. "Yeah" by Usher, blasted from the speaker on the stoop.

A powerful craving filled him. Between the nights of dreaming about her and the sight in front of him, he about blew his load right there. He squeezed his eyes shut and talked himself down.

Imagining skiing in back bowl powder.

Focusing on the morning ice bath he had taken daily during training.

He shivered.

Finally, his hard-on eased. Until …

"Hella Good" came on next. He reopened his eyes and was struck dumb.

Billie swayed to the beat of No Doubt's song, arms overhead, a trowel in one hand and a weeding fork in the other. Lord help him. Once he was sure he was back in control of himself, he exited the truck quietly, ready to talk with her if she noticed him.

She didn't, which wasn't good. What if someone with bad intentions drove up?

He entered the mudroom. Based on what his nose was picking up, she had made something incredible. After their discussion in her bathroom this morning, she left while he was showering, so he polished off most of the apple pie ahead of leaving for the firehouse to do some paperwork. He felt guilty about leaving only a slice for her.

Lee moved into the kitchen and placed the flowers next to the sink. That slice was on the island, on a smaller plate enclosed in a clear wrap he had never bought. He set the Pinot next to it and regarded the pie. For him? Or hers, for later? Had she had any of it?

"Hey, Lee."

"Billie." *Holy fuck.*

Wearing only the bikini, she wiped her forehead with the back of the hand that held the ball cap, smearing fresh dirt on the skin. Her face and limbs were streaked with soil, and delight glowed in her hazel eyes. "Oops." She giggled and then flushed. "I've made a mess."

She needed a shower.

He could use another himself.

His heart pounded and blood surged. His thoughts turned chaotic. He had never seen such beauty or experienced this nature of desire. He barely knew her. *What the hell?* It had to be that chemistry his parents had told him and his siblings about during sex and relationships discussions. They had called it the "spark."

That spark ... It was more intense than when he had first set eyes on Billie during the fire.

Or when she caught him gorging himself on her fabulous apple pie.

Or the palpable sexual tension between them in the upstairs bathroom—when she caught him inhaling the scent of her shampoo. He shook his head to clear the memories. And focus on her words.

"I left your boots by the front door. I'll bring them around after I get a drink," she said, focusing on the tumbler as she filled it, pulling him from his musing. "I'll wash them off and set them in the sun. They'll be pretty dry by the time I put them back in the mudroom. "She drained the tumbler and then set it down, seeing flowers wrapped in brown paper and tied with twine. She faced him, her mouth open, eyes locked on his, the unasked question vibrating in the air between them.

"For you."

Billie pushed up on her tiptoes and slowly kissed his cheek. "Thank you. I love fresh cut flowers." Her breathy words caressed his cheek and reignited the spark, the hunger, in him.

She stepped back and trotted to the mudroom, returning with a small aluminum bucket he had forgotten about. Of course it had been cleaned. She worked quickly, adding water and, after trimming the stems, fixing the flowers in an arrangement to her liking.

"Thank you again, Lee. Oh … Go ahead and finish the pie. I'm going to clean up." Billie looked up through her lashes, smiled, and sashayed out of the kitchen.

Fuck. He didn't want pie right now. What Lee wanted was Billie. He was on fire for her, and she was the only one who could put it out. He waited a few minutes then followed her upstairs after grabbing some condoms out of his room and paused at the bathroom door. She was moving about. The shower went on.

The partly opened door yawned wider when he knocked. "Billie?"

She appeared, still in her bikini, holding up the top by its untied strings. "Lee." A huge grin split her face. "Are you here to clean up with me?"

He reciprocated with a grin of his own. "The thought occurred to me. Will dinner be all right?"

"Yes. I'm so happy we're having an appetizer." Billie yanked him into the bathroom and dropped the ties.

Lee pulled Billie to him and bracketed her face with his hands, lowering his head. His hands trailed over her nakedness. She was more beautiful than his dreams.

She closed the distance, moaning when his lips brushed hers and captured her mouth. Their tongues danced and their hands explored. Panting, they broke apart and moved into the shower, under the spray. They washed each other clean.

Billie was slick, soft, and ready for him. "Please."

"Hold on, baby." He grabbed a condom out of the pocket of his joggers and handed it to her. "I've been craving you since I first set eyes on you." He gazed into her eyes while she gloved him and as he eased into her snug channel.

She grasped his ass. "Deeper, Lee, but slow. I want to savor our first time together."

"Me too, baby," he said, kissing her nose, he chin, the sensitive lobe of her ear as he pumped slowly.

They shattered together and when the water cooled, stepped out of the shower.

Enchiladas were enjoyed by candlelight at the kitchen island. Billie wore her pale-yellow robe and Lee a towel secured at his waist.

The rest of Lee and Billie's story is yet to be written.

About the Author

Sutton Bishop has always believed in happily ever after. Despite beginning her writing
 career while penning nonfiction essays and articles for magazines, her heart belonged to
 romance long before she wrote her first book. After marrying her teenage heartthrob and
 starting her own family, she finally plunged into romance writing and is still yet to come up for air. Sutton's deeply layered and flawed characters are forced to contend with challenging plot twists that reveal their hidden motives and passions in settings that range from America's heartland to the heat of Guatemala, Morocco, Italy, and Spain.

NEWSLETTER, BOOK LINKS, and SOCIAL MEDIA:

https://linktr.ee/authorsuttonbishop
(https://linktr.ee/authorsuttonbishop)

PUCKING MY ROOMMATE

USA Today Bestselling Author

Kristin Lee

1

Flynn

"Gather around, fellas," Coach Sweet shouts as he walks into the redesigned locker room.

It's been a few months since we went to the Frozen Four Championships. The alumni have taken notice and have donated millions to upgrade the facilities. Reed strides in beside me, grinning from ear to ear. Hands down, he is the reason we've made it so far, unless he's smiling because his life is like a movie. Bad boy with a past meets the shy coach's daughter and falls in love with Brooke and her son.

All of the seniors and most of the juniors have girlfriends. Dawes and Christina have gotten back together. I knew that shit would happen. She just needed to fish in another pond to make sure they were marriage material. Dawes is one hell of man—he took her back and never strayed.

The only thing I have is hockey.

I run my fingers over the gold-engraved plate on my locker, signifying I'm a senior. The underclassmen have silver plates.

"Men, have a seat. They've expanded the seating, given us a state-of-the-art mini-jumbotron, and redesigned the locker rooms. All of this will help us recruit top players. I'd like to announce this year's captain, Reed Cross."

Sticks tap against the floor rhythmically as chants of "Captain, captain," echo against the walls. In unison, we say, "Speech. Speech."

Reed's an intimidating figure at six foot three inches and three percent body fat, but these days, he smiles all the damn time.

"Thank you for trusting me... with your team."

Coach Sweet chuckles. "And my daughter and grandson."

"Yes, sir. I've been given the world and although hockey isn't the most important thing in my life anymore, I will work harder than anyone to make this team successful. Last year, I realized that trust is just as important as skills. We have to trust each other on and off of the ice. To you rooks, I'm here if you need me but know that you will pay your dues. Consider carrying our bags a rite of passage because success is much sweeter when you have to work for it."

I hop up and in seconds, the team is surrounding Reed, patting his head, and chanting his name.

Coach says, "Okay. Now that you've heard and seen the good news, I'm afraid I have some bad new too."

Reed lifts his hands, pressing them down against the air until the team falls silent. My first thought is Coach is leaving for a higher-profile job at a northern school.

Coach leans forward on his toes with his hands stuffed into pockets. His lips form a tight thin line before he pops them. "The hockey complex is being demolished."

If I thought it was quiet before, it's like a night in the desert now. Then we hiss like snakes. "What? That's where we live," Dawes says.

Reed looks surprised as the rest of us. Is it possible he didn't know even though he lives with the coach's daughter?

"What the fuck? When?" My voice is strong and full of frustration.

"Sorry, guys. I was just informed. They're knocking down the buildings in two weeks. Because of last year's team, the alumni have raised enough money to build us a state-of-the-art apartment complex with onsite weight and training rooms and a kitchen with a chef during the season, equal to the basketball team. Demolition needs to start ASAP so it's ready for the season." He takes a breath and surveys the mixed emotions in each player's eyes. "The underclassmen will be housed in the same dorm. Upperclassmen, I assume you will want to continue to live in apartments. If you have trouble finding something, see me."

The chatter grows to a low rumbling growl at our lives being uprooted. Reed speaks with authority. "Dawes, Flynn, and I will help whoever needs it."

"Fuck if I will."

Reed's eyes narrow, and I roll my eyes in exasperation. "We'll call it team bonding, and I'll have everyone over for burgers."

Coach adjourns the meeting as Reed and Dawes flank me. "When Janik graduated, I finally had the apartment to myself to entertain the ladies."

"Yet, you haven't entertained anyone," Dawes, our center, says. Dawes and his girlfriend were moving into a different complex since she's graduated and has a full-time position with a law firm.

"Let's go by my house and pick up some of our leftover boxes, and we'll get you packed up. Brooke's subleasing it to someone, but I don't think they're moving in for a while."

"Only if we go to McShane's afterwards for beers."

Reed glances at his phone's calendar. "Caleb has hockey lessons at six, and Brooke has ballet lessons until nine. I'll swing by the bar for a couple of hours."

"You're whipped."

"Yep, and I wouldn't have it any other way."

2

Presley

Focused on my reflection, my thoughts slip to when I was a little girl dreaming of being a teacher, an astronaut, a professional soccer player, or owning a wildlife refuge. I've always been mesmerized by elephants and monkeys.

"You're up," Daisy yells.

My head twitches as I straighten my shoulders and notice the tear crawling from my eye. Quickly, I wipe it away, stand, and adjust the white ruffled lingerie. My act is based on reality—a virgin stripper—every man's version of a wet dream.

I take a deep breath as I hear my cue. "Have those dollar bills ready for our precious Baby Doll."

With my hands clasped in front of me, I act shy and innocent as I walk around the stage, leaving every patron to imagine what's under my sheer robe with ruffles flouncing against my butt cheeks.

Then the music hits a percussion note, and I grab the pole, leaning my body out an angle as I swing. My light-pink hair sweeps across the mirrored floor to several enthusiastic *hell yeahs*.

I can't think about the eyes scraping over my body, or I won't make enough money. Climbing the pole while wrapping one leg around, I hang upside down. Gravity causes the white fabric to fall over my shoulders, exposing the bikini. Untying the satin ribbon, the first layer gracefully floats to the floor.

As I slide my body down the steel cylinder, kicking off it like a cartwheel, several athletes stand at the bar. How do I know they're athletes? Because they're wearing athletic gear with the Stallions Hockey emblazoned across their chests and shorts. It's evident they didn't expect to end up here tonight.

One of them laughs, throwing back his head. I can't hear him over the music, but his smile could light up Las Vegas.

I keep my eyes on him instead of smelly older men in the front or the corporate guys entertaining their clients.

After swirling my hips and teasing the pretty white bow between my breasts, I wait. I've totally messed up my routine. Chills crawl up my legs, and my nipples harden at the thought of the guy with the high-voltage smile seeing me, but I don't want him to see my breasts here with his friends gawking.

Instead, of taking it off at that moment, I rework my routine and get on all fours. The row of men closest to the stage lick their lips while looking at my cleavage. They tuck money into the fabric when laughing hockey guy finally looks my way. He tips his beer towards me, then takes an extra-long pull of his drink. I watch as his throat take it all, and I feel my core clench.

In over a month of dancing, I've never felt this way.

The manager is in the corner, giving me a hardened look and mouths, "Take the top off."

Pushing to my knees, I pull on the satin bow and just as my breasts are revealed, I spin backward. Running my hands under my fake pink hair, I lift it as I arch my back, lowering my head to the floor. The crowd can see the swell of my tits, but they're not on full display. Reaching back with my hands, more men put bills in my hands.

The gang of hockey players all have their backs to the stage, so I take the opportunity to finish my dance. I sway and gyrate as I move the other side. The hockey players have snagged a table.

When my performance is over, I hurry backstage and change into a lace half bra and boy shorts. The way we make our real money is giving lap dances and waitressing. An older man with a stained white t-shirt grabs my wrist.

"Hey, Baby Doll."

"Sorry, I'm running drinks. No lap dances." I keep walking in my five-inch heels, wishing I had on my running shoes.

I lean against the bar and ask Lucy, "Do you have any drinks needing to be delivered?"

She bites back a grin while grabbing her shaker, then pours the alcohol into the steel container. She's so much fun to watch as she throws the shaker in the air, spins, and catches it before straining it into the glass, then placing it on a tray full of beers.

"Why aren't you doing one-on-ones?"

"It's that time of the month, and I'm not in a good mood."

"I know what will put you in a good mood." I lift a brow as she continues. "Deliver these to the hot guys at table ten. They're your age, and you're going to be attending the same college."

"Yeah, I'm not telling them I'm attending the university."

"Don't be ashamed. You have a beautiful body, and you're doing this for a reason. A good reason."

I weave through the tables and as I approach the round table with five extremely hot men, I realize I forgot to ask Lucy about the cocktail. All the beers are the same brand, so I ask, "Who had the cocktail?"

More of my skin is covered than it would be at the beach, yet I feel as exposed as sand in the Mojave Desert. A pair of Caribbean blue eyes lock with mine. He's even more handsome and rugged up close with his square jaw and messy hair.

"If it's a virgin, that would be me," he says, rendering me speechless with his panty-melting low voice.

One says, "Yeah, right. You went through more girls last semester than pages in a Tom Clancy novel." The group explodes in laughter.

He sets his jaw and looks to the red-haired culprit. "Someone's got to get you boys home. Damn, we're being kicked out of our homes so the players next year can live like kings of the campus." He peers back up at me. "Can I taste the drink?"

3

Flynn

"Umm..." She glances over her shoulder to the busy bartender. "I think there's alcohol in it," she says, handing the beers to the rest of the guys.

I stand, peering into her fake violet eyes, but she's fucking beautiful. I find myself thinking about her straddling me, pink hair over one shoulder, hiding one boob. I'd love nothing more than to soak inside her.

"Let me go ask."

I reach for her elbow and her skin pebbles at my touch. As she spins, her nipples poke into the lace. "They keep it cold in here, huh?"

She nods in agreement, her eyes momentarily dropping as a subtle blush creeps onto her cheeks. I grab my drink from the tray and take a sip. "This isn't a virgin, but no worries, I happen to like non-virgins too," I say teasingly, a mischievous twinkle in my eye.

I flash her a playful wink, noticing the sharp intake of breath and the sudden surge of desire evident in her reaction. Feeling the arousal stir within me, I can't help the betrayal of the growing bulge in my pants.

The music and chatter drown out her words, but she leaves, taking my drink with her.

"Flynn." Shearer smacks my arm. "She actually looks like candy—so fucking sweet. I bet you a hundred dollars she's trying to get you to pay for a lap dance."

"Shut the fuck up," I spout with more venom and possessiveness.

She returns with another drink and a bottle of water. "You might need this."

"Thanks. We're leaving in a few minutes." I point to my shirt, displaying the Stallions Hockey logo. "We have practice at five in the morning."

The pink-haired beauty shifts her weight and twists her lips. Her eyes don't meet mine when she whispers, "Do you want a lap dance?"

My asshole friends hoop and holler. I hate it when they're right, which isn't often. Generally getting laid isn't a problem for any of us. Women fall at our feet, hoping to snag an athlete, but I've been sitting out for a couple of months. I'm tired of it all, different girls without an authentic connection.

Desire isn't the right word, for what I want from her, but I want the real her. I want her to take off the wig and remove the contacts. Like an idiot, I say, "Not tonight." I already have an erection, and there's no doubt if she were to grind herself against me, I would come in my pants. And the boys would never let me live that down.

She tucks her lips inside her mouth. "Oh, okay."

"May I get the check? Like I said, early practice."

She nods, pulling out the little black portfolio, and sets it on the table. I focus on her lips as I thank her and sign the check. "And baby." I play with the ends of her silky-smooth pink tendrils. "If you gave me a lap dance, I'd make you come so hard, you would be paying me because I..." I tip her chin, forcing her to look into my eyes. "I will always, always put your needs above my own."

Her face gets so red, I feel the heat she's generating against my knuckles. My hand slides down the column of her neck, and my fingertips trace her collarbone. "See ya around."

My friends wait by the door and toss one last glance over my shoulder, expecting to see her straddling a paying customer. What I see is a girl who doesn't belong here, sitting alone at a table in the corner, braiding her pink hair.

On the way home, Reed's name flashes on my phone. "What's up?"

"Just checking to see if you and the boys needed a ride."

Reed takes his captain responsibilities seriously. "No, we're pulling into the hockey plex now. Fuck, I can't believe I have to move."

"That reminds me. Brooke said you can move into her old apartment. She called the girl leasing it, and she's hard up for cash, so she agreed to take a roommate for the semester. God help her." He lets out a hearty laugh.

I chuckle to myself. "It's amazing how Brooke can turn stressful situations into positive outcomes for everyone. She's helping my new roommate with costs and me with having a place to lay my head and hell, I might get laid."

"Maybe your new roommate isn't your type. Oh, that's right, you'll fuck anyone who walks."

"You would have been proud of me; I refused a lap dance tonight."

"Are you sick? Need an ambulance?"

"Reed 3.0 sucks. He's not near as much fun as he used to be."

"Yeah, but I'm happier than I've ever been. We'll move you in tomorrow after practice. It's my only day I don't have commitments before I pick up Caleb from daycare."

"Sounds good. Thank Brookie Cookie for me."

No doubt he's rolling his eyes as he hangs up.

Just eighteen hours ago, I was frustrated with having to find a place to live. Now, I'm eagerly anticipating this new chapter. Living with a woman has to be a welcome change from the usual scents of smelly socks, beer, and jockstraps.

After unlocking the front door, I toss my keys onto the kitchen counter, quickly gulp down a glass of water, and make my way to my bedroom. As I undress and turn on the shower, filling the room with steam, I can't help but feel a sense of relief.

Standing under the hot water, my mind isn't occupied with thoughts of moving boxes or sharing an apartment with a stranger. Instead, my thoughts drift to the mysterious beauty with pink hair and violet eyes.

4

Presley

Rummaging through the backseat of my car, I find a pair of running shorts and a clean t-shirt. The old, faded concert tee has a musty odor, so I grab my fabric refresher and spritz it around.

I'm excited that beginning today, I will no longer be homeless. Making the move from the hills of West Virginia, where I attended Sutton U, to the University of Kentucky required me to use up all my savings to cover my first tuition payment.

When Brooke called last night and offered me the opportunity to move in whenever I wanted, I was absolutely thrilled. She asked if I would mind having a roommate for a semester to split expenses. I quickly agreed, relieved I'll be able to quit working at Illusions, eventually.

I drive to the moving company to sign all the paperwork to have my belongings delivered, as my thoughts drift to the guy at Illusions last night. It's the first time a man, of any age, has turned down a lap dance from me. It makes me need to know more about him. His self-assured demeanor, confident he could satisfy me, sent chills through my body.

I follow behind the truck and when we pull up to the apartment, two guys are carrying a couch inside. A sigh of relief puffs from my mouth that we'll have a place to sit, since I only have a bean-bag chair from my freshman-year dormitory.

Older men raise the metal sliding door and quickly remove the contents.

I tap on the open door, and a tall, deliciously tattooed man says, "I'm guessing your Presley."

My jaw touches the floor; he's so good-looking with these eyes you can't look away from. I clear my throat. "Yes, are you my roommate?"

"No, I'm Reed, Brooke's boyfriend. Let me show you and your movers to your room."

He leads us into a bedroom the size of my former living room. "It only has one shared bathroom."

"Thank you." Then I point to where I want the bed placed.

"Hey, I'm Flynn. Aren't they going to set the bed up for you?"

I turn to respond and come face to face with the guy from the strip club. My heart skips a beat.

Just my luck.

In a repeat of last night, I stand there without uttering a syllable. What if he recognizes me?

He chuckles, throwing his head back in a way that had charmed me at the club. "I have that effect on women. I'm hot. I know," he teases.

My eyebrows furrow as I figure out whether he's joking. It's possible he's secretly insecure, and the air of cockiness and confidence is a ruse. Sneaking one more peek, I decide I'm wrong. He has every reason to be full of himself.

Luckily, the brutes helping me move in ask where I want the desk, and I direct them to the spot in front of the window. They make a few trips to the truck and in thirty minutes, I have a home.

Flynn's friends wave goodbye and suddenly, I'm alone with the guy who I wanted to rock my world last night.

"Do you need help with the rest in your car?" he asks as he throws some popcorn in his mouth.

"No." My voice is laced with the fear of him finding out I've been living in my car while I saved money for this apartment.

He rubs his hand over his mouth a few times as he studies me.

"Sorry, I'm Presley. I just want to get all of this put away before tackling the car. I threw everything in there that I didn't have time to pack."

God, he's sinfully handsome with his hat on backward and the chestnut-brown hair curling under the hat. The hole on the forehead shows his thick hairline.

"Are you a freshman? Where are you from?" he asks as he grabs the remotes for what looks to be a sixty-inch television.

"I'm a junior. I played soccer in West Virginia, got injured, and lost my scholarship. Kentucky offered me a chance to walk on, so here I am. So, you play hockey?"

His eyes narrow as he looks down at his shirt, and realizes I have no way of knowing he's a hockey player.

Shit. I look around to see if I see any gear and of course, I don't, but lies just tumble from my lips. "Brooke said I would be rooming with an annoying hockey player."

"Oh, she did? Hmm."

Flynn licks the seam of his lips, and I want to push him down on the dark-gray couch and give him the lap dance he thinks he could resist. There was a pull between us last night, and there's a string still tethering us together.

"Do you have any apps you want me to set up on the TV? I have the four main ones but if you want to watch porn, that's where I draw the line." Again, his boisterous laugh fills the room.

I wrap my fingers around his forearm just to see if there's truth beneath the joke, but a jolt of electricity shocks us, and we jump apart.

For a moment, we stand there not knowing what to do. Will he act on the chemistry? Before I can find out, I say, "I better go work on my room. But no apps. I have everything on my laptop." It's the one thing I own that's worth more than fifty dollars.

"So, that's where you watch porn."

"Stop. I don't watch porn."

"Everyone watches porn at this age. It's how we learn."

"Maybe you need a teacher, but I don't." I twist on my feet, waltzing as fast as possible out of the room without being obvious that I'm thinking about having sex with my new roommate. It's like being on a diet—you want what you can't have.

5

Flynn

While I help assemble her bed, she holds onto the headboard as I drill holes and anchor it to the wall. Her fingers turn white as her teeth sink into her plump bottom lip and for a brief moment, we may be having the same thought—what it would feel like to be lying on her bed as she rides up and down my shaft. Holding onto the headboard to steady the erratic movements as we both reach the highest peak. God, what a beautiful scene.

Since that night two weeks ago, where we worked in close proximity, organizing the apartment, and danced around our attraction, I find myself completely enthralled and gawking at her muscular toned legs. Soccer legs.

Presley throws her backpack over her shoulder as she slips her phone into her pocket and hangs her keys around her wrist, knocking me from the memories we've already made.

"Thanks for taking me to the thrift store."

I smirk. "No problem. Every apartment needs twinkle lights."

"They make me happy."

"And I'm here to make you happy." I bend at the waist, bowing to her like she's my queen.

"If that's true, then do the dishes while I'm working."

"Where do you go at night?" I ask, thinking we would see each other more than we do.

Presley's posture hitches as she straightens and takes a breath, hesitating. "I told you; I babysit."

Then she closes the door behind her and what do I do? The dishes. Presley has domesticated me like a cat.

The hours pass slowly, and I'm bored as hell. So, I head to the hockey plex to celebrate its last night. Everyone who's anyone is here, including the vast majority of the campus teams.

Mac Callaghan, a dual-sport athlete, pats me on the back. "Flynnie." He's already buzzed. He lived with Logan and Hagan for a year before moving into the baseball house. "I guess the baseball team will be hosting all the parties this year."

"Where's Reed?"

"With Brooke, Dane, and Lettie, playing volleyball out back."

Someone grabs him so I walk through my old front door and out to the back patio where we always have volleyball and pickleball set up.

"Hey, Flynn. We had fun in your room, didn't we?"

I give her a tightlipped smile. "I need to talk to Reed."

"Find me later, and we can leave this place with an epic memory." Alayna trails her fingers down my chest.

There's not a chance in hell, but I don't want to be a dick. The only person I can think of is Presley. "Yeah, okay."

Lettie, Brooke's best friend, sets the volleyball to Dane Greathouse, an All-American basketball player for the Stallions. Reed heroically saved Dane from a burning building last semester, and they've grown close. Dane spikes the ball, landing it on the other side of Brooke.

In the old days, Reed would have freaked out, not wanting to lose but instead, he grabs her waist and goes in for a kiss.

Lettie jokes, "Are you two trying to lose so you can go home and have nookie?"

"No. Hagan and Adalee are babysitting."

Reed leans down and kisses Brooke. "Cookie, we're definitely having nookie because it rhymes with Cookie."

"Stop making fun of me." Lettie charges them as Dane attempts to stop her and gets tangled in the net.

"Lettie," Dane calls her name before grabbing her by the waist and hoisting her over his shoulder. "I think it's time I take you home."

"When are you two going to stop all the nonsense and sleep together?" I say and suddenly, you can hear the summer crickets.

Lettie and Dane look at each other and for a half second, I see the want in Dane's eyes. He stays silent, then Lettie snaps, "We're best friends. I guess you've never been friends with a girl."

I know I won't win the argument, so I raise my beer and head in the other direction. I sit in an Adirondack chair before a few other teammates join me. We drink all night until I'm mumbling incoherent sentences about my babysitting, soccer-playing roommate.

Why can't I get Presley out of my mind?

I wake up in my bed with no idea how I got home. There's a tap on my door. I groan, struggling to say, "Come in."

"Hey, I brought you some water and some headache medicine." She's a fucking angel, and I realize it's the first time she's been in my room when I'm in bed. Presley is one hundred percent focused on my naked chest and leg that's hanging out of the comforter.

"Thanks." I rise and run my hand over my face.

"I hate to ask, but I still can't afford a trainer, and soccer walk-on tryouts are next week. Would you help me train?"

Being able to spend more time with Presley? That's a hell yeah.

"Sure. Let me shower and eat, and we'll start today." Gulping the water down, I swallow the pills. "Do you know how I got home last night? I haven't gotten that drunk in months."

"Me."

"You came and got me? I rode in that messy-as-fuck car."

"You did. You said you loved slumming." There's a hint of a twinkle in her eye.

I stand and thank God; I have on underwear. I usually don't sleep in any, so I must have passed out. "Thanks. I owe you. I really don't drink as much as I used to."

"I know."

All day little memories come back to me, but I choose to keep them to myself—for now. The way she let me lay my head on her shoulder. The smell of her sweet perfume and how she put her hand over mine. Those memories keep me wishing for more.

6

Presley

For the next week, he gets up at five in the morning for hockey practice, then comes home and runs five miles with me. Our route changes every day. Somedays, we run to the park or through campus. Today, we run to the soccer field. I watch the scholarship players practice from the corner of the field.

"Pres, none of them have as good of footwork as you do. Damn girl, hockey players have fancy feet, but you are next level." We've been doing soccer and hockey drills in the open yard behind our apartment.

Since I confessed that I'm struggling to have enough to pay for college, he has filled the fridge with fruits and veggies as well as chicken and fish, which I hate. But we have a rule if one of us cooks, the other eats it.

"I'm so nervous."

He wraps his solid arm around me. "You've got this. You know you told me about your injury but not how it happened. Were you on the field?"

Brushing off his question, I bend over to stretch my legs. "We should start walking back. By the way, are you going to the football game on Saturday?" The team plays the opener this weekend.

He shrugs his shoulders. "I usually go, but... if you need me to run through drills with you or just take your mind off tryouts, I can stay home."

"I was hoping I could go with you. It'll break up my nerves." He stops in the middle of the sidewalk and looks at me. I wish I knew what he was thinking. I don't have to wait for long.

"Are you asking me on a date, Pres?" He grins, making every nerve in my body prickle.

"No, we're roommates. Can't you be friends with a girl?" I want to be more but don't want to mess up our living arrangement.

"Where have I heard that before? Come on, first one to the apartment cooks," he says with a mischievous glint in his eyes. "And I'm thinking broiled tilapia would be delicious after a hot run."

God, he makes me laugh. Before I know it, he's a quarter mile in front of me.

———

I'm freshly showered, makeup free, with my hair in a loose bun. And the sound of fajitas sizzling pops in the kitchen. I turn the corner, and he's wearing his gray Stallions Hockey tee and expertly tossing the vegetables in the pan.

"I'll never make you eat fish before a big event. My dad always said, 'Eat your favorite meal before a test or the night before a big game.' I know how much you love fajitas, so today fajitas and tomorrow, barbeque."

It's amazing how he remembers every detail of things I say in passing. I mentioned my love for barbecue while running one day as we passed Austin's BBW joint.

I wash the dishes and follow him into the den with a beer in hand. The one time I drink beer is with fajitas. I have a little buzz because I never drink.

"Tell me how you hurt yourself." He leans forward on the couch with his head turned sideways, looking at me.

I pick at the label on the bottle until the edges curl, then take a deep swallow. I feel the tears ebbing from the bottom of my toes to my lids.

"Hey, what's wrong?"

"My teammate and I were at a party, and we were playing beer pong. She was smaller than me but fast as fuck. And if you think I have fancy footwork, Julie was our star midfielder."

A tear falls from my lashes, and he uses his thumb to wipe it away, letting me continue.

"Someone took a video and posted it to social media. The coach saw it and sent the assistant coach to pick us up. On the way back to the dorm, we were hit by a drunk driver. Julie and the assistant coach died in the accident I... I... tore my ACL trying to get Julie out of the car. Adrenaline kept me from feeling the pain of my crushed ankle."

Flynn comforts me as I sob in his arms. "It's not your fault, Pres. It's the asshole who was driving the other car."

"Everyone hated me. My friends and family couldn't bear to see my face. I couldn't look at myself. Once I was well enough to walk, my parents disowned me. I had lost my scholarship and had nowhere to go. Kentucky recruited me in high school, so I called Coach Spangler, and he said I could try out for one of three walk-on positions, but no scholarship."

I lean into his chest as he rubs my back. I want to kiss him so this pain will go away. But evidently, he finally understands being friends with a girl.

He keeps his promise, and we go to the football game together. We sit in the student's section, and I scream and chant until I'm hoarse. Afterwards, we end up at the barbeque restaurant.

When I leave for tryouts Sunday morning, there's a note and a bagel on the counter.

Pres,
Show them your speed. Show them your footwork.
But more than anything, show them your will and fight.
You're a fighter. A survivor.

You need some carbs for energy, and I filled my water bottle for you. It's bigger because I'm bigger. I'm big and your... (he scratched it out.)
Anyway, they'll probably offer you a scholarship on the spot.
I can't wait to celebrate your victory.
Daniel

He signs it Daniel, not Flynn. Butterflies grow inside me. His handwriting is surprisingly neat. I hold the note close to my chest and wish my roommate to be my boyfriend.

7

Flynn

If I knew I would never see her, I wouldn't have helped her train to make the team. The soccer coach offered her a walk-on position this year, and it might turn into a scholarship for her senior year.

It's been two months and between her babysitting job and soccer, combined with my hockey and oh, yeah, we both have class, we literally pass each other coming in and out the door.

I walk in front of her. "We're scrimmaging at the barn tomorrow and then having game night at Reed and Brooke's house... if you want to come." I wink as I stretch out word come. I'd love to make her feel like the woman she is, but there's something sad behind her eyes.

"Maybe. I need the money to pay for school and the apartment."

"I know you want to come... everybody needs a release."

Getting under her skin is my new favorite hobby. I love the way she flushes when I tease her with my words or brush against her while reaching into a cabinet.

Today, her hair is tossed up with deep mahogany tendrils falling loose around her face. Electricity zips through me as she breathes. That's all it takes. I test the distance between us.

Our breaths tangle as my lips move closer. I know she wants this as much as I do.

Say something, please. Give me permission before I take your mouth into mine. Our eyes meet for what seems like hours. I slide my hand to her hips, ready to settle against her but instead of inviting me closer, she pushes me away.

She folds her lips over her teeth, and her eyes water. This is the first time I've even noticed a woman's eyes other than the fake violet ones at the strip club. Hers shimmer with tears, and I ache to wrap her in my protective embrace.

Fuck. What have I done?

Several inches separate us. "I'm going to be late."

"Don't go." I grab the pads of her fingers and curl mine around hers, but they slip apart when she takes two strides out the door.

With one palm on the wall, I tap my forehead against the wall. What has gotten into me? Was it a month ago when she confided in me that she lived in her car for a few weeks so she could save money? Or was it the first week when I saw her wet hair draping along her shoulders, perfectly imperfect when I started craving my roommate?

Shaking my head, I go to my room and hook my phone holder around my bicep, connect my Bluetooth and playlist, and head out for a run. I end up at Reed's new house. He lives with Brooke and Caleb, her four-year-old son.

I hear them in the backyard, so I open the gate. "I need your advice, dude."

He waves me over, as he sets up the tee, balancing the plastic ball. Then he comes behind him, covering his arms. "Caleb, keep your eye on the ball. Line up the bat a few times before you swing."

Reed backs away, and Caleb lines up the bat and ball two times before he swings and hits it over the fence.

"Looks like you have a baller on your hands." I chuckle.

"Hagan kept him two times so we could go to the hocky plex last week to see a play downtown. When we came home, it's all Caleb could talk about."

"Well, at least he's moved on from bull riding."

Reed scoffs, "True."

"Speaking of bull riding, I have a problem."

His eyebrow climbs up his forehead.

"Yeah, I want my new roommate to ride me. Starting a sexual relationship with my roomie goes against every rule ever made, right?" I ask, feeling a mix of nerves and curiosity.

"I wouldn't say it's ideal. But you've lived together for two months. Are you saying nothing has happened?"

"How long did you know Brooke before you..."

Reed throws his hand up. "This isn't about Brooke and me. And we didn't live together. Maybe Logan or Harper would be more helpful, but they're in Louisville for the Thursday night game. What I can tell you is that it was awkward as fuck when they weren't together yet living in the same house. Do you really want to dip your stick in your roommate just to scratch an itch?" he cautions, making me pause and consider his position.

The barn is empty with the exception of family and friends. We're hosting our red rivals. Coach has started a scrimmage league now that we have money to travel. In the stands is Reed's dad, NHL commissioner, along with his dad's wife and his half-brother, who plays professionally.

My parents couldn't make it into town, but that's par for the course. Mom came to two games last year, and Dad came to three. Unlike most of my teammates, my dad never played hockey. My dad is a motivational speaker, and my mom is an emergency room nurse, placing us firmly in upper middle class. I swear they cling to their careers, so they don't have to spend time with each other.

When the first period ends, the score is tied, and I'm playing like shit. Dawes smacks me on the head and says, "Get your head in the game."

"Damn, I need to get laid. Three months, and I'm out of practice."

Reed gathers us and pumps us up. "We're not losing to the Redbirds, got it?" We all shake our heads. "This is our new facility, and we're going undefeated in this building. Understand?"

"Stallions! Stallions!" we chant, bouncing on our skates.

During the second period, Reed does a crossover and slams the rival winger against the boards. That's one thing that hasn't changed: he's just as physical as ever on the ice. He scrambles to steal the puck and, with a quick flick of his wrist, shoots the puck to me. I pass it to Dawes, while Reed splits the defenders. I take the shot, which hits off the bar straight to Reed, and he easily sinks the puck into the net. Two to one. Stallions.

I follow Reed to the plastic shield as he gives Caleb a high five and as he looks at Brooke, I notice the woman beside her—Presley. My smile widens as she bites back her own. Her face reddens as I scan her body—that's when it hits me. She's wearing my Stallions Hockey t-shirt. Shocked, my heart seizes as I bring my stick to my chest. I can't breathe. I can't breathe.

Reed pulls me away "Flynn, are you okay?"

"Presley's wearing my shirt, my fucking shirt."

Judging by the smirk on my best friend's face, he understands what I'm going through –Presley Pains.

"Dude, if that's what she does to you, then you need to explore your options. Talk first. Fuck later." He slaps my back with his glove. "Let's go shut these fuckers out."

For the rest of the game, I skate faster and with more finesse than normal, wanting to show her my skills.

After the game, she's waiting in the tunnel with Brooke, Caleb, and Reed's family.

"Gweat game, Weed."

Grabbing Caleb's chubby fingers, I ask, "Are you going to be a hockey player when you grow up?"

"I like baseball more." Reed and I roll our eyes.

Presley's dark hair is curled in big waves, and I don't think I've ever seen her with makeup on until this moment. "You came."

She nods. "It's my first time. You were impressive."

"I like your shirt." I raise my eyebrows and then give her a flirty wink.

"This old thing." She plays with the hem. "I'm sorry. I don't have any Stallions gear, and it was laying on the kitchen bar."

"Presley, there's only one thing that would make me happier than you wearing my shirts…"

Brooke cuts me off. "Let's get to the house. Caleb is going on a play-date, so Reed and I only have a few hours."

I glance at Presley. "You want to ride with me? We'll pick up your car after."

"Sounds good."

We walk through the parking lot, shoulder to shoulder, with our hands brushing together, but neither of us takes the leap.

I unlock the car and open the door for her, and she looks surprised. As I make my way around the car, I clutch my fist and pump it in the air. She came to my game.

"Hey, thanks for coming. I didn't think you would." I twist my head to see her profile. Her lips tug.

"It was my first hockey game. It was cold."

Unable to resist, I smirk. "I see that." The outline of her nipples shows through the worn shirt.

She lets out a half laugh "You're always so… so…."

"Honest? Yes."

"I was going to say forward or flirtatious."

8

Presley

It may not be full-grown butterflies, but caterpillar hairs tickle my stomach. It's a sensation I haven't had since high school. Until I've met Flynn, that is.

We're greeted by a host of his friends, including Hagan and Adalee who graduated and are now working full time, which is why they weren't at the hockey arena. They introduce us to their best friends Ginger and Joe, then to his teammate Dawes and his girlfriend Christina.

Flynn tugs me towards Reed and Brooke, who are manning the grill.

Brooke grabs my hand, tipping her head to Flynn and Reed. "Come help me with the salads while they handle the meat."

"What if she wants to handle the meat?" Flynn throws his arms up in jest.

Reed opens his mouth to say something, but Brooke's glare pins him, and I guess he thinks better of it.

Their house is filled with homey details, including a picture wall, which includes of lot of hockey players.

"I didn't know until today that your dad is the hockey coach. Who are these people?"

"Reed's family."

"Oh, I love this one of Flynn, Dawes, and Reed." They're carrying Reed, and they've stripped themselves of their jerseys and hockey pads, with their masculine torsos on display.

"That's the game that sent them to the Frozen Four last semester. It's definitely a nice one to get lost in."

She hands me a knife, and I cut the vegetables and toss them into the lettuce, while she grabs a pitcher of tea and one of margaritas.

"How's living with Flynn?"

"It's good. He's such a gentleman."

Brooke blows the margarita out her mouth, spraying it all over the sink. "Did you say gentleman?"

I shake my head. "Yeah, he opens the door for me, leaves a bagel on the table for me every morning before he goes to practice, and he always changes the television station to the soccer channel."

She tips her head like she's processing but switches topics. "Flynn said you babysit almost every night you don't have soccer. I know Harper is looking for someone to take care of Evy while she attends med school during the day. Her maternity leave is up in a couple of weeks, where she has to attend school every day. Maybe you could talk to her, so you don't have to work nights."

"Sounds good."

Flynn appears in the opening to the kitchen, resting his shoulder against the wall. "Ladies, we're ready to eat."

He walks to me and takes the salad bowl out of my hand, and I follow them to the long table set up outside. I've been eating cereal, bagels, and ramen for the past year until Flynn took matters into his own hands. I slice the steak, and it melts in my mouth. I can't contain my appreciation and let out a groan. "Oh my God, this is delicious."

"See, Reed, my roomie loves meat." Under the table, his fingers squeeze my thigh, and I almost moan again. Overloaded with the feeling of his calloused hands, I tighten and out of the corner of my eye, his jaw slides into a smile.

"I do. My dad owned a butcher shop in rural West Virginia. If we didn't have anything else, we had roasts, steak, and hamburger." My words catch as I get lost in a memory of my parents cooking together.

The table quiets, but then Hagan chimes in, "My mom is the main cook in my family, but my dad loves to grill and fry."

"Since my mom left us to work overseas, my dad learned to cook, and I would put him up against anyone when it comes to Italian cooking," Brooke states in an even tone.

"I'm sorry. I didn't know."

"Don't be. People make decisions in their lives, and we have to figure out how to deal with them. She's the one missing out. I have everything I need," Brooke says as she slides the fork from her mouth. Reed wraps his arm around her and kisses her on the cheek.

As a I chew my last bite of steak, I realize I'm not alone—everyone has challenges. Mine may be bigger in my eyes, but most of us have been hurt.

The entire table of couples and the few singles nod in understanding. Hagan claps his hands. "Let's get the table cleared so we can start the card games."

Flynn leans in, whispering in my ear. "From what I hear, Hagan and Adalee are competitive as hell. If we play on teams, I got you." His lips slide over the shell of my ear, and my eyes flutter closed as he pumps his finger against my thigh once again.

As we all gather around the table to play a card game, the atmosphere is lively and filled with banter and laughter. Flynn is seated across from me, and we exchange flirty glances throughout the game. He teases me playfully, hinting at an underlying attraction, and the others are beginning to notice.

Whenever Flynn plays a card, he flashes a charming smile in my direction, causing me to blush. As others get knocked out of the game, it comes down to the two of us. We both draw a card and hold it to our foreheads. We both say a word, and the other answers yes or no, kind of like twenty questions.

I've gotten to know a few things about Reed that I may not have learned in years. He changed his first diaper at twelve when his sister was born. His favorite board game is Clue. His first pet was a goldfish named Mayonnaise because it was white.

"It's a thing."

He shakes his head no, then asks, "Is it a person?"

"Yes."

"Mine's a person?"

"Yes."

We run through a list of questions, then he stops and says, "Wait, what do I get when I win?"

I've had a couple of margaritas. I'm not buzzing but not feeling as shy. "When you win?" I arch my brow. "Don't forget I'm an athlete too. I don't believe in losing, so what do I win *when* I win?"

He looks into my eyes and hesitates before he says, "Me."

Sincerity laces through his tone, and I swallow what feels like a pound of cotton candy.

Brooke's friend Lettie says, "This is getting interesting."

Her friend Dane, who plays for the basketball team, says. "What do you say? You give Flynn a chance if he wins?" Then he mumbles, "Interesting tactic."

I look at Flynn, and he throws his hands out. "Come on, Presley. You know you love me."

Love? Is that what this is?

9

Flynn

"Are you happy I won, Presley?" My hand is on the small of her back as she unlocks the front door. Sexual tension surrounds us like a heated blanket.

She twists the knob, and I step forward, thinking she's walking through. She doesn't, and my body presses into her legs, ass, back, and my lips fall to her ear. "I've been starving myself." I feel her inhale, and I whisper, "I want to feel all of you. I want you to take every fucking inch of me."

I place my hand on the door to steady myself. Instead, it swings open, and we stumble inside. I catch her in my arms before she falls to the ground. Spinning her around, I kick the metal door closed.

Our movements are subtly synchronized, almost as if we're engaged in a secret dance of cat and mouse. Leaning down, I kiss her neck, and she mewls like it's the first time she's been touched. A salty residue covers her soft skin. "Do you want me, Pres?"

"Yes but..."

"No buts."

Hovering over her mouth, I admit, "I know I need you. You've made me a better man since we've moved in together. In two months, I haven't so much as thought of another woman. Have you been thinking about me? Have you been touching yourself at night, thinking about me? Because my hand is sore from dreaming about these muscular legs wrapped around my head and my waist."

She nibbles on her bottom lip as I capture them in mine. She locks her hands around my neck. "What do you want from me, Flynn?"

"I want you to call me Daniel. And I want you to vocalize your needs. Then I'm going to fulfill every single greedy one."

She swallows hard and says, "Daniel, I want you to be the first to have me. I'm not asking for forever, just one night."

I kiss her hard, pinning her against the door. Fuck, her mouth is sweet with a hint of sour from the margaritas. The kiss is desperate and urgent. She wants this as much as I do. But I need to confirm my thoughts as we break apart. "Pres, are you saying you've never been with a man?"

She nods and slides her hands onto my cheeks. "You'll be my first."

"How is that possible? You're so fucking gorgeous, athletic, shy, and kind. You're the poster above every guy's bed, hanging by thumbtacks."

I was being rhetorical, but she answers, "My dad was a preacher, and he kept tight reins on me."

Interlacing our fingers, I lead her into my room and turn on a playlist from my phone. If it's her first time, I want her to remember the romance, fire, and me possessing her in a way she'll never forget and want more of.

With my hands covering hers, we lift the hem of my shirt together, slowly over my head, and discard it on the floor. She gasps as she runs her hands over my chest. Now, it's my turn to remove my shirt from her body. "When we get to round two, you're putting this back on. But I promised to kiss every inch of you."

I rub her thighs before pushing her shorts down to find her bare. "Fuck! I love hot October nights and running shorts."

She smiles. "Built-in panty."

Our eyes collide, and that's the end. We realize we're crossing the line. After months of craving my roommate, I get to dine on her. Fill her body with mine.

I splay my hand over her back, holding her in place as I lay her on the bed. My knee is between her leg as we kiss, soft and sensual. I've kissed a plethora of girls once or twice before getting to the sex, but this feels different. It feels like I could kiss her forever, and I push that thought from my mind to enjoy the moment.

My lips travel down to her breasts, kneading with one hand, sucking her nipple into my mouth. She arches her back, pushing into me, and I slip my arm from underneath her. As I move lower, my dick aches. It's so hard and has been for at least a half hour. Her fingers burrow through my hair as I blow cool air over her center.

"Oh, Flynn."

"Flynn is for the guys and friends. Use my name."

"Daniel, please."

"Has anyone licked your sweet lips and made you come?"

She lifts her head for a moment and whispers, "No."

This adds an extra layer of excitement to the emotion already zipping through me.

I suckle her folds into my mouth, and she jerks at the touch, so I reach around her thigh, interlacing our fingers. "I'll take care of you. I'll go as slow or as fast as you need."

Moans fall from her lips until a wave of her arousal reaches a crescendo, flooding my mouth with her sweetness. "You're perfect."

Passion overtakes me hearing her praise. I like to know what I'm doing makes a girl feel good. More so, I'm hoping this is the beginning of a relationship. I kiss up her body, my hands exploring her sides as I pin hers above her head. "I've never felt this way about someone. I think you're it for me, Pres."

Her eyes glimmer as our lips overlap in sensual kisses until she's tasted all of her juices from my mouth. Presley's fingers graze over my shoulder blades, peering into my eyes. "You need to know something about me. I'm a virgin, but I'm not innocent. I... I..."

"You want me, and I want you. Let me show you how much you're needed and wanted. How much happiness you bring me. How much you make me a sappy puppy dog. How much I admire you for picking yourself up by those West Virginia bootstraps. Everything that happened to you brought you to me. I believe that." I shower wet, warm kisses along her collarbone. "Do you believe I'm crazy about you?"

She nods, sinking her teeth into her plump, soft skin.

I grab her hand, placing it on my erection. "This is what you've done to me ever since the first night I met you."

A small line appears at the bridge of her nose.

"I lied. I have thought of another woman since we moved in together. She has pink hair and violet eyes."

Her eyes stretch open as she turns her head. "I'm..."

"You're a woman who did what she had to. Presley, your secret is safe with me. And now, I want to make you mine."

"For one night?"

"For as long as you'll have me."

She teases her entrance with my tip, and we smile like clowns, gazing into each other's eyes.

"We'll see how you perform," she jests as she lifts her head, and her hands wrap around my neck. "You were pretty cocky about your abilities that night at Illusions."

"Make no mistake, you'll be begging me not to stop." After a soft kiss, I push into her. "God, you're tight. Your muscles inside are as soft and strong as your stomach and legs." I glide in and out until she adjusts.

"Awww."

"Does it hurt?"

"A little. It feels like I ate two Thanksgiving dinners." She giggles.

I kiss her the entire time my hips piston and slap against her skin. Her fingers drag over my ass as she presses me into her farther. "Daniel. Pull out."

"What's wrong?"

"I'm not on the pill. Do you have condoms?"

I look down, and there's a blood spot on the sheets. It's her first time, and I'm the lucky fucker she feels is worth it. I reach into the nightstand and glide the condom over my dick. When I reenter her, she gasps. Within a few minutes, she peaks as I suck her tits, while plunging in and out of her.

"Daniel," she screams as her muscles tighten around my shaft.

She's so damn beautiful and natural. "That's two," I whisper in her ear. "How about a hat trick?"

I turn her onto her stomach and at first, she shakes her head.

"I'm not going there. Not tonight anyway."

I slide my hands underneath her stomach and rub her clit with one hand, while the other slides in and out of her folds. She's wet again in seconds. Pulling one hand out, I keep circling her clit with the other. I enter her from the back, and we make slow love. She holds all of my weight, our sweaty skin sticking together as we reach our climax together.

A rugged roar rips through my chest, and my toes curl. Her hips keep pumping at a slow roll until I pull out and discard the condom. Tracing her lips with my fingers, she says, "I think I'm in love with you."

Getting checked into the boards couldn't knock the smile off my face.

"Glad you're catching up." I press a kiss to her shoulder.

"When did you find out I danced at Illusions?"

"The night you drove me home from the party, I remembered seeing a pink wig peeking out of a tote bag."

"And you still wanted me?" She thinks on it for a moment. "You didn't judge me."

"Pres, I admire you for trying to change your future. Your parents are assholes for disowning you over getting drunk at a party. You're the strongest woman I know. And Presley, I don't want to be roommates anymore."

Her eyes narrow.

"I want to live together as boyfriend and girlfriend."

A surge of energy hits her, and she straddles me. "Does that mean I get a jersey with your name on it?"

"It means you are off limits to everyone but me, and yes, you get a jersey. Now, put my t-shirt back on and let's go for a home run."

She swings her legs off the bed, slides her arms into my tee, and says, "Do you want that lap dance now?"

And she destroys me with her strong, toned thighs tighten around me and her pebbled nipples graze against my mouth through my well-worn shirt.

Presley has many amazing qualities such as being a mentally tough, talented soccer player, but quick learner is at the top of the list.

Thank you for reading Flynn & Presley's novella. To read the first three full length, spicy books in the Campus Stallions series, visit my website: www.kristinleebooks.com

About the Author

USA Today Bestselling Author, Kristin Lee enjoys many of the same things her characters love.

Sports. Small Towns where everyone knows your name. Her family and friends. Kristin's Cavapoo, Milo keeps her warm at night while writing.

If she's not reading or writing, you'll find her at her teenager's basketball and baseball games or attending college and professional sports. Oh, and she loves having a bourbon cocktail while at the horse races.

Come get lost in Kristin's Spicy, Angsty, Swoon worthy Romances.

Join her newsletter to get book recs, recipes from her characters, new releases, sales and freebies.

Roommate Wanted

Skye Blackburn

1
A Matter of Convenience

My eyelids feel heavy as I try to keep them open after a long shift at the hospital. I turn up the volume on the radio and chilly air blasts from the air conditioning to keep me awake on my drive home. My mind wanders back to a little over a year ago when my house became so quiet. My brother and his dog moved out, leaving me alone. My place became a bachelor pad overnight. I decided that I would look for a roommate, not because I needed the rent money, but just to break up the silence when I was home.

Despite posting advertisements at work and in the local newspaper for weeks, I couldn't find a decent male roommate. It's surprising how difficult it is to find a suitable candidate. Unfortunately, the advertisement only attracted two undesirable individuals who were interested in Rae McCarthy, an actor I know. These people were trying to invade her personal life, so my brother Caleb took the position of Rae's bodyguard.

I had given up on finding a roommate when I ran into Kaycee Higgins, my co-worker and friend, in the emergency room. We were chatting, and she informed me that her apartment had flooded, and was looking for a new place to stay. She said she remembered seeing an ad I had posted for a roommate and was hoping it was still available. I had never lived with a female, but seeing her on the brink of tears, I couldn't bring myself to refuse her request.

She told me that all her possessions were ruined and had nothing but a few things she had left in her car. How could any man say no to her? Normally, she comes off as a tough-as-nails, take-no-prisoners type of person, but has a soft interior and a heart of gold when treating patients.

Kaycee is one of the reasons I hadn't switched from the night to the day shift. I found myself looking forward to seeing her beautiful face every day. I know I should have said no when she asked, as one should never mix business with pleasure, but I threw caution to the wind and said yes.

At twenty-six, I knew I shouldn't be crushing like a teenager, but Kaycee does something to me the minute she walks into a room. She's one of those women every man dreams of. She's intelligent, funny, and downright sexy.

I've fantasized about her lips and running my hands along her body. Back then, I just knew at that moment, I would regret my decision. I questioned myself; was living with her going to be a living hell? But… here we are today, a year later and it's been a joy to have her in my life.

We've become closer than ever. Spending time with each other's families and friends and even taking vacations together. If we get an invitation to an engagement somewhere, we always have a "plus one" guaranteed date. I think a lot about our late-night talks, about our dreams and aspirations.

It's nice to have someone I can share dinner with or just sit in front of the TV watching one of our favorite shows. We love watching movies together, sharing blankets and popcorn. Although, on more than one occasion, I've wanted to wrap my arms around her. So far, I've never crossed the line.

One thing I can't deny is that we're an odd pair. She's a complete disaster when it comes to keeping the house clean. While I like to have everything in the house tidy and in its place, she prefers to be a bit chaotic.

Kaycee likes to be loud and boisterous, while I'm calm, cool, and mostly collected. She loves to be the center of attention, while I'm content to keep to myself and observe others. Unlike me, she enjoys taking wild risks, being impulsive, and spontaneous. My personality is more cautious, logical, and level-headed.

Despite our differences, we managed to make it work and have become close friends. We learn from each other and appreciate the unique qualities each of us brings to the table. In the end, we balance each other out and our friendship is stronger for it.

Sometimes I know I come off as arrogant or rude, but it's because I try to keep my distance and not become too attached to people. My family dynamics are complicated, but I'm working on improving my attitude and myself. This helps me to keep my ego in check and remain humble. I strive to be open and honest in my communication without sounding like an ass.

I finally pulled up to the house, and felt a bit concerned. I found out from a colleague that Kaycee had gone home early. It's not like her to not tell me if something is going on. I should have called her to see if she needed something from the store. I don't think she was sick when I saw her at work. Maybe it's that time of the month.

When I walk into the house, I'm hit with the intoxicating smell of maple syrup, sausage, and coffee. My stomach rumbles letting me know I'm famished. Music from the kitchen can be heard throughout the house. As I approach, Truth Hurts by Lizzo, blares with Kaycee singing along at the top of her lungs.

I stopped at the doorway and watched Kaycee. She has a spatula in one hand as she sings and dances around the kitchen. I can't help but smile as her energy is infectious and gives me a second wind.

I want so badly to sing and dance along with her. She turns with a grin on her face. Seeing me standing there doesn't faze her one bit, as she continues to sing. My eyes roam the kitchen. There are bowls and pots strewn across the counter. Flour and chocolate smears are on the apron she's wearing over a T-shirt and shorts.

My mind went blank. Did I forget a special occasion? She turns down the music and comes closer. Her brown eyes study me for a minute. I can't help asking if she's sick or not.

"I take it you're all right?"

"I am!" She says, as the corners of her lips turn into a smile.

"What's going on?"

"Sorry for the mess. I thought I had more time to clean up."

"Do you have someone coming over?"

She slowly shakes her head. "You have no idea, do you?"

My eyebrows narrow as I can't imagine what she's getting at.

How can Dhani stand here looking so oblivious and cute at the same time? He's a brilliant physician, but he can be so clueless, I swear.

"Happy Birthday, Dhani!" I throw my hands up in the air.

"Thank you." He turns his face towards the calendar, as he needs to confirm the date.

"You've done so much for me this past year. So, I wanted to make you a special breakfast. It's just my way of saying thank you." His eyes survey the room. I can tell that he's itching to clean up. "Now go upstairs and take a shower. Everything should be ready in a few minutes."

"Are you sure I can't help?"

"Nope. Now, go on. Get out!" I grab his shoulders, turn him, and nudge him out of the kitchen. Once he's gone, I can't help but imagine wrapping my arms around his shoulders instead of shoving him out of there.

My attraction to Dhani increases the more time I spend with him. I mean, how can any hot-blooded woman not find him attractive? His hypnotizing blue eyes, sandy blonde hair, and chiseled face make it difficult for me not to steal glances his way.

Living with him has been an eye-opening experience. He's such a neat freak. Me? Not so much. I mean, I'm clean, but Dhani definitely takes cleanliness to a whole other level that I was not used to. I place the cooked items on a cookie sheet and place them inside the oven to keep them warm.

I try my best to clean up the mess I made. I pick up all the ingredients, place them back in the cupboard, and wipe down the counter. All that's left to make is some eggs and toast.

Time seemed to slip away from me while I was cleaning. I smelled the scent of woodsy cologne, and knew he was nearby. I stop what I'm doing and look up to find Dhani's eyes watching me.

I can't help but lift my eyebrows. "How long have you been standing there?"

"Only for a minute."

"Please have a seat." I turn on the stovetop, then crack eggs into a bowl and stir them with a whisk. To make them fluffy, I add a small amount of milk. It's impossible not to hum along to the radio. I sprinkle in some salt and pepper, then stir again. I pour the egg mixture into the pan and sprinkle in the vegetables and cheese. I let it sit for a few seconds before flipping the edges and folding them over to make an omelet, then cook for another few seconds. I pop the toast down in the toaster, so it'll be ready about the same time the omelet is done.

"Do you have plans for later today?" I look over my shoulder to see his response.

"No. No plans. Why? What's up?"

"Ryan is going to let me borrow two CDs. Would it be possible for you to take me to his house instead of grabbing a taxi?"

"Sure. I can do that." I set a plate in front of him filled with sausage, toast, pancakes, and an omelet. His eyes go wide with surprise as he takes a bite.

"Wow, this is amazing!"

"Thanks." I beamed with a smile.

"Aren't you going to eat?" He asks. "Make yourself a plate and sit with me."

I make myself a plate with smaller portions and sit next to him at the dining room table. "Thanks for agreeing to take me later. My car is still in the shop."

"It's no problem. It's about time I go see my brother anyway. As you know, I've been so busy at the hospital, I haven't had time to see any of my siblings."

This is great! I can get him to his brother's house without him suspecting a thing. His birthday party should go off without a hitch. I'm so glad he's coming. I don't know what I would have done if he said he couldn't take me. I'm sure he'll have a fun time. I can't wait to see his face when he sees all the surprises I've set up for his party.

We sit and enjoy our breakfast while talking about our day and some of the toughest and most unusual cases we've had come in through the emergency room. It was a long shift, and we're both tired. But even though we're exhausted, we continue to talk. Our conversation flows effortlessly.

I don't know if it's because we work together that we have this close connection, but we don't have much else in common. Despite our differences he still fascinates me. I like the way he thinks and the way he expresses himself. It just adds to the sexy way he carries himself.

I stifled a yawn. I can't hold back the tiredness I feel after working the night shift. Dhani goes to take my plate, and I'm quick to grab his hand. That spark of attraction, that I've felt before with him, shoots to my core as I feel his warm hand beneath mine.

I swallow hard to calm my breath. "This is your birthday. I've got it." I moved quickly grabbing both plates and silverware. I run my hands through water to rinse the dishes, but it does nothing to help relieve me of this feeling I'm having.

"Can I help you?" All I can do is shake my head. How do I tell Dhani the help I need from him is not in the way of cleaning dishes, but in a much more sensual way. "Are you, okay? You look a little flush."

"I'm fine."

He walks over and places his hand on my forehead. "You don't feel like you have a fever."

I can feel my cheeks getting hot at his closeness. I've watched him treat patients with a wonderful bedside manner. This is the first time I've witnessed it firsthand.

"I'm fine."

"There's that word again."

"What word?"

"If I've learned anything from my mother, the word fine is anything but fine, and usually means quite the opposite."

"I'm tired, but I'm fine. Really."

"Are you sure?" I nod my head and smile. "Listen. Leave all that; we can clean up after we both get some sleep. That all can wait."

I do as he requests and make sure everything is turned off, then head up to my room to get some sleep. I put on my sleep mask and lay down. I'm not sure if sleep will come quickly as I look forward to this evening.

2

A Matter of Timing

Our drive to my brother's house is quiet except for the background noise coming from the radio. I'm used to Kaycee talking about a hundred miles a minute. Her quietness makes me feel nervous. I take a deep breath and try to relax. I glance over at her and she's looking out the window and seems at peace. I smile, relieved that she's not feeling uncomfortable.

She shouldn't feel nervous. I know my family has become as attached to her as I am. When I pull up to the house, I automatically step out, walk over to the passenger side, and open the door for her.

I held out my hand to help her. She's dressed in a floral sun dress that flatters her curves. This is the first time she hasn't yelled at me for trying to be a gentleman. I smile to myself as she can be stubborn at times.

The hair on my neck rises, and I have this strange feeling. An overwhelming feeling of being watched. I shake it off as Kaycee walks in front of me. We take the steps up to the front porch and knock on the door.

The door opens suddenly by my sister-in-law, wearing a shit-eating grin on her face. Trouble is brewing in Meghann's head. I can feel it in my bones. I let Kaycee step inside the house first, which allows me time to examine the area. Ryan and Meghann have gotten into surprising each other with confetti cannons. It's become a game for them when you least expect it, and I've gotten caught in the crosshairs a few times. Nothing seems out of the ordinary, though.

"Come on in, Ryan is watching a game in the den." I follow Meghann, but she stops and pulls Kaycee aside. I continue down the hallway and see my brother sitting on the couch just inside the doorway.

"Hey, little bro." The sound of popping from all directions fills my ears. It seems to have gone on for three to four minutes. When I open my eyes, there are shiny, multi-color streamers on my face and entire body. Flashes of light from several cameras go off.

Many voices call out. "Happy Birthday, Dhani!" When I glance around the room, my entire family and friends are there, and a few others I don't recognize. Now I understand the feeling I had of being watched. Someone had to be on the lookout waiting for me to come to the house so they could surprise me. My brother approaches me and places his hands on my shoulders. "Sorry bro but look on the bright side. You look like a Christmas tree. We can put presents around you and call it done."

"Christmas is still far away, so I don't think it will happen anytime soon."

"Maybe not, but these pictures are going to last a lifetime."

Kaycee takes a couple of pictures and places her phone down. She steps in front of me, and I forget about everything else as her smile lights up the room. I get a warm feeling in my chest as she reaches up and removes the streamers from my head.

"Was this your idea?"

"It was. Are you angry?"

I stared into her eyes. "No. Not at all. Are there any more surprises I should know about?"

"If I told you, it wouldn't be a surprise. Now, would it?" The rest of the evening is spent having a beautiful dinner, drinking, and playing games. This is the first time that my family has gotten together since Ryan and Meghann got married a little over six months ago.

Meghann approaches me with a woman I believe to be about my age. "Dhani, I wanted to introduce you to Beth." I nod my head.

"Beth, this is my brother-in-law, Dhani."

She puts out her hand. "Nice to meet you. I've heard so much about you."

"Nothing bad, I hope." I know that Meghann is trying to set me up. How do I get out of this? I turned to say something to Meghann and noticed she's left us alone. My eyes roam the room looking for someone to help me out of this. That's when I see Meghann approaching Kaycee with a guy I don't know. What the hell? Is she trying to play matchmaker for her too?

Kaycee's eyes meet mine, and they look as desperate as I feel. I love my family, but they've gone too far. I block out all the sounds around me hoping I can hear the conversation between them from across the room. But it's no good, it's just too loud for me to hear anything they are saying.

I should feel like an ass. I didn't catch anything this woman said, I don't even remember her name. Frankly, I couldn't give two shits about it. I decided at once, no person is going to come between me and Kaycee. "Excuse me." I leave her side and make my way over to where Kaycee is standing in the kitchen.

Her eyes meet mine as I walk closer. Without thinking about it, I wrap my arms around Kaycee's waist and place a kiss on her lips. The room goes silent as I hold her in my arms. All I can hear is the sound of my heart beating fast. Her plump lips finally touched mine. There could be a band playing and fireworks going off, but I can only concentrate on how her body feels next to mine.

I break away and look down at Kaycee's beautiful face. She places a hand on her lips, and her eyes flutter. There's a good chance she will slap my face because she wasn't expecting it. I prepare myself for the beating of a lifetime.

Instead, she places her hand on my face and kisses me back. I'm stunned. I close my eyes and kiss her, my heart still pounding. I pull away and look into her eyes, and I can tell she feels the same way I do. We stay like that for a few more moments, smiling.

My eyes wander around the room, and everyone is looking at us. Commentary is shouted in all directions. The loudest came from Meghann. "It's about damn time!"

"Did you know Meghann was up to something?"
"No. She is pretty sneaky though."
"She is indeed."
"I don't believe she meant any harm. Don't be angry at her."
"I'm not. It looks like she did me a favor."

———

To my surprise, Dhani stayed by my side for the rest of the evening. Even though this was his birthday party, I felt as though I was going to walk away with the best gift. The party soon breaks up, and people take their leave.

The only ones left are Meghann, Ryan, and the two of us.

"I think Meghann has something to say to you both." She looks between us sheepishly.

"Sorry about this evening. But I had to do something."

"That's not an apology."

"Ryan, I know."

"What do you mean, you had to do something?" I ask as I sip my wine.

"The two of you are so into each other. I think the only ones that didn't see it were yourselves."

"That's crazy."

"Is it Dhani? Do you think you would have made a move on Kaycee if another man hadn't shown interest in her?"

Dhani's eyes fall on me momentarily before he answers. "Honestly, I don't know."

"What about you Kaycee? Would you have finally admitted to Dhani that you have a crush on him?"

"I wouldn't call it a crush." Redness fills my cheeks. "I'm not sixteen."

"Meghann, I think you over-romanticized the situation. You read too many romance novels." Suddenly the room became silent. Meghann's eyes began to twitch.

"That's my job, Ryan. I'm a personal assistant to an author. Are you telling me I should quit my job?"

I hope to defuse the situation before all hell breaks loose. My eyes meet Dhani's, and I cut in before things escalated. "Thank you, Meghann. I appreciate your help. We know you mean well."

Dhani takes hold of my hand. "Ryan don't be upset with her. I know I'm not angry. Thanks sis." He stands and gives her a peck on the cheek. "I think we should get going. Thank you for the birthday party. It was the best one I've had in a long time."

He holds out his hand for me. It's warm and inviting. We took all his presents to the car and said goodbye. The air on the car ride home is different and new. I'm unsure of what to say.

Dhani slides his hand into mine and squeezes. "I don't want you to feel awkward about us. We can take this relationship as fast or as slow as you want it to go."

Warmth fills my chest as I take in his words. I didn't realize how much I cared for him until Meghann introduced Dhani to a potential blind date. A sudden burst of anger built up in my stomach and I wanted to scratch the strangers' eyes out.

Thank goodness Dhani felt the same way. Watching him leave her side and make a beeline for me was surprising. In a thousand years, I would have never guessed that he cared for me too.

Dhani and I carry all the packages inside when we arrive home. I slip off my shoes just inside the doorway and my hands nervously fidget as I take a seat on the couch. What do we do now? Do we discuss our feelings? I take a deep breath, trying to prepare myself for the conversation. Dhani sits down next to me, and I can feel the warmth of his body radiating next to mine.

He takes my hand in his, brushes his thumb along my palm and speaks softly. "Now that we're alone, let's talk about this." He gestures a finger between the two of us. I try to calm my racing heart. I nod and take a deep breath. Dhani squeezes my hand and looks at me, waiting for a response.

I study him momentarily as his icy blue eyes look back at me, waiting for an answer. I move in before I lose my courage and softly touch my lips to his. We stayed in that position for a few moments, our lips connected before I pulled away. I look up at him and smile. We both know we have shared a moment that we will never forget. He grabs the remote and turns on the TV. He leans back and pulls me into his arms.

"Did I thank you for such a great birthday party?"

I tilted my head to look up at him. "No, I don't think you did."

"I meant it when I said that this was the best birthday I've ever had."

"There could be more presents if you're interested?" I lift an eyebrow to insinuate that he could have me.

"More?"

"So much more."

He swallows hard. "Are you sure?"

I nod my head. The corners of his mouth curled upwards into a smile. He stands quickly, turns off the TV and throws the remote down. He scoops me up and carries me up the stairs with purpose. When he gets to the landing, he stops for a moment. He looks down the hallway as he decides whether his room or mine. Instead, he turns right which leads to a guest bedroom and opens the door.

He places my feet on the ground and turns on the light switch. A room with a queen-sized bed, and warm earth tones, fills the room. The bed has a beautiful mahogany bed frame and matching bedside tables. He takes my hand and escorts me to bed.

"Can I ask you a question?"

"Of course."

"Why this room and not one of our own?"

"I want our first time to be special, and what I consider common ground. Nothing that can distract us. Just you and me...making love."

"Wow. That's sexy as hell." I grab his tie, loosen it, and plant a kiss on his lips. When I come up for air, I lift his tie over his head. My hands moved swiftly to unbutton his shirt, as his lips crashed into mine. Our lips and tongues tangled, his finger sliding down my back. The cool air hits my exposed skin as he slides down the zipper of my dress, causing me to shiver.

3
A Matter of Touch

Her body shivers under my touch, and I stop my movement. "Are you okay?"

"I'm fine. This room is a little chilly."

"It won't be for long." I smirk and touch my lips to hers, brushing them softly with mine. I hunger for her touch, her body next to mine. I deepen the kiss as she slides off my shirt and lets it fall. We've barely begun, yet my arousal brushes against her midsection.

Kaycee scrapes her fingernails through my hair, giving me goosebumps along my arms. Pulling away, I look into her eyes to confirm she wants to continue. I want nothing more than to be with her, but the last thing I want is to destroy our friendship. She gives me a sultry smile, and I can't help but be turned on even more.

My fingers grasp her shoulder straps. I slide her dress off and it pools on the ground around her feet, revealing a demi bra and matching red panties. We continue to remove articles of clothing until we're standing pressed against each other, left naked and vulnerable. I take a step back so my eyes can take her in. Her body is unbelievably sexy. My fingers brush up and down her arms.

She pushes me backward on the bed and straddles my lap. She kisses me and grinds her center against my shaft. Her wetness coats my dick, I'm ready to explode. I brace my hands on her hips and lift her slightly so I can slide us back onto the bed.

"Follow me, darling."

She crawled up the bed on all fours, following me, slowly and deliberately. Her movements were graceful and elegant, like a cat stalking its prey. I stop, and she crawls back over me and straddles my waist. I expected her to purr like a kitten as she leaned over and licked my chest.

"I want you to know that I get tested regularly and am clean but can go grab a condom from my room if you want."

"I was tested and got a clean bill of health and haven't had any relationships since. I am also on birth control, so if you're ok with it, I would love to feel you, all of you, deep inside of me."

I lean into her and growl out. "It's my turn." I take her pebbled nipple and swirl my tongue around it. She lets out a moan and its music to my ears as she purrs. She slides back and forth along my dick, grinding increasingly. I grab my shaft, line up with her entrance, and she lowers until she's fully seated. Her eyes shine with want and desire. I thrust in and out of her, slowly at first and then harder and faster. I lean in and kiss her deeply, our tongues intertwining.

Her hips rise to meet my movements. I kiss her gorgeous mouth, nipping at her lower lip. We increase our speed, moving faster and faster. I grab her hips with both hands and pull her closer, our tongues exploring each other's mouths. I can feel her body trembling against mine, and I know she's enjoying it as much as I am. She moans louder and louder until she's lost in her pleasure.

She lets out a hiss as she comes, throwing her head back and calling out my name. I follow her with a curse as I thrust one final time. My cock expended my seed into her sweet pussy. She slumps onto my chest, and we both breathe heavily. I lay still, taking in the moment and appreciating our closeness.

She lifts her head and stares into my eyes. I drag my hands up and down her back. Her skin is soft beneath the palms of my hands. I wrap my arms around her and pull her to the bed so she's lying next to me. Her head lays on the crook of my shoulder, fingers outlining my tattoo.

"Can I ask you a question?"

"Of course. You can ask me anything."

"What made you get a tattoo?"

"I guess you can say I was going through a rebellious stage in my life."

"Did you do it on a dare?"

"No. My dad told me they were stupid, and no son of his was ever getting a tattoo."

"So, you got one anyway."

"I did."

"Just to be spiteful?"

"No, not really. I always wanted one. But, when the old man said no, there was no stopping me."

"I take it you're not close with your father?"

"That's right. I don't consider him my dad. He walked out on my family. The man that I consider to be more of a father figure is my older brother Ryan."

"No wonder you two are so close."

"Enough about my family." I stared into her deep brown eyes, slid my thumb back and forth across her cheek, and went in for a kiss. Her lips taste of strawberries and cream, which stirs my hunger to be inside her again. My cock springs to life for a second time, as she slides her hand up and down my shaft.

We tangled in the sheets, trying various positions, finding each other's likes and dislikes. We're on an entirely new level of our friendship. I want to explore this intimacy much further. I admit that I've never had this before in my life. I've been with other women, but never wanted to cuddle or talk about my feelings. I want this relationship with Kaycee.

We finally expend ourselves and lie together in each other's arms. Before I close my eyes for the evening, I look at Kaycee as her deep brown hair cascades across her pillow. I can't help it, but a smile crosses my face as my heart fills with joy. This evening has got to be the best birthday I've ever had. I don't know if she loves me. But what I do know is that Kaycee doesn't judge me, and she brings out the best in me.

———

When I wake up from my slumber, I'm left with a warm feeling in my chest. The feeling soon leaves when I find I'm all alone in bed. Sun filters through the blinds letting me know that it's later than I thought it would be. I pull the sheets around my body to go back to my room. The overwhelming feeling that I'm doing the walk of shame comes over me. I don't know why I'm tiptoeing.

The sound of footsteps coming up the stairs makes me move faster. I slam the door to my room and pull the drawers to gather my clothes for the day. I stop when there's a tap at my door.

"Kaycee?"

"What?"

"Are you alright?"

"I'm fine."

"Please open the door, Kaycee."

"The door isn't locked."

"My hands are a little preoccupied, I could use your assistance."

With my hand firmly gripping the sheet at my chest, I stomp over to the door and swing it open to find Dhani standing with a tray of food. I take in his tousled, sandy blonde hair and his bare chest. His basketball shorts hang low on his hips partially revealing the V that makes me horny as hell. My tongue voluntarily runs over my bottom lip.

"I'm sorry I left, but I didn't want to wake you. You looked so peaceful."

The anger I felt leaves my body as he steps across the doorway. "You made breakfast?"

"I did, and I made some coffee. Unless you want some orange juice instead."

"Coffee is good."

"I wanted to serve you in bed." He glances around my bedroom, which I haven't had the time to straighten up. "Why don't you get dressed and come downstairs and we can eat in the kitchen."

"That's sweet of you, I'll be right down. I know how much of a clean freak you are."

"I am not."

"Don't kid yourself, I know you are."

"You're right. I was trying to get out of my comfort zone."

"Let's take baby steps." My lips curve into a smile as I appreciate his effort. His eyes fall to my lips. "Go on. I'll be there shortly." He turns with the tray and heads downstairs. I take a minute to go to the bathroom to do my business and run a brush through my unruly hair. When I return to my bedroom, I throw on a sports bra and underwear and wrap myself in a robe. Once I finish eating breakfast, I'll return to take a shower and dress for the day. But for now, my stomach is letting me know how ravenous I am.

When I arrive at the kitchen, the plates are arranged on the center island. A vase with yellow, pink, and lavender-colored wildflowers brightens the room. Dhani places a fresh cup of coffee next to a plate.

"Please, have a seat."

"Wow. A girl could get used to this." I take a seat and remove the plate he used to cover my food. Scrambled eggs, hash browns, and sausage fills the plate.

"If it's cold I can reheat it."

"It's perfect. Come and sit down."

He leans in and gives me a peck on my cheek. When he sits down his leg brushes mine.

"I don't think I can eat."

"Why? What's wrong?"

"Your bare chest is very distracting." He let out a deep chuckle that echoed throughout the kitchen.

"Let me go put on a shirt."

"It's fine. I'm only kidding."

"How about you take off your robe and we'll call it even."

"I'm not bare-chested."

"Damn. That's too bad." His lips turn to a sexy smirk that gives my stomach butterflies. My smile fades as I wonder how it will be when we go back to work. "What is it?"

"We have to discuss how our relationship will interfere with our work."

"There should be no issues."

"Don't you think it will be frowned upon?"

"No. Why should it?"

"People will talk."

"Listen. Nowhere does it state in the hospital policy that employees can't date each other. If people talk, they're going to talk. We can't stop them."

"But...."

He placed his hand on my face to smooth out the worried expression. "If it's going to stress you out, we can keep it professional while we're at work."

"We can?"

"Of course, we can. But that doesn't mean we can't still take a break or have lunch together. People eat together all the time."

"That's true." *Even though I wouldn't mind receiving kisses in the supply closet. It wouldn't be a clever idea to get caught. Ugh, I'm worrying about nothing.* I find myself picking at what's left of my food.

Dhani places his hand on top of mine. "If you're that worried about it, I can change departments."

"No. Please don't do that. I don't think I could bear to work with someone else."

"Okay, then it's settled. We'll just go on at work like we've been doing for the past couple of years as though nothing has changed." I nodded to agree with him. I know I shouldn't worry that this would complicate our working relationship.

"Since we have the day off, let's do something we haven't done before."

"Like what, Dhani? Each other?"

He snickers. "Trust me. We haven't done it enough. We can christen every room in this house, but not today. Do you like to play games?"

"Sure. What are you thinking?"

"Today, I want to do one of those virtual reality rooms."

"Are those the ones where you can shoot up zombies?"

"Yes, that's one of them."

"I'd love to."

"Awesome! I'll set it up." He picked up his phone and set up our date.

I have to say it feels exciting to be in a relationship. Especially with a man willing to try new things and spend time with me.

Our afternoon was spent shooting up zombies. I couldn't believe how tiring it was, even if I was only shooting at imaginary objects. When I took off the mask, I was sweating and knew I didn't look attractive. However, Dhani didn't have an issue with my appearance. He brushed my bangs away from my face and kissed me.

We had a wonderful dinner at a burger joint that we both love. When we came home, we cuddled in front of the TV. I can see myself doing this for the rest of my life with him. But I know I need to take one day at a time.

4
A Matter of The Heart

As the months pass, all I can think about is how I don't want to wait years to ask Kaycee to marry me. The last couple of days, I've been thinking about unusual ways to ask her. After our exhausting evening working in the emergency room tonight, I want Kaycee to know that I appreciate every minute I'm with her.

I watched as she brushed her teeth. I finally realized I couldn't wait any longer and blurted out the most unromantic proposal ever. She blinked several times, trying to figure out whether I was serious or not. The toothbrush sat still in her mouth. She tilted her head to the side, trying to rewind the last few minutes. She removed the toothbrush, spat out the remaining toothpaste, and wiped her mouth with a towel.

"I'm sorry, what did you just say?"

"I asked you if you'd marry me."

"You asked me as if you wanted me to pass toilet paper to you under a bathroom stall."

"I know, I just blurted it out and that was not my intention."

"What was your intention?"

"Well. In my mind, I wanted to plan something romantic like a picnic in the park or a candlelight dinner for two. The server would bring your ring with your favorite dessert. My other thought was to get a flash mob to dance to one of your favorite songs. Another possibility was to rent a beach and have a private sunset dinner. So many ideas ran through my head. After such a challenging evening at work, all I wanted to say to you was how much I love you. How much I want to spend the rest of my life with you."

"Oh, keep talking."

"All I did was screw that up and fumble the ball on the twenty-yard line."

"You know I don't understand football lingo."

I step closer to her and pull her towards me. "For someone who doesn't know football, you know what I meant by the twenty-yard line?" Her lips curled into a smirk.

"Okay, I do know a thing or two about football. But that's beside the point."

I pulled out the ring box I had tucked in my pocket and kneeled on one knee. "You're right. The point is that I've become so eager to ask you to marry me that I couldn't wait for the perfect moment. I wanted to show you how much I care and how much I love you. I wanted to create the most magical moment of our lives. I wanted to prove to you that our love was unbreakable. I was worried about what would happen if I never got the chance and missed out on the best thing that's come into my life. I love you so much. Will you marry me?"

"When we tell our kids about our engagement, can we leave out the part that you asked me in the bathroom?"

"Did you say kids?" She nodded her head in response. "Is that a yes, then?"

"Yes, Dhani. I'll marry you." I stood up immediately and kissed her. Her kisses tasted minty fresh. I ran my hands along her back and held her tight. When we break free from kissing, I look and see a tear running down her face.

"Why are you crying? Is it because I proposed in the bathroom?"

A small chuckle escaped her lips. "No. These are happy tears." I wiped away the stray tear that rolled down her cheek and kissed her.

"You can tell our kids whatever you want. You can even tell them that I proposed in the kitchen where we like to spend our time doing it."

"Dhani, I'm not telling our kids we have sex in the kitchen!"

"I mean, it's where we like to spend our time cooking together." The side of my mouth quirked up in an amused expression. "I prefer your idea more than mine."

"You're exhausting sometimes."

"Yeah. You gotta admit, you love me anyway."

"I do love you, and I don't want to be with anyone else."

I took her by the hand and led her to the bedroom so we could make love or cuddle. I didn't care either way, as long as she was lying by my side. We talked briefly about our thoughts on the wedding. The two of us agreed that we wanted our wedding to be witnessed by a few close relatives and friends. I was content with anything she wanted so long as I was with her.

She yawned and I kissed her forehead. Her eyes closed, breath slowly becoming deeper, as she drifted off to sleep. I found myself falling asleep peacefully, letting her warmth and comfort erase all the worries of the workday.

My hands shake as I prepare to get ready for my special day. Our bedroom has been off-limits to everyone except my mother and Lisa, my best friend and maid of honor. Both have helped me do my hair and makeup. After I slip into my wedding dress, mom puts on my veil and adds bobby pins to secure it in place.

My mom places her hand on my shoulder. "Are you nervous?"

"Maybe a little."

"There's no need to be. We all know how much Dhani loves you."

"It's not Dhani I'm worried about."

"Then what is it?" Lisa's eyes were filled with concern.

"I'm worried about falling on my face in these heels."

"You know you can take them off, right? No one is going to care that you're not wearing four-inch heels. Plus, you'll be walking in the grass in the backyard."

"You're right."

Lisa goes into my closet and pulls out a pair of black and white chucks. She has me slip them on after I put on some socks and helps me tie the laces before leading me out the door.

My mother placed a gentle kiss on my cheek. "I'll see you downstairs."

"Mom..." She stops with the door handle in her grasp. "...thank you."

"For what honey?"

"For always believing in me and standing by my side."

"That's a mother's job. To love our kids unconditionally and guide them on the right path."

"Well, then you did a great job, Mom." I do everything in my power not to cry.

"Don't do it. You cry, then I start to cry, and we all look like raccoons, and we have to redo everyone's makeup." Lisa's comment makes us all laugh, stopping us from tearing up. She grabs a tissue and dries my face from one lonely tear that escaped. "Are you ready?"

I nod my head. In a few minutes, I'll be walking down the aisle, and not only have a new husband, but a large extended family. My mother goes downstairs first and heads to where they'll seat her in the front row next to my grandmother. I take a deep breath and follow my mother's path.

As I walk down the steps, photos line the stairway wall. I'm reminded that it was just over a year ago, I stood at the front door of this house. I came with nothing but a few items of clothing. Who knew after losing all my possessions it would leave me to find the love of my life? Once I've reached the bottom step my father takes my hand.

"You look beautiful, pumpkin."

"Thanks, Daddy."

"Nice shoes."

"Maybe I should go change them." I say as I look down.

"Don't you dare; don't change for anyone." Daddy lifted my head, so I was looking into his eyes. "Always be you, Kaycee." A grin creased his face. He wrapped my hand around his arm.

"Let's do this! We have a party to get to."

"That's my pumpkin."

We stood and waited for our queue to walk down the aisle. All of Me by John Legend, played to let me know it was time. Once the wedding march began, they pulled the curtains back covering the double doors leading to the backyard. The sun shone through the trees. Twinkling lights and flowers illuminated the outdoor seating area. The guests rose from their seats. I felt a rush of emotion as I saw my future husband waiting for me at the end of the aisle.

Dhani stood there, eyes looking towards the ground with his hands together. The wind blew slightly as he waited underneath a wooden arbor, decorated with white chiffon fabric draped across the sides with vibrant colored flowers of yellow and pink. When he lifted his head, his eyes landed on me. His smile grew wider until it reached his eyes.

The minutes seemed to stretch into hours, I thought, as I walked toward him. My father and I reached the end of the aisle, and he squeezed my hand and told me that he loved me. He then gave me away by announcing his permission for me to marry. There was a mixture of happiness and sadness in his smile as he walked away.

Dhani smiled and kissed me on the cheek. I felt the warmth of his lips and my heart raced. We embraced each other, and I knew what we had was special. We took our vows and exchanged rings, and then it was time to celebrate. It was a magical moment that I will never forget. We were surrounded by family and friends as we walked down the aisle, ready to start our new life together.

About the Author

SKYE BLACKBURN

Skye Blackburn writes romantic comedies, suspense, and sports romance, leaving a small piece of herself in each character. As for her heroes, she likes to make them dreamy and thoughtful, sometimes a little mischievous as well. Besides writing, she works in the medical field, daydreams constantly, and is constantly distracted by her book boyfriends.

Sometimes she gets asked what drove her to write. Skye always told her daughters to let nothing hold them back and to follow their dreams, no matter what that is. With her daughter's encouragement, it was time she did the same. The time had come to share her love of romance and to write the stories that were trying to escape her mind.

Skye has lived in California all her life. It is no secret that she has a deep love for the beach. When she's at home, she enjoys binge-watching everything from Marvel, Star Wars, Lord of the Rings, Harry Potter, anime, and K-Dramas. She also enjoys cuddling with her dogs, while watching crime-related TV shows.

She hopes that readers will find something in her work that brings them joy and helps them bring a smile to their day. She also hopes that her stories will inspire readers to take more risks in life and to find their own happily ever after.

Other books by Skye Blackburn

Love On the Rise

Love On the Rocks

Love On the Run

The Breaking Ball

Second Chance At Forever

Meg Napier

1

"Hey Robbie, I know this is kinda last minute and out of the blue, but there's a problem at my apartment, and I need a place to stay. I'll try Alison's number, too, but I was hoping it'd be okay for me to crash at your place tonight and for maybe a couple days. I'll try Alison's number now. Bye. Love you."

Jen disconnected and tried her sister-in-law. She growled low in her throat when Alison's phone also went to voicemail but left a similar message.

What had she expected? Her brother and sister-in-law were both busy, successful people: he as a lawyer for the State Dept., and she as a policy analyst on the Hill. It was Friday night, though, so even the rich and powerful should be winding down.

Jen chewed on her bottom lip and considered her options. Her roommate, whom she loved and trusted completely, had told her during a cryptic but intense phone call that it wasn't safe to stay at the apartment they shared. As that call had come only minutes after an unknown man had come knocking at the door looking for Amanda, Jen had taken her friend's words seriously, packed up a small bag, and gotten out of Dodge.

She was now driving toward her brother's house in Alexandria, hoping against hope she'd be welcome. They hadn't spoken in a couple weeks, although Rob and Alison had both shared pictures of their daughter, Lizzie, in her Taylor Swift Halloween costume that Jen had digitally exclaimed over last week.

If Lizzie was home with a babysitter, would the person even open the door? Jen had a key, but she'd probably scare the sitter half to death or risk having the police called. And the dog would bark, even though he knew her and would jump on her with delight as soon as she crossed the threshold. Lizzie would vouch for her, of course, but who knew how long it might take someone panicking to pay attention to a five-year-old.

She moved her jaw and switched to biting the left side of her lip. She'd just show up and cross her fingers. Maybe they were all watching a movie and had their phones on silent.

Alexandria, an historic DC suburb boasting taverns that George Washington had allegedly visited, wasn't a huge municipality, but it certainly encompassed a wide array of economic prosperity. Her brother and sister-in-law, naturally, had a lovely, decades-old, well-maintained but updated stately home set on a perfectly manicured, deep set plot on a wide street flanked by majestic trees. Jen always felt out of place when she visited. How in the world had she and her brother grown up only a year apart in the same family?

Her salary, after several years working as an RN, wasn't bad, but her student loan payments had only been deferred while she took out new loans to begin working towards her nurse practitioner degree. The apartment she and Amanda shared was in an okay neighborhood, but their digs seemed almost pitiful when compared to how her brother lived.

She squared her shoulders as she got out of the car, having parked on the street since there were already three cars in the long driveway. Yay! Lights were on and cars were parked. At least an arrest for breaking and entering could be crossed from her list of worries.

As she walked up the drive, she noticed voices and caught the distinct smell of popcorn coming from the partly opened window of the front facing kitchen. Her movie night guess had probably been correct.

Jen heard the words of a male voice and stopped. *Chris?* It couldn't be. She really did not want to see her brother's life-long best friend tonight. Yes, she had known him all her life; yes, she had mooned over him for years, but she had spent the last ten years doing everything to avoid him and forget his existence.

"I ended up having to take seminary. There was no other choice."

Of course he was in the seminary. It made perfect sense. Even his damn name was actually Christian, though he had always adamantly insisted everyone call him Chris.

His entire life had been one of decency and service. When his name had come up at Christmas last year—because of course, her mother adored him—Robbie had talked about the incredibly difficult cases Chris worked as a social services director in D.C.

Chris. The wonderful, handsome, honorable *Christian*. That one. The one over whom she had suffered pangs of guilt after they kissed one night in high school when he was her best friend's boyfriend. But those first guilty feelings had paled in comparison to what she experienced after what they did six weeks later.

Both horny, unexpectedly alone, and drunk for the first time in their lives, they had given each other their virginity in an hour of shared, passionate bliss. Then they had turned away in shame and never spoken directly to each other again.

2

Jen stood still, frozen with indecision. It was late, and she was tired and scared. Someone was threatening her roommate, and she had nowhere else to go. Her parents had sold the house she and Robbie had grown up in and decamped to South Carolina two years ago. A hotel in this area would vacuum up every cent of discretionary income she had and really wasn't an option considering she had no idea how long she'd need to be away from her apartment.

She checked the time on her phone. Maybe Chris had come over for dinner and a movie. If they were making popcorn now, that meant they probably hadn't started the movie. "Uncle Chris"—Jen rolled her eyes at the moniker—had most likely said good night to Lizzie, perhaps even read her a story, and they were now ready to start some adult film. That meant what—three hours, tops? She was a big girl. She'd explain her situation, then scurry off to the guest room and leave them to enjoy the movie.

Grow up, Jen. She hissed the admonition aloud as she approached the large front doors and rang the bell. Belatedly she remembered the camera and mic over the door and hoped her words hadn't been audible.

A moment later her brother was there, a typically rueful smile on his face.

"Jen! You called a little while ago, and I meant to listen to your voicemail but then forgot. Is everything okay?" His eyes drew together as he spoke, taking in the duffle bag slung over her shoulder.

"Well . . . yes. And no. I can come in, right?" Her brother was still blocking the entrance, but he stepped back at her words and motioned her in with an apologetic laugh.

"Of course. Come in. Lizzie's just gone to sleep . . ." His words trailed off as Jen stepped inside and an excited and definitely not sleeping five-year-old came hurtling down the stairs wearing a Disney princess nightgown.

"Auntie Jen! You're here, too! Are you going to stay overnight like Uncle Chris?"

The bundle of energy was in her arms, hugging her tightly, and Jen forced herself to breathe as she simultaneously delighted in her niece's enthusiasm and recoiled from the impact of her words. *Chris was staying overnight?* The wild mix of sensations intensified as Pinto, the family's vivacious Labradoodle, began an excited dance around her. How in the world could one moment be at once so perfect and so unsettling?

"I don't know, my angel. I didn't know Uncle Chris was here."

"He is! But it's even better now that you're here, too. Do you want to read me a story? I'm supposed to be asleep, but I'm not tired yet."

Thank God for the babble of little ones. Jen couldn't have resisted smiling even if her life depended on it as the sweet girl held her face between her small hands and demanded her complete attention.

"Maybe one story, if it's okay with your parents. How many have you already had tonight?" She tried to insert some discipline into her voice but gave up as Lizzie began tucking strands of Jen's hair behind her ears.

"Mommy read me a chapter from *The Boxcar Children*, but then we made Uncle Chris read *Fox in Socks*. It was so funny!" The minx erupted in giggles before getting serious again. "But I know *Old Turtle* is your favorite, so we can read that one if you want."

Jen closed her eyes and rubbed her forehead against her niece's bouncy curls. How she loved this child. She was coming to accept that she'd probably never have one of her own, so having Lizzie in her life was a gift she treasured.

She put the girl down and straightened. She could handle this.

Alison had joined them in the spacious foyer and reached out to pull Jen into a hug.

"You've come to join the party and already been bamboozled by the social director! What happened at your apartment? I admit that I'm guilty, too. I just this second listened to your voicemail. Scary things are happening everywhere. I just read about that condo that exploded in Montgomery County."

A shiver ran down Jen's spine—some trickle of memory. Hadn't Amanda grown up in Montgomery County, and didn't her family and a lot of her friends still live there? She hoped Amanda would get in touch with her again soon and let her know what was going on.

She forced a breezy lightness into her words and improvised. "Some kind of wiring issue that they said might take a few days to fix. Better safe than sorry, right? Especially if other buildings are exploding."

Open your eyes wide and make your smile carefree. "But I can easily go stay at a friend's house if you already have guests."

Robbie laughed. "I don't know about guests. Chris is here because pipes were damaged in his building during renovations, and now there's no water. But it shouldn't be a problem. There's room for both of you in the guest room, or I can bunk in there with him and you can sleep with Alison."

"No, no. I don't want to put you out. I can go to my friend Bethany's." Bethany had moved to California the year before, but Robbie didn't know that.

"There's plenty of room in the guest room." Alison's voice was matter-of-fact. "There are two beds, and you're both grownups. But if it's a big deal, we can work out something else."

Feeling trapped and foolish, Jen could only shake her head and plaster a smile to her face.

"One of the beds in the guest room would be perfect. Thanks. And then I'll be out first thing in the morning. I'm beat already, so I won't disturb your party."

"We're just hanging around watching some old stand-up repeats, so you can join us," Robbie said. "And If I heard correctly, Lizzie's already picked out which story she wants you to read. Although it's absolutely, positively the last one."

His last words were directed with a mock scowl at his daughter, who only giggled in response.

"I know, Daddy. Sleep is important to make my brain and my body grow big and strong."

Lizzie's face had taken on a studied adult frown as she spoke, and Jen choked back a bark of laughter. The little girl's adoption of total sarcasm was imminent, and Robbie and Alison would soon have a worthy opponent on their hands.

"Okay, missy. *Old Turtle* it is, and then it's sleep time for both of us. I was up at five this morning, and I'm tired, even if you're not." Maybe she could get herself in bed and asleep, or at least fake being asleep, before Chris even came in.

"Yay!!"

Shifting her niece to her other hip, Jen shot her brother what she hoped was a convincing smile. "I have no problem, but maybe you should check with Chris. He probably wasn't expecting company. He might prefer having the room to himself, and I really can go to a friend's."

"Of course not." Chris, too, had come into the foyer, and as always, Jen's mastery of basic respiration deserted her. He spoke evenly, seemingly without looking up from his phone, but Jen had felt a jolt when their eyes met for just an instant before he looked away.

She forced an inhale. "Okay, then. I'll just head up and read."

Minutes later, Jen surreptitiously studied her niece's bed as she read the familiar beloved storybook. It was a double, and Jen could maybe sleep next to the little girl . . . But no. That would be cowardly. She and Chris had known each other since they were children, and they were now mature adults. *Act like one, Jennifer,* she admonished herself.

She inhaled one last deep breath of Lizzie's delicious scent as she kissed the girl goodnight.

"Sleep tight, Auntie. You're so lucky you get to sleep with Uncle Chris."

Whoa. Jen tried not to react as she straightened to turn out the light.

"Right you are, little one. I'm a lucky lady."

3

Every part of her wanted to slink past the open living room unnoticed and high-tail it to the guest room, but she forced herself to offer a cheery, though exaggeratedly tired, "Goodnight!"

"Come sit with us, Jen." Alison's voice was bright and inviting. "We're watching the new Trevor Noah special. You'll love it. And if you're hungry, there's plenty of lasagna left in the kitchen."

"Thanks, but I'm exhausted. I'll probably be asleep before I'm even done brushing my teeth, so don't worry about making noise when you come in, Chris. I sleep like the dead."

There. She had spoken to him directly, just like a grown-up human being, even if she hadn't looked in his direction while she spoke. And what of it? It wasn't like they had any connection beyond her brother, right? Then why, oh why, did she wish she was wearing something nicer than jeans and a hoodie?

He made an indecipherable noise in response, and Jen gave one last cheery "Night, everyone" before scurrying off towards the guest room.

She could do this. She changed her clothes, brushed her teeth, and washed her face. The ensuite bathroom was three times as big as the one she and Amanda shared, and under normal circumstances, she would probably have enjoyed a nice soak in the oversized tub. But not tonight.

She should shower, but she was too exhausted and in a hurry to get out of sight.

She left the light on in the bathroom so Chris would be able to see when he came in and climbed into the large, beautifully made up bed closest to the window. She would burrow in, shut her eyes, and not show any sign of life 'til Chris left the room again in the morning.

A great plan with sadly deplorable execution. The moment she pulled the blanket up, a nervous energy overtook her, leaving her unable to lie still. She tossed about and tried implementing the relaxation and meditation tips Amanda had shared with her over the years. Amanda was a psychic, as preposterous as that seemed, and sincerely believed in nonsense like meditation. Normally Jen would dismiss it all as hoo-ha, but she had been dumbfounded when Amanda passed on a message from Jen's grandmother about some missing documents that absolutely no one else on the planet could have known about. After that, Amanda had Jen's complete trust, although Jen never mustered sincere interest in meditation despite making a half-hearted go at it every January 1 that usually lasted at least a day or two. But now, as she tried the deep, even breathing, all she really wanted to do was throw off the bed covers and run.

Common sense prevailed, and she forced herself to continue. *Breathe in for four, hold for two, and breathe out for four.* Ever so gradually, her limbs began to relax.

What was she afraid of, anyway? She was a good person, Chris probably a better person, and neither one of them had done anything terrible. Yes, she had pined for him in high school while he went out with her dear friend, Maris. Chris has been everything she thought perfect in a guy: a year older, smart, talented, and so breathtakingly gorgeous. Feeling that way was a traitorous, horrible thing to do when he was her friend's boyfriend, but nothing beyond a bit of illicit but still harmless kissing would have happened if that jerk, Danny, hadn't spiked the punch at Brent's graduation party.

But the guilt she had tried to ignore these many years wouldn't stay buried. She hadn't been *that* drunk. She'd thought the punch tasted funny and had finished only one cup. Everyone their age drank all the time, and many of them sampled or got hooked on the incredible array of drugs easily available. Their particular friend group, however, for whatever reason, didn't. Maybe it was because several of them belonged to the same church youth group Chris and Maris belonged to, or maybe because they were all nerds who somehow found solace in each other's company rather than chemical stimulation. They tended to hang out together with Doritos, M&Ms, and diet sodas and watch movies on weekends when they weren't participating in organized youth group outings. Maris always invited Jen to go with her, and Jen enjoyed the company while wishing guiltily Maris would tire of Chris and leave him unattached.

Jen had tasted alcohol many times. Some of her other friends were major partiers, and her parents never minded if she tasted their occasional glass of wine or cocktail. But she didn't particularly like it, and all these years later, she typically only had one glass of wine or one margarita if she was out with friends.

Chris was most likely still a teetotaler, especially if he was now going to seminary. He had drunk the punch that long ago night though, so if anything resembling coercion had occurred, she was probably the perpetrator.

Jen sat up in bed, efforts at relaxation abandoned as ten-year-old mortification overwhelmed her. She adjusted the pillows, trying to punch them into a sleep-inducing arrangement. What the hell was the matter with her? What had happened between her and Chris was ancient history, but it had definitely been consensual. And though she later learned that he and Maris had technically been on "a break" at the time of the party, the two had gone on to marry anyway. They had divorced after only a year or two, and now he was entering the ministry. And absolutely none of that should be of any concern or interest to her.

Jen had studied and worked hard, gotten a good job, and was now on her way to an even better job. She had dated a few men over the years, and even stayed together with one for almost a year and a half. But none of the guys had held any lasting appeal, and she had come to the sad conclusion that she could handle her sexual needs on her own and would probably never find a soulmate, if such a thing even existed.

But who needed one? She had a family she loved, a niece she adored, and good friends whose company she enjoyed, even though she'd been hard-pressed to find a place she could crash at the last minute.

The lecture she was giving herself was interrupted by his voice.

"Good night, guys. Thanks again for taking me in."

"Anytime, bro."

Damn! She thought she'd have more time, but it seemed like the others were turning in early as well. Why had she wasted time even thinking about Chris when she should either be sleeping or at least worrying about Amanda?

She tucked herself into what she hoped looked like a convincing sleeping pose, her back towards the door, and forced slow and steady breaths. Why in heaven's name was her heart racing? She was behaving more like someone her niece's age than a grown, professional woman.

She glued her eyes shut and willed herself to sleep as first the bedroom door opened and closed and then the bathroom door closed. *S-L-E-E-P!*

Instead of REM induced dreams, her traitorous mind began picturing Chris's image in the bathroom mirror. For ten years she had avoided direct eye contact whenever they were in each other's orbit, but that didn't mean her eyes had remained compliant. They had strayed, studied, and widened whenever they thought the coast was clear, and what they had seen was always pleasing. The years had been kind to Chris. His shoulders had broadened, he had added at least a few inches of height, and the slightly soft contours of his already compelling high school face had firmed into sculpted planes with seductive hints of stubble anytime past noon.

Was his hair falling down over his forehead as he bent down to rinse his mouth after brushing? Were some lucky drops of water caressing those chiseled features as he washed his face? Was he crossing his arms to lift his shirt from his chest or reaching behind to tug it up and over his head as so many guys did? Either way, was his torso underneath as tight and firm as his clad body hinted? And had the light covering of chest hair she had felt ever so fleetingly long, long ago thickened to match the thick dark hair on his head?

Holy fucking hell. What was she doing? *Sleep!* That's what she was supposed to be doing. Not squeezing her thighs together and rocking her hips.

The toilet flushed. She was out of time. *Be still! Breathe!* She called up every trick she could think of. *She was lying relaxed and drowsy on a warm beach blanket with the hot sun beating down on her, the sound of the waves coming and going in the distance.*

The door opened. *Waves! Hear the waves! Feel the sun!* But instead of waves, she listened to the quiet, almost imperceptible sounds of bed clothes shifting, weight lowering down onto the bed, and a phone being placed on a bed table. Had she plugged in her own phone? She thought she had, but she certainly wasn't going to check now. She was supposed to be sleeping. *Breathe!*

"I know you're not asleep, Jen."

No!! Why was he talking to her? She was asleep! Why couldn't he see that?!

"Isn't it about time we enacted a détente and ended this cold war between us?"

Fuck, fuck, fuck! Keep breathing. Her eyes were now wide open, staring into the darkness, but she maintained her stillness. Maybe he'd think he was mistaken and decide she really was asleep.

"No? I never took you for a coward. I was the cowardly one. I'm sorry I hurt you. More sorry than I can ever say, and I'm sorry I acted like such a selfish chicken shit and waited so many years to say so."

What?! Cowardly? A selfish chicken shit? What the hell was he talking about? She would give almost anything to be anywhere else in the world at this moment, but a part of her desperately wanted to understand what he was saying.

Sticking with cowardice was the wiser choice, however, and she remained still.

Finally he sighed, and she heard him move in the bed.

"I thought it was worth a try. But I am truly sorry. And I thought that since your brother and I are still friends, it might be nice if . . ." He paused and then continued, "If at least Auntie Jen and Uncle Chris could be civil to each other, for Lizzie's sake, if nothing else."

She stared into the darkness, trying to process his words.

"What are you sorry for? I was the one who messed everything up."

The words came out of her mouth without forethought. So much for pretending sleep. Obviously her brain and her vocal cords were operating on different frequencies.

More rustling from his bed. He must have sat up since his next words were more forceful.

"You never messed up. I took advantage of you when we were both lonely and confused. You were everything I dreamed about at a time when I had no right even thinking about you."

Wait. He had dreamed about *her*?

"But you and Maris were the perfect couple."

Again, where was her executive function? For someone not wanting to engage, her mouth was spitting out far too many words.

Chris snorted. "Yes. We'd been best friends since kindergarten. Played together, rode bikes together, went to CCD class together—you name it. So when it was time for things like school dances, it made perfect sense for us to gradually think of ourselves as boyfriend and girlfriend."

He stopped speaking, but the silence in the room was thick with unsaid musings. Finally he continued.

"Did you know Maris remarried last year?"

Jen shook her head but didn't say anything, even after realizing he couldn't see her.

"She finally got the courage to stand up to her family. She and Susan are very happy together."

Susan? That meant . . .

Jen sat up and peered towards Chris in the darkness, which wasn't that total, after all. She could make out his own seated form on the opposite bed.

"She's gay? Was she gay in high school?" Oh God, that was an imbecilic question. People didn't "become" gay; they just were. "Sorry, that was stupid, obviously, but did she know? Did you know? Did she tell you?"

And why hadn't she known? She and Maris had been best friends, hadn't they? But after that fateful night, they had drifted apart, and Jen had been "forgetful" about keeping in touch after they went to college.

"Fuck, Jen. Her uncle was our priest, remember? Of course she didn't admit it, at least not out loud. And all I ever knew was that our kisses were about as exciting as physics homework when all my friends were having the greatest sex on the planet. At least that's what they said. I knew it wasn't true, but still, it was more than I was getting. And there you always were, incredibly hot, funny, and smart. That time we kissed in the van . . ." His voice trailed off, and Jen's thighs involuntarily clenched again.

Memories of those stolen kisses, eons ago, had illogically fueled her nighttime fantasies far too frequently, even after ten long years. She had gone as Maris's friend on a youth group trip to an amusement park, they'd made a bathroom stop on the highway late at night on the return trip, and she and Chris had stayed in the van. She'd fallen asleep against him, Maris on his other side, and somehow, as they shifted position as the others closed the door and left them alone, their lips met.

Those few stolen kisses—or had it been one, gloriously prolonged kiss?—had been the best of her sexually boring life. The illicit, forbidden, guilt-ridden encounter they'd drunkenly engaged in six weeks later had been glorious in its own right, but it had also been awkward, clumsy, and a little painful and messy.

Jen sat up straighter. He remembered that kiss, too? After all these years?"

Inarticulate sounds came from her throat. Finally, the worst words possible spewed out.

"But I seduced you! Or took advantage of you, or whatever you want to call it. You were drunk at that party, and I . . . I had my wicked way with you."

More silence. What an idiot she was! She shouldn't have said anything, should have kept pretending to be asleep. But then the side of the bed dipped and he was next to her, kneeling next to her own knees which were now clasped tightly to her chest.

"Maybe you're drunk now, because you're sure as hell not remembering correctly. I pulled *you* away from the rest of the group. Yes, I'd had some of the punch, but it was because you were so goddamn beautiful, and I had just graduated and was somehow terrified I might never see you again. If anything, alcohol gave me the courage to do something I'd dreamed about for months."

Jen tilted her head. Had he added, "and ever since," or had she imagined the words?

His hands found hers in the darkness and held them, his thumbs caressing her knuckles.

They stayed that way for several seconds, each processing the other's admissions. Tears were running down Jen's cheeks, though had she been aware of them, she probably couldn't have explained why.

She finally sniffed, loudly, and continued her streak of inanities.

"You're awfully vulgar for someone who's becoming a priest."

His thumbs stopped moving.

"A priest? Where did you get that crazy idea?"

"I heard you as I was coming up the walk. You're going to seminary. It's fine; it makes sense." Why was she reassuring him?

"I have absolutely no idea what you're talking about."

He had let go of her hands and seemed to have moved further back on the bed. He sounded seriously confused, but she had heard what she had heard.

"You said you were taking seminary. It was just an hour or two ago, so I don't understand why you're denying it."

A moment later he started laughing, but his laughter quickly died and he gave a long, agonized sigh.

"We seem stuck in a pattern of misunderstanding. King Street was blocked off, you idiot. I had to take Seminary Road. I'm not going to seminary. Not now or ever."

"You're not?"

"No. I'd make a pretty lousy priest given how often I still think about making love to you. Except in my fantasies, I imagine doing it properly and not in the grass. Do you think I might ever have a chance?"

4

Jen squinted, trying to see his eyes in the darkness. Had he really just said what she thought he'd said?

"You still think about making love to me?"

Her words came out in a whisper, but he must have heard them because his hands found hers again and gripped them tightly.

"Of course I do. Every time I've seen you for the past ten years I've wanted to kick myself for being such an idiot in high school and not asking out the best girl—the nicest, hottest, and smartest girl—there. And for still not knowing how to put things right and telling you how . . . perfect I still think you are. And it doesn't help that Lizzie suggests I marry you every time she sees a couple kiss on a screen."

"She does?" Her voice was muffled through her tears, and Chris laughed.

"She most certainly does. Hang on. Don't go anywhere."

He stood up and moved to the bathroom, switching on the light. A second later he was back, leaving the light on with the door slightly ajar and carrying a box of tissues.

He sat down on the bed again and pushed the box into her hands.

"Here. Blow. And then talk to me."

She blew, watching him over the top of what turned out to be multiple tissues. It appeared a long stopped up dam had burst.

Finally finished, she scooted back, sat up straighter, and forced herself to meet his eyes.

"Talk to you?"

"Yes, Miss Gaffney. Talk to me. I just spilled my pitiful, heart-heavy, sex-starved guts to you. Is it possible you have any response?"

"I'm about as far from perfect as they come," she said quietly, and then followed it with the inane, "Not totally sex-starved, right?"

"Well, maybe not starved, but certainly not well-fed. And how about you? Do you have a significant other? I've tried to keep track, but I didn't want to seem like a creepy stalker. Even though I think Alison might have caught on to my interest."

She looked into his eyes. It was hard to see in the semi-darkness, but they were the perfectly set eyes she remembered so well, and they showed only naked vulnerability. She wasn't looking into a face she had seen only infrequently over the past several years but into eyes she was sure she had known since the dawn of time.

Slowly she shook her head.

"No. No boyfriend."

His face was only inches from hers, and somehow, their hands were together again. She wasn't aware of either one of them moving, but his lips were now alarmingly, gloriously close to hers.

"Is this okay?" He whispered the words, and she caught them on her inhale, bringing them even closer together.

"I think I desperately want to have my wicked way with you again."

"Wicked away, sweetheart. Wicked away."

It was like coming home. Like coming home, feeling totally at peace, and then being set on fire.

What started out as the barest contact between lips quickly escalated. She wanted—*needed*—to touch, taste, inhale every part of him, and he seemed to feel the same. Within seconds the bed clothes separating them became intolerable, and Chris pushed them aside as Jen pulled at him to bring him closer. His knees and thighs were around her hips as they pressed into each other. She arched back against the fabric-covered headboard, pushing her pelvis up to meet his rock-hard erection.

"I don't have a condom." His voice was raspy. "I'm not a priest, but I'm normally not this desperate or spontaneous."

"I'm on the pill. And I'm clean. We can get tested for free at the hospital." Her words came out in gasps as her head arched back, allowing him full access to her throat, collarbone, and achingly sensitive breasts.

"I'm clean, too."

All too abruptly, he pulled back, and she gasped in protest, sitting up to try and restore contact.

"Are you sure you're okay with this, Jen?"

She reached up and took his face between her hands, searching his eyes once more and finding only fulfillment. There were no years, no girlfriends, no misunderstandings between them. Somehow, the other half of herself she had always thought destined never to find was here with her now, in this bed.

"Okay doesn't begin to cover it. Come back to me. Please."

And he did.

―――

The banging on the door roused them both.

"Auntie Jen? Uncle Chris? Are you awake? Mommy says I can only call you to breakfast if you're up already. Are you up?"

Jen let out an involuntary "ahhhh" as she felt Chris's arms tighten around her waist and his erection push against her backside.

She squeezed her arms around his and pushed back, hearing his own hissed intake of breath. Unable to withhold the huge smile that overtook her face, she nevertheless worked to make her words sound normal.

"We're just waking up, sweetie. Tell your mom we'll be out in about fifteen minutes."

"Fif-teen minutes?!" The little girl's drawn out exclamation of dismay made Jen smile again, even as Chris's fingers playing with her nipples made her squirm and gasp.

"Maybe sixteen," she called, and then she rolled over.

———

It was closer to twenty by the time she entered the kitchen. Chris had beaten her by five, and he now studiously avoided her gaze as he spread jam on a piece of toast.

Alison, however, was not fooled.

"Sleep well, Jen?" Her tone was light, but her eyebrows were raised high above her hairline as she shot her sister-in-law a knowing smile.

Jen's eyebrows lifted right back at her as she pursed her lips. Was Alison on to them? Was she saying she was okay with them? *Had she set this whole thing up?* She glared at Alison, who only laughed. Robbie said nothing, though Jen was pretty sure he, too, was laughing.

"What a lovely day it is," Alison continued. "And how wonderful Jen and Chris were both able to visit at the same time, right Lizzie? Tell Auntie Jen and Uncle Chris what you told me this morning."

Lizzie came bounding over and took Jen's hands.

"If you and Uncle Chris get married, I could get a bee-yoo-tiful princess dress and be a flower girl. Wouldn't that be the best?"

Jen tried to make words come out in response, but all she managed was a sputtering of incoherent sounds. What was Lizzie doing? She was going to send Chris running for the hills.

Chris, however, seemed more in control. He walked around the island and crouched down to meet Lizzie's eyes, adopting a very serious manner.

"I think before we get married, I have to get a pretty ring and get down on my knee and propose, don't I?"

WHAT? Was she still asleep? This had to be a dream.

Lizzie's eyes and mouth both opened wide, and she began to jump up and down.

"Wait, wait!" she gasped. "I'll be right back." She ran out of the kitchen, and Alison doubled over with laughter.

"Smooth move, Chris. Now you're really in trouble."

A moment later, Lizzie was back, holding out a pink plastic ring with a large purple "diamond" in the middle.

"I got this from the dentist office on Wednesday, but it stretches, so I think it will fit Auntie Jen." She spoke excitedly to both of them, but she held the ring out to Chris.

He took it and pretended to assess it carefully.

"It's very beautiful," he said. "And it's very generous of you to share it with us. How about I pretend to ask Aunt Jen now, and she can pretend to say yes. And then, if she wants, we can do it for real again sometime soon?"

Jen snapped her mouth shut, belatedly realizing it had been hanging open. She looked at the three other adults in the room. Alison and Robbie were both grinning, but Chris was gazing at her with . . . could it be love? For once, her vocal chords stayed silent. She stared back at him, and what passed between them was the gradual recognition and acknowledgement of joy. This time, she wouldn't be afraid to reach out and claim it.

Lizzie tilted her head and made a dramatic show of considering his words. Finally she nodded slowly, seeming to have reached a solemn decision.

"That's a good idea. As long as you let me watch when you do it for real."

It was Chris's turn to assume a thoughtful expression.

"How about this: if I do it in private, and she says yes, we'll do it again in front of you."

It took only seconds for Lizzie to nod in agreement. Then, amidst the busy clatter of dishes, a bouncing five-year-old, a dog sniffing happily about waiting for scraps to fall, and four laughing adults, Chris got down on one knee and slipped a gaudy, incomparably perfect ring onto Jen's finger.

And two months later, on Christmas Eve, he did it again with the real thing.

. . .

Thanks for reading "Second Chance at Forever." Find out what led to the frightened phone call from Jen's roommate, Amanda, in the exciting, full-length romantic suspense, SECOND WHISPER, available this summer wherever you buy books!

Afterword

Dear Reader,

    Writing is a lonely business sometimes. Imagine an actor on a stage, valiantly acting out a part. If there's thunderous applause, she knows she's done a great job. If she can hear a lot of whispers, candy wrappers, or the whoosh of an email being sent, she knows she hasn't won over the audience. (Fortunately, not too many theater goers carry literal rotten tomatoes anymore!) For writers, it's a bit harder. So I have a HUGE favor to ask of you. If you enjoyed this story, send me an email at MegNapier@MegNapier.com and let me know. And if there was something you didn't like, send me an email and let me know! Most importantly, remember that posting a **review** of a book you've enjoyed is the greatest gift you can give a writer.

    And if even for a second, you think to yourself: "Huh, I liked that story by Meg Napier. I wonder if she's written anything else," then PLEASE come visit my website. Almost nothing in the world gives me greater pleasure than bringing a sigh of satisfaction to a reader, so if you've reached this page in my story, I thank you, and I truly hope you enjoyed it.

About the Author

Meg Napier had her writing career all mapped out before she started high school, but she gradually put aside her plan to outsell Danielle Steel in favor of practicality and a steady paycheck. Fast-forward through a few careers, a life devoted to the care and feeding of a wonderful husband, three great kids, and too many demanding pets, AND an addiction to reading, and Meg is finally bringing the books she always had bottled up inside her to publication. **SECOND SIGHT**, **SECOND ACT**, and **SECOND STANZA** can be found wherever you buy books, and her short stories appear regularly in romance anthologies, including the widely acclaimed **LOVE AT DAWN**.

Sign up for her newsletter here https://www.megnapier.com/megs-mailing-list/ and receive a free copy of "Second Stanza," and visit her at MegNapier@MegNapier.com.

https://www.facebook.com/MegNapierAuthor
https://twitter.com/NapierMeg
https://instagram.com/megnapierauthor
https://bookbub.com/profile/meg-napier
https://www.goodreads.com/goodreadscommeg_napier

The One That I See

J. Keely Thrall

1

The alarm on my phone hectors me out of my frozen dismay, a shrill reminder that I'm running way behind schedule. Digging through the pile of swimsuits heaped on the narrow dressing room bench—more ruching and ruffles and big, blowsy flowers per square inch of fabric than should be legal—I find the insistent beast and press Snooze.

For the fourth time.

I thumb away the notification banner alerting me to another missed text from David. My hubby, wondering where the hell I am. Right now, I'd say adrift in a sea of self-pity.

A glance in the mirror confirms the reason for my funk. Even accounting for the off-putting fun house warp in the glass, it's an appalling sight. I press my hand over the queasiness that roils through my belly and wish a hole in the ground would open up so I could thrust my head inside and hide.

Playing ostrich is my superpower.

I make a face then turn my back on my reflection. I should have listened to my stern boss-daddy of a husband and got my swimsuit shopping out of the way weeks ago instead of leaving it to the last minute.

Now I'm going to be late to my father-in-law's beach house when I promised to arrive early to help set up for the blowout Welcome to Summer pool party the family holds each year.

My tardiness is David's fault, really, when you look at it from the right angle.

I mean, he's the one who brought up the party way back in March. When any sane woman slogging through the dregs of a New York City winter and daydreaming of sun, sand, a fresh pedicure, and a cute new bikini would leap at the idea of summer fun.

My decision-making process was one hundred percent influenced by the circumstances of his reminder to block off this weekend on the calendar. I'd caught him in the kitchen post-workout, shirtless and sweaty.

At any other time, I'd have thought the implications through more clearly and come up with an excuse. Any excuse. But, shiver me timbers, I'd have said yes to whatever he suggested in that moment, since I was craving something tasty and he was looking like such an absolute snack.

We may have ended up pre-celebrating the party by jumping each other's bones.

It's possible we've been pre-celebrating the party pretty routinely—and definitely spectacularly—the last few months.

All was happy in my world.

Until it turned.

My lips tug down as if twin fifty-pound barbells have attached themselves to the corners of my mouth.

I did not expect to put on a freshman fifteen, inch that foundation up to a sophomore twenty, or chunk my way into a junior... I have no idea how much juniors in college are reported to put on, but my hips alone could provide a good estimate.

And now that I'm dumpy and it would take sixteen bikinis to cover one of my thighs, I don't want to celebrate summer.

I want to eat my feelings.

But I should have known that Responsible David wouldn't let me back out on my promise.

Darn his blue, blue eyes and smooth, voice-of-reason magic talk.

"Everyone's looking forward to you being there," he said this morning after one last go at getting me to postpone my ten o'clock appointment and ride out of the city with him. "You wouldn't want to disappoint them."

Who gave him the right to know which of my buttons to press? Sneaky, wily, tricksy man.

"Everything okay in there, hon?" the sales assistant asks through the door of this tiny box of a dressing room. "Need me to get the next size up?"

I cross my eyes and stick out my tongue—which she can't see but provides me with a jolt of petty satisfaction—and begin peeling myself out of the current catastrophe.

"Nope. Everything is hunky-dory." I wince as my elbow slams into the wall. "I'll be out as soon as I finish changing."

"Okay, hon. Take your time." She leaves, but her perfume lingers, a heavy floral scent that adds to my unsettled stomach. I switch to mouth breathing.

Hopping on one foot, trying to free myself of the clingy material, I catch another peek at my round self before overbalancing to smack into the opposite wall, this time banging my chin.

"Ouch."

Slumping onto the bench, I blink back the prickle of tears. Between the evidence of my extra pounds and this selection of uninspired swimsuits, none of which is a cute bikini, I'm even less thrilled about the weekend than I was when I walked through the front door of this specialty boutique.

I could still bag on the weekend. Tell David I have a touch of tummy flu. Spend the weekend snarfing ice cream, curled up in a king-sized blanket. Get a solid pity party going.

My phone rings, and I answer it without looking at the caller ID, too busy contemplating ice cream flavors to avoid the easy trap. "Hello?"

"Celia! Sis! I'm so excited for tomorrow! I picked up the cutest outfit from La Mer et Le Soleil, a bikini with a wrap that shows off more than it hides in this sweet raspberry color. It's too bad you've put on a few, or I'd have grabbed one for you in teal and we could have been twinsies. Wouldn't that have been too ridiculously adorable? Here, I'll text you a sneak peek. Aren't I scrumptious? Those three weeks at the spa really trimmed me right down. Have you had any luck finding a swimsuit that fits? Or are you going to just do a muumuu? A discreet floral print would work best. You'll want to avoid stripes, especially horizontal ones."

Ava, my older sister, continues without pause, sowing subtle and not-so-subtle shade about my weight into her prattle with breathy enthusiasm. And I take it. I sit there and don't stop her because she's right, isn't she?

My weight gain isn't attractive. It's certainly not something to show off.

Everyone at the party will be disgusted.

The longer she goes on, the bigger I get until my breath starts backing up in my lungs because the dressing room is too small to hold my gigantic ass. Yellow swirls in my vision.

My phone beeps with another call. Foreign prince looking to give me half of their fortune, tax collector threatening jail time, or celebrity with a real deal on a reverse home mortgage—I don't care. Their timing is impeccable, and they are my new favorite person.

"Is Felix still with that drip Lily? Do you think he'd date a slightly older woman? Though, really, I think that last Botox treatment put me back in my twenties, don't you? Wouldn't it be fabulous if we were sisters and sisters-in-law?"

"Ava, I'm getting another call. See you tomorrow."

Ruthlessly, I end the call then lean my head against the mirror, letting my rescuer go to voicemail. I breathe in and out, the yellow washing out of my vision. I love my sister. Even when nerves make her bitchy and brainless. I do. I love my sister, and it would be wrong to strangle her. Very wrong. But satisfying. So very satisfying.

Giving up on the slow breathing, I thump my head against the mirror wall a couple of times to make the "murder is bad" message sink in. No strangling Ava. Not even when she drags me back to the days when my self-worth depended on a number on a scale.

I can do that shit on my own. I don't need my older sister's help.

My phone rings again. Again, I answer without looking at the caller ID. Will I never learn?

"Hello?"

"Celia." My name flows in a cool stream from my husband's lips into my ear and down my spine, sending shivers of delight and alarm to sensitive locations.

"David. Uh, hi."

"What's wrong?"

"Not a thing." I wince at the lie.

The quiet that falls between us makes my heart stutter. Knowing he knows I lied makes it squeeze.

"Are you on your way?"

"Yep. Absolutely." Sticking the phone between my neck and shoulder, I hurry into my clothes before pulling a suit at random from the heap of Lycra. "One hundred percent on my way."

"Could you explain the physics of that, please? Your phone has been in the same location for the last forty-five minutes."

"Traffic jam." Another lie. I'm just racking them up today. "Actually, David, I wanted—"

"I know you're not about to back out on the weekend."

"About that—"

"Dad broke out his inner mixologist and came up with a new drink in your honor."

"He did?"

"And Felix desperately needs your food-prep help. Connor's knife skills remain at the level of 'take the sharp stick away before he pokes his eye out.' The man is almost thirty, but I swear, my youngest brother won't live to his next birthday if Felix is forced to work with him. Plus, Connor wants to show you his new juggling trick."

"Oh, well—" The weight of his family's loving inclusion settles on my shoulders like a damp and clingy beach towel when it's normally more of a warm hug.

"Now where are you, really, and what can I do to help you get on the road?"

"Shopping." He doesn't need to know about Ava's call.

"And it's made you unhappy."

As though his naming the emotion conjured up a storm, the urge to cry my eyes out swamps me, tightening my throat, bringing a sharp sting to my eyes. I nod. He can't see that, so I make a faint, affirmative *mmhh*.

"I told you we'd figure out the swimsuit thing, Princess."

His compassion snaps the lock on my tears, and they run in silent tracks down my face.

"I should have listened to you and gone shopping weeks ago like you suggested. Why am I always so irresponsible?"

"Irresistible. I believe the question you meant to ask was why are you so irresistible?"

"Thbbbt." My raspberry is extra juicy.

"Hey now. We've talked about the consequences of you yucking on my yum. Did you want to start the weekend out with a sore bottom?"

Distracted from my tears, I wriggle as anticipation forces out the sourness in my belly and adds a bright tingle to my butt.

"Let's hear more about this sore bottom. Would it include... spanking?"

"Spanking is only for good girls who don't back out on their commitments. Besides, I might have long arms, but they can't connect with your bottom unless we're in the same room. Which means you need to get your lush tush to the beach house."

"Rats. Foiled by logic."

"And your desire for a sore bottom."

"It's like you get me."

"Princess, I always get you. Now, do you need me to come back and pick you up or are you okay to drive?"

"I'm okay, promise." I scrub the evidence of my tears off my cheeks with the back of my hand. "I'll be on the road as soon as I check out."

"I told you, you don't need to worry about a suit."

"I'm here. I might as well get something so it's not a complete waste of time."

"All right. I'll see you in a few. Then we can talk about what else made you sad."

Gulp.

2

It's as though mentioning the words "traffic" and "jam" reminds all the crazies that it's a beautiful Friday on a long weekend in New York City. Which means they are one hundred percent obligated to take to the road and set a world record for number of fender benders. My drive takes f-o-r-e-v-e-r, and I arrive at the beach house well past dinner time.

Under a glow of lights from the circular drive, I'm greeted by a swarm of Mack men all eager to help me into the house. Felix grabs the roller bag. Connor tugs my backpack away from David with a grin, leaving David only the store bag with the awful swimsuit to carry. Their dad, a smart and strategic man, sidesteps his pack of sons to scoop me into one of his famous hugs.

"There's our girl. We were worried."

"Hi, Johnny." Tired, wired, I lay my head on his shoulder and close my eyes, soaking up his comfort, happy to be out of the car. He sways me back and forth, and I swear I could take a snooze right there.

My stomach growls, making him laugh and release me. "Sounds like someone's ready for some sustenance."

"I'm sorry I missed dinner."

"Don't you fret. There's plenty to nibble." With a pat on my arm, he passes me to David and accepts the bag his oldest passes back.

The spring evening is suddenly quiet as three of the four Mack men trek back inside with my luggage, leaving me on the steps with a narrow-eyed David.

"What?" I reach up to see if my hair is a bird's nest from having the windows down.

"You have a headache."

"It was a sucky drive. Of course I have a headache."

"If you'd ridden out earlier with me, this could have been avoided." His Reasonable David eyebrow arches to punctuate his point as he gathers me into his arms.

"You don't know that." Even to my ears, I sound like a whiny brat.

His other eyebrow gets in on the act, and now both are raised, tacitly calling me out.

"Does someone need to go straight to bed?" He feathers his hands from my waist to my butt and squeezes hard enough to make me dance.

My insides melt with anticipation. Mm, spanky-spank time. He pulls me closer, giving me a hint of his own hard anticipation. I shiver, clenching every muscle that can clench.

I could go to bed...

My stupid cow stomach moos.

"Looks like I'm not heading to my room like a big baby. Yet." My stomach moos again, insistent. "I'm starving."

"What a coincidence." The heated gleam in his gaze promises wicked, lovely things. "I'm starving too."

His kiss makes me forget the drive, my hunger pains, my crappy day. That horrible phone call. My own name. Thorough, slow. Wet, deliberate. Masterful. He lets up only once my knees give out. I'm panting, needy, and rethinking my options.

"Hey, my headache is gone."

"Good." His shoulders relax, and a smile tugs free to grace his sculpted lips.

"Are you okay?" I brush the hair from his forehead, trace the tilted-up edge of his mouth. I should have asked sooner. Should have realized how stressed he'd be until I returned to him safe and sound.

"Okay, and planning on getting even better in the very near future."

He guides me into the house with his hand low on my back. "You sure I can't make you a plate while you head to the bedroom?"

"And miss the world premiere of the Celiatini? The Celiapolitan?" I scrunch my nose. "The Celiarita?"

"Keep trying."

3

We gather in the kitchen, and its million shiny surfaces get busy pointing out the obvious. I'm fat.

Chubby. Pudgy. Dumpy.
Whale. Wide load.
Hefty bag.

Each put-down pricks another hole in my soul until I'm brittle, in danger of breaking. Despite the insistent "feed me" noises in my stomach, even the idea of snacking on Felix's famous three bean dip makes me seasick.

Faking my way through the evening, I do my best to hide my lowered spirits and lack of appetite from David. He would just worry, and he doesn't need that burden when we're supposed to be happy and partying this weekend.

Despite my efforts, I catch his assessing gaze on me more than once. Most of the time, his attention fills my belly with beautiful butterflies fluttering in double time. Now, after pivoting from yet another reflective surface, the only animal moving in my midsection is a snake of doubt.

How can he possibly find me attractive?

When the men start going over morning-prep logistics, I make a show of yawning.

"I'll pitch in wherever you need me tomorrow, fellas, but I'm turning in. I'm beat."

"I'll join you," David says.

"No, no. You're busy. I'm going to brush my teeth and crash. I won't even notice when you crawl into bed, I swear."

What I don't say is we're not having sex tonight and we may never have sex again.

He has no problem decoding my subtext. He cocks his head, giving me another quick head-to-foot appraisal before nodding. "Okay. Sleep well."

I head for the bedroom, oddly more upset that he's letting me have my space than if he'd insisted on joining me.

Damn, I'm a mess.

I speed through my bedtime routine, all the while chiding myself for... everything. Being irresponsible. Arriving late. Letting Ava's insecurities rile up my own so effectively. Gaining so much weight. Making David worry.

I turn from the dresser after snagging one of David's T-shirts and freeze at the sight of my naked body in the large ornate mirror propped against the wall in front of our bed.

Doughball. Chunky monkey. Lard ass.

"Stop. Stop it. Shut up. I'm not listening to you anymore." I say the banishing words, but there's no stopping the litany of mean flowing through my brain.

Yanking on the tee, I stalk to the light switch and plunge the room into darkness. My dramatic gesture does exactly *nada* to slow down the attack. I curl into a ball under the down comforter, trying to make myself as small a target as possible, a tubby lump on the otherwise-flat king mattress. The nastygrams still hunt me down. Still pummel and bruise.

For what seems like hours, I stare into the dark, numb yet throbbing with hurt.

With his customary consideration, David slips quietly into the room. Shutting my eyes tight, I play ostrich, hiding in plain sight. I follow the muted sounds of him getting ready for bed, hoping the familiar, comforting noises will lead me out of hell. A tear lands on my pillow, a second runs down my neck. I squeeze my knees closer to my body, trying to become smaller, trying not to explode, trying not to be a burden.

More of a burden.

A swirl of cool air sprinkles goose bumps down my neck as David climbs under the covers. My heart thumps once, twice, three times in the still silence before all of a sudden I'm sliding toward the middle of the mattress. The unexpected movement shakes me loose of my protective ball and my T-shirt-covered boobs wind up flattened against a hot, hard, naked chest.

For a brief second, before I remember, I curse the cotton between us.

But then my belly touches his, and I flinch.

I try to create some space between us, but he thwarts my attempts. Running his hands up and down my arms and back, he pets me in long, soothing strokes. During our tussle, I encounter fleeting hints of his thick, sturdy interest, but it's clear his focus is on me, not his own wants. He homes in on the chronic muscle spasm at the base of my spine. I inch closer to drooling.

It's very hard to fight against David once he breaks out his magic hands.

I let go of the last of my tension, giving in to my new status of Giant Cooked Noodle.

The moment I relax, my T-shirt disappears in a whoosh.

"There, that's better."

"David—"

"I'm here, Princess. Now, tell me what's going on."

"I don't want to talk."

"All right. No talking." Kissing my forehead, he rubs my bottom right at that ticklish, sensitive spot where booty meets thigh. The spot he likes to spank. "Not tonight, anyway."

The implied threat of those three words—and the teasing action of his fingers—strum my insides into acute awareness like flipping a switch on my hormones, muscling my doubts out of the way. I squirm closer, newly interested in the erection I kept feeling glimpses of during the massage.

If you can feel a glimpse.

I push him onto his back, and he makes sure I hitch a ride so that I'm straddling him when our movement stops.

"Is this pretty for me?" I wrap my fingers around his hard length.

"It's never not for you, Princess." He arches into my hold. "That said, it doesn't need to be appeased whenever it decides to show up."

"But what if I'm pleased to appease?"

"Then, by all means, let's not waste the pretty."

I lean down to begin my seduction with a kiss, but my belly gets in the way of my descent. Confronted by the reminder that my body isn't what I'm used to, I stiffen, ready to withdraw, when David rolls us to our sides.

"This way, hmm?"

"Okay," I whisper, and we try again.

I push into his mouth, alive to all sensation. The slickness of his teeth, the pebbled texture of his tongue. The fresh hit of his mint toothpaste.

We exchange deep, slow kisses, the kind that empty out the brain and leave the body in the driver's seat. In the darkness, we touch, exploring each other, his tantalizing strength, my dampening desire.

A light graze of my fingernails makes him shudder, catch his breath. I call out as he sucks on my taut, sensitive nipples.

Time strings out in a series of moments, gasps and shivers, quivers and moans, a thin wire sparking with anticipation.

He ranges down my front, pressing little kisses on my sternum, across my ribs and breasts.

Over my fleshy belly.

I don't have time to shrink away before he's settled in between my thighs, his mouth doing criminally wonderful things to my lady parts. I squirm and pant, thrusting my hands into his thick hair for something stable to hang on to as my world edges closer and closer and closer to blissful chaos.

Vibrations shimmer up in waves from my core. My skin mists with perspiration. The air in my lungs hitches with each breath.

"Please now, please now." I tug on David, desperate.

He curls two fingers inside me, catching my G-spot as he ravages my clit with his tongue.

My world draws in on itself, an urgent ball of *almost there* stuck just shy of the finish line.

David makes a minute adjustment of his wrist, a long swipe of his tongue.

And I'm gone.

The wire, my world, the bedroom—all of it disintegrates into pure energy as my orgasm rockets through me. I tumble through sensation after sensation, buffeted by a torrent of pleasure.

He tends me through the aftershocks, guiding me back to earth, to our bed, to his sheltering embrace.

I lie there in a puddle of euphoria. The air hangs humid and fragrant with my release. I pat around the mattress until I find his hand. He threads our fingers together.

"Feeling better?"

"Mm-hmm."

"Still don't feel like talking?"

"Nm-mmph."

"Okay, tomorrow it is." He chuckles, threading a lock of hair off my sweat-damp face. "Get a good night's sleep, Princess. You have a lot on your plate tomorrow, what with a spanking and confession session to get through, an appeasement to finish, a barbeque to co-host, and a drink to name."

Too spent to protest that he should have allowed me to take care of that appeasement issue instead of going down on me—and too mellow to worry about the rest of the to-do list—I let him shift us into our usual spoon position.

"Celiahattan," I mumble. "Celiagroni, Celiajito."

"Keep trying. In the morning." He cups his hand over my stomach before purring in his mightiest boss tone, "Now go to sleep."

As I attempt to muster the oomph to place his hand someplace svelter—like my knee—his order kicks in. I succumb to beddy-bye time.

4

The next morning, a wave of nausea kicks off in my stomach, waking me from sleep, reminding me of how little I ate yesterday. How queasy I've been in the early hours the past several weeks. I stretch out like a starfish, a little disappointed, a little relieved, but not surprised that I don't brush against David. He has to be up and prepping for the party.

Yawning, I scoot to the edge of the bed and find a plate of food, a glass of water with lemon slices, and a note on the side table.

Morning, Princess,

Eat (all of it). Drink (ditto). Relax (you'll find your favorite bath salts by the tub. Keep the water warm but not hot).

I'll return at nine for our talk.

Be naked.

David

I rub my forearm over achy, interested nipples. That man. Trust him to turn bossy into foreplay. I test the lemon water first. It stays down, so I turn my attention to the food. Crackers with peanut butter. Slices of banana. I take a sniff and pause. Yep, okay. That'll work.

Chew, swallow, sip, swallow. I make my way through breakfast, staring blankly at the wall, holding off any and all Big Thoughts.

I'm fine through my bath, scheming ways to address the latest "improvement" Roxanne and Pietro want incorporated into the renovations of their family home. Honest to Pete, a Greek Revival portico added to the sleek lines of a mid-century modern gem?

Not on my watch.

By the time I towel off, I've figured out a couple of possibilities that will get the couple the essence of what they want, with the added bonus that I'll avoid making the architectural giants of mid-century design roll over in their graves. *Phew.*

Buoyed by my plan, I slather on various layers of skin care that most days I don't have time for, all the potions and lotions promising miracles. I inhale. They may or may not deliver on their guarantee, but they smell yummy, like herbal tea and lime.

Dewy with product, I walk naked from the en suite into the bedroom and check the time.

Still a good twenty minutes before The Talk.

The resident butterflies in my belly stretch their wings and begin practicing their best corkscrew flips... while somehow also riding an elevator that can't make up its mind whether it's going up or down. I shake my head.

Distraction, distraction, my kingdom for a distraction.

The bag from the boutique perches on the dresser. Do I dare test the aquatic beast once more?

I slept well. I'm not hangry. The lighting is better here than in the shop.

If I still hate every last stitch, I just won't wear the benighted thing.

Decision made, I examine the suit laid out on the bed. It doesn't look *so* bad.

Silver-and-blue swirls glimmer against a black base. There's a built-in bra that might actually provide some support for the girls, who, right along with the rest of me, have grown more substantial this spring.

"You, I don't mind so much," I tell them. "You can stick around."

Getting the suit on takes some strategic heaving, but free from the confines of the tiny dressing room, I don't bang into any walls. Once the bottom portion is up over my hips, I take a moment to shimmy the flirty skirt.

"Okay, now. That's cute. I can work that."

After a deep breath, I stick first one arm then the other through the armholes. Sliding the straps into place, I adjust my boobage so nothing is squished and my nipples aren't drunkenly askew.

Bending, twisting, reaching, I test the fit. Nothing pulls. Nothing pinches. No butt-crack wedgie or scritchy-scratchy bits. My chest fills with lightness.

Yesterday was an anomaly, brought on by the distressing session with my clients, a skipped lunch, and not shutting Ava down ASAP.

David and I won't need to have a Talk after all.

"I'll take the spanking because a gal has needs, but after we can move on to sexy appeasement and fun party and cool drink naming and skip talking altogether."

Seeing no flaws in my plan, I make a crucial mistake.

I turn around.

The mirror reflects a black, blue. and silver butterball perched atop two skinny legs.

Me.

How could I have forgotten?

Not cute.

Fat.

When the door finally opens, I'm trapped in the mirror.

"Celia?"

I wince at David's cautious "Handle Celia Freaking Out" voice, but I can't... I can't pull myself out of my dive.

"How can you stand to look at me like this?" The words grind out as he approaches, shredding my throat as though mixed with glass shards. "I'm bigger than a house. Bigger than Rhode Island. I'll embarrass you out there. Everybody looking at, sniggering at Fat Celia. Maybe that's what we should call the new drink. Add a snickerdoodle cookie as garnish, and now we're cooking with gas. Maybe—"

"Maybe you should stop talking unless you don't mind being unable to sit for the next three days." The silky steel of Stern David pierces my rant.

I blink at him through the mirror as he comes to a halt behind me. In contrast to mine, his reflection shows off a lean, muscled, hunkalicious body, dressed in navy-blue swim trunks and already sporting the foundation of a summer tan.

We don't match. Not at all. My shoulders fall.

He captures my gaze in the mirror, his fiery blue eyes telling me I'm going to be sorry.

Sorry for yucking on his yum.

"I told you to be naked." He snaps the elastic of the swimsuit smartly against my back. "What happens to princesses who don't obey orders?"

"They get spanked." My voice quivers. My chin quivers. My pussy quivers.

Buried leagues deep beneath the garbage dump of my emotions, a small, valiant kernel cracks open, sending out a wobbly tendril of hope. My husband's stern expression holds the promise of sunlight, coaxing that green hope to pulse with eagerness. I love consequences.

The bright pain that yanks me out of my head and into my body.

Into the moment.

Into this room with the two of us, figuring out how to be the best versions of ourselves for each other.

He caresses my bottom, a claim of ownership and promise, tickling tiny bubbles of need into my bloodstream.

"Strip, Princess. I want you bare."

"David, I—"

"Naked. Now."

For a moment, despite my unfurling anticipation, I wish I were the Statue of Liberty. Tall, majestic. Unafraid of taking up space.

Wearing loads more clothes.

I hesitate, searching his expression for one last push of reassurance.

"You can do it, CeCe." He kisses my neck. "Show yourself to me."

In the mirror, his attention follows my hand as I peel off the first strap. My breast releases with a jiggle, the aureole pebbled, the nipple interested but not quite at peak tautness, rosy but not red.

"Nice." The rumble of his voice sends a raft of goose bumps down my body. Boom. My nipples harden into tiny aching diamonds. "Very nice, Princess. Keep going."

I untangle from the second strap. He grunts a sharp noise of approval as both breasts are revealed, heavy and free. I stand a little taller. Yeah, the boobs can stay.

"You're not done."

The hairs on the back of my neck stand on end at his low growl. With a squeak, I push the swimsuit over my hips. The material lands on the rug with a heavy, muted *thwump*.

There I stand.

Open to judgment.

Naked.

Fleshy and round.

Boobs of Unusual Size unharnessed. Hips of Egregious Width nearly filling the mirror from side to side. Belly of Large and Growing Circumference pooching out past my toes.

"Look at you." David's voice is a whisper of wonder. "You're stunning."

"No."

"Sweetheart, we've discussed this."

"Yeah, I know, but—"

"Are you ready for consequences?"

"I— Maybe?" He waits for me to decide. It doesn't take long. I need this. "Yes. Yes, I'm ready."

Smack, smack, smack.

The sing of each spank sounds into the room, a crack of thunder to match the lightning strikes zigzagging across my bottom. I sink into the heat that coils in my core, building, building. Into a pain uncoupled from expectation or disappointment, from past or future. A pain that frees me from overthinking, worry, doubt.

Smack, smack, smack.

Every measured, relentless swat adds to the fire, burning away all the bullshit.

Burning through my fear of not being enough. *Smack.* Of being too much. *Smack.* Of getting it wrong. *Smack.* Getting life wrong, no matter how hard I try.

Smack, smack, smack.

The fire crackles through my blood and bones, scorching through my soul, transforming all the yuck into a blazing corona of yum.

Smack, smack, smack.

A storm of sobs bursts from my inner depths, breaking free from captivity.

I curl over my protruding stomach, wrapping myself around its precious gift, and give in to my tears.

David pulls me into the haven of his arms, turning me until my belly is nestled between us, safe and protected. Rocking me back and forth, he hums wordless comfort into my ear as I drain my sour backlog of stress and anxiety.

Eventually, my crying jag ebbs to sniffles before trailing off into silence.

"Talk time?" He tilts my chin up for a narrow-eyed inspection.

"Do we really need—"

"More spanking? You know I'm always happy to comply."

My hips jerk as he kneads my sore tush.

"Ow. Okay. Fine. You're right. We're done with spanks today."

"Now tell me why you needed them." His touch shifts from squeezing to tracing a featherlight pattern on my sensitized flesh. Spicy little jolts of electricity branch out from each stroke. Down my legs. Up my sides. Most often, they seem destined to find my clit and tits, zaps of need calling me into a wild craving.

"Can we talk later?" I rise on my toes to press a trail of kisses from his jaw down his neck to his chest. "I'm a little distracted."

"You bet, Princess. First, how about we test your eyesight against mine?"

"Uh—"

He takes advantage of my hesitation to face me toward the mirror again. Oh no. I try edging sideways. "Perhaps we should move to the bed?"

"I don't think so." He sets his hands on my shoulders, a usually reassuring weight that right now fills me with pangs of dread. "What do you see in the mirror's reflection this morning?"

My gaze flits to the mirror and away, a hard bounce.

"Um, the unmade bed. Dirty dishes from the breakfast you made me. One hundred percent consumed, in case you wondered."

"Good girl. What else?"

I make a second swift scan.

"You hung the lithograph. I'm sorry I didn't notice earlier. It's stunning, isn't it?"

"A real showstopper. What else?"

My hands start to sweat. I know where he's going with this. I know. I dart another quick glance at the mirror before chickening out.

"You. Standing there all hot, blue-eyed, and bossy."

"Thank you for the compliment." He kisses my hair. "Try again, and tell me what else. What else do you see when you look in the mirror?"

I struggle, again and again, to bring my eyes to the mirror.

David remains a solid, steady presence at my back.

He always has my back.

I keep trying. And failing.

"Do you want help?"

At my nod, he brushes my hair back with calloused fingertips to place a kiss where the vee of my neck meets my shoulders. I squeak. My heart kicks. I do a full-body shudder.

"That never gets old." His low chuckle is pure devil.

"Says you."

"You know what also doesn't get old?" He layers a row of suckling kisses along the slope of my shoulder. "The fact that at the end of each day, I get to climb into bed with the woman who owns my heart."

"Now you're just being schmaltzy." My tone is dry, but it's possible I'm blinking a little leftover wet from my eyes.

"Doesn't matter if she's had a good day or a bad one. If she's fighting demons and trying to protect me by not sharing." He nips the ball of my shoulder. "I sleep more soundly, breathe more easily, and rise each morning like I'm ten feet tall. All because she loves me back."

"I do."

"Then let's fight your demons together, hmm? Let me give you a new perspective, show you what I see. Watch me."

As ordered, I fix my attention on him as he begins to map my body. He strokes down my arms to give my hands a reassuring squeeze, not letting go until I squeeze back. Message sent and received.

He moves to my hips. I bite my lip. The doughy, stretch-marked skin stands in stark contrast to his strong, artistic hands.

But he cups my generous curves as though giving them a hug. As though he can't think of another place he'd rather be. I steal a quick glance at his face to find him absorbed in what he's doing.

What he's touching, seeing. *Who* he's touching and seeing. Me.

His expert thumbs dig into the knots in my lower back. He croons, working me through the achiness, and I groan as he releases the tension.

With a chuckle, he slides his arms around to my ribs, one resting on the high arch of my stomach, the other going north to land under my breasts, relieving me of their weight.

"These last few months, your breasts have been killing me. Every time your shirt pulls tight over these babies, I want to find the nearest closet and get you naked."

"You do find the nearest closet and get me naked."

"*Carpe momentum*," he says without repentance. "Sometimes you have to search for the moment to seize."

"Lucky I like your search and seizures."

He pulls me flush against him, and I purr at the solid wall of muscle I encounter.

Impossibly, he brings me closer yet and starts to caress my stomach in long, slow arcs. I brace for a comment, something to confirm the yuck inside my head. It never comes. The easy, calming strokes loosen the starch from my spine. Up and down, his calluses rasp my skin with just enough friction that I shiver as the goose bumps reawaken along the whole of my body.

My breath deepens. The heat of his thick erection is a promise in the small of my back.

I give him more of my weight.

"That's it. There's my girl." His hand travels farther south. "Spread your legs."

I comply, and he begins a gentle fingertip massage, working his special brand of sorcery into the tiny knot of nerves between my thighs. My head lolls against his chest, my sweat-dampened hair sticking to my face. My cheeks are rosy, eyes sleepy with arousal.

His touch grows more intimate, coaxing my hips to rock, to seek out more pressure, more pleasure.

We lock gazes. Something wild and fierce peers from his dark-blue eyes.

Something primal.

This isn't Reasonable David. Responsible David. Rational David. This is Untamed David.

"Hungry For You and Only You and Always You" David.

My knees give out. He catches me before I fall.

"Do. You. See?" His animal growl reverberates down to my soul.

"Yes." I do.

I'm round and healthy. Proudly, powerfully pregnant. A modern day fertility goddess, beautifully whole.

And I am enough. For him. For me. For us. For our coming child.

Let the garbage go. The judgy voices in my head. My sister's self-absorbed ragging. They don't matter. What's here, between us, is what counts.

"Thank fuck. Brace yourself."

Almost hiccupping with need, I flatten my hands against the cool glass of the mirror, sticking my butt out on the off chance he'd miss it otherwise. Losing the swim trunks, he crowds close, lining himself up to my center.

He thrusts inside me to the hilt. This close, at this angle, my belly looks even larger. Even more beautiful. That's not what captures me in the moment.

No, it's Simply David. One hundred percent my favorite David. Staring at me like I'm the answer to his universe. His next breath. His every Saturday morning. Like all the two a.m. feedings, skinned knees, and exploding science projects will be worth the loss of sleep, the anxiety, the hairpulling. Because we're a team.

I smile and nod. Message delivered and received. This time for real.

He kisses my cheek.

Then precedes to fuck the hell out of me.

5

Post-life-changing mirror sex and round two in the shower to drive his point home, my core pulses with bliss-infused aftershocks. David sits on the bed watching as I use the bedroom mirror to scoop my hair into a messy bun. I'm wrapped in a towel. He's back in his navy swim trunks. More's the pity.

Plucking my swimsuit from the rug, he shakes it out before laying it on the bed next to another store bag.

"Ready to talk?"

"Ready-ish." I wag my hand back and forth. Talking about emotions will never come easily for me, but though playing ostrich may be my superpower, there are times when hiding hurts more than it helps. I sit on the bed, the swirly blue-and-silver Lycra between us. "I thought I was coping well with all the changes in my body. Yesterday took me by surprise."

"What set you off?"

"Ha. What didn't?" It would be easy to throw my hands up in the air and lean into the funny, but his question deserves a more thoughtful answer. "Roxanne and Pietro—the mid-century modern couple?—came to the meeting with an utterly appalling reno idea."

"That usually gets your creative juices flowing."

"True, but usually I'm not meeting with a woman eight and a half months pregnant. Roxanne needed help sitting down, standing up. Even the pitcher of water on the conference room table gave her fits."

"Ah."

"It's so hard for me to admit I need help." I take his hand in mine and hold tight. "Be patient with me, eh?"

"All the patience in the world, Princess." He brushes his thumb across my knuckles. "What else?"

"After the meeting, I felt self-conscious and bloated, as though I were already as far along as Roxanne. The dressing room at the boutique had a warped mirror and seemed duty bound to confirm that I was the size of a house." I pause to swallow. "Then I accidentally answered a call from Ava."

"What did that neurotic—" He clears his throat. "I mean, what did your lovely sister have to say?"

"The same old laundry list of insecurities."

"It triggered more of yours."

I nod. "By the time I arrived here, I was so deep in my head, it's a wonder I passed as a normal human."

"Mostly normal."

"Hey."

"I don't need normal." His sudden grin lights up my insides. "I need you."

"Well, you have me, so winning."

"Damn betcha. Much as I'd rather you hadn't gone through all that shit yesterday, it gave us actionable intel."

"Like maybe I need to block my sister's calls for the next six-ish months?"

"As if that would work. No, like regularly checking in on where you are body-image-wise."

"How might we do that?" Fluttering my eyelashes, I aim for cute, curious minx. "More mirror sex?"

"But of course."

"Damn, I love how you think. Spanking included?"

"Would it even be a check-in without a hearty round of spanks for my princess?"

I beam at him.

"Now, let's talk about today. This"—he dips his chin in the direction of my swimsuit—"is very fetching. You wear it, I guarantee my hands will be itching to get under that flirty little skirt all day." He passes me the shopping bag. "I picked out something that goes in a rather different direction."

Biting my lip to help me focus, I open the bag and place the tissue-wrapped contents on the mattress with the same care I'd handle the most fragile crystal. Folding the edges back, I reveal David's surprise.

A gold bikini and sheer gauze cover-up.

I blink. Once. Twice. Then burst into laughter.

Naturally, David's way through this problem would be exposure therapy.

Bust-a-gut chortles have tears running down my face and my arms hugging my belly for fear I'll give birth early if I don't keep a tight grip on my insides. I laugh, look, and laugh again, each peel buffering away any lingering body shame that might have managed to resist David's intervention. When the whoops settle down, I wipe my face clean.

"You knew. Somehow you figured out what was going on, and you knew." I pet a shiny triangle. "It's perfect."

"You kept putting off shopping. That was the first clue. You started covering up, wearing my shirts to bed. What I didn't know was if our brand of sexual healing would make this"—he points at his gift—"okay. You don't have to wear it. My nose will remain fully in joint if you opt for the other suit."

"Oh no, hubby. I'm one hundred percent wearing this."

"You'll have every eye on you. The belle of the ball."

"The only eyes that matter are yours. And mine and mine," I add when he starts to frown. I cup his jaw. "If I start to struggle, I promise, no more playing ostrich. Instead, I'll send up a bat signal."

He kisses my palm. "It's a deal."

6

During a lull in the party, David and I perch on stools at the poolside bar as my father-in-law stacks the middle layer of my mocktail—a whipped mango pulp in a mouthwatering shade of orange—atop an inch of slushy pomegranate juice. David's arm is slung around my hips, his hand resting on my thigh.

Yesterday shook him more than he's let on. He hasn't been farther than a foot away all day. Even when Ava and I had it out earlier. He kept quiet, but he loomed. Ava won't ever stop being Ava, though she'll think twice before commenting on my body again anytime soon.

"Hey, CeCe, you come up with a name for your new drink yet?" Connor walks up, juggling three neon-pink balls. "How about Celi-aquiri or Celia Colada?"

"Too easy," Felix says as he leans against the bar on Connor's other side. "My vote is for the Celia Slammer. There's mystery there, an intriguing, edgy factor."

"I'm partial to the Celia Sunrise." Johnny finishes pouring the fizzy pineapple juice top layer. "A beautiful time of day to match a beautiful woman."

He skewers three Luxardo cherries and a slice of orange on an umbrella then sets the drink on the bar for us to admire.

"Thank you. It's gorgeous. I'm beyond touched that you created this for me." I take a sip. The effervescence and sweet, tart flavor tickle the roof of my mouth. "Thanks also, guys, for the suggestions, but this morning David helped me land on the perfect name."

"I did?"

"Yep." I move his hand to rest on my stomach and lace our fingers. "You reminded me to focus only on what's important." I raise the glass. "Gentlemen, behold the CeCehama Mama."

With whoops and cheers, the men clink my glass, applaud my mad naming skills, and generally make a big deal. Even after so many years as a member of the family, their exuberance is a shiny, unexpected gift.

That warm hug feeling I was missing yesterday washes through me, and I settle more deeply into my husband's side. Our kiddo is going to be so well loved. David kisses the top of my head.

"Okay?" he asks.

"One hundred percent."

The End... for now

About Keely

Founder and president of the Stays Up Too Late Society of Book Addicts (our motto: "Just one more page, I swear!"), when I'm not reading, I'm writing the stories for the dozens of characters yammering away in my brain.

Liked Celia and David? Catch Connor's story in *The One That I Want*. Details at my website: www.jkeelythrall.com

About the Author

About Keely

Founder and president of the Stays Up Too Late Society of Book Addicts (our motto: "Just one more page, I swear!"), when I'm not reading, I'm writing the stories for the dozens of characters yammering away in my brain.

Liked Celia and David? Catch Connor's story in *The One That I Want*. Details at my website: www.jkeelythrall.com

The Roommate

Mariah Kingsley

1

It's an interesting feeling when you lose your memory. Something as simple as your name is foreign to you. You search for who you are for so long that after a while, you just stop. Stop searching for the past that you may never know and start building something new.

The doctors told my mother my memory would come back in a few days. That was a year ago. So, when the calendar marked a year, I felt I had tried enough to remember; it was time to build a new life. Two months ago I put an ad in the paper for a roommate, someone that would share the bills. Maybe find a friend to share some laughs.

My mother hit the roof when I told her I was moving back to my house. Over the past year, she tried to convince me to sell the cute little bungalow, but after walking through it, I couldn't let it go. Apparently I had a way with interior design. The place was beautiful. Deep purple walls with hints of silver and grays. The moment I stepped in, I felt peace; I hadn't felt peace since I woke up that terrible day in March.

Mother wanted me to stay with her in our family home, but I felt trapped. The expectation on her face every day I woke up was a weight on my shoulders I could no longer carry.. Seven people from the ones I interviewed passed the background check. My mother insisted I ran. But one stood out. James, I know what you are thinking, a thirty-one-year-old woman and a man living together should be a red flag, but the moment James walked into the house, I felt safe.

Safe in a way that I don't think I have ever felt. Well, at least in the last year. He moved in with very little, and I breathed a sigh of relief. I was prepared to share my home, but honestly, I didn't want to change the decor of my space. This seemed to work for him. Things that I learned about myself since moving back out on my own. I was a clean freak, and luckily for me, James was as well. He wouldn't just watch me clean, he would actively participate. During that time, he told me stories of his time in the military and some jobs he did in security. I found them fascinating.

I didn't have to pretend to know who he was. We didn't have a past that he was trying to make me remember. We just went through life, and the company he provided was comforting.

A few weeks after he moved in, he invited me to try a new restaurant. Some tiny place that boasted they had the best hamburgers in town. I didn't really want to leave the house, afraid I would run into someone that knew me in the past. Or worse, have people stare at the huge scar on my face.

James had the perfect suggestion for that. "We can pretend to be out of towners. You can wear a hat and glasses, keep your head down and close to me, and no one will know it's you." I didn't think it would work, but I needed to get out of the house. I was becoming a recluse. Not even leaving for groceries.

I braved the big bad world, put on a hat, and glasses and went to the restaurant. No one even looked in my direction as we walked in. Their attention was on the food, and not on me. When my food arrived, the smell alone had me rushing to open the greasy bag. A huge burger and homemade fries greeted me. One bite and I was in heaven.

"Good, right?" He asked me with a smile. I couldn't trust myself to answer, so I just nodded. He was so damn handsome. Not traditionally handsome, but rugged. He wasn't a man you messed with. But then he would smile, and a little dimple would appear, and you felt at ease.

This started our weekend adventures. We would wake up early on Saturday mornings, drive outside of the city, to a small town, and eat. Then we would walk through the town, visiting shops and talking.

James worked crazy hours. Sometimes he wouldn't get home until late into the night. On those nights, I really missed him. Eager to hear about his day.

My days were boring. I found a job in human resources at a startup company. I did bookkeeping and it was thankless work. I couldn't remember my job at the library, but my mother said I was good at it. I didn't really see myself as the quiet type. Maybe with amnesia I changed?

My mind was elsewhere when the knock came at the door. It was Saturday, and like every Saturday since the first time James and I went out, we had plans. "I'm dressed, come in." The door opened and in he walked, his eyes so bright with happiness.

"You ready, Pretty Girl?" Damn whenever he said that, my heart stuttered. He never flirted, never. In the last few weeks, I have tried to put him in the friendship box, but he just doesn't fit.

"Ready!" I jumped out of the seat at the vanity. The scar that went down my face was the only visible sign something traumatic happened to me. It started at my hairline, missed my eye by centimeters, and went down to my chin.

I have seen photos of the beautiful face I had before, and I don't remember that girl. "You ready?" I looked at him and he wasn't dressed as casually as I was.

I looked down at myself. My pants were baggy, and my tee shirt was two sizes too big.. "I think I should change." His eyebrow went up, and I hurried to explain. "Maybe I should put on something that looks like I care, and not like I ran out of clean clothes." He walked to me, and the grace he carried while doing something as simple as walking was a thing of beauty.

"If you are comfortable in that outfit, you should wear it." I bit my lip and looked away. I felt his finger under my chin, turning my face to him. I hated when people looked me in the face. "I always want you to be comfortable. I am in no hurry, so if you want to, I will wait right here and let you find something that makes you feel as beautiful as you are."

His gaze caused me to shift my weight. There was something working behind those eyes. I just didn't know what it meant. "Well, if I want to find an outfit that matches the beauty I have, then I can keep this on." I said with a laugh, avoiding his eyes.

One moment I was turning, and the next his hand was around my upper arm whipping me around. His eyes flared with anger. "I will not laugh at you putting yourself down." My heart raced. I had never seen this side of him. He always had an easy smile for me. Allowing me to just be me. "Now go find something that you feel beautiful in." He gently pushed me to the closet.

I walked in, dazed. His words echoing in my head.

2

I stood in my closet, trying to shake myself out of the daze James had me in. I had only glanced through my closet once. While I was in the hospital, my mother brought me clothes from home. She picked what I wore when I lived with her. When I moved in here, I just opened the door, getting familiar with what was there. I never even crossed the threshold.

But standing in my closet, I learned a lot about the old me. She loved to shop. When I opened the door, around the corner were shelves and shelves of shoes. All colors and styles. But they had one thing in common: they were sexy.

There were suits, and dresses and even evening gowns. There was also a large island with drawers all around. I walked to it, wondering what was inside of it. When I opened it, my mouth dropped open. Rows and rows of jewelry. Not the cheap stuff, but diamonds, emeralds and rubies. How could a librarian afford this?

I closed the drawers and walked around the U-shaped closet, my hands touching the fine fabrics. Why didn't my mother bring me these clothes? My mind was boggled by what I found.

I was startled when I heard James' voice. "You find something that will make you feel beautiful?"

I jumped and turned around to see him casually leaning against the wall that separated the "everyday clothes" from the extraordinary. "I didn't know this was even here."

"How did you miss it?" He walked to me, his eyes working again. "You don't get your clothes out of here?"

I shook my head. "My mom helped me move back in here. She placed the outfits that I had at her house in the dressers and chest. I've never come in here. He nodded. "Besides, I didn't really need anything. I work from home, a hoodie and sweatpants seemed to be fine."

"Well, I guess you should find something to wear."

He walked over to me, leaned in and kissed my forehead right above my scar. Just as he was out of sight, I asked, "Where are we going?" That would help me figure out what to wear.

"That depends on what you decide to wear." He said, not breaking stride.

———

I went through seven outfits. First, I found jeans. They were form fitting and flattering. Total opposite of what I've been wearing for the last year. After searching for a simple shirt, I found a sexy red silk shirt. The issue was my bra. I looked around the room and thought. *Okay Old me, where would you put a strapless bra?*

I walked over to the island that held drawers on both sides and found that jewelry wasn't the only secret it held. The second drawer there was perfume. I took my time and smelled each one of them. They ranged from sweet to sexy. I picked a sweet smelling one, and when I sprayed it on my neck, a flash, just a flash. But it was there a memory. A kiss. A feather-lightkiss on my neck. "Oh my god, someone kissed me." I tried to reach the memory again, find that spark inside of my brain. But it was long gone.

Was I dating someone? I remember after leaving the hospital, I asked my mother if my friends knew about the incident. Her answer always stuck with me. "You were really a homebody. You never introduced me to your friends."

I thought back to my time at the facility. I was always in the day room talking to people. I hated being alone; it was one of the reasons I sought out a roommate. I heard someone clear their throat and looked up to see James standing there. His eyes warm on me, and like always, there was something more there. "That is a spectacular outfit, Pretty Girl. And I like what you did with your hair."

I wasn't sure about the hair, but with the shirt being so low cut, I thought pulling my hair out of my face would be best. The scar was more visible, but honestly, I would have to learn to live with the looks I received. "Thank you." He extended his hand, and I walked to him, taking it. "You know I have been thinking, my mother says I was a homebody, but why would I have so many evening dresses?" Walking into the common area of the house, I also noticed that there were no photos of my life before the accident. "Do you think I had a secret life? One that my mother doesn't know about?" The very idea was ridiculous.

James opened the door for me, and we walked into the sunlight. The warm air on my skin was much needed. "You should talk to your friends about the past. I am sure your mother doesn't know everything." James led me to his truck. I loved the smell of it. The fine leather wrapped itself around you, causing me to relax.

"No one from my past sees me." And I wouldn't lie that hurt. I mean what kind of person doesn't have one person in their lives that would come to the hospital after an attack like I had. "Sometimes, I think I had to be a horrible person, because no one cared that I almost died." I couldn't hide the hurt in my heart from showing. Another question I was battling with that I never said out loud slipped through. "Do you think I deserved what happened to me?" I couldn't look at him. What if he thought the same thing.

"Tempest," He said, before the question he was backing out of the driveway. Once the question was out, he stopped the car and put it in park. I couldn't look at him. He had to have questions. I know I did. Was I truly safe in my home? Would the person come back to finish the job? Whoever did this to me almost killed me. My body bruised so badly that I was in a coma for over a month.

I heard the click of my seatbelt and felt his arm go under my legs and around my back, and in an instant, I was awkwardly in his lap. "Tempest," he said while looking me in the eyes. "No one, good or bad, should be hurt like you were." He leaned in and kissed my forehead, and the only memory I had from the past slipped into my mind. The feather-light kiss. I couldn't compare them, because he put my face in his neck and held me there.

I breathed him in, and I decided it was time to let the past go. I may never get the answers that I needed, but I could build a new life. I had my mother, and I had a friend in James. Those were the building blocks I needed.

3

Once James helped me get back into my seat and placed the seatbelt around me, we were off. We drove out of our little neighborhood and it was alive on this Saturday morning. People in their yards planting flowers and mowing. Kids playing in the street. There were even a few people jogging.

Maybe I should get out and meet some of my neighbors? Try to make some friends. "Maybe we should have a housewarming party?" I say as we w were just outside of the city.

"How long have you owned the house?" James asked.

"I have no idea. But that doesn't matter. Maybe I can invite our immediate neighbors and make some friends. It's a new me, and I should take some steps to find people to connect with." He nodded and exited the expressway.

We drove in companionable silence for a long while, when he reached over and turned on the radio. When I lived with my mother, after the short stay at the facility, I asked her what was my favorite music? She was always playing some song; I didn't know. I didn't feel a thing when I heard the music. But as soon as I heard the first note to the song on the radio, something inside of me lit up.

"I know this song." I screeched. I reached over and turned it up. For the first time since I woke up, I knew something without thought from my past. "Whitney Houston!" James looked over at me, his eyes dancing. I sang the song, without missing a lyric.

When the song was over, I was kind of sad, and then the next song played. I knew that one too!! I sang along dancing, allowing the music to take over. "So we learned a lot about old Tempest today." He said with a laugh.

We sure did. I couldn't help the satisfaction I felt inside. I sat back in the seat and my arm stretched out, my fingers grazing the back of his head, and I allowed my fingers to rub his hair. Although cut short, it was soft under my fingers. My mind wondered, and I felt him relax.

I didn't realize that he was tense until that moment, a thrill went through me that I could give him peace, in something as simple as rubbing his head. I didn't remember the next few songs, but I enjoyed them anyway. Today I learned more about the old me than I had known in the last year.

We were way over dressed. James took me to a small seafood shack, and when I say shack, I was concerned if a strong wind came through it would fall over. I was so happy; I didn't care. I felt like I was on top of the world. I was following the server and I couldn't help the happiness flowing through me. Many people looked up as I walked down the aisle, but I just smiled and kept walking.

When we were seated and handed the menus, James cleared his throat. I looked up and his expression made the walls of my pussy convulse. "I don't think I have seen you strut." He bit his lower lip, reaching over and rubbing his index finger along my hand. The shiver that went through me was new, but not foreign. "It's sexy." The darkness of those words turned me on like no other.

In that moment, I didn't care about the scar on my face, or the questioning looks people gave me. In that second, I was a desirable woman, and I wanted to be bold. I looked through my lashes at him, and I don't know where the sex kitten voice came from, but it turned me on just hearing it. "Thank you."

With his eyes never leaving mine, he leaned closer. I followed his lead and hated the table between us. His hand cupped my face. "What if I told you I wanted to kiss you?" This man wanted me. He could have any woman he desired, and he desired me.

"You better make it good." He chuckled, stood up, leaning over the table and kissed me so hard and deep I was breathless. He didn't stop until the server came back. She had a smile on her face.

"Brought you some sweet tea and water, no lemon. Maybe that will cool you two down." She looked at us. "But I doubt it." She turned and over her shoulder she said, "Your hushpuppies and gumbo will be out in a few. Keep your clothes on. We have children in the building." I heard a few people chuckle. But something struck me. Something that I have been overlooking since we started this little weekend restaurant thing.

No matter where we went, before I could order what I wanted, James would order for me. It was uncanny that it was always what I was going to order. But once in a while, just like today, the server just brought over food without me ordering. Before I could ask him the question that sparked, the waitress had brought over our order and a little girl wondered over. She couldn't be over seven. "Hey." she said with a wave. Looking at me expectantly.

"Hey." I smiled back at her.

"So, do you have any new stories?" I looked at her, tilting my head.

"Do you know me?" My heart pounded in my chest.

She sat without invitation. "Yep. You're Tempest." This was the first time I met someone that knew the old me. I had so many questions.

"Erin, I told you to stay at the table." A woman took the girl by the hand before I could say a word. Pulling her away. "Please excuse her." She turned away to escape.

"No! Wait!" I stood. The woman turned, and I saw the look on her face. It was brief, only a split second, but I knew she knew me. The hurt she had on her face wasn't for a stranger, but for someone that she had feelings for. "You know me." I said. She looked over to James, and I looked over at him too. They were having a secret conversation, and whatever was said, unnerved them. In the barest of movement James gave her permission.

"Yes, I know you, Tempest." she admitted.

"Were we friends?" I was almost afraid of the answer, but I had to know.

She looked thoughtfully at me. "Not really friends, but you and my daughter were." I looked at her daughter and saw the confusion on her face. "You told her stories, and she looked forward to seeing you." Those few words were like pulling teeth. After she was done, she quickly turned around, walking away.

I looked up at James; he was eating slowly, watching me. His assessing eyes hiding what he was feeling, but I knew he had a million things going through his mind.

"What are you thinking?" I asked quietly. He smirked.

"I was wondering what you were thinking?" His eyes boring into me.

My thoughts were coming together so fast it was hard to pick one. But the one thing that screamed at me was the fear in the eyes of the woman when I asked her if she knew me. "Why would she be afraid of me?" Slowly he took another bite of his food, seeming to think. But I had another thought. "It's obvious that these people know me."

"Maybe they are giving you space. Maybe they don't want to force you to remember them? It could hurt them, to see you struggle." He had a valid point. But something didn't set right with me. "I know you want answers. You deserve them, but can you just allow things to unfold? I think it will all come back to you. Just be patient."

I learned so much about myself in the last few hours. I looked over the room. The only person watching me was the server. I winked at her, and she gave me a sad smile. Yep, she knew me, but she was keeping her distance for a reason. And I wish I knew why.

4

With a full stomach, I wasn't ready to head home. "You want to go window shopping?" James asked while walking out of the restaurant. I smiled up at him, nodding. He took me by the hand and walked us down the street. The town was quant, the homes and businesses mingled together.

"Have you ever been in love?" I asked while we passed a huge Victorian mansion.

He cleared his throat. "Yes, I've been in love." The sadness in his voice caused me to look up at him. Even in these heels, he towered over me.

We passed an older couple holding hands, walking just like us. As we passed, the man placed his arm around his woman, pulling her closer to him. I smiled as I said, "Tell me about it."

"Three years ago, I transferred to another location in my company." He started. "It was a huge promotion, and honestly, I wanted more responsibility. The men that I would work for were all legends in their own right. It was my dream. Our first meeting we were all awaiting our commander, and this woman walked in." I looked over at him, and he was in a trance. He was here with me physically, but in his mind, he was in the office seeing her for the first time.

"She didn't walk, she glided down the hall. You couldn't even hear the click of her five-inch heels. She walked right in and took the seat at the head of the table." He grinned. "This guy we called Buck, saw her and said, *I take my coffee black and sweet, just like you,*" and winked." James laughed. "Buck turned around to Greg, and the way she narrowed her eyes on him, I knew I was in love."

"What did she say?" There was a bench and James pointed for me to sit. I sat hanging on to every word he said.

" '*I don't know what gave you the impression that I make coffee.*' Buck turned to her. His eyes narrowing. '*Second, you call me sweet again, I'll put my fist down your throat.*' She turned to the rest of us. '*I would like to start the meeting on time.*' No wonder he was in love with her. She was badass. "Buck, who wasn't the smartest man on the planet, told her '*Reid, is the commander of this squad. It was on my orders.*' The rest of the guys nodded. She sat back in her chair, crossing her legs. I swear I wanted to know what those legs felt like wrapped around my back. A man passed by the glass wall, and she called out to him. '*Dennis?*' The guy stopped dead, and almost fell over his feet getting to the door. '*Yes, Commander Reid?*' She lifted an eyebrow. '*That was all I needed.*' He nodded and scurried away. She had a board expression, like we were complete idiots. '*For you men to be the best in security, you should have researched and found out that I was a woman.*'"

"She had a point." He looked at me, nodding. "Why did you think she was a man?"

"Let's just say, if she was involved in the case, there was a lot of destruction when it was over." That made me think.

"What kind of security do you do?" I glanced over his background check, but I didn't know the name of the company that he worked for. At the time, I just cared if he could pay the rent. Now, after hearing about this woman Reid, I needed to know more.

"I secure things and people that we can never discuss." Now he really had my attention. "Don't worry, you are safe." I nodded, but I would go back and do some research on the company he worked for. "Anyway, she was the best in the business."

"Men are so sexist." I rolled my eyes. "There are still men out there that think women are fragile creatures. We can do anything they can do while bleeding."

His eyes danced with humor. "You are absolutely correct." His hand grazed mine. And he smiled while looking me in the eye.

"So it was love at first sight for you?" He nodded. "How long before you felt her legs wrapped around your back?" I wiggled my eyebrows.

"Well Tempest, I would have never imagined you wanting to know the dirty details." I laughed.

"Look, I don't even remember sex, so you are educating me." He leaned over and pulled me into his arms. I laid my head on his shoulder and felt peaceful.

"It took us a little over a year and a half before I found out what it would feel like to have her." I nodded.

"What, you just told her you were into her?" Lazily, I made patterns with my fingers on his chest. The muscles under my fingers, shivered. Lust crept up my spin.

He laughed. "Reid probably heard that all the time. One of the reasons that she could get close to the enemy so quickly was because she was unassuming. She didn't look like a threat. She was beautiful, smart, funny. I bet if I asked twenty men that knew her, she was their dream woman."

I nodded. The sound of his heart relaxing me so much that I could have fallen asleep, instead I asked. "So, she dumped you?" I smiled into his chest.

His heart shuddered, and it wiped the smile right off my face. I tried to brace for what he would say next, but I wasn't prepared for what he was about to say. "She went on a mission and never came home." I looked up at him, his eyes facing the water, so far away. I sat up and placed my hand on his face. The sadness in his eyes pulled at something deep inside of me. I leaned and kissed him.

I intended it to be a soft kiss. A kiss to wipe the sadness away, but as soon as his lips touched mine, my body lit on fire. It was like he was fighting to forget losing her, and I was fighting to remember if I ever felt like this before. I doubted it. This feeling can't be erased. Something primal inside of me should have remembered. The way his hands roamed my body. The way my core tightened and wept for more. I wanted to feel him inside of me. I wanted to taste him. Wanted to find what was lost inside of me, through him.

He may never love me. I might be a warm body, but I didn't care, I wanted him. My hands went to his zipper, and he broke the kiss. "Are you sure? People could see us?"

As he spoke, I pulled down his zipper. Holding his thick, long dick in my hand. I could feel it throb with need. "Let them watch." I said while holding his eyes. Slowly I slid off his lap and to my knees. I had to taste him. On instinct my lips went around the tip of his dick. The harsh breath out of his body pushed me to continue as I felt him grow in my mouth.

Taking him deep, he moaned my name. I wrapped both of my hands around his shaft. The wetness from my mouth giving me the lubricant I needed and bobbed up and down, while sucking him deep. I moaned as he placed his hand on my head to guide me deeper. I took my time enjoying the taste and feel of him. The sounds that he made, while I played with his balls. The way his hips moved.

I wanted him inside of me. I could feel the buildup, the way he tried to contain the moans. The feeling that anyone could catch us in this moment thrilled me. Just as I pushed him deep inside my throat, he picked me up, the abrupt movement made me wonder if someone was watching? When his mouth hit mine, all thought left me. I wrapped around his body his hardness between us.

I pushed back and looked into his lust filled eyes. "Not here." I moved to protest. He held me tighter, his voice speaking to the animal inside of me. "It's fifteen minutes to get home. Don't touch me, please." He pleaded. The thought of not touching him was disappointing, yet I wanted to feel all of him. Every inch. I would do as he asked.

I slowly got off him, grinding down on his erection, watching his eyes blaze. He stood not looking at me and fixed his pants. I walked to the car. Swaying my hips on purpose. I never looked behind to see if he noticed, but I could feel his eyes on me. When we reached the car, I took my time getting in the truck.

Moments later he followed, getting in and not making a glance in my direction. With each mile the anticipation built. I had to shift in my seat, the friction intensifying the need that was overwhelming. He sped through the expressway, weaving in and out of traffic. Speeding and with every mile the anticipation built. I mapped out in my mind what I wanted, how I would taste him, feel him. A flash went through my mind, hands, my hands against a chest, smooth, hard. I could feel his heart beating so rapidly. My eyes traveled the path of my hands, lower and lower— the door to the truck opened and I snapped back into the right now. James standing at the door, questioning eyes on me.

I wouldn't focus on a memory when reality was right in front of me.

5

James' hands shook so hard as he tried to place the key in the door. I took them from him, and he stepped out the way. The door opened, and the familiarity of the house I lived in for the last few months didn't feel the same. It was missing something. Something I couldn't put my finger on. I didn't have time to think because I was pulled into his arms, turning me around he lifted my hands, and slid his hands down my body. My shirt off in a flash, the sexy demi bra on display. He pulled me to him, his head going into my neck, licking, kissing and biting. It sent a shiver down my spine.

With the precision of a surgeon, he removed the rest of my clothing. I stood bare in front of him. My boldness slipping, until I saw him, his breathing uneven, as he reached out his fingertips to touch my body. The awe in his eyes, the gentle touch as if I wasn't real, as if this was a dream, made me pull him into me. My hands going to his face holding him to me. Kissing him softly. The emotion made me wonder. Was he thinking of her? Did he wish I was Reid?

I couldn't follow that thought, I took him by the hand and led him to my bedroom. On the way I looked at the bare walls and I swore something should have been there. Photos maybe? Walking into the room, things were out of place there as well. Maybe the bed, or— James interrupted my thoughts, turning me as his mouth crashed down on mine.

My hands roamed his body under his shirt, the soft skin over hard muscle felt so good under my hand. His hands roamed as well, cupping my ass and pulling me into the hardness in his pants. I wanted to feel him inside of me. Not in my mouth like in the park, but deep inside of me. I wanted him to touch my soul..

My hands went to the hem of his shirt and pulled it over his head. Feeling his chest was one thing, but seeing it was something else altogether. I counted eight indentions where his muscles met, I placed my hands on his broad shoulders my hands feeling the ridges as I went down, down until I reached his belt buckle. My eyes went to his heated ones, as I unbuckled and pushed his pants along with his boxers down.

With a smile on my face, I walked so close to him, I could feel his heat on my skin. Wrapping my hands around his neck as he wrapped his arms around my body. He pulled me into him, lifting me, and my legs went around his waist.

Walking towards the bed, I broke the kiss and looked him in the eyes. Something inside of him pleaded, and I didn't think it was about what we were about to do. As he placed me on the bed, coming down on top of me, a flash went through my mind. A man, his head between my legs, his eyes, so familiar watching me as he licked and sucked. The flash was gone in an instant, and it was as if James read my mind, because he slid down my body, his mouth kissing me softly as he went.

My body hummed at each touch it had me squirming underneath him. "Be still." His dark voice almost made me climax. Spreading my legs, he smiled up at me when I stilled, and then bit my thigh, not hard, just enough to make a shock go through me, and I couldn't hold back a moan.

I felt his fingers at my entrance, and his warm breath over my clit. I wanted to force him to taste me, but I refrained. My reward for waiting was only seconds later, when his fingers slipped in, and his thick lips went over my clit. In tandem, his mouth and fingers worked. The pleasure that ran up my spin caused my back to arch.

This man played my body like an instrument, building up the music inside of me, until the climax was so hard and loud that I screamed.

Another vision, I was on the side of a building. Facing the brick wall, my hands bracing me, as a man fucked me ruthlessly from behind. One hand beside mine, the other over my mouth to muffle the screams as I climaxed.

I almost came again from the memory. The sound of a condom wrapper brought me back into the room. Watching him holding his thick, long dick I couldn't help myself, I had to touch it. I took the condom out of his hand. His eyes blazed as I sat up and rolled it down. I loved the feel of his dick, how heavy it was in my hand. "Thank you, baby."

Those words made my legs spread wider, and he rewarded me, sliding inside of me so slowly my eyes closed. In a whisper I heard, *"Does this feel like fucking to you?"* My eyes snapped open, and I saw his eyes looking at our connection.

"What did you say?" He pulled out and glided back inside deep. Damn that felt good.

"I said you feel amazing." I couldn't analyze what was going on because he moved. His hips thrusting in slow circles, hitting my walls. He leaned down without missing a stroke and took my nipple into his mouth. His hips moving, the sucking and— Damn, did he just bite? "Oh, my god!"

I wanted to moan his name, but it felt wrong to say James. My hips moved to meet his, and my legs wrapped around his waist. His free hand went to my ass, cupping it. His mouth released my nipple and took mine. The kiss was deep and meaningful. My hands holding his head to mine. I didn't want to lose those soft lips. Another flash, me licking a set of beautiful lips. I couldn't see anything else, just the smile on those lips.

I didn't want to think of some faceless man, from a past I had no connection to. I wanted this man. In a motion I wasn't even sure about I pushed him on his back, not breaking the connection and rode him. My breasts bounced and like beacons his hands found them.

It was like muscle memory; I rode him hard, gripping his dick with my walls, and the sounds of his moans pushing me to climax harder. I was close, but didn't want it to end. I stopped, and his eyes questioned me, until he saw me move my feet flat on the bed, and I began to bounce on his dick, and then grind down. It felt so good, we both moaned. He was so deep, this was perfect. His hands came to my hips and held me still, and then he pushed me back and quickly pulled me forward.

The sensation so overwhelming that the sounds in the room reminded me of an animal. I felt it build, and I wanted to slow down. I didn't want to feel the universe close into itself, not yet. The world fell away, it shifted right under me, as the truth and pleasure spread through me.

My body was moving violently and I could feel the explosion that his body produced. Memories flooded my mind. The first meeting, the way his eyes never left me. The first time he kissed me after I saved his life in the jungles of Peru. So many memories of who I was, accompanied with the feeling of absolute pleasure sent me over the edge, the last thing I screamed was "Axel."

6

I don't know how long I was out, but when I awakened, every question I've had in the last year was answered. Axel wasn't in bed with me, but I knew where he would be. I got up and walked to the bathroom, grabbing my robe, putting it on as I walked through the hall to the kitchen. I didn't cook, but Axel did.

Before we became a couple, the only time I came into the kitchen was to go into my secret office. I walked over to the bookshelf and picked up the figurine of a cardinal, and the door slid open. Revealing a thumb pad that glowed red. I placed my right thumb on it, and after a quick scan, it opened.

As it opened, I thought about the man that I loved. We were in Serbia on a mission. We barely got out alive. Three soldiers didn't. Axel and I were lying low in the dirtiest hotel I had ever been to. We didn't bother taking off our clothes, with one hand on our weapons and the other hand holding each other. We laid like that for a long time, in the silence. Finally, he asked me, "Do you ever wish you hadn't picked this life?"

I looked over at him, and huffed out a laugh, saying, "Yes. Especially on days like today."

He squeezed my hand, "What would life look like if you never joined The Organization?"

I didn't have to think long. "I would live in a regular house. Stylish, but practical. I would be married to a man" I thought of the most generic name, "named James. And he would have a job that sounds exciting but was boring as hell."

Axel laughed, "Like what?"

I loved when he smiled. He didn't do it often enough. "He would be in security. Nothing crazy. He would be home most nights, and we would go for long walks in small towns, trying food, and dreaming about retirement."

We laughed at this fake life I would have had. I turned the corner and knew what I would find. Axel was sitting at my desk. Eight monitors all doing something different. He turned in my seat, and tears were in his eyes, something I hadn't seen even when I accompanied him to his father's funeral.

"I thought I lost you." His words, soft and the hurt in his tone, made me move to him. He opened his arms, and I sat in his lap, resting my head on his chest.

"Why didn't you just tell me who you were?" Deep down I knew the answer, and then I remembered. "We were supposed to be married three weeks before the attack." I searched his pain-filled eyes, and I didn't have to wonder why he didn't come to me, and just tell me when I woke from the attack.

"When you woke and didn't remember who you were, your mother, she thought it was best if you created a new life." His warm body and arms holding me to him was the only thing keeping me from losing my temper.

My mother hated my job. I could see her using this to get me out of the life. But keeping Axel and my friends, no my family away from me, was inexcusable. I held my anger at bay, not wanting to lose focus of what Axel gave me. "So you became the man of simple Tempest? The man I told you about in Serbia?"

He nodded, "Yes. And watching you struggle with the boredom of this life was killing me." I was bored. I couldn't put my finger on it, but I knew something was wrong. I hated getting out of bed and looking at the same screen all day.

I had one question, but I think I knew the answer. "What if I had never gotten my memory back?"

I tilted my head back to see his face. He looked down at me. A sad smile on his face. "I was leaving The Organization." I closed my eyes.

"But you love your job." We all did. Our biggest fear was retirement. The skills in this job couldn't just transfer into civilian life. And Axel loved the rush. There were many times I thought he would have done the wild things we did for free.

"Baby, there is nothing in this world that I love more than you." My heart melted. "I would have been a security guard at the mall if I got to lay next to you every night." My hand went to his face, and I captured his lips.

We were made for each other. Even without my memory of him, I knew in my soul; he was someone I could trust, depend on, maybe even love. My heart hurt that our wedding never happened. We lost a year together.

"I love you Ax." tears swam in his eyes and leaned down to kiss me, just as the monitors flashed, and my back went straight.

Axel turned us around to face the screens. The static screen showed nothing, but I knew she was there. "Well, you finally remembered who you are." The Executive was the faceless commander of The Organization. A secret army that controlled every major decision in all the world.

I didn't have to ask how she knew I had my memory back; she knew everything. Well, almost everything. "Do we know where Navir is?" The man that drugged me, and then took his knife and carved through my face. I didn't remember what happened next, but the hospital said I had severe blunt force trauma to the head.

"We both know you are the only one who can find him. You understand his mind better than any of us." It was true. It was why he came after me personally. Three days before, my team and I had dismantled his operation. Leaving him with little money, and nowhere to hide. Or so I thought. It shouldn't have taken a year to find him. He would have been out of money in three months and not able to hide, if my calculations were correct. But with my memory gone, he would have time to find new allies.

"I need to know what hole he ran to after almost killing me." I would track him down and find him. I didn't care how long it took, or how many bodies I left behind.

"Before we go any further," Axel said. "Reid and I have some unfinished business." He leaned up and pulled out the drawer, reaching in. In a second, he pulled out a ring. My ring. The ring he gave me the night he asked me to marry him.

Reflexively, I lifted my hand, and he placed the ring on my finger. "I can have the jet ready in thirty. First stop Vegas. You two get married, and I will give you forty-eight hours for a honeymoon. Then you bring me Navir."

I nodded, "There won't be a place on earth he could hide." I would find him. Make him pay for what he did to me, to us. I looked at the man I loved. The world was about to lose one of its greatest warriors. Luckily, that didn't happen. It might have taken a year, but I was back, and more determined than ever. Navir wouldn't be able to hide from us.

The monitors flashed, and the static disappeared. It was just me and Axel. "Are you ready for this adventure?" Axel asked and kissed my nose.

Looking into his eyes, seeing nothing but love, I replied, "Absolutely."

Too Close For Comfort

Regina Frame

1

Logan

The alarm went off with the sound of the chicken dance. That shit tears me up every time I hear it. This was not one of those times.

"You set a timer?" The blonde chick riding my dick stopped mid thrust with a scowl on her face.

"That's to remind me that I have a meeting in exactly twenty minutes. Time to go, babe. I still need to shower." I slapped her on the ass and moved her off my lap.

"Oh my God! You're a jerk, Logan!" she shouted, jumping from the bed and grabbing her dress from the floor. "Do you even want my number?"

"No, darling."

"You're everything the tabloids write about you! The only person you care about is you!" she spat.

"Look, Mary…"

"It's Misty, you jerk!" She shimmied her dress up over her hips.

"You came three times. You're a greedy little cunt, aren't you?" I don't normally use that word, but this chick was beginning to piss me off.

"That's what they make Viagra for. You could use some work in the stamina department if you ask me!"

"Do I look like I need any help?" Now she really pissed me off. "You need to get dressed and go. I'm running late," I said as I walked to the bathroom and closed the door behind me.

I jumped in the shower and washed all the necessary parts. Brushed my teeth and pulled my damp hair back into a manbun. When I walked back into the bedroom she was gone. I hated it when the groupies cried and went into full on clinger mode. This shit was getting old. *I was getting too old for this.* Maybe one day I'll find the one. I grabbed my cell and fired off a text to let the guys know I'd be there in ten minutes. I jumped on my bike and headed for the freeway. It took me exactly twenty minutes to get to the studio because the damn paparazzi was on my tail. I finally lost them around Fifth and Vine.

When I stepped into the room JC, our drummer, was sitting at the table with his feet propped up and Marco and Jamie were in the studio messing around with their guitars. JC stood and knocked on the glass and motioned for them to join us at the conference table.

"So, what's this all about that it couldn't wait until later? I had the sweetest..." I didn't get the chance to finish because JC cut me off.

"We all know you like pussy, but this is important, and I didn't feel that it could wait," JC said. "I received a call from Carl over at Silver Tone Records and he thinks he's found a base player for us. He thought she'd be a perfect fit."

"She?" we all said in unison.

"Yes, and don't give me shit about it! I've been told she's one of the best there is. She played for Pierce Morgan's band until he wanted a little more than just her guitar skills so don't you shit heads get any ideas. She's a bandmate and off limits," JC demanded. They were good but definitely no match for High Voltage.

"Don't we get a say in this? We would like to hear her play before the ink dries on the contract." I growled.

"She's on her way. She should be here any minute," JC explained.

A few minutes later, a beautiful blonde with legs for days walked into the studio with a guitar case almost as big as she was.

"Guys, this is Sydney Frost. She's played bass for ten years and won numerous awards." JC went around the room and introduced each of us and what part we played in the band.

"It's nice to meet you, Sydney. It's hard to believe you've played for ten years. You barely look eighteen," I said.

"I'm twenty-six. I started young. My dad taught me how to play."

"Speaking of playing. We're one of the top grossing bands in the last ten years. We've scored more gold records and grammys than I can count on one hand. Do you think you can keep up with that?" Marco asked.

"Stop being a dick, Marco!" I growled. "Show a little class whether you have some or not!"

"I'm just saying she better be good if she's going to keep up with High Voltage."

I looked to Sydney, whose eyes were narrowed on Marco.

"Why don't I show you? Care to jam with me?" She lifted one blonde brow. "If you can keep up?" She smirked at Marco, which seemed to piss him off even more. We all grabbed our instruments and took our places in the recording studio. "How about When Danger Calls?" That was one of our top selling records and very complicated to play for someone outside the group who didn't practice it every day.

2

Sydney

When I was told High Voltage was looking for a new bass player, I couldn't believe it. If I could land this gig, it would be a dream come true. It would be everything that I've worked so hard for over the years.

"Don't let Marco get to you. He's a dick sometimes but when it comes down to it, he's got your back," Logan said.

Logan was the lead singer. His voice was raspy and caused all my girlie parts to tingle. He was tall at least six feet, with a bright smile and piercing blue eyes. And he smelled delicious. Like Sandalwood and something else. My eyes were drawn to his sexy lips as he flicked the piercing with his tongue. His lips curled up, and I realized he'd caught me staring again. Embarrassed I'd been busted, I felt my face flush with warmth, and I was pretty sure my face said it all.

Marco cleared his throat from across the room, breaking through the uncomfortable awkwardness. Thank God. "Are we gonna jam or what?" he asked.

I grabbed my guitar case and walked across the room and took my place in front of one of the mics. JC tapped his sticks three times and

Marco joined in with guitar. I blended in and Logan belted out the lyrics to the song. His voice did things to me that I couldn't explain and that scared me. The rest of the session went by in a blur. We blended together as if we had been together for years. We practiced and even had a recording session so that we could play it back to see how we sounded together.

I was beyond excited, and the guys were pleased with it. It was pure magic. It was a relief to know that I wasn't going to be sent packing before I ever got the chance to play on stage with them. I was thankful that I was getting the opportunity to peruse my dream with such a prestigious band.

"Wow it's getting late. I need to find a hotel room. Do you guys know of one close by the studio? In my rush to leave, I forgot to make a reservation. I need food and a long hot shower."

"I have an extra room. You're welcome to stay with me," Logan offered as he hefted his guitar onto his shoulder.

I continued to scan for area hotels, but none had openings. Looks like I'd be spending the night with the black hair guitarist with the ice blue eyes. I had been so distracted with the thoughts of what it would be like to meet the guitarist face to face, so finding a place to stay never entered my mind to tell the truth. I just hoped I could control my hormones around him. That was not part of the plan, and I was not entirely sure that I could do it, but I guess I'd find out.

I followed Logan on his blacked out Hayabusa to a ritzy neighborhood in the hills of California. He punched in a code and the big gate swung open revealing a long winding drive through emasculate landscape. We reached the end of the driveway to reveal a two-story brick mansion. There was a beautiful fountain in front surrounded by colorful begonias.

Music had been kind to Logan, because not only did he have a motorcycle, but he also had a red Hummer and a silver Porche, which had a mirrored finish. I'd never seen anything like it.

I got out of my car and grabbed my bags from the backseat and waited for Logan to get off his bike.

Logan

On the drive home I couldn't get Sydney out of my head. She was a gorgeous blonde with emerald-green eyes that sparkled like gems. It was going to be hard to keep my dick to myself. She had colorful ink traveling up her right arm in the form of a Toucan bird. I loved a chick with ink. It was bad ass! There was nothing sexier. I couldn't help but wonder if she had any other tattoos hidden beneath those clothes. It was probably a bad decision to let her stay with me, because JC warned us all before she arrived to keep our dicks to ourselves. She was off limits according to him. I took one look at her and realized how screwed I was. JC said it could cause problems within the band. Could he honestly expect me to live with her and not touch her? That was like giving a kid a lollipop and telling him not to lick it. That was some fucked up shit. I'd love a taste of her.

"Cool ride," she said as I flung my leg over the seat and removed my helmet.

Girls got good taste. "I love the black on black. It looks badass."

"Thanks. I'll take you for a ride sometime."

I didn't miss the flush of her cheeks. I pictured her riding my dick, tits bouncing as I thrust inside her. Fuck. Now I was hard. She walked over to my Porche and trailed her fingers along the door, and I could tell that she was wondering about the paint job. It was an unusual, mirrored finish, and mine was one of ten that were made.

"I've never seen anything like this. It's sharp," she said.

"It's one of ten that were made. The beauty of this is that when the paparazzi are trying to catch a money shot, it's practically impossible because of the flash from their cameras.

"Here let me take that," I offered, taking her suitcase from her hand. Her sweet coconut scent filled my nose, and I had to bite my lip to keep the groan from escaping my throat. "Come on. I'll show you around." I flicked on the lights and tossed my keys on the counter as we walked through the house. I pointed to each room and explained what they were.

I was pretty proud of the place. It had dark hardwood floors, neutral walls with white crown molding, and floor-to-ceiling windows in the den that looked out over the pool. The only thing I changed about the place was the kitchen appliances. I had them all replaced with state of the art, stainless steel, restaurant grade quality, because believe it or not, I liked to cook, and I was pretty damn good at it if I do say so myself. I hired an interior decorator so that the furniture and everything else would match. I was shit at matching anything...even my damn clothes. That's why I had a stylist.

"Do you get much privacy in this neighborhood? Aren't they curious about the rockstar that lives next door?"

"No. That's what's great about this place. The neighborhood is made up of celebrities. It's pretty close to Clairmont Pictures. The recording studio, and some of the major television networks. The neighborhood was built with that in mind. We walked down the hall and I stopped just outside a white door. "This is your room." I pushed the door open wide. "And that room is mine." I pointed to the room next door. "All I ask is that when you have sex, please don't scream or make cat noises. I need my sleep. All play and no sleep makes Logan an asshole." I laughed.

Her eyes widened.

"If I do, you'll be the first person I call." She reached up and pinched my cheek between her thumb and finger. The warmth of her touch sent a tingle to my balls, and just when I thought my dick couldn't get any harder, it proved me wrong. The asshole. I grinned and leaned in close, my lips brushing against her ear.

"Oh, and one other thing; I sleep in the nude, and sometimes I sleep walk, so consider yourself warned." I breathed against her neck, causing her body to shiver against mine and a small gasp to leave her full pink lips. I wanted to kiss her. Taste her. And if I was reading her body language correctly, she wanted me, too. *What the fuck are you doing? She just got here and already you're thinking with the little head.* "Pizza?" I asked, and forced myself to take a step back. If I weren't careful, I'd do something we'd both regret. It was going to be hell trying to control myself around her.

"Are you saying I smell like pizza?"

She was flustered, and her cheeks were a light shade of pink. I loved that I did that to her. It was such an honest reaction; not like that of the chicks that hung around after our shows. Nothing, and I mean nothing, embarrassed them. They'd done and seen it all. I chuckled and gazed into her emerald eyes. They narrowed, and her spine stiffened. I thought for a minute she was going to slap the shit out of me. She thought I was toying with her, but I wasn't. I just had a lapse in judgement was all. I really needed to get a hold of myself before I did something we might to be able to move past.

"No." I chuckled." You know, Pizza? It's round and has stuff like cheese, pepperoni on..."

"I know what pizza is, smartass!" She covered my mouth with her hand as I continued to talk, and just for spite, I licked it, causing her to frown and wipe her hand down the front of her jeans.

"No need for name calling, Syd." I placed my hand over my heart like she'd deeply wound me.

"Are you always like this?" She cocked her head to the side and studied me like I was some type of alien life form.

"Like what?" I arched my brow in question, amused by the expression on her beautiful face.

"Like a kid in a toy store whose been told they can have anything they want."

"Always." I laughed.

"Why am I not surprised?" She shook her head and laughed. "I'm going to shower and change clothes," she announced, and flipped her blonde hair over her shoulder where it fell in silky strands.

"Need help with that? I could scrub your back if you want?"

I took a step forward, only to be stopped when she placed her warm hand in the middle of my chest to stop me. A surge of sexual awareness crackled in the air around us. She may not have admitted it, but it affected her, too. I saw it in the way her breathing changed when she touched me.

"Okay. I'll order pizza," I said to the door, before turning on my heel and walking toward the kitchen. I stared down at my hard dick where it pressed against my zipper. "Not tonight, buddy. You should be ashamed of yourself. She's a visitor."

3

Sydney

I closed the bedroom door and leaned back against it. Closing my eyes, I took a deep breath in an attempt to stop the pounding of my heart. *Get a damn grip.* My body was humming with sexual energy from that simple touch and a strong pulse had started between my legs. If this was any indication of what it will be like staying with him, I may need to purchase new dildos and fresh batteries.

I would be lying if I said I wasn't a little disappointed when he pulled away. I'd fantasized plenty of times about kissing him...among other things. I guess, for the time being, that would have to do.

I dropped my bag just inside the closet door and fished my phone out of my back pocket. I had felt it vibrate several times today but didn't have time to check it. Just as I thought, I had several texts and a voicemail from my best friend. She was asking me to call her to let her know that I'd made it safely, and asking if the guys were even hotter in person. I sighed and sat on the side of the bed to type out a message to her.

I'm here. We were in the studio all day. And yes, the guys are even hotter in person.

She responded immediately, just like I knew she would. Her damn phone was always in her hand.

Bitch, where's my picture?
What?

I shook my head and sighed.

If you remember correctly, I didn't promise anything, and if you call me a bitch again, I promise you won't get shit!

That calmed her down.

Oh yeah! I forgot to tell you to Google Logan Blackwood. There are nudes! Full frontal. I'm tellin ya! Wow!

There is no way I'm searching for Logan Blackwood's dick! I responded.

Girl, you have got to see this!

There were several eggplant emojis and a startled cat face that followed the text.

That's it! Drop it or you won't get any pics!

I knew that would get her where it hurt.

Damn. You play dirty, girl!

I giggled to myself as I scrolled through my phone, doing the very thing I swore I wouldn't do. Damn! She wasn't kidding; there were pictures of Logan posing for some calendar called Hot Stud of Music. He was Mr. March. And Oh My God! He had a Jacob's ladder! I'd never dated anyone who had one, but I heard they felt amazing.

Once I finished with my shower, I dug through my suitcase and pulled out a pair of black leggings and an oversized sweatshirt that hung off one shoulder. I opened the door and was greeted with the delicious smell of pizza and garlic. I walked into the kitchen and grabbed a paper plate and tossed on a couple of slices before heading to the den where I found Logan sitting on the floor playing x-box. A tiny yorkie sitting by his feet.

"You have a dog." It came out more a question than a statement, because I hadn't seen the dog when I came in.

"This is Thor." All three pounds of him.

"Where was Thor when I came in?"

"My neighbor watches him while I'm out. Walks him, feeds him, talks to him and all that shit. He gets really moody if you don't pay attention to him."

The tiny dog was sitting beside Logan with his eyes on me. I stepped closer and said, "Hi Thor. Aren't you a cute one?" This dog growled at me and yapped.

"Yeah, I should have told you he doesn't like to be called cute. Isn't that right, Thor? He prefers handsome." I snorted.

"Well, he *is* cute!" This time, Thor started this nonstop yapping. It was the most irritating sound ever.

"You've officially hurt his feelings. You'll never be able to make it up to him."

"I'll get over it." I snorted. "What game are you playing?"

"Halo."

"I love Halo," I said around a mouth full of pizza. He paused the game and turned and looked at me.

"You've heard of it?" He looked at me like I had grown a third eye. "I can honestly say that I've never met a chick who knew what an x-box was, let alone Halo."

"I guess the girls you hang out with have other things on their mind." I smirked.

He tossed the dog a piece of pepperoni and said, "Thor, say goodnight to the beautiful lady." I felt my face go up in flames. Logan Blackwood thought I was beautiful. The dog made a snort/sneezing sound and walked out of the room with his head held high.

He ran his hand through his long black hair and grinned. I squeezed my thighs together to help ease the little drumming that had set up between my legs.

"What kind of movies do you like?" he asked. Good. Anything to get my mind off this wild attraction I have for him.

"I like any type of action movie. You know, like Fast and Furious, and I love anything horror. I love that rush of adrenaline," I said with way too much excitement in my voice. Both sides of his lips curled up into a sexy smile.

"You're the perfect woman," he said, and flicked the ring in his lower lip. There went that pulse between my legs again. I shifted in my seat again.

"What kind of movies do you like?"

"Porn," he said with a laugh. "Nah, just kidding. I like anything with blood and car chases. We're the perfect match! Will you marry me?" he joked. We both laughed. "I guess I should have asked if you had a boyfriend before I proposed to you."

His blue eyes on me caused a shiver of desire to run down my spine. "I'm pretty sure you have women lined up for a taste of Logan Blackwood after every show." My face heated when his cocky grin appeared, and I realized what I'd said. "I think it's probably time for me to go to bed."

"You don't want to watch a movie?" he asked.

"Nah, it's been a long day."

"Want to make a movie instead?"

It was my turn to grin. I couldn't help it. I don't know what made me do it, but it was a full out grin.

"Ah ha. My little sunshine has a dirty side." He stood and placed his empty plate on the coffee table along with mine.

"Good night, Logan," I said, walking toward my bedroom.

When I turned to say something more, he was on me. Hands and lips everywhere. I could barely breathe. This man kissed the shit out of me and weakened my knees.

He backed up a long enough to ask, "Is this, okay?" When I nodded, his hands went to the hem of my shirt lifting it over my head and dropping it to the floor.

Logan

I tossed her shirt to the floor and walked her backward to the bed where I stripped off her leggings and the tiny scrap of lace between her legs. There was only one word to describe my sunshine. Beautiful. And she had her clit pierced. Fuck me. I had to have a taste. I leaned forward and licked up her slit before taking her piercing between my teeth and gently tugging. She gasped and threw her head back. Her blonde hair hung down her back like a curtain of silk.

"This is not fair," she said, breathless pushing on my shoulders. What? I looked up into her green lust filled eyes. "You're not naked." I quickly stripped out of my shirt and then my jeans. I wasn't wearing underwear. Never had. I liked to let my junk breathe. Her green eyes widened when she saw my dick. "You have a Jacob's ladder," she breathed.

I reached out and pulled her to me, her body soft against mine. Silky and smooth. Her hair smelled of coconut shampoo. Our eyes locked and there was definitely a dangerous little flicker behind those emerald greens. I trailed my tongue down her throat and along her collar bone. Her nipples pebbled beneath my fingertips as I pinched and plucked them. You taste just as sweet as I knew you would. Her teeth tugged at my bottom lip and she sucked on my lip ring. She threw her arms around my neck and climbed me like a tree, and when she rubbed her warm center over my throbbing dick, it was every man for himself. Her lips went to my ear.

"Fuck me, Logan," she moaned in my ear.

"Fuck, Sunshine. You're beautiful," I whispered against her pink lips as I lie her on the bed. Her fingers went to my hair, gripping the long strands, tugging, trying to pull my mouth closer to her throbbing clit. My tongue snaked out and flicked that little gem, causing her legs to tremble beneath my palms.

Her heavy breathing and chorus of soft moans were the only sounds in the stillness of the bedroom. They were like music to my ears.

"Fuck me, Logan," she pleaded with a shaky breath. Her fingers traced over my abs and along my trimmed pubic hair and my legs trembled. She took me in her hand. My dick was hard as steel. If she stroked me once, I'd probably go off like a rocket. I crawled up the bed and hovered over her.

"Are you sure?" I asked again.

"I've never been surer."

I grabbed a condom from the bedside table and rolled it on. Positioning myself at her entrance, I took my time pushing in slowly. I stopped a few times giving her time to adjust to my size. I began to move in and out. Sex had never felt so good. "Eyes open, sweetheart," I commanded.

Lacing our fingers together we began to move at a faster pace. With our eyes locked, we spiraled together over the edge into blissful release.

"Fuck," she said.

"Regretting it already?"

"Hell no! I was just thinking how much I'm going to love this whole roommate situation."

I wrapped my arms around her and pulled her on top of me. "I think I'm falling for you, Sunshine."

"I'm already there," she said, laying her head on my chest. Within a few minutes her breathing evened out and I knew she'd fallen asleep. I planned on every night being like tonight for as long as she'd have me.

Titles By Regina Frame

Finding Forever
ROCKSTAR SERIES
DIRTY AFFLICTION
Honesty
Lyric
Heartstrings
Harmony
Melody

Trapped with Temptation

Lori Ann Bailey

1

Three minutes.

That was all it took for Emma Mitchell's world to implode.

Minute one: She'd used her old key to let herself into her childhood home and left her luggage by the front door.

Minute two: She'd collapsed onto the familiar worn sofa. Memories had flooded back: days of doing her homework, walking the dog, evenings helping her mother make dinner and doing dishes while music floated in the background, nights playing board games with her family. And the evening that on this very sofa, her dreams had come true, then her world shattered.

Minute three: She'd frozen at the clunk of a door shutting. Her brother was in Europe. The house should be empty. Petrified, Emma remained motionless as a rustle of shuffling feet sounded through the laundry room and into the kitchen.

She needed a weapon. She jumped up, grabbed a giant book from the coffee table, and slinked towards the noise.

A shirtless man with lean shoulders and dark wavy hair rummaged around the fridge's contents. Anxiety rushed through her. Even before he turned to face her, she recognized those shoulders, the hair, the stance, the strong legs, and the man who had been the infatuation of her entire existence.

Mason Gray. An intruder would have been easier to deal with. An intruder could be reasoned with or run from. An intruder wouldn't steal her heart. Oh crap, she found herself wishing for an actual intruder.

Mason straightened and turned. When his eyes landed on her, a moment of shock skittered in his chestnut eyes. He smiled.

Emma's heart skipped a beat—no, two beats. Perhaps it stopped beating altogether because her body went numb and refused to move.

In those endless seconds, a world of emotions grabbed her and yanked her back through time. Her brother's best friend had taught her how to throw a football, helped her study for her AP World exam, came to her for advice on the endless streams of girlfriends that flocked to him, and encouraged her to dream big.

Three minutes. That was all it took. One. Two. Three. Three minutes to undo three years of moving forward.

Mason had been here to comfort her after her mother's death when she'd come back her junior year of college. When Emma had returned for the holidays her senior year, he'd made love to her on the sofa on New Year's Eve. It had been magical and beautiful and the realization of all her desires.

Then he'd received a text. His ex-girlfriend, Kaylee.

He'd suddenly lost interest in her, as if he were a million miles away, pulling all his clothes on and saying, "Oh shit. It's Kaylee." Then he'd disappeared.

The next afternoon, when she'd not heard from him, she'd searched his social media, which he never posted to. Nothing.

She had checked Kaylee's, and her breath caught. Mason's ex had shared a picture taken of them only that morning.

Kaylee wore full makeup and wowed in a stunning, sparkling dress. Kaylee had been the most beautiful girl in Mason's senior class. In the photo, her arm coiled around Mason's waist, while his arm draped lovingly on her shoulders. The image was captioned "Forever My Hero" with three heart emojis. He was still wearing the clothes he'd left her house in.

With her heart officially broken, Emma had turned her phone off, packed her things, and driven back to her apartment in Columbus, Ohio.

She hadn't answered Mason's text late the next evening that said, *Sorry about last night.* Or the text that asked, *When will you be home again?* Or the text three months later: *Happy Birthday, Em.* Or the text, *Congratulations,* when she graduated from Ohio State. She didn't answer the phone when he'd tried to call. She didn't ask her brother about him.

Three years had passed faster than the last three minutes. Emma blinked.

"Em."

Her name on Mason's lips warmed her, and her heart pumped again. Unfortunately, it now beat with a thud, thud, thud that thrummed in her ears.

"Mason. What are you doing here?" she asked through a constricted throat.

"I'm house and pet sitting while your brother is in Europe."

"Oh," she replied as her mind raced. She couldn't stay here. Not with Mason in the house.

"How long are you in town for?" His smooth voice comforted and tortured at the same time.

"I'm moving back, and I'll be here at the house until I find an apartment. I can watch Riley." She was trying to tell him he could leave without telling him that he had to go.

Mason's smile blossomed as if the news pleased him. She wanted to cry but also to wrap her arms around him and forget the hurt that had plagued her with his rejection.

For her sanity, she needed to come straight out with it. "You can go home since I'm here."

"Wish I could, but there was a fire in my neighbor's apartment last week. They won't even let me back in to inspect the smoke and water damage."

"That's awful," she said.

"So it looks like we're stuck together for a little while." Mason shrugged.

He actually appeared pleased at their predicament.

This was going to be torture. She was stranded for this evening, but she'd get out early in the morning to search available apartments. Her brother, Andrew, wouldn't be home for weeks. Each moment with Mason brought back memories and longing and pain.

"I'm making dinner. I'll toss in enough for both of us," Mason said.

"Thank you," she managed as she debated jumping in the car, grabbing takeout, and securing a hotel, but she didn't want to blow through her savings, and she would need a deposit for a new place. She was trapped.

"Chicken okay?"

"Yes," she said. "I need to unpack." Unpack her clothes, unpack her life, unpack the emotions that had been carefully stowed away and left to fester like hidden treasures in the storage facility of her mind.

2

After a long shower and a million attempts to tell herself she could face him and not break, Emma shimmied into her favorite low-cut, skin-tight pre-game top and a pair of black jeans. She ran the straightening brush through her hair. The attempt was partly to show Mason what he'd missed out on but, secondly, to give her the confidence to face him and banish the thoughts that she'd not been enough.

She stopped in the hall bathroom to check herself one more time in a different light. Mason's toiletries were lined neatly on one side of the counter: toothbrush, shaving cream, a razor, and cologne, Polo. The scent on him had always made her weak in the ankles, knees, elbows—every part of her that had craved him. Even now, she caught a whiff of it, and she found herself leaning into the faint traces in the air.

Reaching for the bottle, she almost lifted it before thinking better. She flipped the light switch off, walked down the hall, and was greeted by another enticing aroma. Her stomach stood up and yelled, "Finally," sending signals to her mouth, which watered with anticipation. She'd had two boiled eggs and a piece of cheese before leaving Ohio this morning and chosen not to stop for lunch.

Mason was pulling the chicken from the oven when she stepped into the kitchen. While his back was to her, she took a moment to study the table. He'd set the surface with napkins, silverware, and glasses of water.

After placing the food on the counter, he smiled at her. The smile that he'd worn when he'd teased her about her first boyfriend, the smile he'd given her when they'd hijacked a golf cart at his parents' country club and torn through the course at "grip onto the seat for your life" speed, the smile she'd craved every day after falling in love with him in seventh grade when he'd barely known she existed. Her heart still stopped at that smile.

"Just in time. Can you grab a trivet?" he asked, falling right back into a world where he belonged here with her family. Back into a time when she was simply his best friend's little sister. She wanted to scream, "No, I will not do anything for you," but she fell right back into doing whatever he asked.

"Sure."

"Thank you." He stood aside. "I hope you're hungry. I made enough to feed the whole D-line."

"Do you still play?" she asked.

"I'm in a flag league. It gives me something to do on the weekends."

She almost asked, "What does Kaylee think of that," but Emma decided to keep things light since they were trapped together for a while.

"Sounds nice."

"Grab a plate." He left the food on the counter so they could serve themselves buffet-style.

As she sat down with a plate full of chicken, roasted squash, peppers, onions, and a dinner roll, a sense of anticipation for the meal filled her.

"What are you doing back in Charlottesville?" he asked as he slid into the chair nearest her.

"I'm looking for a new job."

"I thought you liked the one you had." Concern darkened his eyes.

How did he know? Perhaps her brother had told him. She'd assumed Mason had done what she had. Anytime she'd seen her brother the last few years, she'd stuck to her "don't ask what you don't want to know the answer to" policy.

She had no idea where Mason had ended up.

"I did, but the family that owned the business decided to sell. A larger group came in and bought them out. The new owners already had a big accounting firm that manages their books. I was no longer needed." Funny, she thought, that seemed to be the story of her life. She gave her all, and then she was no longer needed.

"That's awful."

"Yeah."

"Do you have any leads?" he asked, then filled his mouth with a forkful of chicken.

"I do." But she didn't want to talk about her. She'd refrained from asking about him for so long that now her curiosity boiled over.

"Where are you working?"

"At the local college."

"You got the job!" she almost squealed. It was what he'd always wanted. Despite what had happened between them, he deserved to be happy, and history had always been his passion. "What are you teaching?"

"Oh, just your favorites. The rise and fall of empires, plagues, civic engagement, and a little bit about cultural revolutions."

She laughed, surprised at how easily it came to her. Numbers had always made sense to Emma. History was too brutal and subjective: civilizations learning from their pasts, forgetting what they'd learned, tearing down structures to build them back up again, and going to war. History had been her least favorite subject, but she'd always found joy in watching Mason's passion for humanity's past.

The conversation flowed.

Soon, they were done and clearing the table, moving to the sink to wash the dishes side by side, going through the motions of being who they were before. All the hurt faded to the back, and a bit of relief settled into the casual routine as if they would make it through this forced time together without angry sparks flying.

He washed a plate and handed it to her to dry. Their arms brushed, and they both froze. The touch was innocent, but it ignited the awareness that no matter how she attempted to squash it, he still hung the stars in her version of a perfect universe.

"I've missed you," he said, so low that it was almost a whisper.

She inhaled sharply.

"Why didn't you answer my texts and calls?" he asked, breaking their truce.

Blood rushed to her head, the heat of it reminiscent of the time her brother had snuck a ghost pepper into her BLAT sandwich. Then, Mason had been the one to grab her a glass of milk and soothe the pain. This time, he was the cause of it.

"Don't go there, Mason. You know what you did was wrong."

His face went slack, and the rosiness drained from his cheeks.

"What did you expect me to do, Em? I was a horrible friend."

Friend, friend, friend, friend. The words repeated over and over and over in her head, a drum that tattooed out "fuck you, fuck you, fuck you."

Her lip quivered, but instead of breaking down, she held her chin up and unleashed her pent-up hurt. "Yes, you are the worst sort of *friend*." She let the last word drag and hang in the air.

Mason turned off the tap, set the wet pan on the counter, grabbed his keys, and fled from the house. He'd destroyed her heart for anyone else, but somehow, the hurt she'd heaped on him magnified back on her. The shattered bewilderment in his eyes tore her in two.

3

Emma scrubbed the makeup from her face, climbed into her pajamas, and pulled out a Scottish historical romance novel by her favorite author. The one part of history she did find intriguing—the dynamics of Highlander life—instantly swept her away into a world of warring clans, divided loyalties, and a love story that would always end happily ever after.

A pounce alerted her to Riley's presence. Riley was an orange short-haired tabby her brother had inherited from a psycho ex-girlfriend whom Emma had never liked. Riley was a sweet cat, the only thing good that had come from that relationship. He kneaded his paws on her thigh, then glanced up and gave an urgent "meooooow."

"Alright, alright. Looks as if Mason left without doing his job."

She set her book down and moved toward the laundry room. The cat was so close to her heels that he was halfway tapping along beside her and almost under her feet. He reminded her of the cat their mom had brought home when she and Andrew were still young. Emma missed that cat... and her mom.

Her father had moved into a small condo and sold their childhood home to her brother. Andrew had taken over the master bedroom, which meant that Mason must be staying in there, one door down from her old room that she'd never quite moved out of.

As Emma leaned to fill Riley's bowl, Mason walked in through the garage door. When he saw her, he quickly glanced away, but it wasn't fast enough to hide the sadness and regret that ate at the corners of his tired gaze.

"Excuse me," he said as he skirted past her and headed toward the back of the house.

His shoulders drooped as they had on the day his mentor, the football coach, had been carted off the field with a fatal heart attack. He looked utterly devastated, and she wanted to go to him and soothe the hurt, but that would only lead to more pain for her.

Emma and Mason successfully avoided each other for days. Her priority was finding a job, so most of that time was spent scouring the internet and filling out online applications. On the third day, she answered a call from a local department store she'd applied to. They'd been expanding, and the owner was having difficulty managing her accounts.

The position sounded perfect, and an interview was set up for the following day. Feeling confident, Emma left the house to hunt for a new place to live. Even if Mason were only temporarily in her brother's house, she couldn't stay there indefinitely. She loved Andrew, but as her older brother, he took it upon himself to be a little overprotective.

He had scared off most of her boyfriends. With his size and position as center of the football team, he'd dominated the halls. Everyone moved for Andrew Mitchell. Even after he'd graduated, Andrew kept tabs on her through the younger players who had admired him.

By the end of the day, she was exhausted. She'd seen rooms for rent in houses and apartments that were either above her budget or full of college students. Neither would do. She needed a quiet place with well-established people who wouldn't be keeping her up all hours of the night.

The early darkness of the December evening closed in. Instead of getting the winter blues, the cool, crisp air cleared her thoughts and brought clarity. Despite her rocky start, something about being back in Charlottesville—perhaps the familiarity with the quaint little city, the friendly people, the holiday lights strung on neighbors' homes, or picking up Chinese from her favorite takeout—was refreshing and comforting.

When she stepped into the house, Mason's scent hung in the air and hugged her in a warm embrace. He reclined on the sofa, the book she'd almost thrown at him the other night in his hands, and Riley sprawled in his lap.

"Hey," she said. Then she attempted to look uninterested when what she really wanted to do was curl up next to them and soak in their warmth.

"Hi," he returned. Although not as bright as the other evening, his smile still melted her to the core.

Perhaps it was because she'd made progress in her searches and didn't feel vulnerable now. It was also that she wanted to make amends for driving him from the house the other evening. So she held up the bag. "I picked up from Golden Noodle."

"I'll eat whatever you have left over." An eager glint twinkled in his gaze.

"You won't have to. I ordered you cashew chicken."

His eyes practically sparkled. She used to live for moments like that. Just seeing the sheer pleasure he found in food.

"You're the best." He set his book on the sofa and cradled Riley, picking him up, then resettling him on a blanket nearby.

As they ate, the conversation turned to football, then Mason's parents, then they talked about Andrew. It was natural and comfortable. Maybe it was time to let go of the past.

"I'm sorry about the other night."

"No worries. I'd forgive you almost anything. And besides, you know the way to my heart," he teased.

Her breath caught. Oh, how she wished she had known. She was being more serious than he could know when she asked, "What's that?"

"Cashew Chicken." He laughed. "Or really, any food, for that matter."

She giggled along because it was true. Mason enjoyed food.

"Let's start over then. I miss our friendship." And it was true. She hadn't let herself realize that in hoping for more with him, she'd given up on the one person she'd confided all her childhood secrets to.

They may not be destined to be together, but they would always share a special bond. She'd just have to tamp down the sexual frustration she felt around him.

They could be friends again.

She could do this.

4

Emma aced her interview, connected with the owner of the shops over their shared love of Charlottesville, and was offered the job right on the spot. She was going to take the evening to think it over, but she was leaning toward saying yes. The pay and benefits were good, and the commute would be a breeze as their main office was downtown.

On her way home, she stopped by the grocery store, which was unusually crowded, to grab ingredients for dinner and then by the ABC store to pick up a bottle of Pinot Grigio for tonight and a Cabernet Sauvignon to keep on hand. She planned to make them dinner tonight. Although she was focused on regaining her friend, she couldn't ignore the butterflies of excitement that still coursed through her anytime she was near Mason.

After buckling herself in, she started her Honda Civic and glanced up. A familiar shock of silky blonde strands caught her eyes. Kaylee. She was still as beautiful as ever. Emma knew why Mason had been drawn to her. Everyone was. She had been the cheer co-captain when Mason was a senior on the football team, and she'd been a genuinely nice person. They'd been a perfect match.

Kaylee held a toddler with hair even lighter than hers as she headed into the grocery store. She appeared to be singing to the child and had a glow on her cheeks from the cold, brisk wind. Her belly was round, and she cradled it with the hand not holding her boy.

Jealousy slammed into her, quickly replaced by happiness for Kaylee. Despite Kaylee being more than three years older than Emma, the woman had always been kind to her. Kaylee now had a beautiful family, everything Emma had always wanted, but… Mason was not living with her.

A sudden rush of cheer filled Emma's chest.

Emma put on the Christmas music she used to listen to with her mom when they would wrap presents together. She'd not been able to listen to it the last few years. Since her mom's passing and then Mason's dismissal, she'd only driven home for Christmas day to be with her father and brother, then returned to Columbus posthaste.

Nothing was the same without her mother. Bittersweet memories played in her head on the way home and she thought for the first time that it might have been hard on her dad and brother to go through the holidays with both her and her mom absent. She would do better this year and make it a holiday to remember.

Once she accepted her new position, she'd have to get out and do some holiday shopping. There were still a couple weeks to go.

The house was empty when she arrived, so she kept her music going as she moved around the kitchen, chopping vegetables for roasting, boiling potatoes for mashing, and marinating salmon for baking.

She was a glass into the Pinot Grigio and belting out "Winter Wonderland" when Mason appeared. He had a computer bag slung over his shoulder and wore glasses with ebony frames slightly darker than his thick, wavy hair. He had the college professor look down, and he was hot.

Her mouth fell open. She must appear like the awkward kid she'd been when she'd made cookies for Mason under the guise of baking them for all of her brother's friends who had been throwing around a football in the backyard.

Then, she'd not beat the sugar and eggs together well enough and accidentally gotten sugar-free chocolate chips. Her attempt had fallen flat, and not only did the cookies look like squashed, overcooked, bubbly pancake batter, but they tasted awful.

Mason had said, "I'll help you next time, Em." And he'd eaten them anyway while the rest of the boys had snuck their cookies into the waste bin.

He had helped her the next time. And treated her as the kid sister he didn't have. She'd learned two things that day: her infatuation with him was hopeless and that when you screw up a recipe, adjust and don't give up.

As a result, she had perfected this salmon recipe.

"Well, this is a beautiful sight," he said. His eyes rested on her with the tray of salmon in her hands.

"I remembered how much you like salmon."

They sat down to eat, and again, the conversation flowed. She learned about the classes he was teaching, that his parents had moved to Tampa and that his Hyundai, Old Reliable, was making weird noises and needed to go into the shop. Nostalgia needled at her as she remembered all the days she'd watched out the window, waiting for a glimpse of the champagne-colored, beat-up car he'd mowed countless lawns to purchase. Mason's dedication had always amazed her.

"What happened with you and Kaylee?" After seeing her today, Emma finally had the courage to ask.

"Oh, that was over a long time ago." Mason shrugged his shoulders. "She's married now to John Wall."

"No kidding." She was stuck on the part where he said they'd ended a long time ago.

"Yeah, they're pretty happy."

She wanted to ask if he was seeing anyone else, but that seemed a bit too far for the peace they'd recently brokered. She didn't want to fuck it up.

They'd finished and cleaned up, but she wasn't ready to go back to her room and dive into her book. She was enjoying herself.

"Want to watch a movie?"

"Hell yeah," he said. *"Die Hard?"*

She'd watched it so many years with Mason and her brother that she knew it by heart. Even if she'd rather watch something new, there was comfort in it.

"Perfect."

"I don't have class tomorrow, and we're supposed to get four to five inches tonight."

"Well, that explains the grocery store," she said.

"Was everyone rushing out for bread and milk?" His laugh was smooth and a balm to her soul.

"I think it was the whole county."

With everything else going on, she'd not looked at the weather, but with that in mind, a night inside curled up on the sofa, watching a movie, sounded like a perfect idea.

"You want to get it set up? I'm going to put on pajamas," she said.

"Sure."

Emma hurried to pull on an old t-shirt and cozy shorts, then brushed her teeth and fastened her hair into a messy bun. When she came back into the room, not only did Mason have the movie ready, but he had also changed.

Mason unfolded the large blanket that was kept in a basket by the sofa and then settled in. She should have thought to put on pajama pants and a long-sleeved shirt, but she'd been flushed from the conversation and the wine. Now, she shivered as they made it through the opening scene.

He tossed the end of the blanket toward her. "Here. I'll share."

She pursed her lips, wondering if she could handle being so close to him.

Sensing her hesitation, he said, "I'll be on good behavior."

She swallowed hard. Emma wasn't certain she could match his resolve.

Under the soft velour, she began to thaw, but her side was still cold because the edge of the blanket didn't wrap around one arm or her legs. She scooted across the cushion so that they could both enjoy the warmth without her pulling it from him.

Unfettered excitement built in her chest. The last time they'd been this near on the sofa, she'd experienced heaven. Suddenly, she wasn't paying attention to the movie or the way her heart had felt when he'd abandoned her that night long ago.

He smelled of bergamot and pine and pepper and perfection—Polo.

For her, breathing became labored. And she could swear he was focusing too hard on the movie, his breath too even and measured as if he were fighting the same urges she was.

Her hand slid over and took his. A soft sigh escaped from his throat as he accepted her fingers and cradled them as one would an heirloom crystal glass, carefully and steadily.

She struggled to control her heart, which pounded thump, thump, thump, louder than the base on the speakers. She struggled to reign in the warmth that radiated from her core. She struggled to pay attention to anything but Mason's thumb, which was making gentle caressing circles on the pulse point of her wrist. To hell with it, she wanted to lose control and the struggle.

Turning into him, she trailed her hand up and down his leg, feeling the length of tight muscle that he meticulously maintained. His breath hitched, and there was no doubt he was holding back as well. On her next swipe up, she continued all the way to his penis, where his pajama pants had tented. He was hard, and he moaned as she trailed her fingers from the base to tip.

"Em," he pleaded. "I don't want to mess things up again."

"Then don't," she responded as she rose and swung her leg over his to straddle him. When she glanced down, he was staring at her with an intense hunger in his dilated eyes. She understood. He wanted her. Wanted her as much as she needed him.

This time, she wouldn't expect him to stay. She wouldn't expect more than one night. She wouldn't expect him to change for her. She was a grown woman. She could handle the heartache, but she couldn't handle regrets. And she knew if she didn't take advantage of this situation, she would have major regrets.

Her head dropped, and she took his mouth with hers. His lips parted, and as her tongue entered his mouth, his hands slid higher and gripped onto her hips, holding her gently, but also strong enough that it seemed as if he were saying, "Don't leave me."

As her tongue dueled with his, desire exploded in every part of her body. It was as if there was no past between them, no future they had to plan. There was only right here and now and their need.

When she drew back, his eyes bore into hers as if she were the sun, lighting his universe and keeping him rotating. The thought of how much he desired her made her heady with the power of it.

"Are you sure you want this?" he questioned. His tenor was as strained and as stretched as the flannel covering his penis.

"Yes. I want this. I want you." Her voice was husky and unrecognizable.

His eyes dilated more as his brown gaze focused on her as if he were a man waiting for a life vest tossed from a ship to save him in the middle of a storm.

"Not here," he said as he coiled his arms around her waist and stood. "Wrap your legs around me."

She nodded and did as he said as he carried her down the hall. She took advantage of the moment, dipping her head to kiss and nip at his neck. He tasted of salt and honey and heaven.

When they reached her room, he slowly released her to slide down his solid form. Gooseflesh erupted on her skin as tingles of awareness, arousal, and anticipation surged through her core and limbs.

His mouth crashed down on hers, urgent and hungry and drowning with thirst. She savored every move he made as his strong hands gripped her waist, then inched up, removing her t-shirt with the action.

He pulled back from their kiss to tug the fabric over her head and toss it to the floor. In the muted lamp light, his gaze reflected heat and pinned her with a need so fierce, it sent shivers straight to her toes.

As he leaned in, his lips met hers once more, then trailed kisses across her cheek and to her neck, where he teased and licked and sucked. Fire exploded in her core as he continued and nibbled at the tip of her ear.

She gripped his sides and arched into his touch. His hands roamed, exploring her, caressing her, encompassing her, landing on the waistband of her shorts and underwear and gliding them from her body.

He drew back and feasted his eyes on her as if she were a fancy meal and he'd not eaten in a week. The approval in his stare made her feel desired and treasured.

He shed his clothes—the whole time watching her, drinking her in, lavishing her with longing and lust.

She soaked in the view and admired his form. A body forged in the gym and on the gridiron, a temple built on healthy habits and honed to sinewy perfection. Mason was a god.

Closing the distance between them, she trailed her hand across his rock-solid abs and up to his chest, where her hand rested above his heart, the thing she cherished most in the world. His eyes indicated that he felt it, too, a connection so deep that time and hurt couldn't erase or diminish it.

Then, they were a tangle of limbs, feeling, exploring, worshipping each other. He backed her to the bed and gently guided her down. She lay, and he examined her as his chest rose and fell in a beat out of time with his typical calm and cool.

She reached up for him to join her, and he gave her his smile, but it was different. The curve of his lips still melted her, but at this moment, they smoldered her insides with yearning. Then he pulled back abruptly.

"Oh, hell. Stay right there," he said, then emphasized, "Do. Not. Move." He turned and rushed from the room, returning mere seconds later with his wallet. After ripping a foil packet from the inside pocket, he tossed it across the room to her dresser.

When he climbed next to her, he groaned as he again surveyed her curves and body, memorizing the smoothness and dips and arches of her bare flesh and awakening her senses fully.

As he clasped her cheeks in his hands, he turned her face to him. "Are you certain?"

"Yes," was all she could rasp out, then her tongue darted out to wet her lips.

He nodded, then positioned himself between her legs, ripped open the package, and put on the condom.

Their eyes met, and nothing else existed.

He lowered himself. With one measured push, he was inside her, and pleasure consumed Emma. He stilled for what began as a second—then the moment stretched into a perfect moment of time where they were in sync, a snatch of time worth waiting an eternity for. Mason's hand cradled her face as he studied her, his eyes swimming with need and emotion and something that broke the wall she'd built around her heart.

With each thrust, a new emotion burst from somewhere she'd hidden inside; longing replaced by contentment, hurt replaced by hope, loss replaced by fulfillment, unreturned love replaced by unconditional love.

There was no denying it to herself. She still loved him. Always would.

She dug in, savoring each second that his pelvis rubbed against her clit, his penis filling and completing her, his passion igniting sparks of rapture.

And… she was falling into nirvana, into sated bliss.

Her breath caught and released in short, strangled gasps as she let the ecstasy pull her under. As she did, Mason's gaze fixed on her, and his strokes became erratic. It sounded as though he said, "Em," before he was panting, and his whole body went rigid with tension as he came.

Mason stayed on top of her, caressing her cheek, kissing her lips, watching her as if she were his salvation.

A few moments later, he rolled to her side and said, "Let me get rid of this." He stood and walked over to her bathroom trash, then returned and turned off the lamp.

Just as Mason was returning to the bed, a phone on her nightstand buzzed. It lit up the room like an emergency flare at a crash site.

Her chest tightened.

Fear and the rotten, festering memories of being abandoned enveloped with the stench of panic.

Mason reached for the phone.

Her eyes stung, and her stomach churned.

But she was going to be a woman now, and she'd prepared herself with no expectations for the future. Still, she'd held out hope.

The phone buzzed again.

She wanted to weep with the unfairness of it.

Mason silenced his phone and set it face down on her nightstand. Her eyes watered with joy and relief. He wouldn't take off like before. He wanted to be here with her.

He settled in and cradled her close, his arm wrapped protectively around her. "We have so much to talk about," he said.

"Tomorrow," Emma pleaded. "I just want to enjoy this right now."

"In the morning, then." He kissed the top of her head, then inhaled.

Before long, she was asleep.

And when she woke… Mason was gone.

5

Emma scoured the house. Mason was not in her brother's old room. He wasn't in the kitchen. And he wasn't in the garage, which, to her surprise, her brother had apparently turned into a home gym. What shouldn't have been a surprise was that he'd disappeared again, but somehow, deep inside, she'd thought this time would be different. That they'd grown as people. That he saw her as more than a kid. That he could envision her as something more than his best friend's little sister.

Snow blanketed the driveway except for a Hyundai-shaped patch of pavement where his car should have been.

Emma did not check social media. That had ended poorly last time. And Emma would lose her mind if she found him on someone else's account this morning, his arm wrapped around another woman when he should be cradling her.

After deciding she'd been childish the first time by ignoring him, she picked up her phone and searched for Mason. The old text stream materialized, and her eyes watered. He'd said they needed to talk. She'd not addressed her hurt then and buried it like a dead body under a mound of dirt, not wanting to perform an autopsy to discover what had happened.

She was done playing the uncaring coroner. She did care.

She typed out, "I'm ready to talk," and pressed the arrow.

Minutes went by.

No reply.

Hours went by.

No reply.

Time became a jumbled mess of slowing and speeding up and not moving at all.

Emma had to get her mind on something else, so she retrieved her book and settled in on the sofa to be swept away, but even her favorite author couldn't keep the pain at bay.

Riley jumped onto the sofa and meowed before claiming a spot on Emma's lap. "Where did he go, Riley?"

He answered with a hearty murrrrrr, murrrr, murrrrr.

She checked her phone.

No reply.

She texted, *where are you?*

No reply.

Once she had turned on the TV, she restarted the movie. But instead of getting lost in the story, it reminded her of what she and Mason had just done. Again. As the movie played out, she closed her eyes and counted her breaths—anything to calm the anxiety that had taken root and grown like morning glory, a beautiful weed climbing onto the framework of the life she'd hoped to rebuild.

She woke to yells and gunshots on the TV.

But she was no longer sitting on the sofa. She was lying down, and her head was cradled in Mason's lap. He watched the movie, but his fingers threaded her hair and messaged her scalp.

He glanced down and gave her that smile. She melted.

For a moment, she leaned into his touch, welcoming the comfort of his attentions. But then she remembered the pain of rejection as it seeped into the surreal scene. The pent-up frustration and fear had fomented and forged with the hurt feelings of the past. Her heart metastasized and morphed into a blob of anger.

"Where were you?" she asked.

"I wanted to let you sleep." His voice was smooth and soothing, innocent and enticing.

"Oh," was all she could say as she let the years of regrets coalesce into a cool façade. She sat up, then jumped to her feet. She needed distance between them to think.

Mason continued, "It's almost the end of the semester, and I have essays to grade. When I opened my bag, they weren't there, so I ran to my office to get them."

"But you were gone for hours." Emma crossed her arms, hugging herself.

"I know. Old Reliable died, and I had to walk to a shop to get them to tow it."

"But you could have called." Her calm demeanor had broken, and even she could hear the hurt in her voice.

"I would have, but I left my phone on your nightstand, and I didn't have your number memorized." Mason stood and stepped toward her as if he wanted to ease the worry lines she imagined were streaking across her forehead.

"You didn't go to your ex's?"

"Why would I do that?" He blinked and appeared taken aback.

"That's what you did last time." The bitter words flew from her lips like a predator swooping to collect a helpless baby bunny in a wide-open field. The accusation cut to her heart and dredged up the old pain.

His brow crinkled, and his irises sharpened as if he were reaching back for unclaimed memories. The confusion marring his lovely features couldn't be faked. Mason had no idea what she was talking about. And somehow... that made it hurt more.

"What are you talking about?" he asked.

"Kaylee."

Mason's puzzled look deepened, and he held his palms up as if to say, "What's the big deal?"

Emma continued, "Our night meant so much to you that you ran out to party with her as soon as we'd—" She couldn't finish. Her chin scrunched, and she sniffed. Her shoulders collapsed in as she fought back tears. She would not cry in front of him.

"That's not what happened," he protested.

"She shared it. You had your arm wrapped around her, and she called you her hero."

"I don't understand. You ghosted me." Now Mason's tone amplified.

"What was I supposed to do? You said you were sorry about what happened, and you ran off to Kaylee."

"Kaylee and I weren't together," he insisted.

Emma pulled out her phone and scrolled to Kaylee's account, swiping past years of baby, marriage, and engagement pictures until she reached the image that had destroyed her heart. She held it up for Mason to see. He squinted.

"Kaylee and I were friends."

"That's not what it looked like. We were together, and then you left me to answer her text."

"It was John who texted. Kaylee's car had run off the road, and he was worried she was hurt."

"John Wall?"

"Yes, that's who she was dating. They were already engaged."

Emma's face burned. Had she made a mistake?

"When I got there, she was fine, but I had to go home. We needed Dad's truck with the hitch to pull her car out of the ditch."

"Why didn't you come back and tell me?" Emma asked as she sank back onto the sofa.

"It was daylight by the time I got home, and I was covered in mud. I took a shower and fell asleep trying to figure out how to justify my actions to you and to Andrew."

"What do you mean?"

Mason sat next to her and shook his head. He inhaled, then met her gaze, pinning her with his sincerity.

"I'd betrayed my friend and slept with his sister on his sofa while he snoozed in the other room."

The silence boomed as his rationalization rammed her with the reality of that night.

"I was sorry I'd not told you what you meant to me. I was sorry I'd not taken better care of you. I was sorry I'd been disloyal to my friend, but the one thing I wasn't sorry about was the way I felt for you."

A tear slid down her cheek. Queasiness oozed in her belly. He'd texted that they needed to talk, and she'd run away like a frightened child. She'd been so afraid she'd been relegated back to a friend that she'd not even given him the chance to explain.

"And I left town." Emma's stomach twisted with a sudden stab of shame.

"I'd known for years that you were the person I wanted to be with, but you were my best friend's sister and still in high school. Then you were off in Ohio, and you were grieving for your mom."

"I'm so sorry," she whispered.

"I had wanted to tell you what you meant to me and make our first time perfect, but instead, I lost control and was embarrassed. When you didn't return my texts and calls, I thought you didn't want me."

She took Mason's hand and stared straight into his brown eyes. "I've always wanted you."

He gave her that smile and twined his fingers with hers.

"How do you feel now?" she asked.

"Like I want to start over. Like you and I deserve a shot. Like we should do things right."

Emma nodded. The tight knot of rope that had constricted around her chest loosened, and a dizzying, thrilling lightness lifted her up to the skies.

Mason continued, "One night, after a few shots of whisky, I came clean to Andrew. I told him everything—how you'd broken my heart and how sorry I was for not telling him how I felt about you. He said he'd always known, but he was going to let us handle it without his interference."

"Maybe this is the one time he should have interfered." A giggle escaped from the back of her throat.

"Or maybe we should have both spoken up sooner." Mason dipped his head to rest it on hers.

"Agreed. We will have to work on our communication," she said, then she tilted her chin up and claimed his lips with hers.

The connection between them sizzled and popped, sending sparks sliding down her spine and out in every direction. Satisfaction seeped into her soul on the very sofa where she'd found salvation and sorrow and now, sweet serenity and faith in a man she'd assumed long lost.

After the kiss, Emma relaxed, nestling near Mason. He draped his arm around her shoulder and drew her close. Hope for a future together blossomed in her heart. It was tentative and new but at least they had the chance to see what might grow between them.

She took his hand in hers and they talked about the past, the present, and precious memories yet to come.

At a pause in their conversation, she examined her emotions. Shock and awe and elation zipped through her veins. Emma was back in the town she adored, ready to start a promising job, and getting a new chance with the man she'd spent most of her life pining for. Okay... so the apartment hunting and roommate question was still up in the air, but she was happy right here for now.

It seemed too good to be true. Then, she remembered she hadn't asked him one very important question.

"Are you dating anyone now?" she asked.

"Yes. Yes, I am," he said, drawing her hand to his chest and resting it above his heart.

"You, Em. It's always been you."

Lori Ann Bailey

Lori Ann Bailey is a best-selling author and winner of the National Readers' Choice Award and Holt Medallion for Best First Book and Best Historical. Lori writes brawny highland heroes and strong-willed independent lasses finding their perfect matches in the Highlands of historic Scotland. When not writing, reading or sharing her love of history and romance, Lori enjoys time with her real-life hero and four kids or spending time walking or drinking wine with friends. Lori adores hearing from readers on Facebook and Instagram. Please visit Lori on her website to sign up for her monthly newsletter.

https://loriannbailey.com/

Also by Lori Ann Bailey
Highland Pride Series:

Highland Deception

Highland Redemption

Highland Temptation

Highland Salvation

Highland Obligation

Highland Misfits Series:

To Have a Highland Thief

To Covet a Highland Criminal

To Save a Highland Sinner

Surrender of a Highland Smuggler

The Highland Knight's Revenge

The Highland Guard and His Lady

True Love Delayed

J.T. Bock

1

The right side of his house stood intact. The left side had crumpled under a tree uprooted from his front yard.

Finn couldn't find a better metaphor for his life. Career perfectly erected. Personal life flattened.

"It's a disaster," he said to his friend Mandy, standing on the pavement in front of his half house.

"Could be worse," she said.

"A tree squashed my home."

"You could've been inside when it fell."

His neighbors had reported that the tree fell around 5:30 p.m., during a freak rainstorm. Had he been home, he would've been in his bedroom changing for his evening run after stocking the kitchen for his daughter's stay. Fortunately, the kitchen—along with his favorite pans—hadn't been destroyed like the rest. He'd never been as grateful to a client for keeping him late at work.

So, yes, it could've been worse. But that didn't solve his other predicament.

"In two hours, I pick up Ana from Susan's. If my ex learns I have no home, she'll keep Ana for the rest of the summer."

A year ago, his ex-wife had accepted a job in Finn's hometown. He'd moved across country from Virginia, where he'd lived for the past eighteen years, back home to be near his daughter. Last month, Ana had been traveling with her mom and stepdad—the longest he'd been apart from her since the divorce.

Finn had spent that time furnishing Ana's bedroom—now obliterated, like her planned stay.

"Still nothing to rent?" Mandy asked.

Finn shook his head.

Mandy and her husband had offered their couch until he could find a short-term rental. Nothing was available and he'd run out of time.

Chainsaws revved. The contractors began the arduous task of extracting the tree from Finn's house before estimating the damage.

Mandy led him across the street to his car.

"With the biggest pop culture convention in town, I knew it would be difficult," she said.

"Short-term rentals and hotels are booked through next week. The only places available are over an hour outside the city." And away from his job and Ana's theater camp. "I just need someplace until the con ends."

"I have an idea."

"I'll take it."

"Hear me out first."

"I'll take it. I'm in a bind."

"Then I'll let Robin know you're coming."

"Wait, what? *Robin?*"

"Yes, Robin. My sister, your old girlfriend. The one you've been avoiding."

"I haven't been avoiding her. Between moving, starting a job, and having a tree crush my hopes, I didn't have time."

"Right, in the year since moving here, you've had no time."

How he'd missed that Wright sisters' sarcasm. "We didn't part on the best terms."

"No need to tell me. After you broke up, she didn't sleep or eat for days."

He hated to be reminded of the pain he'd caused. "You're making my point."

"I'm joking, sort of. I found bowls of half-eaten mac and cheese in her room, so she didn't starve."

"She hates me."

"She can't hate her first love."

"Which is why she never returned my calls or replied to my letters?"

Finn had never hated Robin, had never stopped wishing for a reunion in their first year apart. Then he'd met Susan and had a child, and eighteen years had passed in an instant.

"She's stubborn. Besides, you're friends on Facebook."

"That doesn't mean anything." He lurked through her feed, never commenting, afraid she wouldn't respond.

"You aren't to blame for what happened. You were at different places in life. Plus, if Robin hasn't forgiven you, why did she agree to let you stay?"

"You asked her?"

"This morning, but based on your expression, you don't believe me."

"I don't believe she agreed willingly."

"Maybe she wouldn't have, if she didn't need the money."

"What's wrong?" Not that he should be surprised. Robin had never excelled at bookkeeping. Finn had planned to manage Robin's business after he became a CPA. Then his father had died, and his mother had needed him more than Robin, it seemed.

"It's not her fault. Christopher—"

"Her boyfriend?" Occasionally, photos of a man sporting a scraggy goatee and long hair crossed his socials from Robin's page. Finn ignored them, or tried to.

"Boyfriend *and* business partner. He stole her clients and assistant, stiffed her on rent."

"I'll pay whatever she needs." And more, if it meant mending the rift between them.

"What she really needs is a friend."

He could use another as well. Being in his home city again, going to the places he used to frequent with Robin, highlighted how alone he was.

"Considering how I left things between us, I don't know where to start."

"You said you'd come back to her, and you're here now."

"I also told her to grow up."

"Trust me, she's forgotten about that," Mandy said.

———

"You know what he said before he left?" Robin shoved random pots into a kitchen cabinet.

"That he'd come back—"

"To grow up!" She cut off Mandy's response on her way to the living room.

Robin scooped up several costumes stacked on her sofa for clients attending *the* ComicCon this weekend.

"I thought you cleaned?"

"I did." Robin balanced the armful of costumes. She kicked open the door to her office/sewing room/whatever-didn't-fit-anywhere-else room. She tossed them onto a chair and shut the door.

"I vacuumed, dusted, cleaned the bathrooms."

Robin scowled when Mandy rubbed her fingertips along the one or two or, okay, three spots she missed while dusting.

She nabbed a rogue fabric scrap from the floor and uncovered sealed condom packets that she remembered tossing out. Robin dusted the coffee table with the scrap. Then she stuffed it and the condoms into her back pocket.

"I cleaned and disinfected Rodent's room."

"Rodent?"

"Don't make me say his name."

"Okay."

"I took his remaining stuff to Goodwill."

"That must've been hard. I could've helped," Mandy said.

"It's been seven months. Time to move on. It was cathartic, really."

Especially when she'd sold his collectibles for less than they were worth but enough to pay the rent he owed her.

"What about your old room?" Mandy asked.

"What about it? Finn's sleeping in your old bedroom, where Rodent slept. The finished costumes are in my old space."

"Oh."

"Oh?" Robin arched a brow at her sister's odd tone.

The doorbell ding-donged off-key. She meant to fix that. Meant to fix many things when the ex was here and she'd the time and money to do it. Through the window by the door, Robin caught sight of Finn's hand holding a frying pan.

Did he think she wasn't grown enough to have pans?

Her hand both itched to open the door and shook at the idea of opening the same door she'd slammed in his face eighteen years ago.

Mandy grabbed the doorknob. Probably doubting Robin would let him in.

She elbowed Mandy aside, plastered on a smile, and swung open the door.

"Hey, Neighbor Boy ..." She lost her words, shocked by Finn's pressed gray suit, steel-colored tie, and starched white shirt—a far cry from the thread-bare t-shirt and ripped jeans he'd worn the last time she'd seen him. Wavy black hair that used to fall to his shoulders was now cropped at the sides. A few curls escaped the mounds of gel he must have used to keep it down. Far from the boy she'd grown up with, Finn was a handsome man.

"Hello." He smiled then hesitated.

Robin sensed he wasn't sure what was appropriate: handshake, hug, or simple hello.

Crossing her arms, she made the choice for him.

"What's that?" Robin pointed.

"My daughter." He moved aside to reveal a young teen. A felt cap sewn with purple flowers covered black hair like Finn's. Her fingers tapping on the screen of the cellphone she held, she didn't notice—or pretended not to notice—the adults watching her.

"Not that. Although we'll get to *that* in a minute." Robin side-eyed Mandy, who scurried into the living room. "In your hand."

"My frying pan?"

"Why do you have it?"

"It's the best pan for frying sausages. The surface cooks evenly—"

"You didn't think I'd have a pan?"

"Of course you do."

"But not this special pan."

"Do you have one of these?"

"Is it expensive?"

"Yes."

"Then no."

Next to him was a suitcase and next to that his daughter.

"I don't have one of these either." She nodded at the girl.

"Too expensive?" He flashed a grin.

"Among other things." Robin graced him with a half-smile. She couldn't let herself get comfortable. He was only here for a few days, not the rest of her life.

"This is Ana."

"Anastasia." The girl pocketed her phone then held out her hand to Robin.

"Great name." As they shook hands, Robin admired the teen's fingerless gloves, the same purple flower pattern as her hat.

"That's why I don't use Ana anymore." She shot her dad an exasperated look.

"Did you make your hat and gloves?" Robin asked.

Anastasia nodded.

"They're lovely. Nice, even stitching on the flower details."

"Thanks. I just started playing around."

"Robin creates costumes for cosplayers. Remember? I told you in the car," Finn said.

"I've worked on theatre and movie productions too," Robin added.

"Awesome!" Anastasia's face lit up. Robin found herself excited as well. Something she hadn't felt about her work since it, well, became work.

"Hey, you're dressed alike." Finn's gaze swung from his daughter to Robin.

In unison, they scanned each other's outfits. Dark jeans (Anastasia's baggy), black Converse (Robin's worn), and Nirvana concert shirt (both new). The shirt memorialized a concert that Finn and Robin had wanted to see with Mandy. But they couldn't afford it and were too young to attend anyway.

"Why are you still outside?" Mandy came up behind Robin. "Come in."

"Yes, come into *my* home," Robin clarified. "You'll find it hasn't changed or grown up at all."

Finn sighed and brought Ana's suitcase into the house. So much for Robin forgetting what he'd last said to her.

Stepping inside transported Finn back in time. Instantly, he felt comfortable, as if almost two decades hadn't passed.

He wanted to express this sentiment to Robin. Instead, he said, "You're right. Your parents' house is the same."

Mandy groaned.

"*My* house," Robin replied. "The sofa and TV are new. We also removed the wall to the kitchen to open the space."

There were other changes too. Flanking the flatscreen TV, built-in bookshelves overflowed with vintage toys jostling for space around books. Her parents' landscapes hung amongst fantasy posters, displayed as art on the limited wall space.

The compact living room started at the door to her dad's old office on the left and stretched into the kitchen where a two-seater dinette filled the kitchen's center.

"Whoa!" Moving past the sofa to place his frying pan on the dinette, Finn slipped on a fabric scrap.

Robin touched her back pocket before picking it up.

"I cleaned before you arrived."

"You did?" Finn joked. Robin's pride was her costuming, not housework.

Both sisters and Ana glared at him.

Finn retreated to his car for groceries and luggage filled with new clothes. After hanging up his blazer, he set his suitcase in the alcove and the bag of groceries in the kitchen. Then he looked for Robin to inquire about their rooms and noticed she and Ana were missing.

"Where are they?" he asked Mandy.

"Upstairs." She stopped him from going up. "I didn't mention Ana."

"Why?"

"Didn't want to complicate things."

"Maybe we'll stay outside the city after all."

Raucous laughter exploded from the second floor. Ana hadn't laughed like that since before the divorce.

Finn raced upstairs and down the narrow hall, skidding to a stop at Robin's childhood bedroom. Mannequins in various stages of dress crowded the room. Movie posters and photos papered the walls. The wood floor hidden under fabric scraps, pins—he scooped those up—and beads needed a good vacuuming.

Her wrought iron bed was pushed against one wall like he remembered.

"Dad, Robin said I could sleep here."

"On that bed?" His face burned with a memory never to be shared with his daughter.

"I'll move my stuff." Robin gathered up the material piled on the mattress.

Walking past him, she whispered, "It's a new mattress. If you recall, the springs gave out on the old one."

He ran his hand over his face to mask his discomfort. His ex-wife would hate this place. His mother—he shook his head at what she'd say—didn't need to know.

"It needs dusting. Your allergies—"

"Whatever." Ana sniffed.

He began picking up costume debris. "Let's move these mannequins to give you room."

"Dad, these are superheroes. Badass women."

"Language."

"Only saying what Robin said."

"Don't do that." Especially if her grandmother heard her. "What were you laughing about?"

"Yeah, that." She squeezed behind a mannequin clothed in a skin-tight Westley costume from *The Princess Bride* movie. "Check it out." Ana unpinned a Polaroid from the wall and handed it to him.

The summer before college he'd dressed as Dr. Frank-N-Furter and Robin as Magenta from *The Rocky Horror Picture Show* for the same pulp culture convention, albeit much smaller, as the one in town this week. That was the night their relationship changed in this bedroom.

Three years before his father died and everything changed again.

"Isn't it funny?" Ana's grin faded when he didn't laugh. "I thought you'd like it."

"I do."

"No, you don't. You're not even smiling. You used to be fun. What happened?"

"Life happened," Robin replied for Finn, as she entered with a vacuum in tow and a feather duster sticking out of her back pocket.

"Here." She exchanged the photo for the duster.

After pinning it back to the wall, she gave the photo a wistful look. "Your dad had great legs."

Ana squealed in a mix of delight and embarrassment then flopped onto the mattress. Finn wanted to crawl under it.

"You dust. I'll vacuum," he said to Ana.

Ignoring him, she ran from the room after Robin.

"As you wish." He rolled up his sleeves.

"Whatcha doing?"

After she'd dropped that comment about his legs, Robin didn't need to embarrass herself more. "Hiding from your father."

"Me too." Anastasia jumped down the final two steps to the first floor.

Robin shoved her office door open.

"Cleaning that room next?" Mandy asked from the sofa, where she was replying to a text.

"I'm going to work." Robin took in the haphazard piles of props, costumes, and unopened bills and wished for a tree to smash her house too.

"Can I help?" Anastasia asked.

"I'm beyond help."

The vacuum whirled to life from the second floor. Anastasia slid past Robin and into the office.

"Since everyone's settled, I'll go. The kids texted they're finished at soccer practice." Mandy headed for the door.

From inside the office, Anastasia sneezed.

Robin opened two windows behind her desk. She retrieved a box of tissues from the windowsill.

"Here." She handed Anastasia the box.

"I'm fine. Grandmom makes a fuss but it's nothing."

Robin believed that. Finn's mother could make a volcano out of an anthill if it got her attention.

The front door shut.

"Be right back." Robin left Anastasia, eyeing a crown perched on a chair, and hurried after Mandy.

In the alcove, she tripped over a suitcase and into Finn's blazer hanging on a hook next to her sweater. His cologne, the same woodsy and bergamot scent she'd gifted him years ago, clung to it. She tossed it over the suitcase so the smell wouldn't infect her stuff.

She reached the porch as Mandy stepped off. "I should never have agreed to this."

"It's only for a weekend."

"I have deadlines. The con first, then the play. It's only me now." After Rodent had left, taking her assistant with him, she'd struggled to find time to shower let alone host houseguests.

"You already put Finn to work. I'm sure he can help with cooking or —" she wriggled her eyebrows "—storming castle drains."

"Excuse me?"

"Cleaning your pipes, furnace, that dank basement filled with cobwebs."

"My cobwebs have been cleared, furnace filter changed, and pipes drained. I don't need a man for that."

"Sounds painful."

Robin rolled her eyes. "I need to focus on work."

Mandy gave her an overly sympathetic look. "I understand how hard it is. Finn is fit. And he still wears that cologne you gave him."

"Didn't notice."

"I'm sure you didn't."

Robin stalked down the steps. "I don't know what you're playing at, sis, but—"

The front door banged open. Anastasia shouted, "Robin!"

"What's wrong?" The teen's frantic tone set Robin on guard as if the IRS was calling.

"My grandmother wants to talk to you."

"Mrs. Cary?" She'd rather be audited.

"And I'm out." Mandy hurried along the driveway, disappearing around Robin's van.

Anastasia shoved the phone into Robin's hand. Mrs. Cary's polished face filled the screen.

Oh, joy. The woman was wielding FaceTime to check on them.

"Hello, Mrs. Cary."

"It's Mrs. Guest."

Robin had forgotten she'd remarried a year before Finn married.

"Right, Mrs. Guest."

"How are you, Robin?"

"Busy."

"I see. Ana showed me your office."

"It's not normally like that," she lied. "Once this convention wraps—"

"Maybe Finn should take Ana back to Susan's, as much as I despise that woman."

Robin stepped onto the lawn away from Anastasia in case Mrs. Guest said anything more about Susan.

"No," Robin said with a conviction that surprised herself.

Mrs. Guest's eyebrows shot up. "You're Finn's ex-girlfriend."

"From eighteen years ago. We were best friends before that."

"He's a father now."

"And?"

"You never left your childhood home."

"I bought the house from my parents when they retired. Properties are expensive here."

"You're still playing dress-up, I understand."

"I own a professional costume business." One that did well, until Rodent had stolen half her clients.

But this woman didn't deserve an explanation about Robin's life. In the decades she'd lived next door, she'd never bothered with Robin's family. She'd carried herself like a rose amongst buttercups, afraid their pollen would pollute her delicate petals.

As children, Robin had felt for Finn, struggling to meet his mom's expectations and become a copy of his doting dad.

"Just admit that you've never grown up."

Oh, no, she didn't. "What did you say?"

"Robin?" Finn came up behind her.

Turning, she tossed him the phone.

"Mom, what do you want?" he demanded.

Robin strode across the lawn and back up the porch steps to where Anastasia waited with her arms crossed.

"Sorry, Grandmother can be a bitch."

Robin took a deep breath. She wasn't about to correct Anastasia's language when she thought the same thing. But she could share what had taken her a decade to conclude. "People say things they don't realize are cruel when they're scared."

"Scared of what?"

"Losing control."

Her son and granddaughter had moved over a thousand miles away from her. Now they were rooming with someone she had never approved of.

Even more, Mrs. Guest disapproved of Finn cosplaying, the one way he would rebel against his mom. Where he could try on a fantastical life of his choosing.

This thought gave Robin an idea.

"I could use your help with something." She motioned Anastasia inside.

Finn cut across the lawn, following the same path his teenage self had taken to visit with his girlfriend. Although this time, it wasn't for a make-out session, but to apologize for his mother.

She'd lectured him on how bad it looked for her granddaughter to stay with his ex-girlfriend. His stomach turned, imagining what his mother had said to Robin.

During his divorce, Finn had started therapy. The discussions had moved from Susan to his mother and then Robin. He'd wondered whether his mother saw his free-spirited father in Robin. His dad had played in a jazz band until he'd married his mother who'd settled him into a level-headed career in accounting. Maybe his mother feared she couldn't change Robin like she had his father. Maybe she feared Finn would float off if not kept grounded.

Maybe she was a narcissist.

The therapist had never confirmed which before he moved. However, those sessions gave him the confidence to finally say what *he* wanted to his mother.

He'd informed her they were staying.

Finn only hoped Robin still wanted them to stay.

He discovered her placing a crown on Ana's head in the office. Hanging on a wall to their right, a television displayed a scene from *The Princess Bride* with the character Buttercup wearing the same prop.

Nirvana's *Come as You Are* played in the background.

"Your daughter liked the t-shirt but didn't know the band. I'm rectifying that."

"They rock." Ana bobbed her head to the song. Robin righted the crown before it fell.

"Don't move."

Ana straightened and lifted her chin imitating the actor's regal pose.

Robin glanced from Ana to the television.

"Looks perfect," Finn said.

"Thanks. I finished gluing the stones last night." She lifted it from Ana's head then put it in a hatbox.

Robin opened her laptop, set atop paperwork scattered across the surface of the wide desk that had belonged to her father.

"Do you need help with costumes?" Ana asked.

"I'm finished sewing. But if you're here next week, I'm starting a new job and could use you."

"Will we be here, Dad?" Ana asked.

"If Robin allows it."

"Then your mother gave you permission to spend the night?" Robin smirked.

"No, but I don't care," Finn replied.

"Can you pack up this crown?" Robin asked Ana.

A printer hidden behind a box of tissue paper churned out a label, which she handed to Ana. "Cushion the crown with tissue, close it up, then affix this label to it."

Ana did what she was asked. He'd never seen his teen so eager to work.

"Let's pack the other costumes from this movie next," Robin said.

"What movie?"

"The one on the screen."

Ana shrugged.

"It's the red dress and black pirate shirt from *The Princess Bride*. Finn and I used to—" Her cheeks flushed the same red of the dress draped over a chair.

His face was probably as red from a memory of Robin wearing the dress, the fabric sliding along his face when he lifted the skirt to find she hadn't worn any underwear.

Finn moved to the far end of the desk.

"I thought this was Raven from UltraSecurity." Ana pointed to the black shirt next to the dress.

"That's upstairs and totally different. He's a superhero and the Dread Pirate Roberts, aka Westley, is ... wait a minute, have you *never* seen *The Princess Bride*?"

"Never," Ana said.

"Really, Finn?"

He tore his attention from overdue tax notices sticking out from a pile of mail.

"What?"

"Your daughter hasn't seen our favorite ... uh ... this classic movie?"

"My mom isn't into movies," his daughter replied.

"What she said," Finn added.

"Another thing to rectify while you're here." Robin opened an empty box and folded the red dress inside. "These costumes are for a play based on the movie that they're previewing at the con. I'll take you when it opens."

"I'd like that."

"Ana." When his daughter didn't acknowledge him, Finn said, "*Anastasia,* can you unpack the groceries in the kitchen so I can start dinner?"

His daughter looked at her new boss—not her father—to give her leave. Robin nodded and she left.

"Do you have dinner plans?" Finn asked.

"No time." Robin stared at her laptop and hit the delete key multiple times.

"In that case, I'm making a special dinner to thank you for hosting us."

"Whatever you want." Her fingers flew over the keys, gaze focused on her screen.

Finn stood next to the desk, trying to find a reason to stay. Being in this room enveloped him in such an ease that he swore it was only yesterday that they had their final fight.

"Ah, your check."

Robin stopped typing to watch him reach into his pocket then hand her the check.

"This is too much." She tried to give it back. He sidestepped her.

"No, it's not. Given the rents in this city, that's a bargain."

With a sigh, Robin slumped into her chair. "Mandy told you what Rodent did?"

"Who?"

"Christopher. He stole clients, but I have loyal ones left," she made a sweeping motion with her hand, "Financially, I'm okay now."

"But you're late with your taxes." He grabbed an envelope from the desk. "The fees will add up. I can help and talk to the IRS, get them lowered."

She snatched it from his hand and tore it open. "Rodent swore he paid this. I didn't know it was there."

"We can fix it."

"We? You're not my accountant."

She tossed the notice onto her desk. Her eyes watered. Instinctively, he reached to comfort her.

Robin held up her hand for him to stop. "More proof that I've never grown up, huh?"

"I didn't say—"

"You did when you left. And your mom just said it to me."

"I'm sorry for what she said. For what I said then. You never gave me the chance to apologize."

"Then it's my fault?"

"No, that's not—"

"I got your letters. Mandy read them to me when I refused to open them."

"Then you know, you knew."

"You made your choice. You chose to leave."

"I told you I'd come back."

"You're late."

Ana bounded into the room oblivious to the tension. "Everything's unpacked. I'm hungry. When are we eating?"

"In a minute," he replied, then said to Robin, "I may be late, but am I *too* late?"

She didn't answer, so he took it as a positive.

"I'll start dinner. Is there anything I should know about the kitchen?"

"It's old and small, and the appliances are overtaxed like me." She turned back to her laptop, dismissing him as she began typing.

Finn asked his daughter, "Can you help with dinner?"

"Do you need me?" she asked Robin.

"Not now. I must review my late taxes, thanks to Neighbor Boy."

"Neighbor Boy?" Ana glanced from Robin to Finn.

"What Robin used to call me," he said.

"I never stopped." Robin continued typing.

Finn kept his composure when he wanted to pump his fist in victory from the office to the kitchen. Robin never stopped using her beloved nickname for him. She'd never reverted to a disparaging one like with those she hated.

A sign that she still cared?

He hoped so. Because being in her presence confirmed another thing he'd considered during his therapy sessions.

That he was still in love with Robin.

———

While Finn cooked dinner, Robin sorted through notices buried on the far end of her desk, where Rodent used to manage the books.

Or not manage the books as these late fees proved.

She stared at the inconceivable numbers—the interest was more than the original taxes—but considered something else inconceivable.

Finn apologizing to her in person—and Robin forgiving him in person.

Well, not *saying* she forgave him, but admitting she'd never stopped calling him Neighbor Boy.

For years after he left, Mandy had begged Robin to forgive Finn. Now she could admit—again, not out loud—that her 24-year-old self hadn't been mature enough to unpack her stubborn anger and forgive him.

She had been afraid of Finn leaving again, breaking her heart again, choosing his mom over her again. Robin's parents, both painters, had set aside their art for soul-depleting corporate jobs with benefits and money. Mandy, a talented writer, had followed suit until she'd married and quit to raise children.

Robin didn't want to wait until retirement to create art. Sacrificing stability, she'd turned her hobby into a business until a poor partner choice threatened it.

She laid her head on top of the tax notice. Her laptop dinged with a message.

"No!"

The actor hired as Raven to promote the UltraSecurity series at the con had dropped out. His replacement was taller and—she checked the measurements against the new ones—broader. The fabric stretched, but it might not be enough.

"Dinner is served." Finn carried in a plate piled with cheesy noodles.

"I'm not hungry." Her stomach growled, giving away her lie. "Okay, I'll have some."

Finn set down a fork and the plate.

Her mouth watered. "What's this?"

"An adult version of our favorite dish, macaroni and cheese with hot dogs."

"I haven't eaten this since ..." Since he'd left.

The sumptuous cheesy noodles and chopped sausages—not hot dogs—beckoned Robin to shut up and eat.

"You've never had this version. I made it from scratch with aged cheddar and Gruyère."

"Not Velveeta?"

"Absolutely not."

She speared the meat with her fork. "This isn't a hot dog."

"It's homemade chicken sausage."

"How'd you learn to cook so well?"

"Susan and I took cooking classes when we first dated. I loved it and kept going after we were married."

Robin dragged the plate closer. She took a bite, then another.

"After Anastasia was born, I learned how processed our foods are. I cook from scratch when I can. Although that," he motioned to her dinner, "isn't healthy nor wholly unprocessed."

"But it is delicious." Robin scraped her plate clean.

"I didn't mean to upset you." Finn took her plate.

She glanced at the tax notice she'd used as a placemat. Melted cheese stuck to its edge.

"It's fine."

"Not that. But it isn't fine, and we will fix it."

There was the "we" again. This time it didn't bother her.

"I want us to be friends again. Anastasia even asked if we could stay with you through the summer instead of finding another place to rent."

Robin started to respond yes but didn't want to appear eager. "Let's see how it goes."

"I'm not asking. I wouldn't impose for that long. I just wanted you to know you've made an impression on her."

"It's no imposition. I could use the money from a housemate, especially given these bills."

"Can we call a truce then?" He held out his arm like they had when they were young imitating the arm shake used by warriors in their beloved fantasy films.

She rose and grasped his forearm. They stood, gripping each other's arm longer than the five seconds usually allotted.

Robin let go first, scared at how she instinctively began pulling him closer.

Finn turned to leave. But after rereading the email on her screen, she stopped him.

"You're 5'11", right?"

"I am."

Robin slid papers and scraps around her desk until she uncovered the tape measure.

"Turn around." She took the plate from his hand and set it on a box.

"What are you doing?"

She unwound the tape across his back. "You're the same size as the new actor playing Raven."

"So?"

"Anastasia, can you help me with a costume in your room?" Robin called out.

The teen appeared in the doorway. "The UltraSecurity ones?"

"Yes, I want your dad to try one on."

"What?" Finn and Anastasia exclaimed.

"The original actor dropped out. Your dad is about the size of the replacement."

"This will be good." His daughter chuckled.

Finn grimaced.

"Dad, come on. You could stand a glow up."

"Yeah, dad," Robin joined in.

Although she did enjoy Finn in the shorts and tank he'd changed into before dinner. His legs still had it.

"I was going for a run."

"Wait until after the fitting. Don't want you stinking up the costume."

"You used to like my stink." He leaned into her as she walked by.

Robin sniffed him. "Is that the cologne I gave you?"

"The only one that ever worked on me."

Smiling, Robin darted upstairs before she read more into his comment than what he meant.

With Anastasia assisting, she removed the costume from the mannequin, then handed it to Finn.

"They're small." He held the shirt and pants up.

"They stretch."

His daughter shooed him across the hall to his room.

"No photos!" He shut the door.

Robin and Anastasia shared a giggle and went downstairs. She turned on the overhead light in her office. Underneath it, they cleared a space for a circular platform where Finn could stand so she could measure and make any adjustments.

"I don't know," Finn said from outside the room.

"What don't you know?" Robin asked.

"If I'm supposed to look this good."

He leapt into the doorway and flexed his arms and legs under the skintight outfit. A black robber-style mask wrapped around his eyes.

His daughter burst out laughing.

Robin's jaw dropped. The new actor might be out of work.

She fanned herself then tried to recover by batting her hand toward the platform. "Enough posing, Raven. Get over here."

"Raven?" He sprang onto the stand.

"The character you're cosplaying as."

"I'm not a sexy Westley?"

"Raven is a hero from the UltraSecurity series." Robin rolled a cart of sewing supplies closer.

"Never heard of it."

"Not many have. He's a thief, but not like my ex. Raven steals stolen artifacts and returns them to the rightful owners. Not clients and my assistant like Rodent did. Although he was fu—" She stopped herself from saying an R-rated word. "Dating her behind my back."

"What a dick!" Anastasia exclaimed.

"Language," Finn corrected, then to Robin, "What she said."

Dings from phone texts sounded from the kitchen.

Anastasia felt her jeans pockets before sprinting to the kitchen. She grabbed her phone from the dinette.

The doorbell rang.

"Are you expecting someone?" Finn asked Robin.

"No."

Anastasia ran to answer the door. Finn hopped down to intercept her.

"Wait!"

But she was too fast. As Robin entered the vestibule, an unfamiliar teen girl chirped, "What is your dad wearing?"

Finn's face flamed red.

The young teen let out a nervous giggle.

Anastasia explained, "He's helping Robin fit a costume for the con. Oh, and that's Robin."

Robin waved hello.

The girl seemed unsure how to respond. She glanced at Anastasia for direction.

"Why is Mel here?" Finn crossed his arms.

"I was supposed to spend the night at her house and go to camp with her tomorrow."

"You never told me."

"I texted her when we got here, because I wasn't sure."

"Wasn't sure about what?"

Anastasia looked down. "If I'd like Robin. But she's cool. Now I want to stay."

"My mom's going to be mad. She rented a movie for us and got your favorite doughnuts for breakfast," Mel said.

Finn took out his phone. Where he'd been keeping it in the skintight costume, Robin had no idea.

"Let me ask your mom." He stepped into the living room, leaving Robin with the two teens.

"Can we stay here, please?" Anastasia begged.

"That's not for me to say." Robin peered out the door where a car idled in front of her house. She couldn't see the driver but motioned they'd be another minute. The car's headlights flashed in response.

"But you should keep your promise to Mel if your parents allow you to go." She shut the door.

"My mom knew. I forgot to tell my dad."

"Get your clothes and toothbrush." Finn returned, sliding the phone into the waistband of the pants. "Next time, tell me. I haven't seen you in a month. I was hoping to spend time together tonight."

"I'm sorry, Dad."

"Apologize to Robin too."

"Sorry, Robin." Anastasia trudged up the stairs.

Mel shrunk back against the door as if she felt responsible for the tension. Finn's shoulders slumped in disappointment. Robin squeezed his hand before she went after Anastasia.

"What?" his daughter asked when Robin poked her head into the bedroom.

"Maybe, if you still want, you and your dad can stay the rest of the summer."

"Really?"

"Really."

Anastasia gasped as if struck by an idea. "Could you help make the costumes for my camp's play?"

"I'd love to. But only if you spend this weekend with your dad."

"I will."

"And tomorrow, I could use help packing my van. Then we can find other costumes for your dad to try."

"Promise?"

"Yes." She held out her arm and grasped Anastasia's forearm. Just like she had done with Finn. "And true friends don't break promises."

Robin returned to her office while Finn escorted both girls to the car.

After shutting the front door, Finn entered the room. "That was embarrassing."

"The costume!" Robin clasped her hand over her mouth.

"Tried to explain it to Mel's father, but he was too busy razzing me. I dread the next PTA meeting. You have no idea how much dads gossip."

"We'll get you out of it soon." She cringed. "I didn't mean it that way."

"What way?"

Robin rolled her eyes at his feigned innocence and changed the topic. "Are you okay?"

"Yes, you get used to a thirteen-year-old forgetting that parents want to be around them. What did you say to her? She said she's excited about tomorrow."

"That I had other outfits for you."

"Not the—"

"Yep, the infamous Frank-N-Furter."

"Can't believe you kept it."

"I won my first contest with that costume, of course I kept it."

"No way I can fit into it."

"I think you can." Her gaze trailed over him, top to bottom, before she forced her eyes away.

"I also told Anastasia that you can stay the summer."

"What?"

"Sorry, I should've checked with you first."

"We can't impose like this."

"Now you won't waste your precious time together moving again. Plus, I can support a budding costumer and her theater camp."

"That's generous."

"Selfish actually. The too-big check you wrote will cover your weeks here."

"I owe you more."

The way he stared caused Robin to wonder if he was insinuating something other than money.

She turned to the desk behind her. "Let me check the measurements again."

Robin stretched over her desk for the laptop. Flipping it around, she leaned on her forearms and reread the actor's measurements.

"Okay." She rose to find Finn facing the door. "I need you to turn around."

"Not yet." He wriggled while his hands shifted in front of his waist.

"What's wrong?"

"How do men wear these costumes?"

"With a dance belt. Didn't I give you one?"

"What's a dance belt?"

"It's what male ballet dancers wear under tights. Do you at least have underwear on?"

"I do, but I tucked *it* under and now—" his hips jerked back and forth "—it's stuck."

"What's stuck? Ohhhh, why is it stuck?"

"Why do you think? You leaned over the desk, and it moved."

A tingle started low in her stomach in response. Neither of them needed this complication.

"Go upstairs and change."

"No, I want to do this for you. Do you know how hard it was to put this on?"

"I know one thing that's hard."

"Don't joke. Don't say a thing."

"A thing," she said then realized, "The windows are open."

She'd opened them to air out the room for Anastasia. She yanked them and the curtains shut. Finn finally turned around.

"Thought that would work. Nothing switched you off faster than fear of getting caught."

"You remembered."

"I do." *And much more from this very room.* Robin shifted to the task at hand. "I need to check the hem."

"This is humiliating."

"Growing up together, we experienced many awkward moments. You're like my brother."

"That did it."

"Good."

She marked minor adjustments to the legs before sliding his phone from the waistband.

Finn sucked in a breath.

"Need me to repeat how you're my brother?" She circled his waist with the measuring tape. It didn't need any adjusting. The pants fit his trim waist as if sewn for him.

"It's just ..." He shook his head.

"Spit it out." She moved to his back.

"It's been a while since I've been touched."

"Does Anastasia know Susan cheated on you with her current husband? Because she reacted strongly when I mentioned Rodent had cheated on me."

"I never told her. We explained that we'd grown apart, which was true."

"How long was she cheating?"

"She claims only a month."

Robin snorted.

"We hadn't been intimate long before that. What about you and ..."

"Rodent."

He chuckled. "You love giving nicknames to those you hate. What was mine?"

"I told you before. You were always Neighbor Boy." She stared at the measuring tape until the numbers and tick marks blurred together.

"Why wouldn't you talk to me then?"

"Because I was devastated." She edged backward until the desk stopped her retreat. "If we spoke then I'd forgive you and risk being hurt once more. I couldn't survive that pain again."

Finn's eyes were unreadable under the mask. She recalled a movie character stating that you can't trust those in masks.

"I'm sorry. My mother was broken after my father died. I wanted to be there for her. You seemed fine—"

"Fine?"

"You were focused on your business."

"You're implying I wasn't there for you?"

"You didn't notice that I needed you, and I was too immature to know what to ask for."

Robin crossed her arms and leaned on the desk. He was right. She'd been focused on networking, growing her business, traveling to cons every week. She'd never seen how his grief affected him.

She hadn't been mature enough to understand Neighbor Boy's pain.

"I should've been there for you," Robin admitted.

"You couldn't have known. It took years of therapy for me to recognize my grief. Plus, you wouldn't have your business had you followed me."

But I would have you.

As if he'd read her mind, he took her hands. "I'm here now."

"I can't do this." Robin slipped her hands from his.

"Why?"

Because I'd never recover when you leave. "We're finished. You can change."

Robin put her back to him and opened her laptop. She noted his measurements in her spreadsheet. When he grunted behind her, she looked over her shoulder to find the shirt stuck along with his arms over his head.

"There's a zipper." She slid the shirt back down. "I'm lucky you didn't rip it." She unzipped it, breathed in, and savored his cologne.

He removed the shirt. Their eyes locked.

"Are you going to take off the mask?"

"Maybe this is the glow up I needed. It's comfortable."

Sexy is how she'd describe the way it accentuated his lips, fuller than in her memories. She shivered recalling their softness pressed along her neck and under her earlobe.

"Why are you doing this to me?" she asked.

"What?"

There was that feigned innocence again. The game they used to play. He loved to bait her into making the first move.

"People in masks can't be trusted," she said.

"I'm not leaving again."

"How do I know?"

"I promise."

Finn put out his arm. Robin grasped it. This time neither let go.

———

Robin slid her hand from his forearm up to his bicep. "Do you need help with the pants?"

He nodded and stepped down.

"It's tricky." Robin moved her hand to the waistband and tugged. The hidden Velcro gave way. She wiggled the pants down his legs then draped them and the shirt over her sewing machine.

"Looks like you need help with something else." Robin cupped his bulge, and he grew harder. Her other hand settled behind his neck to draw him into a gentle kiss.

Testing the waters, Finn let Robin take the lead before he broke from their kiss to brush his lips along her neck to her earlobe. She moaned and dropped her head to the side.

Finn slid his hand under her shirt and over her breast.

She moaned again. "I have the Buttercup red dress. It's tight but I can—"

"Can't wait." He kissed her.

Robin peeled off her shirt, unfastened her bra. From her back pocket, she fished out condoms.

He raised his brows when she handed him one.

"Don't ask. It's been a long time for me too." Robin removed her jeans and panties. "Now take me against the desk like you did before."

When they were twenty, and her parents were at the store and there wasn't much time.

"As you wish." Finn slid off his underwear.

Time had rounded her curves, softened her middle and made him crave to touch her body again, to relearn every precious inch of it.

Finn trailed his hands along her sides to her rounded rear. With deliberate movements, he spun her to face the desk. A swift swipe of her arm sent papers and fabric bits fluttering to the floor. She planted her hands and arched her back, ready for him.

He almost came putting on the condom. Positioning her ass, Finn grabbed himself and entered her.

Robin pressed against him, pressing him further inside. She moved forward and back, forward and back.

"We have all night. No one is coming," she said.

"I am." With that, Finn felt a release that shook him to his soul.

After catching her breath, she whispered, "I want more."

Robin threaded through a maze of packed boxes in her living room. She checked off the deliverables on her tablet and yawned. Reconnecting with Finn was worth the exhaustion today.

He'd dragged himself to bed at one o'clock, while Robin finished the alterations. She'd fallen asleep, curled up next to him. Before he left for work, he kissed her cheek like he used to, like eighteen years had never separated them.

Her cellphone rang.

"What happened last night?" Mandy asked when she answered.

"With what?"

"You know." Kids shouted in the background before Mandy shut a door and muffled them. "I called Finn."

"Didn't trust me?"

"Didn't trust that you wouldn't be difficult. Finn sounded different."

"Different how?"

"You tell me."

Her doorbell let out a choking ding.

"Gotta go."

"Tell me."

"I don't make love and tell, sis."

"You didn't!"

She hung up on Mandy to open the door.

"Hey." Anastasia stood on the other side with her overnight bag slung over a shoulder.

A car pulled away from the curb. Mel waved from the passenger seat.

"Where's Finn … err … your dad?" Robin hoped the teen couldn't tell how hard her heart thumped in anticipation of seeing him.

"He's working late and said to eat without him. What did you and Dad do after I left?"

"Your dad exercised, and I sewed." Not a total lie.

"Are you hungry?" Robin took the duffel from Anastasia and set it on the floor.

"Yeah."

"Let's eat the leftovers then pack my van."

The macaroni was better the second day. Fueled by carbs, they cleared out the living room, stacking boxes in her van for tomorrow's deliveries.

Finished, Anastasia jumped from the back of the van onto the driveway. She paused with her hand on the door.

"I wish you and Dad would've stayed together. He would've been happy."

"Don't say that." Robin squatted on the edge to meet her eyes. "Because you wouldn't be here, and he loves you."

Anastasia surprised her with a hug.

Robin squeezed the teen tight before letting go.

"Go to my office. I found his Frank-N-Furter outfit."

Laughing, Anastasia hurried inside.

Robin stepped from the van. She pulled the door closed to find Finn standing there.

"Ack!"

"Didn't mean to scare you."

"Which is why you're creeping around?"

Finn drew her to the other side of the van. "I overheard what you said to Anastasia."

"I meant it." Robin glanced at the house to confirm Anastasia was inside before embracing Finn. "And I've grown up enough to recognize that true love never dies, but it can be delayed."

The End ... for now.

About J.T.

J.T. Bock conjures pulse-pounding tales like her UltraSecurity series (superhero romance) to share with kindred readers looking for a fun escape. Her alternate identity enjoys spending time with her workaholic husband and their sidekick rescue dog and traveling to interesting locales. Check out J.T.'s latest stories at www.jtbock.com.

A Room with A Groom

A Kingsmill Courtships Novella

Sharon Wray

1

Sophie Sinclair was sure of one thing. She wasn't a nervous bride. When she handed her menu to the waitress, she even smiled confidently. Then she sipped her soda and studied the courtyard of the café in Middleburg, Virginia. She couldn't be more at peace because tomorrow, once she became Mrs. Ben Mosby, all would—*finally*—be well.

After years of running and hiding from violence and loneliness, her life would be physically and emotionally safe. Her and Ben's dangerous past would no longer matter.

Her cell phone rang and, after glancing around the almost empty courtyard, she answered, "Ivy? Are you at my apartment?"

She hated being *that* person who spoke on the phone in public, but she'd been waiting for this call from her best friend and maid of honor. Ivy was supposed to have arrived yesterday, but an accident closed the interstate between Boston and Washington, DC.

"I'm here," Ivy said. "Now I can study the maid-of-honor stuff."

"You haven't read my wedding document? Or the cross-referenced indexes?"

Ivy snorted. "I thought you were a new and improved low-key bride?"

"I am." She brushed stray hairs off her damp face. She hated the

August humidity. "But there's nothing wrong with being prepared. I promise I'll be the most easy-going bride ever."

"If you say so. But you were right about Kingsmill." Ivy's voice sounded wistful. "Everyone I've met is straight out of central casting. Although I'm not sure if they're in a sweet holiday movie or in a horror flick where the nice locals turn tourists into zombies."

Sophie laughed, and when a warm breeze swept across the courtyard, she closed her eyes. Since leaving Salem, Massachusetts—and her best friend almost a year earlier—she'd missed Ivy's take on the world. "I promise Kingsmill is more of a holiday movie. Although I'm not always sure which holiday."

"That's *not* a resounding *no* on the zombies."

She smelled something *off*, opened her eyes, and looked up at the sky. It seemed grayer than before. "Don't worry. Kingsmill's quirky inhabitants are charming."

"Last week you called them annoying."

"Because Nana Ruthie, the town's matriarch, wanted to take control of my wedding."

Ivy laughed. "What did you do?"

"After talking to my future sisters-in-law, I handed Nana Ruthie my wedding planning book." The truth was, it'd been one of the best decisions she'd made lately. Other than agreeing to marry Ben. "Since then, I've updated it fourteen times."

"Only fourteen?"

She frowned at the disbelief in Ivy's voice. "I didn't want Nana Ruthie to think I was a control freak."

"Whatever you say. So..." Ivy made a thumping noise, like she'd dropped onto the bed. "Where are you?"

"Ben and I picked up my wedding gown and his tuxedo. We're a few hours away." Ben, who stood across the street near his blue Ford truck, noticed her and waved. She waved back. She'd gone to the café to get a table while he'd carried the clothes to the vehicle. Except now he leaned against the truck's hood, his phone pressed against his ear.

"I love my dress. It fits perfectly," Ivy said. "Thank you for... you know."

For paying for the dress. As a florist, Ivy lived on a tight budget.

"You're welcome. I went over the measurements with the designer multiple times to make sure it'll fit." She paused as the town's church bells rang three times. "I may have annoyed her."

"I doubt that."

Sophie ignored Ivy's laughter. "I just ordered our lunch. We should be home by six."

"Okay—wait, someone is knocking on your apartment door."

Sophie heard muffled words. A moment later, Ivy said, "I was summoned to the café beneath your apartment by a woman wearing a WWE T-shirt printed with the question 'does *your* sport have blood time?'"

She'd been worried about this. "That was Nana Ruthie."

"What should I do?" Ivy lowered her voice. "I'm afraid if I don't go, she'll hurt me. Although she did bribe me with lemon cupcakes."

"You need to go, and Lily's lemon cupcakes are great. Make sure, when dealing with Nana Ruthie and Lily—the woman who owns the café and my apartment—you don't show fear. Otherwise you'll end up running the town's sunflower festival. Trust me."

"I can hold my own. *Mwah!*" Ivy blew a kiss and hung up.

Sophie searched for Ben again. He was in the same position, except now he was looking up.

The sky was darker, as if a veil had been draped over the town.

"Here you are." The waitress placed the food on the table.

"Thank you." While she'd ordered a club sandwich, Ben had wanted two cheeseburgers, a chocolate shake, French fries, and onion rings.

The waitress handed her a ketchup bottle when Ben rushed over, still studying the world above.

"I'll grab to-go boxes." The waitress disappeared.

Sophie's nose itched, and she smelled something acrid and bitter. *Smoke.*

2

"Why do I smell smoke?" Sophie waited for Ben to kiss her before adding, "What's going on?"

"Don't worry." He sat and grabbed some fries. After eating, he wiped his hands on his napkin and went for the ketchup.

She grabbed it first. "Tell me."

He sat back and sighed. "Wildfires."

She handed him the ketchup. That explained the smoke. "How close are they?"

"Miles away." He dumped ketchup on his plate. "I'm not worried."

She watched him eat ferociously. He was either being vague because he wasn't stressed or because he didn't want her to panic. He'd been holding info back from her lately. As the sheriff of their small town, he often dealt with things he couldn't talk about. But sometimes it bothered her.

"You should eat." He motioned to her lunch. "I want to leave ASAP."

Their waitress returned with to-go boxes and the check. "We're closing early because of the fires."

"Thank you." Sophie took the boxes and packed her sandwich and chips. "I hope you get home safely."

Ben found his wallet and took out cash for lunch and a tip. "To leave town, head east. If you hit a barricade, they'll direct you to the best detour."

The waitress took the cash with shaky hands. "Thanks."

Sophie reached for his plate only to discover he'd eaten everything. Because the man she loved devoured food like a shop vac.

A minute later, she hopped into the truck and stowed the food on the floor on the front passenger side. But she'd noticed bags filled with granola bars and bottled water on the floor behind her seat. He'd shopped while she'd been trying on her wedding gown?

Ben stood outside, phone against his ear again. His eye squint told her he was stressed. When he finally got into the driver's seat, he didn't mention the phone call and she didn't ask.

She pointed to the back seat. "You bought water and snacks?"

"In case we need them at the reception."

His tone told her that wasn't the entire truth. But while she wished he'd open up more, he kept things to himself because he either wasn't allowed to talk about them or he didn't want her to worry. What he didn't understand was that sometimes his lack of communication made her even more anxious.

When he pulled onto the road, he drove toward the Shenandoah Mountains.

She snapped her seatbelt. "You told the waitress to head east. Why are we driving west?"

"I want to check in at Mt. Weather."

"That super-secret government military bunker covered in antennas that everyone knows about but pretends doesn't exist?"

Pretending not to notice military/government activity was a thing in this part of Virginia since Washington, D.C was less than fifty miles away.

"Yes." He relaxed his grip on the wheel. "The State Police set up a station there." He nodded to the clock that registered half past three. "We'll still get home before the rehearsal."

"Okay." She studied his clenched jaw. "You need to stop grinding your teeth when you're upset. Tomorrow is our wedding day. We're supposed to be happy."

"I'll try." Once Main Street turned into a narrow highway, he glanced in the rear-view mirror. Then he pulled off to the side of the road and stopped. A second later, the roar of engines drowned out all other sounds. On their left side, a dozen motorcycles raced by. Even though they were going twice the legal speed limit, she identified their leather cuts. The top rocker said *Devil's Renegades*, and the logo showed a skeletal death head surrounded by angel's wings.

They belonged to the Devil's Renegades Motorcycle Club, Virginia, Ravensburg Chapter.

Once the bikes disappeared around a sharp turn, Ben sent a text. Then he started driving again.

He didn't say anything. They both had a difficult history with outlaw motorcycle clubs. He'd once been a member of the Devil's Renegades while she'd dated a member the Black Jacks, a rival MC from Massachusetts. "You're not going to pull them over?"

"No. But I notified my colleagues." He stepped on the gas again, and they sped down the silent country road.

A moment later, she asked, "You're armed. Right?"

He winked at her, obviously trying to lighten the mood. "I'm always armed." It was the way he spoke, with a sexy—maybe even dirty—undertone that made her laugh with relief.

She hit his hard bicep with her smaller fist. "Alright, Mr. Sexy. Let's see the secret government facility so we can get home in time for the rehearsal. We have less than nine hours left."

"Left before what?"

"Before I have to hide from you." She settled into her seat, determined not to fret. "It's bad luck for a groom to see a bride before the wedding."

"I promise to get you home before midnight."

"Before six is better." She checked her watch again.

He shook his head, muttering about his *chill* bride.

She ignored him and studied the sky. Was it getting darker out?

A few minutes later, a text popped up on his phone. Because it was tilted in his direction, she couldn't see it. He gripped the steering wheel until his knuckles turned white, and he turned onto a dirt road. "What's wrong?"

"We're going to miss the rehearsal."

She frowned. "*Why?*"

He glanced at her, and his eyes appeared darker than ever. "We're trapped by wildfires."

3

Three hours later, Sophie got out of the hot truck. She'd finally accepted the truth that they weren't going to make it home for the rehearsal and had called Ivy to let her know.

They'd run into so many roadblocks on their way here that it felt like they'd been driving in circles. Ben stood on the other side of a twenty-foot tall fence lined with razor wire, talking to people in uniform. They'd already gone to Mt. Weather and those people had sent them here, to some secret spot near the West Virginia border. Because Ben hadn't shared what he'd learned, she wasn't sure how they were going to get home.

Now Ben was waving his arm toward mountains that loomed around them.

She coughed and got back in the truck. It was half past six in the summer, but it seemed much later. Ben opened the driver's door, and a waft of smoke made her cough again.

She opened a water bottle and handed it to him. "What's going on?" She understood his need for secrecy, but she was beyond frustrated.

He drank deeply and used his fist to wipe the water off his chin. Then he turned on the ignition. It didn't take long to leave the base and head westward. "Good news or bad news first?"

"Hmmm." She focused on the mountains ahead of them. Now that they'd left the foothills, plumes of black smoke rose from the southern and northern ridges.

He headed down the narrow road, toward the darkest part of the sky. "I'm sorry we're missing the rehearsal. Pastor Mark promised we can still get married tomorrow."

She nodded and hid her disappointment. "Good news first."

"The fires haven't made it to Kingsmill."

"That's great." She took a granola bar from the box situated between their seats. "Can we go home now?"

"No." He glanced in his rear-view mirror. "One of the two pieces of bad news is that since we're farther north, we're boxed in by fires and we'll have to find a safe place to wait it out."

"Why can't we head east, toward D.C., then head south, and then west again?" Like making a circle around the fires.

"The roads heading east are closed so emergency vehicles can move west. And I need to do something before we head home."

"Ben?" She bit into her granola bar and struggled to keep the annoyance out of her voice. "I'm resigned to missing the rehearsal, but at midnight I have to go into hiding until I see you at the wedding. I don't want any bad luck following us into our marriage. We've had enough of that during the ten years we were apart. If I had my way, I'd forget everything about my past."

"Sophie, we agreed that from now on, we're not going to let our past define our future. And for the record, I wouldn't want to forget any of it. I loved the woman you were then, and I love you now."

She smiled. "I'm not going to be a hypocrite and deny I was highly attracted to your younger, darker, motorcycle-riding, leather-wearing persona."

He sent her a triumphant smile. "Tell me more."

She laughed, grateful for the release of tension in her chest. "When I first saw you—one of the infamous Devil's Renegades—riding on a black Harley with no worries and no fear, I thought you were sexy as hell and as dangerous as sin. And now that we're a decade older..." She paused to find the right words. "I crave the man you've become."

He took her hand and kissed it. "I promise we're getting married tomorrow." He slowed the truck when the road became an unpaved lane. "But I need to do this first."

"Can you share what *this* is?"

He turned to her with eyes tinged with sadness. "This is me not letting my past define our future."

She rubbed the back of his neck. "Which past? The near past—like last week when you saved your niece's cat from that coyote? Or the farther past…. the one where we got to know each other in an adult way, secretly, without the Black Jacks or Devil's Renegades knowing?"

A secret love affair that almost got them killed and led to their decade-long separation.

"The farther past." They'd finally entered the woods, and the trees pressed in while branches scraped the roof. They were on an old logging road, still going up the mountain. "I need to make sure my younger self's mistakes are behind us before we get married."

"We escaped those motorcycle clubs. You left the Devil's Renegades and are now a sheriff. And I'm done with the Black Jacks. Unless the Black Jacks are trying to restart their chapter here in Virginia?"

When he didn't answer, she turned toward her side window only to have her visibility limited by smoke and foliage. "This doesn't feel right, Ben. I'm scared."

"We're miles from the active blazes. Because we're lower on the mountain, the smoky air is settling downward. When the southern roads are clear, we'll go home. Until then, I need to do this."

"Why do we have to do it *now*?" Couldn't he have done this soul searching weeks ago?

"I need to prove I'm not responsible for this fire."

Whoa. "We've been together all day. Why would you be responsible?"

"I didn't start the fires, but I think I know who did and why. And it's the *why* that might be my fault." He turned on his emergency radio and staticky voices came through.

The sounds of back-and-forth chatter of emergency personnel filled the truck. While she knew he wasn't responsible, she also knew there was nothing she could say to make him feel better. With the radio on, he obviously didn't want to talk about it anymore. He was using his work to shut her out. Again. "Why do you keep looking in the rear-view mirror?"

"It's the second piece of bad news." He hit the gas despite the road's terrible condition. "We're being followed."

She looked behind but only saw smoke and trees. "By whom?"

"Black Jacks."

4

Four hours later, the smoke and sunset had forced them to drive with little light, except for their headlights and the flames flicking the tops of distant pines. Ben was taking her to a safe house, but the profound darkness still frightened her. And, of course, they'd lost cell service an hour ago. "Are we close?"

"Yes." They passed a sign tacked to a tree. The headlights exposed the original words *Camp Bobcat* which had been crossed out and replaced with the crooked, handwritten words *Camp Bones*. "We've lost the Black Jacks."

"Thank goodness."

He stopped the truck in front of iron gates attached to ten-foot-tall brick walls that spread out in both directions. The gates automatically opened, and Ben drove through.

"Who owns–" she paused because a man appeared in a pool of yellow light cast by a lamp above his head. He leaned against his motorcycle and watched them approach.

Ben raised two fingers in greeting, and the man, with long blond hair and a matching beard barely covered by the bandana over his mouth, nodded in return. He looked like an extra in a Viking movie–except for his Devil's Renegades black leather cut.

"That's Fate," Ben said. "He came to Salem with me–the same trip where I met you."

"I remember." She'd protected all of her memories about that week because it'd changed her life.

Fate stared at her, and she shivered. "Why are we here with the MC?"

"My cousin Hawk is VP of the Ravensburg chapter. I asked him to come, and he'd never ride alone." Ben drove slowly, probably to appease the other Devil's Renegades hiding in the shadows. She couldn't see them, but she *felt* them.

"Don't worry." Ben took her hand and squeezed. "No one will hurt you."

"Why did you ask Hawk for help? You're not a member anymore."

"I spent years with these men and despite moving on with my life–"

"And becoming a sheriff–"

"We still have a strong bond. I'm also related to a few of them." Ben parked the truck in front of a wooden shack with a "Camp Director" sign posted on the door. Mold decorated the siding, the windows were covered with oilpaper from the inside, and green things grew out of the gutters. "You must remember what life is like with a MC."

"I do. That's why I left."

He shut off the truck. "My cousins, my brothers, and I used to spend our summers at this scouting camp. When my brother Kane and I were members of the MC, we recommended the club buy this property. It's a perfect hideout, and a great place to run summer bike rallies." He sent her a grin, despite the danger that soaked the air. "Like a camp for grown men."

"Whatever you say." She waited until he came around and opened her door. She coughed from the smoke irritating her throat.

He led her toward the shack. The lights over the door blinked, and a generator hummed nearby. "I don't hear the crickets."

"All animals, no matter how small, run when they sense danger."

She knew the feeling.

The door opened. A tall, muscular man wearing a black leather cut over a black T-shirt and jeans appeared on the stoop. His long blond hair was tied behind his neck, and his uncanny resemblance to Ben ID'd him as a Mosby.

"Hawk." Ben embraced his cousin, and they hit each other's backs.

When they separated, Ben motioned her forward. "This is Sophie."

Hawk drew her into a hug. He smelled of pine trees and bourbon. "You're as pretty as Kane said."

She smiled. Instead of responding, she smoothed down the skirt of her blue cotton sundress, wishing she had a sweater to cover her halter top.

"Come in." Hawk waved them into the dimly lit room with leather couches, two battered desks covered in computer equipment, two mini fridges, and a door leading into another room.

Two men wearing MC cuts appeared, and she reached for Ben's hand. He squeezed three times–their secret code of reassurance. These men were as tall as Hawk and Ben, but one had a bald head covered in tattoos that matched tattooed sleeves on his arms. The other man wore his long hair braided down his back and had a patch on his cut that said *Enforcer*.

An MC's enforcer was the club's protector. The guy you wanted on your side of a tough negotiation. He was also the man who stayed behind long after the talking had failed.

Both men greeted Ben with hugs. Then they stared at her. Her face heated up, and she glanced at Ben who'd moved behind the table to study the laptops.

"Love what you've done to the place, Hawk." Ben's voice held a tinge of laughter, probably to break the room's tension. "Especially the high-tech upgrades."

"Kane redid our security set-up." Hawk gripped the enforcer's shoulder. "Sophie, this is Thor." Hawk nodded to the bald man. "That's Drac."

She cleared her throat. "Hi."

Another man came through the front door in a leather cut with a prospect patch. Where Thor and Drac carried a threat level of ten, this man's wide smile collided with his high cheekbones. The prospect, with his ginger red beard, long hair swept back from his forehead, and green eyes, was the most handsome man she'd seen in a long time. Other than her fiancé, of course.

"I'm Cali. The prospect." He nodded at Ben. "Glad you two made it safely."

She released a breath. Cali was more approachable than the others, including Hawk. Maybe because he was a prospect and didn't have to carry the weight of being scary all the time.

Thor sat behind a desk and pounded a laptop keyboard. "What's up outside, Cali?"

"No sign of Black Jacks. But that fire–" He motioned toward the west-facing window. "It's blowing toward us."

Hawk opened the door. "Wind's shifted." He pointed at Thor. "Whatever we're doing here, brothers, let's do it quickly."

As the men made plans, she moved toward an uncovered window that overlooked the back of the camp. Behind the cabin, a long gravel lane stretched between two long houses with rustic front porches. Beyond the buildings, trees stretched for miles. The place reeked of loneliness and serial killers.

Cali came up and pointed to the left building with doors and windows every ten feet. "That's the barracks for the MC members." He motioned toward the building across the road. "That's the mess hall."

"I didn't know your club owned this place." She wiped her forehead with her forearm. It was hotter than a few minutes ago. "I never heard the Black Jacks mention it."

"That's good news," Cali said. "Hopefully those Black Jacks following you got trapped by fires."

She wrinkled her nose. She had no love for the Black Jacks, but she didn't want them burned alive.

"Ben," Hawk asked. "Do you really expect those Black Jacks following you to show up here?"

"Yes," Ben said as he typed. "But right now the LEOs and firefighters are focused on containing the fires instead of going after the men who potentially started them."

"Black Jacks started those fires," Thor said sharply. "As revenge for what happened last month. And J-Reb's—I mean Ben's—part in it."

"What are you talking about?" Her voice sounded shrewish, but she didn't care. She was worried about the fires, terrified she'd miss her wedding, and tired of being left alone in the metaphorical and physical dark. "Are these fires retribution for the *big thing* that happened last month in Ravensburg?"

Hawk frowned. "What do you know about that?"

"Nana Ruthie told the town that Black Jacks attacked the Devil's Renegades' Ravensburg clubhouse. Feds arrested members of both clubs."

Ben mumbled something unpleasant about Nana Ruthie, and Hawk cursed.

She crossed her arms. "Since I may not make my wedding tomorrow, I deserve answers."

Ben came toward her. Deep lines had formed around his eyes, and she took his arm.

"Ben, whatever this is, we're in it together."

"Sophie–"

She touched his lips. "When you're not honest with me, I get anxious. When I'm anxious, I spin stories in my head about horrible things happening to you. And before you say I'm being ridiculous, horrible things *have* happened to you. To me." She waved her hand to include the other men. "Probably to all of us."

"Okay." Ben tossed his keys to his cousin. "Hawk, would you and the others grab supplies from the truck? I have water, snacks, and ammo. Then move the truck so it's safe."

Hawk nodded. "Got it."

Once Hawk and the others left, she tapped her foot. It was time for answers. "If Black Jacks started these fires in retribution for their arrests, how is that your fault?"

He retrieved two water bottles from a mini-fridge and handed her one. "Remember when I was gone for three days last month?"

"Yes." She opened hers and drank, appreciating the cold water against her dry throat.

"I was in Boston." He also took a long drink. "I was a witness for the prosecution in the case against those Black Jacks and Devil's Renegades members. Because of my testimony, four Black Jacks were sent to prison for fifteen years. My testimony also freed the Devil's Renegades members, a situation that annoyed the Black Jacks even more."

This was not good news. "How is this relevant now?"

He finished his bottle and tossed it into a nearby trash can. "I gave my testimony behind closed doors, as a confidential informant. But yesterday the DA's office leaked the transcripts." He took her hand and led her to the leather couch so they could sit.

"Do you know the leaker?"

"No." He leaned forward, head down, forearms over his thighs. "But Black Jacks know I'm the CI that put their brothers in prison."

She wanted to know why he'd not shared this burden with her earlier, but now wasn't the time to question him. "Why did you ask Hawk to meet you here?"

"I wasn't sure I'd lose the Black Jacks following us." He glanced at her with shuttered eyes. "So I led them here, where I knew Hawk would offer backup."

Her chest felt tight, and she stood to pace the room. Her body demanded physical action to keep up with her racing thoughts. "You're hoping the Black Jacks will follow us here so you and the club can ambush them?"

Ben nodded. "Unfortunately, only six of the Ravensburg Chapter club members are here. The others passed us earlier today, on their way home to protect their town."

She didn't know what to say. He'd known, all day, that they were in danger from more than the fires. He'd known their past was barreling at them, faster than a bullet train, on the eve of their wedding, and he'd said nothing.

"Ben, I want this marriage to be a team effort." She sat down and forced him to meet her gaze. "I brought some terrible people with me when I ran away from Salem, but I'm not the woman I was. I can handle knowing things like you being a CI."

"I wasn't allowed to tell anyone."

"Can you tell me how you're going to take down the Black Jacks with only six MC brothers?"

"I don't know." He returned to the laptops. She followed and stared over his shoulder at the images from the security cameras along the camp's perimeter.

"Ben—" Something appeared in the upper left frame of a screen. Ten motorcycles riding toward the camp's gates.

The door opened and banged against the wall.

"You were right, Ben." Hawk strode in. "Black Jacks are here." He took her arm and led her to the back room, which held a queen-sized bed and a bedside table. "In here, both of you. Don't come out until I say."

Ben grabbed Hawk's wrist. "No way am I letting you fight the Black Jacks alone."

Hawk released Sophie and pressed his fist against Ben's chest. "No way am I letting a Mosby man lose his life before his wedding. The family already hates me, but if you get hurt they'll never forgive me. Now get inside so I can lock that *fucking* door."

Sophie sank onto the bed just as the lights turned off. The generator's rumbling stopped, and she heard the door lock click. "Ben?"

When he didn't answer, she realized the truth. She was alone.

5

She banged on the door locked from the other side. When no one answered, she tore the paper off the window. The blackness surrounding the camp crept through the window cracks like deadly shadows... except for the horizon that blazed in shades of yellows and reds subdued by gray smoke. The fire was coming closer.

Gunshots, followed by male shouts and loud engines, shattered the silence, and she ran back to the door where she banged until her fists ached. When no one answered, she sank to the floor. After many minutes of listening to gunfire and yells outside, she heard two male voices from the other room.

"Don't be an ass, Ben." Hawk coughed. "Protect yourself and Sophie. The MC has this covered."

"There are twelve Black Jacks to seven Renegades. Six if I hide like a coward."

Ben still considered himself a Devil's Renegade?

"No one could ever call you a coward, cousin. We've faced worse odds."

"This is my nightmare." Ben's voice sounded scratchy. "I brought it back to life."

"Kane told us this might happen if you got involved with Sophie again. He was worried your combined pasts would resurrect old shit that didn't need resurrecting."

Sophie inhaled sharply. Never being able to escape her past had been her biggest fear since leaving Salem and reuniting with Ben.

"Kane should've kept his fucking mouth shut."

"I told Kane he was wrong," Hawk said. "We all joined this club–the same one our grandaddy Caleb co-founded–because for a long time it was the only family we had. But Kane has no fucking right to judge your choices. Especially not after the shit he's pulled the last few years."

"Can we stop talking?" Ben said. "We have a fight to win."

"Everyone is regrouping," Hawk said. "I also reminded Kane that everything that has ever happened to us is what brought us all to this exact moment. Now we have a choice. We can run away or fight for the life we want. The life that's meant for us."

"That's what I'm doing," Ben said.

"Except this isn't just your fight, Ben. Your testimony kept me and the brothers out of jail and sent a few Black Jacks to prison. But this war between our clubs belongs to our grandfather."

"Caleb?"

"Fuck, yes. He lived a rough life and died a rough man. He threw away love with both hands. Don't let his blood-soaked legacy ruin your future. You deserve to be happy with Sophie. Don't allow guilt or other emotional bullshit to sabotage your future."

Hawk's words made her eyes sting with unshed tears, and she released a deep breath.

"When did you get all metaphysical?" Ben asked.

"When I fell in love."

"I don't believe it."

"I don't give a shit." Hawk paused. "Ben, when was the last time you were on a bike?"

"I don't know. Years? What the fuck does it matter?"

Sophie chewed her bottom lip. Since she and Ben had reunited, they'd never gone riding because Ben sold his bike.

"It matters because your bike was once a huge part of who you were, and the man Sophie fell in love with."

Ben scoffed. "This is ridiculous–"

"Did you know Caleb's original name for our MC was the Dogs of War?"

"No."

"Caleb believed war was all he was ever good for. A combat-tested veteran who came home from the battlefield still fighting everyone and everything."

Gunshots and motorcycle engines started up again, and she pressed herself closer to the door with no shame about eavesdropping.

"Hawk? Why are we talking about Caleb when we should be fighting Black Jacks?"

"To make you face the truth. Years ago, you left the club our grandfather started and almost got yourself killed. Why? To live the life you wanted. Then you became sheriff of the small town you despised while growing up. Why? To live the life you wanted. Now you're marrying the woman you love—the woman who carries as much dangerous baggage as you do–and you're willing to fight an army of Black Jacks to protect her. Why? To live the life you want with the woman who completes you."

"So your woman completes you?" Ben asked.

"Yes." Hawk's laugh carried erotic secrets. "Izzy also taught me the most important rule in long-term, intimate relationships–never forget you're in a partnership based on love and respect. That means you don't lie or hold secrets, even in the name of protecting each other. That is the fastest way to lose the one person you'd give your life for."

Sophie wiped her damp cheeks with her forearm. The lock unclicked, and she sat on the bed just as the door opened.

Hawk pushed Ben into the room. "Let your brothers protect you, like you protected us last month. Let us help you get your happy ending."

"But–"

"Shut the fuck up, Ben." Hawk winked at her. "And take care of your bride."

Before Ben could respond, the door shut and the lock clicked.

Outside, distant gunshots echoed, followed by the roar of motorcycle engines. But Sophie kept her gaze on Ben.

His black T-shirt was streaked with ash, and his strong arms were covered in dirt.

"Ben, when you told me our past had been buried, you didn't believe it, did you?"

"No." He sat next to her. Their hips touched and she held his hand. He exuded the acrid scents of smoke and defeat, both of which reminded her of the last night they'd spent together before their ten-year separation. A night filled with passion and danger.

She squeezed his hand. "Why did you lie about how you felt?"

"I wanted to protect you."

"Secrets only lead to suspicions, suffering and solitude."

"You sound like Hawk." Ben lowered his head. "I love you, Sophie. Those years without you broke me. I wouldn't survive another moment if I lost you."

She kicked off her sandals, straddled his lap, and held his face between her palms. "From the moment we say I do, we'll be together forever. In this world and the next. But hiding your feelings, no matter the reason, separates us. We need to remember that regardless of the danger, we're always stronger together. And the best way to stay close isn't to fear the people we once were or forget our past, it's to accept it as a part of us. To embrace our history. Turn it into our canon. All of the stuff we've lived through taught us to trust. Our past doesn't define us… it sets us free."

He gripped her waist and flipped her onto her back. His hips ground against hers, and he held her hands above her head. Her skirt rode up, rough denim rubbed the inside of her thighs, and she squirmed beneath his erection.

"Sophie, while I'm ashamed of things I did when I was younger, it brought me to you. I'll be forever grateful for everything–all the terrible things–that we had to do to find each other again. I promise, when I say those vows tomorrow, I'll never break them."

Loud shouts, followed by screaming engines and the staccato pops of gunfire, sounded closer. Yet that outside battle wasn't the only one being fought.

"Don't be afraid." Ben's whispered voice caressed her cheek. "My brothers have this."

Before she could answer, his lips met hers in a frenzy of heat and desire. His tongue drove into her mouth, and he demanded a powerful response. A part of her wanted to hide beneath the bed, but the more feminine part of her focused on the man making love to her.

One thing she knew from her time with the MC was that no matter the danger, women were *never* involved. They weren't consulted for their opinions or included in decisions. Although Ben wasn't a member of an MC, he could read the threat level. If he wasn't worried, then neither would she. Trusting him was part of loving him. She'd spent too many years alone fighting that truth.

So when he untied her halter dress and found her bare breasts, she closed her eyes and whispered, "*Oh, Ben.*"

She held his head while he nibbled and sucked until her lower limbs melted away. Until his watch alarm dinged.

"Wait." She lifted his head only to find his gaze unfocused and shiny, his breaths irregular and rough. "It's midnight. I need to hide in the bathroom."

"*Why?*"

"It's bad luck to see the bride on her wedding day."

He brushed stray hairs off her cheeks, but she closed her eyes.

"Sophie?" His kisses began at her neck and traveled down to her breasts. "You can't be serious."

"I am. We can't look at each other."

He laughed, and she tried to push him off–except he wasn't moving.

"Please, Ben."

"Nope."

Annoyed, she attempted to kick him off. "We don't need the extra bad luck."

On cue, Hawk yelled at someone outside the window, and more gunshots fired in the distance.

"Look at me." Steel lined his low voice, and she peeked at him. "This superstition isn't true."

"But–"

"No." He nuzzled the soft space between her breasts. "If we're not going to be defined by our pasts, we're not going to obey ridiculous customs."

She closed her eyes again. "We can't risk it."

"Don't move." He slid off of her. A moment later, he said, "If you want to play this game, we play my way."

She opened one eye. "Where did you get that?"

"The bedside table." He held up a red bandana. "It's clean." His smile held a secret. "Now let's keep your eyes closed."

She nodded. Once he tied it around her head, she touched the smooth cloth covering her eyes. "Neither one is supposed to see the other. This only takes care of half of the problem."

"I make my own luck." He kissed a trailed down from her neck to her waist. Somehow her dress and panties disappeared. Then she felt his scratchy face against the inside of her thigh. Her stomach clenched, and she gripped the quilt beneath her.

"Please, Ben. *More*."

While she lay spread out in the dark, with the violence outside, his mouth and hands took control. They skimmed over her body, loving and adoring her. When his mouth found her nipples, they tightened.

Suddenly, he moved lower, between her legs. His hands slipped beneath her bottom, and his thumbs met her soft folds. His breath promised paradise.

"Say it," he commanded in a rough voice.

"I want you."

His mouth descended, sending her flying. The strokes of his tongue, his thumbs massaging the sensitive skin, and the feel of his scratchy face against her tender thighs shook her with such force he had to hold her hips still while he continued his intimate invasion.

Finally, her body shuddered, leaving her tingly and numb. His tongue gave a final caress, and he moved his body over hers. His erection felt hard and hot against her stomach.

When had he removed his clothes?

Their bodies moved rhythmically against each other, both seeking and pulling away at the same time. He lifted her hips, and his ragged breaths told her he was close to the point of no return. The rough feel of his skin, combined with his musky scent, almost sent her over the edge as well.

"Sophie?" He took a hard nipple into his mouth. He teased and taunted with his teeth until she grabbed his head.

"*Yes.*" She gave her permission and wrapped her legs around his waist. When he entered her, the force sent her up the bed until her head banged against the headboard. His long strokes pounded into her, and she surrendered to his powerful thrusts.

Everything exploded at once. An orgasm ripped through her, and she screamed his name. He arched above her as his powerful body drove into her three more times before collapsing. Then a burst of noise, light, and chaos from outside broke the bathroom window.

"Sorry!" Cali's voice, laced with laughter, came from beyond the bathroom.

She wanted to laugh. She wanted to cry. She wanted to cover herself with a sheet in case anyone entered the room. But all she had the energy to do was take off the bandana. Ben padded naked across the room, slammed the bathroom door shut, and found a blanket in the closet. By the time he covered her naked body and returned to bed, she was mostly asleep. The war outside didn't matter. She was safe and loved within the arms of her groom.

6

"Sophie?" Ben's voice woke her, and she sat up. Grayish light peeked through the window.

"What time is it?" she asked.

"Four a.m. The Black Jacks are gone." Ben, who was already dressed, handed her her dress. "The fire jumped the break. We're leaving ASAP."

She found her panties and sandals and ran into the bathroom. After a quick shower, she met Ben and Hawk in the main room near the laptops.

"It's a canopy fire now." Hawk pointed to the screen. "Between the strong winds, steep slopes, and dry fuel, we have twenty minutes to evacuate."

Ben kissed her cheek "Go to the truck. I'll be there in a minute."

Hawk led her outside, and she coughed on the smoke-filled air. An eerie light outlined the horizon and exposed new holes in the cabin's siding.

She'd had great sex during a firefight, and she hadn't cared. She wasn't sure what to make of that new personality quirk, other than to remind herself that she'd trusted Ben to keep her safe. And he had.

Drac and Cali were loading crates into the truck's bed. When they saw her, they nodded. A hot flush flooded her cheeks. Had they heard what she and Ben had done earlier that night? Then she decided she didn't care. It was her wedding day. If she wanted to have wild monkey sex with her groom, in the middle of an MC battle, that was her choice.

"Hawk?" She pointed to the crates. "What's this?"

"We're loading ammo from our storehouse, in case the fire reaches the camp."

Yikes.

He held open her door, and she hopped in. Before closing it, he said, "I know this has been stressful, but today is about celebrating new beginnings. Leave the past buried in the days and years you'll never see again."

"Thanks." She paused when Ben exited the cabin. "Hawk, what happened to those Black Jacks?"

"They discovered that stupid actions have serious consequences." Hawk smiled as if none of the previous night's violence mattered. "Don't worry about anything. All of my brothers are unhurt, and today is about you and Ben getting married."

When Ben slipped into the driver's seat, he turned on the truck and grinned. "Is my bride ready to get married?"

She smiled until her face hurt. "Yes, please."

Nine hours later, she wasn't smiling. "It's almost one o'clock. Our ceremony begins in an hour."

"I know." Ben stopped the truck in a road pullout, behind two motorcycles parked on the side of a mountain, thirty minutes from Kingsmill. The four other Devil's Renegades had gone in different directions to report road closures and other obstacles.

Hawk and Cali stepped off their bikes and removed their helmets. Hawk then pulled out a SAT phone and started talking. Something was wrong, besides the fact they'd spent hours circling mountains to avoid fires.

She and Ben walked toward Hawk's bike.

"What's wrong?" Ben asked Hawk.

Hawk pointed toward a southern mountaintop. "We're close to Kingsmill, but the only road leading into town is blocked by downed power lines and trees. The truck can't pass."

She squeezed Ben's hand. "Will we make the wedding?"

Hawk shrugged.

Cali smiled at her. "Don't worry, darlin'. We'll think of something."

Ben dropped her hand to pace the narrow highway. They were blocked on one side by a steep slope and the other side dropped off into a 500-foot deep ravine.

"Can we walk?" she asked Ben.

"It's too far." Ben stood on the edge of the road and looked down. Then he turned to see the mountains on fire behind them. Finally, he eyed Cali's bike. "But I have an idea."

Cali's grin lit up his beautiful face, and he tossed his keys to Ben. "That, my brother, is an inspired idea. And I'll watch the truck."

She glanced at Hawk. "What are they talking about?"

Hawk laughed. "How do you feel about changing into your wedding gown in the woods and arriving at the church on the back of a Harley?"

Twenty-five minutes later, when Ben turned the bike onto Kingsmill's Main Street, Sophie relaxed her hold on his tuxedoed waist. A few miles ahead, the church steeple shone in the afternoon light.

The breeze blew her gown behind her, and the hum of the bike's engine sent tremors along the inside of her thighs. Although she'd tucked her veil around her waist, it'd come loose to fly high above her dress's train. Cali's helmet kept the veil's comb attached to the French braid she'd managed in the reflection of the truck's rear-view mirror.

Ben gunned the engine, and she closed her eyes. It'd been years since she'd ridden with Ben because, since she'd arrived in Kingsmill, they'd buried every aspect of their past.

But no longer.

The church bells rang twice, and she opened her eyes. When Hawk's bike pulled up to escort them, she raised her hands. She couldn't remember any time in her life when she'd felt this happy, this loved, this free.

Once they stopped in front of the church, she removed her helmet, gathered her skirt and veil, and hopped off. Two people ran toward them. Ivy, wearing a blue strapless gown, carried two bouquets and a pair of white satin stilettos, while Ben's brother, Kane, in a black tuxedo, followed.

They both stopped a foot away, their gazes filled with relief, shock, and exasperation.

Ivy shook her head and handed the shoes to Sophie.

Kane frowned at Hawk as he tossed his helmet onto his bike, and she hid her grin. Hawk still wore his jeans, black T-shirt, and his leather cut–all covered in ash, dirt, and probably dried blood.

"Come on, brother." Kane took Ben's arm. "Everyone's waiting."

Ben handed Hawk the keys to Cali's bike. "You're staying for the wedding."

Not a question. Just a statement filled with emotion and gratitude.

Hawk nodded, and Kane dragged Ben away.

Ivy gave Hawk the bouquet of mini sunflowers and white roses. "Meet me in the vestibule when you're ready." She kissed Sophie's cheek and whispered, "Apparently, I'm running the Bonfire Night Festival in three months."

She laughed, and Ivy followed Kane and Ben into the church.

Alone with Hawk, she slipped off her sandals and used his shoulder for stability while she put on a stiletto. "I can't thank–"

"Don't thank me." He held her elbow so she could slip on her other shoe. "We're family. In more ways than blood."

Her vision blurred. "Last year, my step-father died. Other than Ivy, I've no family with me today."

He gently squeezed her shoulder. "I'm sorry."

"Thank you." When her shoes were on, she fluffed her skirt, retrieved her bouquet, and smiled at him. "Would you walk me down the aisle?"

His brown eyes widened, and he motioned to his messy hair and dirty cut. "Are you–"

"Yes, Hawk." She took his arm, and they headed toward the church stairs. Her dusty train floated behind while her wrinkled skirt and lace veil drifted around her. When she heard the entrance music, she walked faster. She was marrying the love of her life, and they were going to have a glorious future. "I've never been so sure of anything in my life."

The End... for now.

Enjoy the story? Please leave a review!

About the Author

Sharon is the *USA Today* Bestselling Author of the *Deadly Force Romantic Suspense Series, Devil's Renegades MC Romance Series,* and the *Kingsmill Courtships Contemporary Romance Series.* She's repped by Deidre Knight and Kristy Hunter of The Knight Agency.

Visit Sharon at www.sharonwray.com to sign-up for her newsletter for sneak peeks, giveaways, and updates on upcoming releases.

Roommate Deal

Ashley Zakrzewski

1

Chloé Laurent is one unhappy girl. How her best friend and ex-roommate could do this to her is beyond her understanding! To move out is one thing. She found her hearts other half in Devin Wilson. To move in with him is right and proper. But to insist his nephew takes her place! *No!* This makes her so upset.

"He is a good guy. Sweet and respectable." Iris reminds her.

She doesn't get it. Chloe doesn't want a new roommate. She is happy with the one she has, and learning to cohabit with someone new is too much stress. *Ugh!*

"I don't want a man as a roommate!" She reminds her through clenched teeth.

Iris knows the issues I have with men, and it's despicable that she already told this Michael guy that he can move in and take her room. Chloe have seen the movies and she doesn't want to be part of a low-budget romcom.

"I know. I'm sorry Chloé. He has his own classes. Different times then you. You will hardly see each other."

She would move out but the apartment is too affordable. It's also in Iris's name, so she gets to choose the other occupant. So, unless she wants to pay more than she can afford as she finishes her medical training, she must bear it. *Damn it!* The only reason he is moving in here is because he is currently living with her boyfriend, and would be a third wheel. So now apparently, he's Chloé's problem.

Iris, rosy with new love ignores her friend's mood and finishes packing. Michael will be there soon. Chloé helps her. She is happy that she found the man that makes her flow, but every box filled means he is closer to being here. She isn't ready for that. "I will miss you despite what you're doing to me."

Okay, so maybe she shouldn't hold a grudge against her best friend, well her only friend, because of this...

"Chloé, he's a hunk. You'll be thanking me."

"I doubt it." She mumbles under her breath.

She doesn't want some guy staring at her. There goes walking around in her underwear. This sucks. Why can't he find somewhere else to live? The location of the apartment is one that everyone on campus wants, and Chloe wouldn't have an issue finding a female roommate. Iris didn't even give me a choice in the matter.

"I will miss you too, but we'll still see each other at college and will get together." The last box is taped up when the bell rings. "Oh, Devin is here!" her face goes from lovely to ethereal at his name. Chloé can't help the joy that fills her heart at this, even with her discomfort with the other guy with him.

They are rung up. Devin enters first. She falls into his arms, leaving Chloé to introduce herself to his nephew. "Hello. I'm Chloe." She puts her hand out to him.

"Michael." He was a hunk, as Iris said. But Chloé was not in the market for hunks. Not after...

"Nice to meet you. I'm sure you're a very nice guy. An adequate roommate. Just understand, I'm not, nor will I be looking for more. Understood?"

She wants to make certain he knows that she isn't interested in extra benefits. He just needs to pay his share of the rent on time and clean up after himself. Nothing else.

"Wow. Someone thinks highly of herself. I've got a girlfriend. Thank you. Iris, show me where to put these and I'll help Devin carry your stuff down." She does before scolding Chloé.

"Well, you made a strong first impression."

"I wanted things clear."

"Oh, they're clear. You know you can't live your life thinking all guys are going to be..."

"Don't!"

"I beg you, Chloé, get help. Talk to someone. This isn't healthy."

She doesn't want help. Just a few friends, her studies, and her apartment.

They are alone with the last of Iris' things in the boot of Devin's car. Michael comes back up to find Chloé sitting on the couch, her knees to her chest.

"Well, that is it? They're off. How long do you think until we're invited to the wedding?" she looks up at him with her honey eyes darkened to molasses.

"If she is smart, never. Moving in with him is bad enough. She loves him." A deep sigh as she drops her eyes again, resting her head on her knees. "Love just leads to pain and heartache."

"Voice of experience?" She doesn't answer, keeping her head down and mouth shut. "Okay then. I'm going to go look around. Okay?" A shrug that he takes as consent and slips out.

The apartment is very clean. Decorated by a hand that knows what it is doing, he hopes it was partly Iris, as his uncle's can use the same. He walks back in to find Chloé in the same position he left her in.

"It's quite girly." He comments, hoping to get her to laugh. Instead, her head jerks up and fire comes out of those unique eyes.

"Two girls lived here, after all."

"Yes, true. I didn't mean to offend. I just was ah - saying. I won't disturb what you've done. It's very well decorated. I won't mess with that. Just my own room."

"It's your room." She says with unconcern. "If Iris wanted it to stay the same, she wouldn't have moved."

"Chloé, I know you don't want me here. I'm sorry." Her head is back down and she is back to ignoring him. He sighs and heads to his own room.

This is going to be more difficult if she won't even speak to him. There is no need to make it more awkward. Michael isn't excited about living with a woman either, and his girlfriend, well she is on the fence.

With that attitude, she has nothing to worry about, that's for sure.

2

In a small part of her injured heart, she feels bad for the disdain she is showing her new roommate. She knows it isn't his fault. She just can't help that her distrust of men rubs off on him. She shudders under the memories she can't keep out.

Going to college at age eighteen where she met her first lover. She thought herself finally free only to be trapped in a different type of nightmare. Justin, call me Malcolm, seemed perfect, at first. A university professor. Steady, old enough to help her deal with her daddy issues (as her therapist later explained) but completely different than him.

The first time he hit her, for going to class too provocatively, she knew she deserved it. It was followed by pets and kisses, gentle loving. A pattern developed. It might have still been going on if he hadn't have raped her. It pushed hidden memories to the surface.

She had left, just wrapped in a sheet, to arrive at Iris door. She told her all about Malcolm. She has been here since. But even Iris doesn't know about her dad. Only her mom and therapist. If she did maybe she wouldn't. No, she would still say she needs to understand not all men are like Caelan and Malcolm.

She tells herself over and over that not every man is like her father or

Malcolm. So many times that it's become a mantra, but no matter what, it doesn't stick.

She sighs and stands to go make tea. The polite thing to do would be to see if Michael wished some also. She turns towards his door and knocks.

———

Michael opens and looks at her. Chloe sees he has started putting away his things. Already she can feel Iris's presence disappearing. She sighs.

"Yes?"

"Right. I was going to make some tea. You want some?"

He started to ask if it was a peace offering or something equally snarky but, she seems to be trying. Michael settles for, "Yes thank you." He follows her out and feels and sees her tighten as he gets close. He stops and lets her get a few steps ahead before slowly following. Who had hurt her?

She sits a quite lovely tea set on the kitchen table before starting the kettle. "Beautiful. It's old."

"Yes, a gift from my uncle." She gathers up tea bags, sugar, milk, and crisps before the kettle whistles. The hot water is transferred to the tea pot. Chloe pours. She wasn't speaking and he decides it is up to him to get the conversation going.

"Your uncle, he must be a special man?"

"He tries." He frowns at this answer and look that runs across her face. "Look Michael, family is off limits, okay?"

"Yes. Alright Chloé. You're studying medicine, right?"

"I am." She takes a sip of her tea, a bite off a crisp.

"I want to help, you see, where I can."

Her eyebrows go up. Good, he has her attention. "I'm studying psychology. Want to be a therapist."

She stares at him before her whole demeanor changes. "Does Iris know?"

"My field of study?"

"God damn her straight to hell! I stopped going so she brings a therapist here!" She stands with jerky movements, hurrying away.

"Wait Chloé! What?" He hears her bedroom door slam. *Shit! This will not do.* He gets up and fetches his phone and rings his uncle. How does she already Michael so much?

3

It rings and rings. Finally his Uncle Devin answers, a bit breathless. "This best be life or death important nephew!" He swallows hard. It isn't yet dark. He didn't think...

"Ah sorry for interrupting. It's Chloé. She...." he hears a rustling and the phone is handed off to Iris.

"What is wrong with her?"

"That is just it, I don't know. We were having tea and talking. She wasn't perfectly relaxed but better. We talked about college and I told her my field of study. She reacted quite intensively. Stormed into her room and then slammed the door. It would have been nice to know I was moving in with a girl who despises therapists!"

"Not therapist, well not all therapists. Just one but..."

"I need some idea of what I'm dealing with here." He pleads. He doesn't wish Iris to break her friend's confidence but...

He hears a deep sigh on the other end. "Alright. She had a bad relationship. Real bad. I think there's more she hasn't shared. Her last therapist was a madman. Told her to just get back on the horse. No way would she be able to start dating again. She quit. I couldn't convince her all therapists are not alike. All guys are not alike. She's hurting badly. I didn't know how to reach her..."

"So, you sent me here to..."

"Be a trustworthy man. Just someone to help her get used to the opposite sex again. I imagine she thinks it more."

"Oh. She wished you straight to hell." He doesn't hear her come out. Until she is at his side. She is quick, jerking the phone out of his hand before he has a chance to react.

"Damn right I did! You had no right! What did you tell him? How could you..." She throws the phone back to him and slams back into her room. He lifts the phone back up to his ear. They are both silent for a moment.

"Shit!"

"What now Iris?"

"Let her be. I'll come by tomorrow. Try to explain." He agrees and rings off.

Now what?

He cleans up from their interrupted tea. He needs a non-threatening way to reach out to her. Something to show he is here for her as a roommate and a friend without making her more uncomfortable. A note. A note slipped under her door. That may do.

He carefully washes the last of the China, placing it in the drainer and goes to find paper and a pen. Sitting down on his own bed, he begins.

Hi roomie,
I apologize for ringing Iris and seeming to get in your business. I wasn't trying to make an already uncomfortable situation worse. I was just attempting to see what I could do to help.
She didn't tell me much. Just your ex was a huge jerk. I'm sorry about that. Look, I'm here to get through school, the same as you. I do have a girlfriend, Rose. I'm not wanting to be your therapist or lover, just a roommate.
This is my schedule. Rose and I also have a standing date night every Thursday. We can be at her flat if that makes you more comfortable. You

do what you need to be okay with this. My schedule allows you to avoid me if that is your wish.
Again, I'm sorry for overstepping.
Michael.

He slides it under her door and waits.

She lays curled up on the bed, sobbing out her anger and hurt. She is thankful her new flat mate isn't the type to try to not give her space. It was something. It really wasn't him. It was Iris. To tell him anything! She just wants to forget. How can she when people keep bringing it up? She hears him at the door and braces for a knock. Instead, a paper is slipped under her door.

She slips up, wiping her eyes to retrieve it. A note. She perches on the edge of her bed and reads it. When done, she breathes a sigh of relief. He really is given her space. She gets her own stationery and pens him back.

Thanks roomie,
It isn't you specifically. It is Iris and all males. He was more than a jerk but not talking about him. Thank you for your schedule. And the info on you and Rose. Her place would be better for a bit. Thanks.
I need to stay alone now. I will come out when ready or when I need to go to class. Don't worry about me. I've had worse betrayals.
Thank again.
Chloé.

She slips it under her door. A few seconds later it is retrieved. She climbs back on her bed.

4

She arrives quite early the next morning hoping to catch Chloé before she heads on to class. Michael opens the door for her. "How is she?"

"Well, I haven't seen her. I heard her, up and about, after I went to bed."

"So, you haven't talked with her at all?" He shakes his head as he leads her into the kitchen for coffee.

"Didn't say that. We've been passing notes under her door. Seems a bit kid-like but it works. She's still mightily upset and hurt. I needed to make sure she was alright while respecting her need for silent solitude. This works for that. Well, I'm off. Have an early class." She sees he has coffee set-up for Chloé with a note.

"Thank you. You handled the situation better than I did."

"Don't beat yourself up. You were trying to help your friend." He lifts up his backpack and leaves. Iris goes over to Chloé's door.

A knock. "I know you're heading to class Michael. Thank you." Her voice is rough from crying. Iris feels like doing some crying herself.

"Michael has left. He made you some coffee and left a note."

"Iris? What're you doing here?"

"We need to talk." She waits, hearing her move around behind the door. It opens showing a tear stained face. She is still in pajamas and wrapped in a robe. "Oh my dear." She reaches for her.

"Don't! I will listen to you but don't touch me." She moves towards the kitchen with a chastened Iris following. Chloé takes a seat and lifts up the folded note.

Chloé,
I pray this day allows you to find some peace. Call if you need me.
Michael

It brings a ghost of a smile to her face. That smile is replaced by a frown when Iris asks, "What did he say?" Seeing her reaction, she holds up her hands, calling for a truce. "Sorry. Sorry for everything. It wasn't my intention to make you think or feel that I chose Michael because of what he's studying."

"Wasn't it though? You've been begging me for months to see a new therapist. Then the guy you move in with me is studying to be one?" She glares at her as she picks up the coffee cup, taking a sip as she awaits her answer.

"No. Look his field of study helps. But not," Her hand goes back up as Chloé is ready to explode again. "For the reasons you think. It shows he's a sweet, compassionate, kind hearted, man. Someone the polar opposite of…"

"Don't!" her face turns pale and the hand holding the cup shakes. Iris starts to reach for her and stops. She places the cup down and holds her hands tight together on the table.

"He needed a place he could afford and Devin and I needed privacy. That is truly all. I should have told you but you were so adverse to the idea…"

"I was and am. He's better than expected but still a man."

"A man that has been dating the same girl for over a year. He won't try to be more than your friend. You think I didn't vet the guy moving in with my best friend!"

"Devin is your best friend now."

"Best female friend then. I love you like a sister. I would never do anything to deliberately harm you. I'm so sorry."

"I know you wouldn't. I forgive you. I just assumed…"

"You know what they say about assumptions?" This gets a full smile.

"Yes, and I was an ass. I didn't let you explain. I'm sorry."

"It's alright. Are you going to class today?"

"Yup. Oh, the time!" She quickly stands.

"Go get ready. I'll clean up here."

"Thanks." She hugs her and Iris returns it.

He returns from class to find her already home. To his surprise, she sits on the couch, books stacked in front of her. She looks up at his entrance.

"Hi Chloé."

"Hey, thanks for the coffee this morning."

"You're welcome. I thought a note was best." He sits his backpack down and eases his shoes off, placing them by hers at the door.

"Thanks for that too. I know I was…"

"Who you needed to be." He takes a seat across from her. "Don't worry. "She gives him a small smile.

"I don't know where you study but, you may join me here, if you wish. The table is big enough. I don't want you to think this isn't your apartment too."

He knows what that cost her. "Thank you, Chloé." He pulls his backpack up and they are both soon engulfed in their studies.

Made in the USA
Columbia, SC
03 August 2024